Destiny's Dream

Sybilla knew the next move was hers. "Perhaps you could wash my back." She passed him the soap root and hiked up her hair with one hand.

Hawk made no move to touch her. "What's wrong?" she asked.

"Is it the custom in England to bathe in your underwear?"

She smiled. "As a matter of fact, it is."

"Then I'll just have to work around it." His rough hands, slick with lather, massaged first her shoulders and then her back through the flimsy fabric, sensuously thrumming her taut nerves like a mandolin's strings. As he rubbed the sweet-smelling lather over her back, Sybilla turned and looked deeply into his eyes. Slowly she untied her camisole.

"Tell me what you need," he said.

"You'd make me say it?" she asked, lowering her gaze. She watched his lean brown hands play upon her pale skin.

"I need to hear you say it . . ."

Destiny's Dream

Joanna Jordan

AVON BOOKS ◆ NEW YORK

DESTINY'S DREAM is an original publication of Avon Books. This work has never before appeared in book form. This work is a novel. Any similarity to actual persons or events is purely coincidental.

AVON BOOKS
A division of
The Hearst Corporation
105 Madison Avenue
New York, New York 10016

Copyright © 1990 by Debrah Morris and Pat Shaver
Inside cover author photographs by Larry McDade
Published by arrangement with the authors
Library of Congress Catalog Card Number: 89-92488
ISBN: 0-380-75790-7

First Avon Books Printing: June 1990

AVON TRADEMARK REG. U.S. PAT. OFF. AND IN OTHER COUNTRIES, MARCA REGISTRADA, HECHO EN U.S.A.

Printed in the U.S.A.

RA 10 9 8 7 6 5 4 3 2 1

Chapter 1

Tucson, Arizona Territory
April 1887

All hell was breaking loose. Or so it seemed.
Hawk Devlin tipped his chair back against the wall of the Palace Cigar Store and calmly unwrapped a cheroot. He propped his feet on a nail keg and yanked his wide-brimmed Stetson down to shade his eyes from the bright afternoon sun. He didn't know what was causing all the ruction, but judging by the level of braying, neighing, and screaming along Congress Street, it was fearsome indeed.

Most likely it wasn't the renegade Maloche. He hadn't been reported this side of the border in the six weeks since the boys over at Fort Lowell had sent him slithering south to whatever rock he lived under.

Nor was it Hawk's distant Apache relatives. Geronimo and his band had surrendered last September, and the government had declared an official end to the war by shipping what was left of them off to rot in Florida. Regarded as a foreign nation, the Apaches had been deprived of their native lands so that the rest of Arizona could live in peace at last.

So what was destroying the peace on such a grand and robust scale? Hawk bit off the end of his cigar and spat it into the dust. Whatever it was, it was

1

none of his business. The good citizens had appointed a police chief to corral the desperadoes who considered it their sacred duty to take up where the Indians had left off.

Kept the law busy, too. Without the Apaches to worry about, white folks had more time to kill one another.

It didn't really matter what was causing the commotion, so long as it didn't disturb Hawk's smoke. In fact, he didn't care if the devil himself was being driven through the streets in leg irons. Nothing was going to stop him from enjoying the cigar he'd ridden all the way into town for.

He'd been out prospecting his small claim, hoping to finance his next sojourn into the Superstition Mountains to look for the gold his ancestors swore was hidden there. But since his claim was showing every sign of petering out, he'd used his dwindling cigar supply as an excuse to come back to town.

Once he finished his smoke, he planned on having a leisurely soak at the public bathhouse before sitting down to a steak supper with all trimmings.

Afterward, he'd head over to one of the good-time houses on Maiden Lane if he could find one where he was still welcome. Not that he wasn't a good customer, but several of the madams had complained that his appearance at the door caused so much bickering among the girls vying for his attention that a few catfights had broken out. More than a little furniture had been broken too, if gossip was to be believed.

Lazily flicking a match with his thumb, Hawk held it to the end of the cigar and drew deeply. An unbelievably rank odor assaulted his nostrils, and they flared in disgust. Something smelled worse than hell on house-cleaning day, and whatever it was, it was getting closer. He narrowed his eyes against the cigar smoke and looked around.

Up and down the narrow street, horses whinnied and bucked and unseated their blaspheming riders.

Prospectors chased runaway burros, the rattling and clanging of the animals' packs adding a quaint musical note. One of the loads ruptured in the dusty street in front of Hawk, spewing pickaxes, tin cups, beans, hardtack, and red flannel unmentionables in all directions.

Small children screamed for their mothers, and frightened women snatched them up and dashed into the safety of storefronts. Some of the men ran toward the source of the bedlam, but Hawk blew lazy circles of smoke and watched them drift away on the still dry air. The spectacle was sure to reveal itself sooner or later.

He didn't have to wait long.

Hawk had lived in Arizona most of his life, among both the whites and the Apaches. He'd seen things no man should have to see. But nothing in the vast experience of his twenty-eight years had prepared him for the almost biblical sight of a camel caravan lumbering down Congress Street.

"Well, I'll be damned," he muttered. His chair rocked down with a thud, and Hawk shoved back his hat for a better look.

The horses tied at the hitching posts along the street went wild as the strange-looking beasts approached, but Hawk paid them little attention. His unwavering gaze was riveted on the lead rider. The handsome young woman managed to appear serene and unruffled atop the ugly, swaying camel. She looked straight ahead, as if unaware of, or perhaps unconcerned by, the chaos she had unloosed on the citizenry.

Never had Hawk seen such a beguiling sight. The girl's delicate features were shaded from the hot April sun by the brim of a ridiculous domed hat that looked more like a helmet than a proper John B. A gauzy white scarf tied around it fluttered behind her like a banner.

Her light-colored shirtwaist resembled a military blouse with its brass buttons, epaulets, and dark

green tie, but its masculine cut was made remarkably feminine by the way she filled it out. Fine
leather boots disappeared under the hem of a heavy,
green calf-length skirt split for riding astride.

There were eight camels in the unlikely parade,
and Hawk estimated the ungainly animals to be at
least eight feet tall. Big patches of fur, the color of
dirty sand, were falling out of mangy hides. Each
camel was fitted with a framework that formed a box
around the hump and carried either rider or pack.
Small copper harness bells tinkled merrily above the
din, and the still hot air was made stifling by the
dust stirred up by the beasts' big splayed feet.

The other riders in the moth-eaten entourage included a well-dressed and dignified-looking old gentleman wearing a monocle and an uneasy smile; a
small, dark-skinned man swathed in white robes;
and a wild-haired woman decked out in the colorful
garb of a gypsy. All and all, it was an exotic assemblage.

Hawk appreciated a good show as well as the next
person, and watching the locals contend with their
fractious animals provided solid entertainment. Tucson, with all its grasping for civilization, had become
a mite boring lately, and it did Hawk's heart good
to see the community's fine upstanders with their
mouths hanging open.

He hid his amused interest behind an unsmiling
facade. He'd learned early in life to keep his
thoughts and feelings to himself and to make the
most of whatever advantage such reticence provided. His temper, banked like a well-tended fire,
was slow to blaze. But when it did, its heat could be
deadly. He did what he had to do to survive, but he
was never impulsive. In this country, a rash man
was a dead man.

There had been those who'd mistaken his quiet
reserve for passivity. There'd even been those stupid enough to misread the hard-eyed loner and prod

him to the breaking point. The fools had lived to regret their poor judgment.

Hawk hadn't trusted anyone since his mother died. He'd thought himself in love only once, but he'd since put so much physical and emotional distance between himself and those memories that they no longer seemed to belong to him.

His primary interest in women now was in what their bodies offered him, but even so, women were usually more nuisance than not. He doubted he'd ever meet one worth the trouble required to get to know her. However, as he watched the straight-backed, honey-haired stranger ride toward him, looking for all the world like some haughty desert princess, Hawk felt unfamiliar stirrings of curiosity and excitement.

Sybilla Antonia Hartford was acutely aware of the effect her arrival was having on the local inhabitants. Being completely British in attitude and manner, if not in blood, she managed to hide her misgivings behind an air of authoritative calm.

She had considered leaving the camels behind at the railway station and searching for the man called Hawk Devlin alone, but one look at the ruffians loitering around the depot had changed her mind. One thing she had learned since her arrival was that there was safety in numbers. Though a veritable oasis of civilization by Western standards, Tucson was still a rough-and-tumble outpost by her own.

Replies to her inquiries about the best guide for the expedition had been unanimous, but her attempts to learn Devlin's whereabouts had garnered little more than diffident shrugs and an occasional "Beats me, ma'am." One bristle-faced fellow claimed no one ever knew where Devlin was until he "sorta appeared" among them.

She had hoped the unusual sight of the camels would create enough uproar on the streets to lure the man out. Surveying said uproar with an aplomb that Queen Victoria would have been proud of, Sybilla now feared she'd made a dreadful mistake. She could only hope she wasn't breaking any laws.

She noticed a young man standing agape on the wooden sidewalk. Guiding Jezebel with a single rein and driving stick, she halted the camel in front of him and asked in the crisply modulated tones of the well-bred, well-educated Briton, "I wonder, can you help me? I'm looking for Hawk Devlin and was told he might be in town. Would you perchance know his present whereabouts?"

"Beg pardon, ma'am?"

"Hawk Devlin," she pronounced slowly for the lad's benefit. "Do you know him?"

"Why sure, ma'am. Everybody knows who Hawk is."

"Splendid. Then perhaps you can direct me to him."

The boy rubbed his freckled chin. "Well, ma'am, nobody ever knows *where* he is."

Sybilla sighed in frustration. What was the man, some phantom will-o'-the-wisp? "I was told he resided near here. Is he in town or not?"

"Don't rightly know, ma'am." The boy stared at the camel, who curled back her lips in a superior sneer and batted her long, curling lashes.

Sybilla had been told Americans spoke English, but since her arrival in the country she'd concluded that if they did, it was some primitive dialect known only to themselves.

"That's a camel, ain't it?" The boy was clearly proud of his perceptiveness.

"It is indeed. Now if you will be so kind—"

"How came it to be so ugly?"

Sybilla sighed her frustration. "No doubt its appearance is the result of a weakness in its genetic composition. An evolutionary problem with which I am sure you can most strongly identify." She looked around at the gathered crowd. "Can anyone tell me where I might find Hawk Devlin?"

"Right here, lady." Hawk stepped into the street, his curiosity aroused more by the woman's beauty than by her bizarre arrival.

Sybilla turned toward the deep voice just in time to see a man throw down a cigar and grind it under his heel. He tugged down the wide brim of his hat and crossed the street with deliberate strides. Could this man be the legendary Devlin? He was hardly the grizzled old desert rat she had expected.

"You looking for me?"

"Are you Hawk Devlin?"

"Who wants to know?"

Although her behavior indicated a thorough lack of manners, Sybilla found herself staring at the man. She had been told Devlin was part Apache, but this fellow did not conform to her expectations. He was taller than any Indian she'd ever seen, and his long-limbed muscularity was quite different from the squat, stocky physiques she'd come to associate with Athapascan peoples.

His hard body was taut, as if conditioned to expect trouble, and his skin was burned bronze by the sun. Its darkness served only to emphasize the startling quality of his arresting blue eyes and long sable-brown hair. His features, which included a straight nose that was more Celtic than Indian and full, unsmiling lips were, in a word, compelling.

Yet his overall countenance was one of a dangerously uncivilized man. Sybilla could not remember ever seeing a more overpoweringly masculine example of God's handiwork. As he stared back at her, she experienced a shivery chill despite the ninety-plus degree temperature. She also had the unsettling sensation of not having donned enough undergarments.

"I asked you a question, lady." Hawk took inordinate pleasure in the way she looked him over.

Sybilla kept her eyes on Devlin. She was loath to look away and told herself it was because he was the sort one did not turn one's back on. "Forgive me. I am Sybilla Hartford."

She said it as if it was supposed to mean something, but Hawk wasn't impressed. "So? What do you want with me?"

"I wish to hire you."

Hawk looked up at the Englishwoman and, despite his good intentions, felt drawn into the golden depths of her pale brown eyes. He'd never seen cat eyes like hers in a woman, nor had he ever met a woman with enough self-assurance to match him gaze for gaze without flinching.

Her tawny hair, half hidden by the ridiculous hat, was firmly secured against errant breezes. Her skin had the pale luster of old cameos. She looked as though she'd been reared in a misty rose bower away from sun and hardness.

Hawk surprised himself by looking away first. Most of the mutinous horses had been led down the street, and a form of peace had been restored. People came out of hiding and stood around gaping, obviously intent on hearing what the lady had to say. To them, an Englishwoman was a creature as rare and alien as a camel.

"I don't have all day to stand in the street smelling your stinking camels," Hawk informed her. His voice was intentionally gruff to mask her effect on him. "What do you want to hire me to do?"

Sybilla flicked Jezebel's flank with the stick, and the ponderous beast bent her front legs. She knelt with a jerking movement, folded up her hind legs, and fell to the ground with a dusty thud. Dismounting gracefully, Sybilla handed the rein to the white-robed man who appeared suddenly at her side. "Thank you, Ahmed. Wait here please."

The little man bowed deferentially. "Yes, missy."

She noticed the others in her entourage had also dismounted and were chatting amiably with the bystanders. Uncle John was placating a blustery-faced lawman, and she hoped they would not be fined for disturbing the public peace. She could ill afford additional expenses.

Turning to Hawk, Sybilla said, "Come, Mr. Devlin, our discussion is best held in private."

Hawk was amazed. The woman was no bigger than a child. Atop the camel she'd seemed much taller, and he wondered how such a small young person could command so much authority.

"Well? Are you coming?" she asked archly.

"I don't know if I am or not. What do you want with me?"

"I told you. I wish to engage your services." That statement was met with considerable jeering and elbow-poking from the gathered crowd. "Hey, Devlin, you reckon those gals over at Mae's have been blabbing again?" someone called out.

Hawk ignored them and looked her up and down. Little or not, she carried her weight in all the right places. All that starch and polish concealed a fine figure of a woman. "And what services would those be, exactly?" he drawled, his lips hinting at a grin.

Sybilla was charged with awareness of this bold stranger and could not understand her reaction. She'd felt little more than indifference toward the few men who had previously expressed such interest in her. She wasn't like the simpering little fools whose coy flirtations and empty-headed gushings attracted equally empty-headed men.

She would not pretend to be something she wasn't for any man, nor would she defer to their "superiority." Those who couldn't accept her ambition or allow her to lead the life she chose, she disdained. Fools that they were, the men of her acquaintance had allowed themselves to be so treated, reinforcing her opinion that there simply was not a man in the world for her.

Sybilla's cheeks burned at Devlin's undisguised appraisal of her attributes. This rough Westerner was not a man to be scorned. By her or anyone else.

"I'm fairly parched," she said with concealed

trepidation, fanning her face with her hand for emphasis. "Could we perhaps go somewhere and have a drink?"

"Somehow I can't picture you bellying up to the Dusty Devil bar and belting down a few shots of whiskey."

Sybilla's eyes widened at the image. "I should think not," she said indignantly.

"Then maybe you'd better tell me what you had in mind."

The man was still staring at her, and she felt his eyes all over her body like a sudden fever. "Water. Is it presumptous of me to assume there is water in this town?"

"I think I can scare some up." Besides being curious about what she was doing here, Hawk figured it wouldn't hurt to find out what she wanted from him. After all, it wasn't every day a pretty, refined lady offered him money to do God only knew what.

He took her elbow and steered her across the street into the U.S. Bakery. Officially, it was the Uncle Sam Bakery, but when the thrifty owner ordered the sign, he'd economized.

They stepped into the dim shop, and Sybilla was grateful for the respite from the unrelenting sun. The inside temperature was considerably lower due to a slowly rotating ceiling fan that stirred air cooled by several blocks of ice set in tubs around the room. The arrangement was ingenious and effective.

Devlin ordered Sybilla a glass of lemonade with ice and two gingerbread cookies. He watched her take off her helmet and place it on an empty chair. Why would a woman with such glorious sun-kissed hair want to gather it into an unbecoming knot at the nape of her slender neck? he wondered.

Devlin ordered nothing for himself, and Sybilla concluded that he was not the lemonade type. No doubt he felt more at home in a saloon filled with other rough-and-toughs than in a bakery filled with muffins and pastries.

Seated at one of two small tables, Hawk watched Sybilla with the intensity of his namesake. The dainty way she sipped the lemonade was hardly how a "parched" person would consume liquid. "Okay. You got your drink, you got your cookies, now tell me what you want."

Finding no napkin available, she reached into her pocket, withdrew a lace-edged handkerchief, and dabbed her mouth. "I shall come right to the point."

"That would save time," Hawk muttered.

"I am planning an expedition into the Superstition Mountains and was told you know more about the area than anyone else."

Hawk's sable brows drew together. "Who told you that?"

She shrugged. "Everyone I asked. You seem to be something of a legend in the area."

"Yeah. Anyone who goes into the Superstitions and lives to tell about it becomes a legend real fast."

"I also queried the magistrate in Tombstone, and he was kind enough to recommend you. He said you were a pathfinder par excellence."

"Oh, he did, did he?" Hawk leaned back in his chair. "What else did the old coyote say?"

Sybilla hesitated, wondering if she should tell him. The lawman had admitted that while Hawk Devlin was certainly the best man for the job, she would be better off hiring a rabid wolf. Or words to that effect. No, she decided as she studied him across the table, she wouldn't mention that. It might provoke him, and he was clearly not the type one would intentionally wish to provoke.

She smiled sweetly. "He said you possess faultless integrity, and are scrupulously honest and totally trustworthy."

Hawk's eyes narrowed suspiciously. That didn't sound a bit like something that old dog of a lawman would say about him. Especially not after he'd run Hawk out of Tombstone last month for no good reason. He couldn't be held responsible for a couple of pretty senoritas trying to give each other a hairbob with shivs. Hadn't he assured them there was enough of him to go around?

"What did you lose in the Superstitions?" he asked.

"Lose? Why, nothing. I am hoping to find something."

Hawk groaned and shook his head. "Don't tell me, let me guess. You're looking for a gold mine."

Sybilla smiled and her face lit up. "Precisely. You see, I have—"

"A map?" he supplied mockingly.

"Why, yes. You are indeed perceptive, Mr. Devlin. I believe we shall get along famously."

"I doubt it. You see, I'm not interested." He scraped back his chair to leave, but her hand shot across the table to stop him.

"Once you've heard me out, you will be. My map is authentic in every detail. All I require is an honest guide who knows the country."

"Lady, for every so-called lost treasure, there are hundreds of genuine, sure-thing maps."

She smiled. "Not like mine there aren't."

"You got any idea how many people have died in those mountains looking for gold?" He should know. During the years he'd been on a similar quest, he'd buried a few of those unlucky souls himself.

Sybilla expected resistance and dealt with it impatiently. "Quite a few, I'm sure. That's where you come in."

"Wrong." He stood up. "That's where I go out."

"I'm willing to pay you handsomely."

He paused. His claim was playing out, and he could use some cash for a stake to continue his own search. "Up front?"

It took her a moment to understand. "In advance, you mean?"

"Yeah, in advance. Taking tenderfeet into the Superstitions isn't exactly a reliable business. I prefer to get my money before my clients saddle a cloud and ride for the Great Beyond."

That bit of Western humor failed to amuse Sybilla. "I'll pay you after the gold is located."

"Good day, ma'am." Hawk shook his head. It was a shame such a fine-looking woman was also a fool; he wasn't about to waste any more time with her. There was something strange about those pale eyes of hers. The way they burned, she had to be off her mental reservation.

"If you would only listen."

"Lady, you're crazy. A woman like you wouldn't last two days in those slag dumps of hell."

Sybilla folded her hands primly in her lap. "Is that the real reason you will not accept the job? Or won't your male pride allow you to work for a woman?"

"No. I'm just looking out for my own hide. If I haul you into the mountains to die, the men around here would string me up quicker than hell can scorch a feather. In Tucson it's against the law to waste good womanhood."

Sybilla's smile was patronizing. "I can assure you I have no intention of dying."

"Folks hardly ever do, lady. I've lived around here most of my life, and there's one thing I do know. There are a thousand ways to die in the desert, and none of them are pleasant."

"I am not frightened."

"You should be." For some reason, the thought of anything happening to her was upsetting. He stood abruptly. "I believe that concludes our business."

But as he opened the door, she called to him. "Mr. Devlin! I must insist you hear me out."

Her imperious tone of voice only strengthened Hawk's resolve to see the last of her. Without turning around, he said. "Lady, you can insist till you turn blue and keel over, for all I care."

As his broad back disappeared through the door, Sybilla's fist smashed down on the wobbly table in an uncharacteristic display of temper. Since she'd

arrived in this country, it had become harder and
harder to restrain what her father had called her
Spanish impulses, those hot fits that were a legacy
from her criollo mother.

How dare Devlin speak to her in that manner and
then walk out! He was nothing but an ill-bred bar-
barian and had no more manners than the other
street ruffians. Where was his sense of adventure?
What kind of man refused to assist a woman in
need?

Sybilla had imagined a man of Devlin's ilk would
be eager to earn a bit of easy money. But perhaps
he didn't believe in honest work. When she realized
she was muttering to herself, she shot the rotund
proprietor a look calculated to discourage questions.
Scraping back her chair, she flounced out of the es-
tablishment.

She slammed the door, and it shuddered on its
hinges. The baker drew a relieved breath.

A moment later the bell over the door tinkled, and
Sybilla slipped in. She picked up the hat she'd left
on the chair and retraced her steps to the door. ''The
cookies were delicious and the lemonade most refreshing,'' she said as she eased the door shut
gently.

The Hartford party established a tent camp on the
outskirts of town that was soon humming with do-
mesticity. Sir John Collings was small of stature but
big of heart. He worked diligently to clean the desert
sand out of his camera box, mumbling all the while
about the indignities of camp life.

''I find it utterly preposterous that there is a perfectly good hotel and restaurant in town, and we are
reduced to sleeping in tents and eating goulash prepared by a witch.''

''For shame, Uncle,'' Sybilla scolded. ''Zora is not
a witch.''

''She acts like one,'' he insisted.

"Telling fortunes in a circus hardly constitutes practicing witchcraft," she pointed out.

As if to give lie to Sybilla's words, the gypsy Zora canted loudly and unmelodiously as she leaned over a bubbling pot at the campfire. The long black rope of her hair hung over one shoulder as she stirred, and big golden hoops swayed in her ears.

John raised his brow, and his monocle dropped from its niche. "Looks like a heathen to me," he harrumphed.

Sybilla would never admit it aloud, but the fey gypsy did, at times, seem a sorceress. "She is an accomplished cook. Ahmed is very religious and, as her husband, he will keep her waywardness in check."

Ahmed, seated near the fire, mended the harness of one of his beloved camels. Unpacked and hobbled for the night, the creatures rested in the waning sunlight, chewing their cuds contentedly.

John shrugged eloquently. "He does seem to try, poor fellow. A difficult task, that."

Sybilla, hands clutched behind her back and head lowered in concentration, paced around the camp kicking up a miniature dust storm. She was still irritated at Devlin not only for refusing her offer, but also for laughing at her.

Well, she thought begrudgingly, perhaps he hadn't exactly laughed, but he had tried his utmost to make her feel foolish. The angry thought that she had allowed him to get away with it quickened her step.

John watched her for a moment. "What's all the bother, Sybilla? Why all this stalking about?"

"He turned me down, Uncle." Her determination wavered for the first time since they had begun this trip. "Our quest might end right here. Without Devlin's help we might never find the gold."

"Perhaps he'll yet change his mind?" John suggested optimistically.

"He was adamant. The Montoya gold is the only

legacy from my mother's family. And if we fail to find it, I shan't have another chance to prove to the Bureau of Ethnology that I am a qualified ethnologist in my own right."

"Surely, my dear, that is of no further consequence. The directors of the bureau have already withdrawn the research grant."

And so they had, immediately upon notification of her father's death. They had also withdrawn all support and suggested in no uncertain terms that Sybilla give up her foolish idea and stay home where members of the "weaker sex" belonged.

But she couldn't do that. She no longer had a home. Her late father, noted ethnologist Dr. Thomas Hartford, had sold what was left of Hartsmoor, the family estate, to make this trip. Over the years, he had disposed of it stick by stick, using the money to pay his debts and finance scholarly expeditions around the world.

Weakened by a years-long battle with malaria and a heart condition that had almost destroyed his health as well as his career, he had become obsessed in his last years with the idea of going to America to search for the Montoya gold.

With it, he felt he could prove that the map and diaries he had inherited from his wife were authentic and that Sybilla's mother's ancestor, Ricardo Montoya, was not the deluded lunatic everyone believed him to have been.

Montoya had claimed to his dying day that during his explorations of the area now known as Arizona territory, he had helped a tribe of friendly Indians who had rewarded him by leading him to a fabulously rich gold mine—a mine whose location was revealed on the crumbling, two-hundred-year-old map now in Sybilla's possession.

Even after several months, it was still hard for Sybilla to believe her father was gone. Though he'd been a virtual stranger during much of her childhood, he'd always been her hero—dashing, intrepid, resolute.

His sudden death had left Sybilla ill-prepared to take charge of family affairs. She'd been forced to shed her tears and mourn her loss in private while worrying about her own uncertain future. Her lack of public emotion did not mean she hadn't loved her father.

Rather, she felt she had to be strong for Uncle John. Dear old John, who was really her father's uncle, had been alone and homeless after the sale of Hartsmoor, and he was now her responsibility.

The absence of choices had made her decide to make the trip without her father. Uncle John had insisted on accompanying her. He pointed out that his fondness for dime novels featuring Deadeye Dick made him almost an expert on Western culture. He also had some expertise as an amateur photographer and had appealed to her sense of glory by persuading her that he could use his dubious skills to document the journey.

They had boarded ship in London and docked in New Orleans, then traveled overland across Texas and New Mexico on an endless and forgettable series of smoky trains and bone-jarring stagecoaches.

They had encountered Ahmed and Zora in Tombstone, where the couple was having problems with the owner of a broken-down circus. Recognizing the value of camels in the desert, Sybilla had convinced them to join her quest, and the party had traveled by rail to Tucson, where they'd arrived earlier today.

Sybilla had endured a lot to get this far, but she was running out of options. She had enough money left to outfit the expedition, but what good was that without a knowledgeable guide to lead it? Devlin was purported to be the best man for the job, and she wanted the best.

She was accustomed to getting what she wanted. She had neither the wish nor the funds to return to England. All that pastoral peacefulness would assure her untimely expiration from boredom. If she was to remain a spinster—and at twenty-three she had resigned herself to that fate—she would have a career in ethnology. She was not about to spend her life sitting in some quaint dooryard feeding pigeons.

"Sybilla, dear," Uncle John chided her gently, "won't you stop that dreadful pacing and have a spot of dinner?"

"I'm really not hungry. I must think."

"I've never seen you so agitated, my dear. Do you want to tell me what happened when you spoke to Hawk Devlin?"

Sybilla whirled around. "Hawk! What kind of name is that? It is not a proper name at all. However, I suppose it suits him, for he is not a proper man."

Uncle John set aside the camera box and attempted to rise. "Did he say or do anything untoward, my dear? Shall I thrash the young devil?"

Sybilla was touched by the offer. Protecting her was so important to her elderly uncle that he would pit his feeble pugilistic skills against those of a man as strongly virile as Devlin. "No, dear, he did not insult me. Though I am sure he tried. I made him a fair offer, and he tossed it in my face."

"Unsporting of him, I must say."

"Indeed. The man is nothing but an uncouth ruffian, and if he is the best Arizona has to offer, I can only wonder at the future of this territory."

Uncle John smiled. "It isn't at all like you to give up so easily."

"I am not giving up. In fact, I intend to find Devlin right now and demand he escort us." She wheeled around and stalked off toward town.

"Oh, Sybilla, dear?" Uncle John called politely.

"Yes, Uncle?"

"Shall I accompany you?"

"Thank you, no. I must do this myself."

"Very well. But one last question. Are you quite

sure demanding is the best way to proceed? Mr. Devlin does not strike me as a gentleman who takes orders kindly.''

Sybilla laughed. Her uncle was right. Making demands would only fuel an already raging fire. She would persuade, bribe, threaten, or cajole Devlin into leading her into the Superstitions.

''The problem is,'' she mused aloud, ''Mr. Devlin does not strike me as a gentleman at all.''

Chapter 2

Hawk eased back in the big copper bathtub and sighed his pleasure. The hot, sudsy water was sheer luxury to a desert rat who thought nothing of riding five miles to the nearest water hole. It was almost sinful to waste so much water bathing, but since he'd never been opposed to sinning on a grand scale, he settled down to enjoy the decadence.

"Wo Chin!" he called after a suitable period of ecstasy.

"Yes, Mista Hawk?" The little Chinese man bobbed and bowed, his long queue swinging behind him.

"Fish one of those cheroots out of my vest pocket, will you? I didn't get a chance to finish the one I started earlier."

Wo Chin unwrapped the cigar and placed it between Hawk's white teeth. He produced a match from the folds of his loose garments and held it while Hawk inhaled. The little man beamed.

"Is good, Mista Hawk?"

Hawk dried his fingers on the towel draped over the edge of the tub and pinched the cigar between his thumb and forefinger. "The best," he drawled. "Lucky thing I require so little; a good cigar, a hot bath, and the biggest steak in town puts me in tall cotton."

"Yes, Mista Hawk. You hoppy man alrighty."

Wo Chin bowed and backed away. Hawk watched

a chain of connected smoke rings float upward in the humid, soapy-smelling air and considered the Chinese man's assessment. It wasn't exactly accurate, since he'd long since stopped expecting happiness. He'd hardened his heart for so long that he didn't feel much emotion anymore. He didn't ask much of life and was content with what he had. Right now, that consisted of a good horse, a petering-out claim, and the ability to live with himself.

In that regard, he considered himself well off. There were plenty of men who couldn't coexist with their consciences, whose past deeds would haunt them until they ended up in hell where they belonged.

The last man Hawk had trusted was his father, and that had been a long time ago. Captain Malcolm Devlin had chosen to return to Virginia when his Western tour of duty ended. Despite his many promises, he'd preferred his "real" family over a half-Apache laundress and the son he'd fathered. Hawk had been a trusting four-year-old then, and his mother, Mirry, had never given up hope that the dashing cavalry officer would return to them.

But that had never happened, and Hawk had gained enough experience in the meantime to know better than to call any man friend. Likewise, he had no enemies. He didn't let anyone get close enough to love, hate, or even know him.

When he got tired of prospecting, a solitary occupation that suited him fine most of the time, he found work breaking horses for the army and local ranches. He had the well-deserved reputation of being able to ride anything on four legs, and less talented individuals paid good money for his expertise.

The time he spent among people was usually short-lived. It didn't take long for him to grow weary of the backslapping camaraderie of the soldiers and cowboys. Nor was it many weeks before the close quarters of the bunkhouse and barracks induced in him social claustrophobia. He used the stakes he earned to purchase a few months' supplies and, packhorse loaded, headed back to the peace and quiet of his small claim north of town.

Wo Chin's quavery voice, raised in indignation, drew Hawk out of his thoughts. He paid the disturbance little attention since he couldn't understand the Chinese man's Gatling-gun lingo anyway. He sat up straight a moment later when he heard Wo Chin beseech in broken English, "No, no, no, missy. You can no come in here. Bath for mens only."

Missy? Hawk had never heard of a woman storming the doors of the public bathhouse; not even the shamelessly bold residents of Maiden Lane had that much brass. No woman in her right mind would enter the all-male domain.

No woman in her right mind? Now who did he know who fit that description? Nah, it couldn't be. Even she wasn't that crazy. He clenched the cigar between his teeth and craned his neck toward the entrance, observing Wo Chin's valiant attempts to bar admittance to the inner sanctum. The little man was shrieking, jumping up and down, and waving his fists.

His worst fears realized, Hawk groaned at the sight of a bright head of primly pinned hair bobbing up behind Wo Chin. Wide, golden eyes peered over the Chinese man's shoulders into the tub room.

"Is Hawk Devlin in there?" an unmistakably British voice demanded. "The desk clerk at the hotel said he was coming here, and I wish to see him. It is a matter of utmost importance."

Wo Chin, clearly shocked, continued to flap his arms and scream. "No, no, no. You come in here you see too muchy."

Hawk heard Sybilla demur prissily, "I'll be the judge of that," before feinting to the right. When Wo Chin jumped to block her, she deftly slipped around him and strode purposefully across the water-splashed plank floor. Dumbstruck by the

unheard-of sight of a female in the bathhouse, cowboys and prospectors ducked down in their tubs and
snatched up towels to protect their modesty.

"What the hell are you doing in here?" Hawk's
voice was deadly quiet as he bit down hard on the
cigar.

Sybilla hadn't thought past the idea of bearding
the lion in his den, but facing so many unclothed
men brought home her folly. Now she fervently
wished she had waited outside. But it was too late
for that; she would just have to brazen it out.

"I came to see you."

"When you get an eyeful, you can just turn
around and get right back out again," Hawk
drawled.

Sybilla's cheeks flamed at the insinuation, but
with strained British aplomb she managed to keep
up a pretense of detachment. She settled her gaze
on Hawk's face, thinking it the safest place for her
eyes. When his lips curved in a knowing grin, her
body was invaded with a slow heat that only added
to her confusion.

She gripped her hands behind her back and focused her attention on a spot just beyond Hawk's
shoulder. Another fatal mistake. One of the other
patrons, hoping to make good his escape, was just
stepping out of a tub. Realizing his exposure, the
man froze like a jackrabbit in a hunter's gunsight.
With one foot in and one foot out of the tub, he
clutched a skimpy towel before him.

Her shocked gasp sent the poor man bolting for
cover. She closed her eyes against the sight of so
much white flesh and willed herself out of the horrid
predicament. Her humiliation increased tenfold
when the other men laughed at her distress.

She opened her eyes cautiously and found Hawk
struggling to contain his own mirth. Attempting to
regain control of her suddenly unruly emotions, she
proceeded to explain away her rash actions.

"You would not hear me out earlier, so I came

here to make a captive audience of you, as it were."
Sybilla shifted from one foot to the other. Waiting
for Devlin's response, she let her gaze slide down
to the visible pulse beating within the brown column
of his neck.

"Even captives have a right to privacy," he insisted.

Sybilla realized he had a point, but did not know
how to back down and still save face. Jamming her
hands on her hips, she tried to bluff her way
through. "I am here, and here I shall stay."

"Have it your way, lady." Hawk found Sybilla's
discomfort entertaining. Watching her wrestle with
her riled-up sensibilities was as good as seeing any
show staged at the opera house. Getting in on the
act, he picked up the cake of soap and rubbed it
enthusiastically over his chest.

Not knowing how to proceed, she hesitated, and
her gaze followed his movements with a will of its
own. His bronzed, soap-slick muscles rippled as he
scrubbed, and she realized that Hawk appeared to
be tan all over. How could that be? She'd glimpsed
tan faces and hands on the other men in the bathhouse, a sharp contrast to their pale bodies.

"Must you do that?" she sputtered.

"Do what?"

"*That!*"

"This *is* a bathhouse. If you had any sense, you
would haul your skinny English butt out of here
right now. No decent woman would dare come in
here." He feigned a studied indifference he didn't
feel by applying the soap to his scalp and scrubbing
it into a lather.

Skinny? How dare he! Sybilla had almost decided
her outrageous ploy had backfired and was prepared to wait for him outside. But his insult changed
her mind. She would not be ordered about in that
derogatory manner.

"Perhaps the decent women of this dusty little

burg are not quite as desperate as I. I shan't leave until you agree to talk to me.''

Hawk slapped the bathwater with his palm, and it splashed up and extinguished his cigar. ''Dammit, now look what you've done. That's the last straw.'' He tossed the sodden cheroot away.

Her gaze was momentarily drawn by the movement, which parted the soap film around Hawk's lap. Before she did indeed see "too muchy," she averted her gaze. When she could speak with some semblance of dignity, she said, ''All I ask, Mr. Devlin, is a fair hearing. You owe it to me to find out what I have to offer.''

''I don't owe you mule squat,'' he said amiably. ''And I'm not about to sit here in my altogether and listen to you either.'' She straightened her shoulders, showing him all too well what she had to offer, which was another problem. He closed his eyes and vigorously scrubbed his head.

Sybilla, vexed at being dismissed and ignored, spied a bucket of rinse water. Without thinking her actions through—a newly acquired fault since she'd met this infuriating man—she hefted the bucket and dumped the water over his soapy head. Snidely pleasant, she said, ''Allow me, Mr. Devlin.''

While he sputtered and cursed at the cold drenching, she upended the bucket on the floor and plopped down on it. She grabbed the towel draped over the side of the tub and held it away from him. Hawk was left with no covering save a few rapidly disintegrating soap bubbles.

''Dammit, woman, you've gone too far.''

Yes, she had. But it was not in her nature to admit it. ''On the contrary. I am not going anywhere. I plan to sit right here until you change your mind and agree to discuss the proposition I offered you.'' Or until she swooned from the sight of so much male virility, she thought.

Hawk glared at the smug-faced woman. Who would have guessed she possessed so much arrogant nerve? "Wo Chin! Fetch the law and have this trespasser hauled out of here."

"It would be much less complicated if you simply agreed to talk to me." Sybilla wasn't about to back down now, despite Devlin's murderous looks and her own trembling knees. "If you do, I will leave promptly. If you do not . . ." She allowed her words to trail off for effect.

They glowered at each other for several long moments while Hawk's awareness of his imminent exposure grew. And that wasn't the only thing growing. Sybilla Hartford's brazen behavior was having a disastrously arousing effect on him. What a time for his body to betray him, and after all he'd done for it too. He didn't want to give her the satisfaction of knowing her little ploy had worked, but neither did he want his embarrassing situation revealed to every rock-headed cowboy and desert rat in the place.

Sensing she was near victory, and saying a little prayer for his cooperation, Sybilla inquired politely, "Shall I wait outside while you finish your toilette, Mr. Devlin? Or would you prefer to see me arrested and incarcerated in what the locals so colorfully refer to as the hoosegow?"

"Dammit, Devlin," called a water-logged sourdough. "Tell the little lady you'll talk to her so we can get outta here. This water's gettin' cold, and I'm shrivelin' up somethin' awful."

Shriveling was the opposite of Hawk's problem, and he didn't like being outnumbered. Not one bit. His anger boiled up again when he realized he had no choice. "Dammit. All right. Wait outside."

Relieved beyond belief, Sybilla could not hold back a triumphant smile. "Shall I trust you to keep your word?"

Hawk revised his earlier assessment. The woman *was* crazy. "Get out of here before I change my mind and have you arrested for taking indecent liberties with an unarmed man."

"Certainly, Mr. Devlin. You will not regret your decision."

He watched her rise from the bucket, dust off her absurd skirt, and walk primly toward the door. He slapped the water again in frustration. "Hell, lady, I already do."

Sybilla waited impatiently outside the bathhouse for what seemed an interminably long time. She was beginning to think Devlin had sneaked out the back way and eluded her. She tried to tell herself it didn't matter, she would find the Montoya gold without him if necessary, but she knew her chances of doing so were what the people out here called slim and none.

A block away on Meyer Street the town's nightlife was getting under way with rambunctious gusto. The street was lined with beer gardens, saloons, gambling parlors, and worse. The establishments attracted blighters of the worst sort: so far she had turned down four improper proposals from passing cowboys, all promising to show her "the time of her life."

Somehow she doubted that was possible; Tucson was clearly a rough frontier village with little of cultural interest to recommend it. The opera house's current offering was billed as a program of "talented and artistic knife-throwing." Not exactly what one would call edifying entertainment.

It was obvious the town was undergoing severe economic depression. She had seen several boarded-up stores as well as a large number of able-bodied men loitering in the streets when they should have been more profitably engaged. Perusal of a copy of the *Arizona Star* revealed that all major industries, including mining and cattle, were experiencing hard times.

According to the article, business was so bad in Tucson that the population had declined to just over five thousand. Looking around, she didn't find that at all surprising. Why would anyone who had a choice wish to live in a godforsaken place where the landscape was unaesthetically composed of prickly flora, hostile fauna, and an unrelenting sea of dust?

Apparently, one sign of the difficult times was an increase in lawlessness; vivid accounts of murders, robberies, and rapes filled the headlines. Many of them had been attributed to a cutthroat gang led by a local badman named Maloche.

Recalling those stories, Sybilla glanced about nervously. It was growing dark, and she hadn't seen another woman on the streets since taking up her vigil outside the bathhouse. Perhaps coming to town alone had not been such a good idea after all.

She jumped when a deep voice spoke behind her. "I've been thinking over what you said."

"Oh, Mr. Devlin, you startled me." She turned around and noted the improvement in his appearance. He'd had a shave and looked much younger now that his face was devoid of bristly whiskers. His hair, worn short on the sides but longer in back, was still slightly damp from his bath, and he smelled of some spicy tonic. His boots were polished, and he wore a fresh blue shirt, leather vest, and clean denims. She tried not to notice the way the taut fabric of his trousers melded to his heavily muscled thighs, for she had seen enough of him in that washtub to realize just how beautifully put together he was.

Aware that she was staring again, she murmured, "I am pleased you have reconsidered."

Hawk was struck once more by Sybilla's small stature. He was sure his hands could span her narrow waist and was sorely tempted to prove his theory on the spot. A few wayward tendrils of hair had escaped their pins during her tussle with Wo Chin, and the dishevel lent an air of vulnerable femininity to her otherwise no-nonsense appearance.

"I didn't say I reconsidered. I said I thought about it. I've decided that no amount of talking is going to change my mind, so let's just save time by skipping the discussion.'' He turned to leave but knew he couldn't possibly get off that easily.

Sybilla remembered what Uncle John had warned about making demands and bit back a sharp retort. Swallowing her pride, she managed to underscore her words with an amazing degree of helplessness. ''Please, Mr. Devlin, I beg of you. Do wait and hear what I have to say before you reject it.''

Hawk stopped in his tracks. She begged of him? Now, why did he doubt that? Knowing he should keep right on walking, he ignored his better judgment and relented. ''All right. I'm hungry enough to eat a saddle blanket, so if you want to tag along with me to the hotel, I'll give you ten minutes while the steak's cooking. But that's it.''

She tried not to smile, fearing she would appear too smug. ''Splendid, Mr. Devlin. That's most generous of you, I'm sure.''

''Stop calling me Mr. Devlin. You've seen enough of me by now to call me by my first name.''

''Perhaps so,'' she admitted. ''But I do think we should endeavor to put that embarrassing encounter behind us. Therefore, a certain formality must be maintained, Mr. Devlin.''

Good idea. Especially since he was planning to send her on her way as soon as he could.

They walked in silence the two blocks to the hotel dining room. Sybilla struggled to keep pace with his long stride and maintain a ladylike decorum. Once they were seated at a gingham-covered table, she declined his offer of supper, claiming she had already dined.

She hadn't, but her stomach was so full of butterflies she couldn't eat a bite. She blamed her excitement on the forthcoming journey and refused to admit it might be Devlin's presence that had such an effect on her.

While he ordered his steak with instructions to ''just hurt it a little'' and asked for a side order of something called calf fries, Sybilla tried to organize her thoughts. The task was made difficult by the disconcerting way Hawk watched her, his blue eyes taking in her every movement.

She felt self-conscious and worried that this could very well be her last chance to persuade him to guide her into the Superstitions. If she failed, the expedition would be as good as lost, for she had made additional inquiries and had found no one else even remotely qualified for the job.

As soon as the waiter departed, Hawk's impatience became evident. "Okay, let's hear it so you can be on your way. I'd like to enjoy my supper in peace and quiet, and somehow I get the feeling that wherever you are, peace and quiet are as scarce as jackrabbits on a reservation."

Sybilla ignored the rebuke, relieved that he made no further reference to the bathhouse incident. Her memories of Hawk in that tub were troubling enough without him bringing it up again. Perhaps he wasn't such a bad sort after all. She took a deep breath and began. "Have you ever heard of Dr. Thomas Hartford?"

"No. Should I?"

"My father was a highly respected ethnologist associated, until his retirement, with Cambridge University in England. For the last five years he worked on his own, and I trained at his side. Due to poor health, he suffered a few professional setbacks, but his last dream was for us to come to Arizona Territory and search for the gold he was convinced was here. We sold all we owned to finance the trip, but he died just months before we were to depart."

Hawk had no experience at offering comfort, so he merely mumbled "I'm sorry." Secretly he thought the old man had a lot of nerve even to consider dragging his daughter along on such a wild goose chase.

"Thank you," she said stiffly. "His death was sudden and most unexpected, though he had suffered for some time from bouts of malaria which weakened his heart. Uncle John and I are here to continue the quest.''

Hawk noticed how the other men in the dining room looked at Sybilla, their glances coveting her rare, delicate beauty. She seemed totally unaware of her effect on them. He wasn't exactly immune himself. Hawk leaned forward, his elbows on the table, and offered the best advice he could. ''Go home. You don't belong here.''

''Perhaps not,'' she said softly. ''But I am here nonetheless.''

''You have no idea what you're getting into.''

''I assure you, I do.''

Hawk shook his head. More people had died from complacency in this country than from Apache arrows. ''What is it you want?''

''It is my intention to find the Montoya gold and prove to the scientific world that it has not heard the last from the Hartfords.''

Hawk was in the process of swallowing a sip of the hot coffee the waiter had poured, and her words made him sputter. ''The Montoya gold? Is that what this is all about?''

''It is.''

''For crissakes, lady, why didn't you say so? You could have saved us both a lot of trouble.''

''I'm afraid I don't understand.''

''I know you don't. That's what's so pitiful.'' He sipped his coffee more carefully this time. ''This country is full of legends about lost gold troves. It started with El Dorado, and the stories have been gaining steam ever since. The Lost Padre, the Lost Pegleg, the Lost Frenchman, the Lost Soldier, the Lost Pesh-La-Chi. The list goes on and on. They even have a saying out here that the mines men lose are always richer than the mines they find.''

Sybilla listened patiently to the longest speech she'd yet heard from Devlin. ''What does all that have to do with me?''

''Haven't you been listening? The lost Montoya

gold is the unlikeliest of all the unlikely lost-gold myths.''

She waved his assessment aside with her hand. ''I have documents that prove it is not a myth at all.''

''Oh yeah, how could I forget about your so-called treasure map?'' he asked mockingly.

Suddenly aware of the interested onlookers, Sybilla lowered her voice. ''How much do you know about the legend?''

He shrugged. ''What everybody else knows, I guess. Sometime in the sixteen hundreds a Spaniard named Montoya led an expedition into the area. He turned up alone in Mexico a couple of years later, claiming his whole party had been wiped out and he was the only survivor. Then, to make the story sound better, he also claimed he'd discovered a fortune in gold. Which, unfortunately, he'd had to leave behind.''

Sybilla sighed. It seemed everyone thought her ancestor either a lunatic, a charlatan, or worse. She heard the snide insinuation in Devlin's voice, and suddenly it was important that he think well of her family.

''Ricardo Montoya was an ambitious criollo nobleman,'' she continued. ''Born in Mexico of pure Spanish blood, he set out from Mexico City in 1657, ostensibly on an exploration for the Crown. His destination was the Pimeria Alta, the far land of the Pimas, which, as you know, is now Arizona. Most likely his primary goal was to find enough gold to buy himself a position of power among the New World politicos.''

''And you think he found it?''

''According to Montoya's diaries, which have been in my mother's family for generations, the conquistadors were led to the mine by a tribe of friendly Indians, probably Pimas, as a reward for helping them fend off attacks by hostiles. The Spaniards shared their technology with the Indians, who in turn helped them erect an *arrastre*, or primitive mining operation."

Hawk's eyes narrowed. "So the gold was mined and the Indians were exploited."

"Not at all. Montoya and his men helped them."

"Helped themselves, you mean."

"The work went on for several months, and untold riches were eventually wrested from the earth. During this time, Montoya fell in love with a Pima maiden. He planned to take her home with him to New Spain when the expedition returned."

Hawk smiled wryly; he knew all too well how those kinds of promises turned out. "I bet he did."

His sarcasm was disappointing, but Sybilla continued her tale. "The mining crew was decimated by illness and hardship as well as harassment by hostiles." She smiled. "Apaches, I believe."

"We hostiles have a long history of decimating white men."

"Apparently the Apaches objected to the whole process."

Hawk understood that. "According to the People, gold is sacred. I'm sure they resented the Spaniards' theft of the Earth Mother's gold. If they were given to upholding cultural traditions, they would have called upon the wicked *gans*, mountain spirits, to curse those who stole the sacred ore."

"Well, it seems the Spaniards were indeed cursed, as they fell victim to one tragedy after another, some of which can only be described as unbelievable."

"Ghosts are bad medicine." Hawk shrugged. "I'm surprised the Apaches didn't just raid and be done with it."

"They did. On the day of the final raid, Montoya and his Indian girl were away from the mine professing their love for each other in"—she blushed prettily—"a physical manner. From their hilltop hideaway, they were helpless witnesses to the attack. The Spaniards were all killed, but a few Pimas escaped, including the brother of Montoya's lover."

"And old Ricardo, who by now could read the handwriting on the wall, just moseyed on back to New Spain?" Hawk guessed.

"He knew he had to return with the news of the expedition. He said goodbye to his love and what remained of her people, swearing to return for her and the gold. He gave her an amulet, a golden cross, as proof of his love and set off in the general direction of New Spain."

"That's an amazing story."

"Incredible, isn't it?"

"I don't believe a word of it," Hawk scoffed.

"But it is true." It disturbed Sybilla that she cared so much about his opinion. She tried to tell herself that she was interested only in persuading him to accept her offer, but she felt something else. Something akin to longing.

Her statement did not merit the emotion in her voice, and when Hawk looked at her closely, he glimpsed a vulnerability that he'd thought she lacked. "How the hell did Montoya get back to Mexico alone?"

"He was aided by Spanish friars who had established missions to the south."

"How convenient. I take it he didn't keep those promises he made to the luckless maiden."

"Unfortunately, no. He never returned to the Pimería Alta and the woman he loved."

"Why not? I'd think the gold, if not the girl, would be a powerful incentive."

"He soon settled into the relative comfort of his family's hacienda and an arranged marriage. After his terrible experiences, he had little inclination to return to that savage land again. Besides, no one really believed his tales of glory since he was half mad from his ordeal."

When Hawk had sat down at the table, it had been with one thought—to dismiss Sybilla's story as nonsense and get back to the comfortable existence he'd known before she blew into his life like a cyclone.

But after only a few minutes, he felt drawn to her for reasons he couldn't identify. "You mentioned that the documents were in the possession of your mother's family. How so? I thought you were English."

"On my father's side. He met my mother while lecturing in Mexico City. Vittoria Isabelle Maria Gabriel y Montoya was Spanish, the last of the Montoyas."

Hawk sat up a little straighter. "You mean you're actually a descendant of Ricardo Montoya?"

"Yes, the last one in fact."

"And you believe the story?"

"Oh yes. I've read his diaries, remember. My mother also believed it with all her heart. She was orphaned at an early age, and I think it gave her comfort to think she possessed a golden legacy. That's why she clung to the map and other documents so zealously."

Hawk frowned. "There's something I don't understand. If the Montoyas had the map all along, why didn't any of them try to find the mine before? Surely, in two hundred years, someone in the family would have gotten a little curious."

"You must remember that after Coronado's explorations failed to discover the Seven Cities of Cibola, the Spaniards for the most part abandoned the idea of finding wealth in the New World, and gold-hunting expeditions fell out of fashion. I imagine they reasoned that if a great *conquistador* like Coronado couldn't find gold, how could a novice like Ricardo Montoya do so? Also, according to his diaries, Montoya was considered somewhat eccentric by his family."

"You mean they thought he was crazy?"

"Something like that. But it was understandable considering that he wrote at length about supposedly supernatural events. He was convinced that the mine was cursed."

"Maybe it was."

"I hardly think so. Montoya died relatively young and without credibility. There were those who said his own poor leadership and folly killed his men, that he never made it to Pimeria Alta and made up the whole story."

"That I can believe."

"The family tried to keep him quiet and suppressed his story for years, but eventually the legend outpaced the man."

"Legends have a way of doing that," Hawk agreed.

"But legends almost always grow out of fact."

It wasn't that Hawk didn't believe her. If Sybilla Hartford said she was the last of the Montoyas, she probably was. It was just that the story was too farfetched and full of holes for him to swallow whole. He didn't have time to consider it at length, for she warmed to her subject and prattled on about the historical significance of rediscovering the lost mine and the artifacts it contained.

He admired her enthusiasm and admitted that she had a way with words. The longer she talked, the more intrigued he became, especially when he considered the similarities between her story and the legend of the ancient, gold-hungry white-eyes he'd heard from his mother's people.

The Apaches didn't call it the Montoya gold. They had their own names for the long-lost horde and the spirits who protected it. He'd looked for it off and on for years, and in the process had gained a lot of knowledge about the Superstition Mountains.

He had yet to find so much as a lost nugget, either Montoya or Apache. The kindest thing would be to send this proper young Englishwoman packing, thus saving her a lot of grief, perhaps even her life. But curiosity made him want to hear more.

"There's a lot of real estate in what old Ricardo called the Pimeria Alta, and it's probably changed some since he was here," Hawk put in when she stopped for breath. "God redecorates every now and then with earthquakes, landslides, and other disasters. What makes you so sure the mine is in the Superstitions?"

"Numerous landmarks helped us narrow things down. The two rivers on the map are undoubtedly the Salt and Gila, and those haven't changed since Montoya's day."

"Okay. Let's say for the sake of argument that you're right. The Superstition area is made up of over two hundred and forty square miles of the most savage land you'll ever encounter. How do you expect to find the exact location?"

"That is precisely why I need you, Mr. Devlin. It is essential for the expedition to have a guide who knows the terrain intimately."

He gazed into her excited eyes, and the word "intimate" took on a whole new meaning. He swallowed hard. "What makes you think I won't take you out into the desert, slit your throat while you sleep, and keep the map for myself?"

His words were unsettling, and Sybilla realized that he might very well be the brigand he made himself out to be. But as she looked deep into his eyes, what she saw there reassured her. "As cold and hard as you try to appear, I cannot believe you are a man who murders innocents."

"And are you an innocent?"

Sybilla had never met such a blunt man. "In some ways," she answered, fearing the turn of the conversation.

"And what makes you, a self-proclaimed innocent, such a good judge of character?"

"Intuition. It tells me you don't kill without sufficient provocation."

"Is that a fact?" Hawk's glance drifted slowly from her pale eyes down to her gently rising and falling chest, and he felt the deep stirrings of what could only be called lust. "In that case, you'd do well to worry, Lady Hartford, because you're just about the most provocative female I've ever met."

Sybilla was quite speechless. Her stomach fluttered, her face grew warm, and she longed to escape the man's steady gaze.

"We do have something in common," he said. "We both trust our gut feelings. That's why I'm telling you to go back where you came from and give up this wild goose chase. Regardless of all the stories circulating about lost gold in the Superstitions, there is no proof that there are any glory holes, abandoned mines, buried caches, or sunburned nuggets lying around waiting to be picked up. Believe me, I've looked. Those mountains are nothing but lava rock, and the only gold you'll find is placer gold."

"Placer gold?"

"Gold that's been weathered and washed out of gold-bearing rocks. Pan any stream in the area and you'll find a trace of color, but you can pan until you turn gray and never amass a fortune, not even a small one."

"But my ancestor described the mine as a vertical plug that pierces the lava rock. Geologically, it is possible for such a deposit to exist. The ore could have been melted and pushed upward through the landmass by volcanic force. If that happened, it would have hardened into a vein of almost pure metal."

"Maybe," he allowed.

"It is also possible for a lava flow to carry a landmass over a vast distance. Is it not equally possible for that bit of earth to contain gold?"

"Maybe."

"Have there been any such discoveries in the area?"

"There've been a few wild-eyed prospectors and old be-damners who claimed they found something, but I've never seen proof of it. There's an old Dutchman in Phoenix, name of Jacob Waltz, who says he found a mine worth a hundred million dollars, but most folks think he's sun-touched."

"Has anyone ever seen his claim?"

"Plenty have tried, but those who follow him into the mountains don't come out alive."

Sybilla shuddered. "We cannot be sure it is the same mine."

"We can't be sure it isn't, either. One thing in your favor though—the old man never has produced anything even close to a hundred million dollars worth of gold. He showed up with some ore, but I think he high-graded it in from somewhere else."

"That is reassuring to know. I was becoming distressed by the thought that someone had beaten me to the Montoya gold and possibly destroyed the artifacts I seek. I have no doubt we will find the gold that my ancestor attested is there."

Hawk shook his head. "Every hoodoo with gold fever thinks the same thing."

"Gold fever?" She tried to listen, but it was difficult to concentrate when she kept being sidetracked by Hawk's mesmerizing gaze.

"What do you think makes farmers and clerks desert their homes and families to join the stampedes into the gold fields?" he asked her. "What makes lonely old prospectors dare the devil in search of an end-of-the-rainbow dream?"

"Greed?" she ventured.

"It's not that simple. Gold fever makes a rational man act crazy, a peace-loving man violent. It turns brother against brother, friend against friend. When a man has gold fever he doesn't give up until he's rich or dead."

Sybilla wrested her thoughts into control. "Rest assured I do not have gold fever, nor am I likely to contract it. As a scientist, I have simple needs. My primary goal in finding the mine is to prove to the world that it exists and in doing so to redeem Ricardo Montoya's reputation."

"That's mighty noble of you. I'm sure Ricardo will rest easier in his grave knowing you're on the job."

Sybilla was not amused by Hawk's relentless sarcasm. "I also want to retrieve the artifacts for science, but most of all I want to make my father's dream a reality."

"The gold doesn't really matter then?"

"Of course it matters." She almost blurted out that she was practically penniless, but pride saved her that humiliation. "With the gold to fund future expeditions and studies, I can guarantee Uncle John a comfortable old age and myself a living."

"Finding it won't hurt your own scientific reputation either, will it?"

"It can only enhance it." She thought of Dr. Handelman at the bureau and his condescending letter withdrawing the foundation's support. "There are those in positions of authority who feel women have no place in ethnology. I mean to prove otherwise."

It was just as hard for Hawk to believe that anyone, even a chilly-hearted English lady, was immune to the timeless lure of El Dorado as it was to believe there was anyone who did not take Sybilla Hartford seriously.

"Look, Miss Hartford, I understand how you feel, and I think what you're trying to do is admirable."

She straightened her shoulders, anticipating his rejection, hoping it wouldn't come. "But . . . ?"

"But I don't think you know what you're doing."

"I know exactly what I am doing."

He glanced at the rare steak the waiter had set before him while they were talking. It was growing cold in a puddle of congealing juice and no longer looked appetizing. He forked a few of the calf fries into his mouth and chewed thoughtfully.

"I get the idea you think we can just dash into the Superstitions, find the mine the first day out, and dash home again. What you propose is no Sunday school outing, you know."

"I am prepared to endure primitive conditions, so please do not concern yourself on my behalf. I am quite at home in the desert, having spent several months with my father in Egypt."

"I don't know much about the Egyptian desert, but I do know the Superstitions. A lot of capable men have died there, but that's not too surprising. The amazing thing is that ten times more haven't. There isn't a more inhospitable place, except maybe hell itself, than those mountains. They just weren't created for you to make yourself at home in."

"What could be so terrible?" Sybilla asked.

Hawk talked around the food. "Try pumas, rattlesnakes, scorpions, Gila monsters, and tarantulas the size of this plate. Bristle-backed wild pigs. Javelinas have tusks like razors and rotten personalities. If that's not enough for you, how about scorching hot days and freezing nights? Then there's landslides and flash floods to take up the slack.

"The devil himself made canyons filled with a hundred kinds of cactus, the worst of which have barbed spines that actually jump off and embed themselves in your skin as you walk by. There are no more than a dozen reliable water holes in the entire area, and then you have to know where to look." He waved his fork for emphasis. "Am I getting through to you, lady?"

"Thank you for your concern, but it isn't necessary. I have been up and down the Amazon, in and out of the pyramids. I've crossed India on elephants and hacked my way through tropical rain forests filled with headhunters armed with poison darts. I sincerely doubt any force at work in your mountains can deter me from my purpose."

"Those were just the natural things that can kill a person. I haven't told you about the unnatural ones," he said casually.

"Unnatural ones? Really, do you take me for a fool?"

"You're a dreamer, and that's worse than a fool. The Pimas have a name for the Superstitions. Mountain-with-Something-Wrong-with-It. Once you see them, you'll understand why. There's a cliff top where an entire tribe was turned to stone for disobeying their god. A race of pygmies is said to have guarded the mountains in the old days, and some are still spotted from time to time. A lot of people believe evil spirits are behind all the mysterious goings-on there."

A chill slipped up and down Sybilla's spine at the images Hawk conjured up. If indeed the mountains were as harsh and unforgiving as he said, she would need his guidance even more. "If you are trying to frighten me into changing my mind, you can save your breath. I have no intention of turning back because of a lot of silly, primitive beliefs and legends."

Hawk slammed his fork onto the table. "Then how the hell do you explain the fact that your whole expedition is based on silly beliefs and legends?" He didn't wait for an answer. "You said yourself legends are usually based on fact."

"So I did. However, I have documentation to prove my story. Do you?"

"Just because the People didn't keep journals doesn't make their stories any less real."

"But undocumented legends grow in grandeur the farther they are removed in time and space from their source of origin."

"That brings us right back where we started," Hawk told her. "The lost Montoya gold is just another legend. Forget you ever heard it." He was beginning to suspect that the Montoya gold and the Apache gold he sought were one and the same. But he did not dare reveal that suspicion to Sybilla. Any encouragement he gave her would send her straight to the Superstitions, and possibly to her death. He wouldn't want that on his conscience.

He turned his attention to his now-cold steak. He'd done his duty by discouraging her from venturing into those mountains. From here on out she was on her own.

"Does that mean you refuse my offer?" Light-headed with hunger, and a feeling that was less identifiable, Sybilla fought her disappointment.

"That's exactly what it means." Hawk chewed the cold, tough beef, regretting that he hadn't gotten a look at that map of hers. But there was no way he was going to share with this woman what he had already sweated and suffered untold hardships to find.

Sybilla had never needed anyone in her life the way she needed this impossible man. She was crushed by his refusal to help her and knew she must escape before he saw the hot tears in her eyes. "Is that your last word, then?"

"My very last." He pretended interest in the bloody steak.

"Very well, then. Thank you for your time, Mr. Devlin. Enjoy your dinner." She rose gracefully.

"Enjoy your trip back to England."

"Oh, I'm hardly giving up. I'll have to look elsewhere for a man with a more adventurous spirit. Someone who is less intimidated by geography and more impressed by scientific methods. But I'm sure I'll find him." With that she strode out of the dining room, her head high.

Hawk watched Sybilla's stiff-backed departure, knowing he should be relieved she had given up on him so easily. That proud, graceful woman was ten times more dangerous than a dozen knife-wielding senoritas, and only a fool would give her the opportunity to prove it.

Of course, there was still the chance she'd take his advice and go home. But it was a very small chance. She was stubborn enough to take her stupid camel train into the Superstitions alone. Or worse yet, dig up some treacherous malcontent who would take advantage of her the first chance he got. The thought of any man laying hands on the pristine Miss Hartford tied Hawk's insides up in knots like twisted barbed wire.

Thinking he hadn't finished a single thing since he'd met the fool woman, he took a last fond look at his uneaten supper, slapped a silver dollar down on the table, and kicked back his chair, growling to himself the whole time.

Dammit, a person would think he actually wanted to protect her! He'd never played the Sir Galahad role before, so why in blue blazes was he starting now? It wasn't like him to act against good sense over a woman, and the fact that he was doing just that made him madder than a bee-stung bear.

By way of rationalization, he told himself that what he was really protecting were his interests. He'd been looking for that gold mine a lot longer than Miss Icicle Hartford, and he'd be damned if he'd let some Janey-come-lately find it first.

Knowing beyond all shadow of a doubt that he would live to regret this hasty decision, Hawk snatched up his hat with a muttered curse and followed her out the door.

Chapter 3

"**M**iss Hartford!"
     Sybilla stopped, closed her eyes, and offered up a prayer that Devlin had changed his mind. "Yes?" she answered with studied indifference, despite her hammering, hopeful heart.

"I wish you'd reconsider and give some thought to going home."

Upset that he still didn't take her seriously, Sybilla marched down the wooden sidewalk. "Not at all. As I tried to impress upon you inside, with or without you, I am going into the Superstitions. I will find that gold or die trying."

Damn, Hawk swore silently. Why was he letting this woman get to him? What did he care if she took off and never came back? Most women would appreciate his concern, but not this haughty beauty. Left to herself, she would surely perish. "I believe 'die' is the operative word. Come on back here and let's talk turkey," he said grudgingly.

"What a quaint phrase." Sybilla could scarcely believe her good fortune; this was the first time Devlin had shown any real willingness to escort her party. Suddenly she was almost giddy with joy, and that was disturbing in the extreme. Why was she experiencing this absurd elevation of spirit at his capitulation? Could it be her excitement stemmed from Hawk as a man and not as her guide? Of course not!

She told herself that she was merely happy that

things were finally settled, that within a short time the party would be under way and she would be closer to finding the gold. That was all. She walked back to him. "Here is what I propose—"

It riled him that he'd fallen for her helpless act, and he cut her off rudely. "You don't do the proposing. I tell you my rules, and you tell me if you can live with them." If he went along with her crazy scheme—and he still wasn't sure he was going to— she'd have to meet his price. Pathfinders par excellence did not come cheap.

"Very well. Proceed."

"First thing, I want to see the map, up close and in person. I want to verify it for myself before I go tearing off on some suicide mission." Her so-called map would be the first tangible evidence that the long-lost mine was real and not just another story passed around Apache campfires. His decision had nothing to do with the way she made him feel.

"Absolutely not. I am not quite the fool you think me to be. I refuse to share the map with anyone." Especially a prospective guide of such questionable reputation, she added silently.

"Then how am I supposed to know if I'm taking you where the hell you need to go?"

"I will reveal it in stages as the expedition progresses," she promised quickly when she noticed the furious glint in his eyes. "I believe you said there were other stipulations?"

"Yeah," he said, clenching his jaw. "The first is, I'm absolute boss on the trail, and everyone takes orders from me." He ticked the items off on his long brown fingers. "Two, no whiskey allowed. It just causes trouble. Three, I have the final say-so when it comes to any decision affecting this outfit. Four, you get rid of those damn camels and buy some regulation burros and horses. Five, my going rate for wild goose chases this week is fifty percent of whatever's found."

"I should say not! My counter offer is ten percent of the gold, Mr. Devlin, and not a tuppence more."

Hawk bristled. "Just a damn minute here. I have reason to believe the Montoya gold is the same gold I've been looking for, for several years. Why should I be willing to lead you to it for a measly percentage when I could have it all?"

"You forget that I hold the map, Mr. Devlin," she pointed out smugly. "Ten percent of something is much better than one hundred percent of nothing, wouldn't you say?"

"You've got a point there. But what's to keep me from taking it all, once I've had a look at that precious map of yours?"

"Integrity?" she asked hopefully.

"Who says I have any?"

"I do," she said with conviction. "Ten percent, take it or leave it."

"Oh, all right, have it your way, but I also want twenty dollars a day for expenses. Is it a deal?"

Sybilla tamped down her temper and pretended to mull over his ridiculous demands. The only one she agreed with was the ban on whiskey. Some of his restrictions were so absurd she wondered if he was trying to provoke another argument.

Of course, *she* would have final say in decisions affecting *her* expedition. The camels would definitely stay, as they were eminently more suited to rough desert terrain than horses and burros, and far more reliable. That's why she'd paid so dearly to have Ahmed and his caravan released from his agreement with that circus.

As for remuneration, she was prepared to pay Hawk his ten percent, as he would surely earn every penny. The twenty dollars per diem was nothing short of highway robbery, since locating the mine could take weeks. She might pay it if the find was as big as she expected. If not, he might have to forgo his expense budget.

However, knowing she must tread gingerly lest

he change his mind and back out, she decided to agree to his impossible demands now and make needed adjustments as they went along. He would come around in due time, she thought as she crossed her fingers behind her back.

"Agreed. When do we get started?"

Hawk was suspicious of Sybilla's quick surrender. She didn't strike him as the type who did anything the easy way. He'd expected an argument, or at the very least, negotiation on a few points, especially the one about who had the last word. He looked at her, and she smiled pleasantly.

"It'll take you a few days to round up supplies," he said finally. "If you have any trouble buying the dynamite, let me know."

She raised a delicate brow. "Is dynamite really necessary?"

He regarded her impatiently. "Can't move mountains without it. I'll make up a list and bring it by your camp in the morning. You buy the goods and get them packed, and I'll meet you in the cottonwood grove north of town in three days. Fair enough?"

Sybilla frowned. He wasn't planning to expend much energy earning his ten percent. "Three days? Is that the best you can do?"

"Lady, don't push me. We haven't shaken on this deal yet."

"Is that how things are done out here? A handshake instead of a contract?" She was by no means blind to his attraction, and she had deliberately steeled herself against his presence. But touching him? That was unthinkable.

"That's right. If a man's not as good as his word, he's no good at all."

"Very well." She extended her hand and waited, nervously anticipating the moment when he would take it.

Hawk was reluctant to clinch a deal that was sure to cause nothing but headaches. Also, he was worried about how he would manage to keep his hands off her once they touched that silky skin. He stared at her small white hand for a long moment before clasping it in his large brown one. With a sinking feeling, he pumped it up and down twice.

"Good show!" She extracted her hand from his as if she were pulling it out of a worm jar. "I must get back to camp and tell the others the good news."

She turned to leave, and he fell into step beside her. "I'll walk you back to your camp. You shouldn't be out here alone this time of night. It isn't safe."

Touched by his concern for her welfare, and ever cautious not to reveal his effect on her, Sybilla stiffly inclined her head in agreement. "As you wish."

"In fact, you probably shouldn't be camping out there at all. Some drunken miner is liable to . . ." He wasn't sure how to complete the sentence since ladies like her were sure to have delicate sensibilities.

"Do something unseemly?" she finished with a smile.

"Yeah, very unseemly." He could think of a few unseemly acts he'd like to perform with her himself. At the very least he wanted to pull her into his arms and kiss some of that starch out of her.

Hawk's eyes gleamed, and from the way he was looking at her, Sybilla thought he might just show her what he meant, then she felt his withdrawal. For one awful moment she was disappointed that he hadn't acted upon whatever impulse had put that sparkle in his eye.

"Do not concern yourself. I sleep with a loaded revolver under my pillow and I am quite adept at using it."

The lady was just full of surprises. "Spend a lot of time target shooting, do you?"

"Enough to keep my skills honed."

The note of false modesty in her voice grated on Hawk's nerves. "There's a big difference between aiming a pistol at a paper target and aiming one between a man's eyes.''

''I am well aware of that, Mr. Devlin, and even though I abhor violence, I assure you I am quite prepared to do whatever is required to ensure my survival.''

''You ever hear the phrase 'When in Rome, do as the Romans do'?''

''I am familiar with it, yes.''

''Then I suggest that while you're in Arizona you try to talk like ordinary folks. You spend words like they were six for a dollar.''

''I was taught one must never lose sight of one's upbringing, even when in primitive surroundings.'' She felt it would be well to remember that advice when faced with the rather primitive longings which only Hawk seemed able to provoke. Maybe that's why she continued her sermon. ''Father always insisted on maintaining decorum, whether in a steaming jungle or in a barren desert. Lowering oneself to the standards of the masses only diminishes one's own dignity.''

Hawk whistled through his teeth. ''Dignity must be mighty important to you.''

Sybilla tossed her head in a consciously superior manner, realizing that she'd made a complete fool of herself this evening. ''It is to be maintained at all costs.''

Hawk decided he should feel honored that such a flossy, highfalutin gal would even stoop to associating with a member of the unwashed masses. Lord almighty, what had he gotten himself into? ''I'll see that gets on your tombstone,'' he said dryly.

Sybilla said nothing to that, and they walked on in silence. ''Here we are, then,'' she said, feigning cheerfulness when they reached the camp. No one was in sight, apparently having retired into tents for the night. She almost thrust out her hand for another handshake but thought better of it. She'd experienced a warm yearning that was quite improper when Hawk had touched her earlier. For a moment she'd felt herself under the spell of a mesmerist. Her heart had stopped beating for the length of the handshake, then raced quite alarmingly.

Hawk's voice intruded on her thoughts. "Looks like everyone's gone to bed."

She smiled with false brightness. "Yes, well, cheerio then, Mr. Devlin. I shall expect you to deliver your supply list in the morning, after which Uncle John and I shall begin our shopping. We shall rendezvous in the cottonwood grove at dawn on Thursday, three days hence."

"Provided you drop the Mr. Devlin and call me Hawk."

"Very well, Hawk."

He nodded, seemingly satisfied at the sound of his name on her lips. Then he spun on his heel and strode away.

"Oh, Mr. Devlin? I mean Hawk?"

He stopped but didn't turn around. No way was he going to subject himself to yet another tempting glimpse of Sybilla Hartford this close to bedtime. "Yeah, what?"

"Thank you," she said simply, honestly.

"You're welcome." He hurried toward town and a good night's rest in his bed at the hotel. At least that was one place the arrogant little wench couldn't invade.

Sybilla watched Hawk melt into the darkness like a wary jungle cat. Such an unsettling man. He inspired longings she had never experienced before and dreams of being crushed within his embrace. He radiated a vitality that she found nearly irresistible. But resist it she must, for such an attraction might prove perilous.

Her intuition warned her to run as fast and as far from him as she could. But that was impossible. No matter what happened, they were definitely in this together.

She needed him much more than he needed her,

and that fact undermined the inner confidence that normally helped her overcome setbacks. As she slipped into her tent and closed the flap, she could only hope she had exercised good judgment in ignoring those internal warnings.

She lit a lamp and turned the wick down low. Sitting on the edge of her cot, she opened a small leather-bound trunk and pulled out a gilt-framed photograph of her parents and a small music box that had belonged to her mother. She tipped up the heart-shaped lid, and the tinkling strains of "The Blue Danube" waltz filled the tent.

How her mother had loved that composition. She had taught Sybilla to play it on the pianoforte when she was scarcely big enough to reach the keys. Sybilla had been a serious child and had worked laboriously to coax the melody from the instrument. As she played, her mother had waltzed around the room, as light on her feet as gossamer on a gentle breeze.

Sybilla remembered her as she'd been before the tuberculosis had robbed her of health and beauty. Vittoria Hartford had been pretty and graceful and full of life. Perhaps because she had been reared in a convent, where she'd been forbidden to give in to her more fiery impulses, Vittoria had encouraged them in her daughter. Sybilla's inherent restraint and her proper English grandmother had forced her to wage a constant battle with her latent spitfire passions.

As a child Sybilla had longed to be like her mother, perpetually happy and optimistic and free from the restraints of society. In reality, she was more like her staid Grandmother Sybilla, for whom she'd been named, always concerned more about appearances than self-fulfillment.

After her marriage, Vittoria, who was twenty years younger than her scholarly husband, had insisted on accompanying him on his expeditions. Then Sybilla was born in a jungle outpost in the Yucatan, and Thomas Hartford insisted his wife and daughter return to his mother and uncle at Hartsmoor. Vittoria had objected strenuously, but in the end she'd realized that for Sybilla's sake she must defer to her husband's wishes.

So for the first twelve years of her life, Sybilla had two homes; her grandmother's country house in Chelmsford where mother and daughter lived when Thomas was out of the country, and the snug brick town house in Cambridge where they lived when he was at the university. She was never really content in either home and often begged to be allowed to travel with her brilliant and dashing father.

Grandmother Sybilla had scolded her for being silly. Pretty little girls did not go on scientific junkets. They stayed at home and learned to speak French and play the minuet. They spent their days in gentle pursuits such as embroidery and tatting. They read the classics and trained their minds in order to become fitting companions for the husbands they would someday attract.

Disappointed but lacking the temerity to rebel openly, Sybilla could only mutter that there didn't seem to be much advantage in attracting a husband if one had to sit at home and tat while he went about having all the fun.

Vittoria had consoled her. She'd advised her daughter to set her sights as high as the stars, to aspire to whatever her heart desired. It was no crime for a girl to have brains and ambition, and someday she would meet a man who would appreciate those qualities.

The music box stopped and Sybilla rewound it, drawing comfort from memories of the mother who had died when she was twelve. After that, she'd stayed on with her grandmother and Uncle John. It was to him that she'd turned when she'd needed guidance. The dear man had lavished his fatherly attention on Sybilla, never having had children of his own. When her father visited, he had seemed uncertain of his paternal duties and was more like a jolly family friend on holiday.

She finished her education, and when she was seventeen, Thomas Hartford suffered a severe attack of malaria and returned home, forcibly retired from his professorship.

Her father's convalescence was slow and complicated by depression over his own mother's death from old age. Demonstrating her knowledge of ethnology, garnered from books and lectures, Sybilla convinced him that they could travel and study on their own, applying to various scientific foundations for support.

The thought that he might not be doomed to retirement proved good medicine for Dr. Hartford, and it wasn't long before they'd sold off a portion of the estate, left Uncle John in charge of the rest, and departed for Egypt for an extended study of the ancient pyramids. Sybilla had never been so happy as she was the day she first saw Giza.

She clutched the photograph to her breast and steeled herself against the loneliness that washed over her as the melody played. Despite their many early separations, she and her father had developed a close relationship during his last years. She missed him as much as she still missed her mother. Except for Uncle John, she was alone in the world now, and at times like this she felt that fact keenly.

"Don't worry, Papa," she whispered. "I'll find the Montoya gold, and the scientific world will once more recognize the name Hartford."

Thursday morning, the sun had scarcely topped the eastern horizon before its heat burned away the last vestiges of the cool night. Birds flocked in the cottonwood grove to celebrate the new day, and Sybilla once again paced impatiently.

"Where is that man?" she asked no one in particular.

Ahmed's wife, Zora, shrugged in her inelegant

Romany way, and her Persian husband shielded his eyes from the bright sunlight and stared toward town. "Not here, missy," he informed her unnecessarily.

"Perhaps Mr. Devlin was detained, my dear," offered Uncle John.

"Perhaps the cad has reneged on our deal. I knew I was asking for trouble with nothing more than a handshake to seal our bargain. I should have gotten it in writing." Sybilla glanced at the patient camels, who had been packed and waiting for nearly two hours. She caught sight of the two nervous young Mexicans she had optimistically recruited to help excavate the mine when the time came.

The Ruiz brothers, Juan and Miguel, were eyeing the camels and their new boss warily, and Sybilla feared an imminent mutiny. Speaking flawless Spanish, she had tried to reassure them that this was a minor delay.

At least she hoped that's all it was. If Hawk Devlin had indeed deserted her, she would recommend him to the first lynch mob she encountered. She had turned the town upside down looking for the high-priced dynamite he'd required, filled his supply list, overseen the packing, and arisen before first light to make sure the caravan was ready to depart. How dare he now jeopardize everything in this thoughtless and self-centered way!

Furious beyond bearing, Sybilla turned to Uncle John, who was fanning himself in the sparse shade of a cottonwood. "It looks as if I must go to town and find out what happened. Wait here and don't let those Mexicans out of your sight." She opened a flap on her saddlebag and retrieved her revolver. Spinning the chamber, she made sure it was loaded and then gently released the hammer.

"I shall bring Hawk Devlin back with me, even if it's at gunpoint." She stalked away in high dudgeon, her destination the Hodges Hotel.

* * *

Hawk woke up sweating from a nightmare in which Sybilla Hartford figured prominently. Since delivering the supply requisition to her as promised, he'd worked hard to get the cat-eyed woman out of his mind. His attempts to ease his frustration in Maiden Lane had been largely unsuccessful, and in the end he'd been forced to buy two bottles of rotgut in hopes of blotting her from his thoughts.

Through eyes that were no more than slits, he noticed the brilliant sunlight streaming through the greasy window and tried to figure out what day it was. He attempted to sit up but couldn't balance his enormous head on his shoulders, and fell back on the lumpy mattress with a moan.

The whiskey had not been a good idea. He never had been much of a drinker and figured his inability to tolerate spirits was inherited from his mother, the half-breed daughter of an Apache warrior and his white captive. It sure hadn't come from his father, who'd earned the reputation of drinking his fellow officers under the table without showing the effects.

Knowing he needed a last binge before riding off into no-man's-land with that crazy Englishwoman, and knowing also that it wouldn't do his reputation any good to be seen incapacitated, Hawk had brought the bottles up to his room yesterday to get likkered-up in private. Or had it been the day before? His poor drink-soggy mind would not release such insignificant information.

It didn't really matter how long he'd been holed up trying to obliterate Sybilla Hartford from his thoughts. He could drink until he died from alcohol poisoning, and that would never happen. He groaned aloud and wondered for the thousandth time what it was about her that had captured his imagination.

He'd seen prettier girls, but her delicate appearance fairly screamed ''Don't touch me'' while taunting him to do just that. She had a good mind, but it was clearly of the one-track variety.

Her manners were what was termed impeccable, but all the good breeding in the Queen's realm wouldn't do her a damn bit of good in a country that placed top premium on the ability to survive. And she had about as much chance of that as a snowflake in a firestorm. She was a rare rosebud just waiting to be crushed beneath the harsh heel of reality.

He groaned and held his head. Damned if that rotgut hadn't flat made him poetic, a trait passed on from his Celtic forebears. He tried to get up again, but the movement was too painful. Easing back this time, he decided he could do little more than sleep off the results of his intemperance. Despite the fact that his eyeballs felt as if they were studded with tiny cactus needles, he closed them and prayed either to die or to get better.

Sybilla paused momentarily outside Hawk's room. The desk clerk had assured her that Devlin hadn't been down since day before yesterday, but he'd been loath to reveal which splintered door concealed the man's lair. In the end, the owl-eyed simpleton had succumbed to her sternly phrased demands.

Angry at the thought that Devlin might have escaped his obligations by dying, Sybilla doubled up her fist and pounded furiously enough to wake even the dead. "Devlin, I know you are in there. I demand you open this door immediately."

Hawk tugged the pillow over his head. Some chain gang had gotten hold of his brain and was going at it hammer and tongs. Muddleheaded as he was, he couldn't mistake who was out there screeching at him. She hadn't respected his privacy thus far. Why should she begin now?

"Go away," he called hoarsely.

"Devlin! If you do not open this door promptly, I shall be forced to kick it in."

"You and what army?"

That did it. The last of Sybilla's control snapped.

Drawing back as far as she could in the narrow hall, she turned her shoulder to the door and rocked back and forth to the count of one, two, three. When she slammed against it, the unlocked door flew open and spilled her unceremoniously onto the floor of the musty room.

Glancing up from his deathbed, Hawk tugged the blanket to his chin. "Well, I'll be damned. You must be stronger than you look."

Sybilla covered her embarrassment heroically by jumping to her feet and dusting off her riding skirt. Her shoulder throbbed, and she was sure to have an angry bruise for her trouble. "How dare you lie there like some great overgrown slug while I wear myself down scouring this unholy town for the supplies and then packing them all for the journey! Your lazy inconsideration has made a number of people—people who were depending on you, I might add—wait for over two hours."

"What are you talking about? What day is this?"

Her sharp intake of breath was far more eloquent than her words, which were delivered with a splutter. "You don't even know what day it is! It is Thursday, you sot!"

Each outraged syllable was like another knife thrust deep in Hawk's aching skull, and he prayed for immediate death. He'd probably go to hell for his actions, but then he could use the holiday. "Go away, lady."

"I will not go away! We shook on a bargain, and I mean to hold you to it. Now get out that bed immediately."

"Sorry, I can't do that."

Sybilla didn't think he was a bit sorry. "What do you mean, you can't do that?"

Improvising was difficult in his present state, but Hawk managed a reasonable explanation. "I'm sick and, as you can plainly see, in no condition to travel. Just go away. I'll be better tomorrow, and we can take off then."

Sybilla clenched her hands into fists at her sides. Ladies do not take the Lord's name in vain, she repeated silently like a litany. She spotted an empty whiskey bottle kicked up against the wall and another protruding from under the bed. That explained why the place smelled like a taproom. Sick, indeed! It was several moments before she could respond in a civil manner. "Your illness is nothing more than the result of your overindulgence in spirits."

"That's right, and I've got a headache that won't fit in a corral. Now just get on out of here before I do something . . . unseemly."

Producing the loaded pistol and waving it around, Sybilla stood her ground. "I am not leaving until you come with me. Get up!"

Hawk groaned. Hadn't he endured enough? Hadn't he been afflicted enough? Hadn't Sybilla Hartford butted in his life, his thoughts, his dreams, enough? He was in no mood to be ordered around at gunpoint by a hidebound, starchy-aired female. Evidently there was only one way to get rid of her and her high-handedness.

Drawing on nearly depleted reserves of strength, Hawk asked calmly, "Are you sure you want me to get out of bed?"

"Immediately," she demanded in proper harridan fashion.

"Are you *absolutely* sure you want me to get up?" he prodded innocently.

"Yes! I want you to get out of that bed now." Her jaw hurt from clenching it so tightly, and she cocked her weapon menacingly.

"Put that gun down. Nobody's ever said that Hawk Devlin wouldn't oblige a pistol-packing lady," he said with a pained smile as he thrust back the covers.

It had never occurred to Sybilla that he might be naked beneath the blankets. Civilized people slept in nightclothes, and the sight of so much proud,

bronzed virility was nearly enough not only to
knock the wind out of her sails, but also to make her
pull the trigger. She put the gun down before that
happened.

She had never seen a naked man up close except
in paintings and sculptures, and then there had always been the ever-present fig leaf to conceal what
Hawk was so blatantly revealing to her now. To her
credit, she did not swoon or rush from the room in
gasping hysterics, as he obviously expected her to
do. Nor did she betray her shock and, dare she admit it, her arousal. She was a maiden lady alone in
a tawdry hotel room with a naked man of mixed
blood and few scruples. The shame of it!

Striving for unruffled forbearance, Sybilla folded
her arms coolly across her brass-buttoned chest and
fastened her gaze on Hawk's Adam's apple, the safest part of his anatomy to stare at. ''Do get dressed,
please.''

Hawk couldn't believe his ploy had failed. Right
now she was supposed to be lying on the floor in a
dead faint. Any sensible lady would rather die than
gaze upon a buck-naked man. But Miss Iron Britches
wasn't collapsing with the vapors. She was waiting,
her gaze unwavering, for him to get up and don his
clothes. He did so, all the while keeping his dark
blue gaze locked onto her pale brown one. It wasn't
until he began to button his pants that her bold audacity embarrassed him. He modestly presented his
back to her, and fastened the fly over his evident
arousal.

When he turned back around, Sybilla was holding
out his hat. Without betraying her breathless state,
she managed to speak quite calmly. ''I can see you
are not yet packed. How much time do you require
to gather up your scattered belongings and be ready
to ride?''

Hawk couldn't believe the turn of events. Here he
was, hotter than a stag in rut, and she was still as
cold as a knot on the North Pole. He'd been a fool

to entertain notions about her, even if they had been drink-induced and sleep-fevered. A sinner would have an easier time tiptoeing through hell unnoticed than a man would have getting within seducing range of Sybilla Hartford's prickly hide. Hawk yanked his hat out of her hand.

"Five minutes, give or take a couple."

"Fine. I'll be waiting in the lobby."

"I don't need an escort. I have a few things to tend to, so you go on ahead."

She regarded him doubtfully. "Very well, but if you are not there in a reasonable time, I shall be back, and next time I won't be in such a forgiving mood." She spun around on her heel and traipsed down the hall.

Damn! Hawk slapped his hat against his thigh in an effort to relieve some of his frustration. She could watch him get dressed from a natural state, but she couldn't watch him pack? He grabbed up his belongings and stuffed them into his saddlebag.

He'd been within his rights to cleanse the earth of unnecessary scum more than once, but he'd only killed in self-defense. It just wasn't in him to commit cold-blooded murder.

But he waited in the room the full five minutes, knowing he was in serious jeopardy, right now, of succumbing to the urge to nail Sybilla Hartford's hide to the wall with bullets.

Chapter 4

$\sim\!\!\sim\!\!\odot\!\!\bigcirc\!\!\sim\!\!\sim$

Hawk smelled the camels before he actually saw them.

So did his horse, a six-year-old gruello stallion aptly called Diablo. The big gray's unpredictable behavior had earned him his name, and he was not a tractable specimen under normal circumstances. With snorts and shudders, he was doing his damnedest to tell Hawk there was nothing at all normal about these particular circumstances.

Cursing the sun for being so bright and fate for allowing Sybilla Hartford ever to cross his path, Hawk urged his rebellious mount into the cottonwood grove where the Hartford caravan had assembled. The muted sounds of their activity were only slightly louder than the incessant racket of a million cicadas singing the only tune they knew.

He rode the skittish Diablo into the dappled shade, and his narrowed eyes quickly accounted for the members of the party as they went about various tasks. Sybilla's uncle sat in the sparse shade packing photographic equipment with care. The old man was wearing a jacket and vest that matched his trousers, a white shirt, and a tie. Probably the height of fashion back in merry old England, Hawk mused, but most unsuitable for the dry desert heat.

The gypsy and Persian were at the creek filling canteens and waterskins. Though it was hard to tell, due to the language barrier, they appeared to be engaged in one hell of an all-out squabble. Their lightweight clothing was more atuned to the climate, but Hawk wondered if the woman would have enough sense to cover her nearly naked shoulders and chest once they set out.

The two silent young Mexicans were apparently more accustomed to the demands of desert life and dressed accordingly in lightweight garments. Their clothing, which would reflect the sun, would keep them relatively cool. They might know how to dress for the occasion, but they seemed to have no more to do than stand around looking confused.

All things considered, Hawk figured he had to be crazy to take this motley crew anywhere more strenuous than an ice cream social.

The animals responsible for the stench, and for Hawk's anger, knelt in the sun, placidly chewing and blinking, looking right at home.

"What the hell are those camels doing here?" Hawk thundered when Sybilla approached him. Protesting the tight rein, Diablo whickered, tossed his head, and did an equine version of the flamenco around the tiny woman. "I thought I told you to get rid of them."

She stood firm, exhibiting an annoying lack of respect for the ill humor of both horse and rider, who by this time were equally wild-eyed. Although Devlin looked frightening and sounded intimidating, Sybilla refused to be either frightened or intimidated. But maintaining a civil tone required self-control. After all, less than an hour ago she had seen the man in all his naked splendor. She well remembered the powerful masculine beauty concealed beneath his nondescript ensemble of denim pants, black shirt, and buckskin vest.

A striped Mexican serape was tossed over his shoulder, and his wide-brimmed hat was secured with a chin thong. Strapped around his lean middle was the one article no well-dressed Westerner left home without: the ever-present leather holster and sidearm.

Sybilla, who was more accustomed to issuing orders than to taking them, answered curtly. "So you did. Fortunately for this enterprise, I chose to ignore that ill-gauged directive."

"You what!"

"I excercised my superior knowledge in the matter."

"Lady, you deliberately disobeyed an order." She was too strong-minded to suit him, and he'd do well to remember that the next time he felt his defenses slipping.

Sybilla's patience was growing short, and if there was anything she detested more than waiting, it was having someone bluster at her. They had agreed upon a dawn departure, and already the sun was a glittering, white-hot globe in the sky. Though it was early morning, the heat was oppressive and could only get worse as the day wore on.

"I wasn't aware that this was a military operation, Mr. Devlin, nor that you were my superior officer."

Hawk dismounted and tried to calm his nervous animal. Pain pounded through his head at the sudden jarring impact of booted feet striking solid ground. The hellish sun had assaulted his senses the moment he'd stepped out of the dark hotel, and his temples had throbbed violently ever since. He longed for the relief of a Comanche war club between the eyes.

Since there were never any renegades around when you needed them, he chewed vigorously on a piece of peeled willow bark instead. The Indian remedy for a headache usually worked, but Hawk had a feeling there weren't enough willow trees in all of Arizona to cure the megrims this woman was destined to give him.

With conscious effort he managed to turn the wince of pain into a glower of contempt. Sybilla's attitude made the task easy. Although the temperature was already inching toward one hundred, she looked as cool and starchy as ever. Today she was wearing the standard British colonial uniform: crisp khaki blouse, divided skirt, leather gloves, tall boots, and pith helmet. Her bright hair was pinned securely beneath the helmet.

She matched him glare for glare with her arms folded across her chest, her small pointed chin jutting defiantly. Gold or no gold, he had to be loco to agree to go anywhere with such a hardheaded woman. "You're going to be hell with the hide off, aren't you?" he asked conversationally.

Sybilla wasn't familiar with the colorful phrase, but its meaning was obvious. "I have the best interests of this expedition in mind and shall do everything within my power to ensure its success. However, as the inimitable Horace said, I swear allegiance to the words of no master."

"When wiser men are talking, let your ears hang down and listen," he countered grimly.

"Who said that?"

"Damn near everyone who's been to the Superstitions and lived to tell about it." He turned to tie his prancing horse to a new-blooming paloverde tree, and a miniature cloud of sulphur-colored butterflies fluttered to a nearby mesquite. "No camels."

"Just how extensive is your knowledge of the beasts?" she asked with irritating superiority.

"Sorely inadequate, thank you very much."

"Then perhaps you are not aware that camels are ideally suited to desert survival. Much more so than either horses or burros."

"Horses and burros do just fine."

"But I was under the impression that water is scarce in the Superstitions."

"There're maybe two score so-called permanent springs and streams in the whole area. Out there water has roughly the same value as blood."

"A point well taken. Camels have a unique ability

to drink a large quantity of water and retain it in their systems. They can store over fifty quarts in special cells in their stomach linings that act like sponges.''

In his present state, Hawk had a hard time understanding how anyone could work up any enthusiasm over something as inherently uncharming as a camel. ''You don't say?''

''I do indeed. Why, some camels have gone for as long as three months without drinking water. Human beings require no less than a gallon of water a day in this climate, and the camels can carry it. On the other hand, horses, mules, and burros drink far more. We would need mules to pack water for the horses. Surely you see the obvious disadvantage in that.''

On a good day he might, but right now Hawk was in no mood for logic. Not when he felt as if he'd been flogged through hell with a buzzard gut. He shot the wonders in question a look of derision. ''I've heard they're bad-tempered, stubborn, and completely lacking in intelligence.''

Sybilla bristled at the slur on her livestock. '' 'Tis true they can be somewhat irascible. But they can carry up to a thousand pounds and travel up to twenty-five miles per day. That could prove quite useful when we begin packing out the gold.''

The strength of Hawk's objections was tempered not only by the pain in his head, which he had no wish to aggravate by arguing, but also by visions of eight camels marching out of the desert bearing thousand-pound packs of gold. ''They stink.''

''I admit they are possessed of a rather pungent odor, but one quickly becomes accustomed to it. Unfortunately, horses do not. I'm afraid you will have to leave yours behind.''

The thought of being horseless was more than Hawk would tolerate. ''Now wait just a damn minute. Camels may be all right for pack animals, but you're not going to get me on one.''

Sybilla looked pointedly at Diablo, who was pawing the ground and bucking at his short tether. "Take my word for it, Mr. Devlin. Stock not trained to accept the camels' scent are completely uncontrollable. A high-spirited creature like that would cause no end of trouble on the trail."

"I can handle Diablo," Hawk assured her. "I break horses for a living."

"So I've heard. But not even one with your skill can make a horse accept a camel. It's quite impossible."

"He'll accept what I tell him to. I can ride anything that moves."

"Then a camel should present no problem for you." With brisk efficiency, Sybilla turned to one of the cowering Mexicans. Dropping a few coins in his hand, she commanded him in flawless Spanish to take the horse to the livery stable in town.

Scurrying to do her bidding, the boy removed Hawk's bedroll and saddlebags and dropped them in the dust. Then he scrambled into the saddle and galloped away. His sandal-clad feet, too short for the stirrups, flopped wildly against the gray's sides.

Hawk's fury grew as he watched his horse disappear. He wasn't worried about Diablo. The livery owner knew him and would take good care of the animal until Hawk came for him. And since there wasn't a man in Tucson with enough guts to steal Hawk Devlin's horse, Diablo would be safe enough.

What made him madder than a new-made steer was that, thanks to Miss Iron Britches's high-handedness, he was in serious danger of losing control of this so-called expedition.

"There's something we need to settle before things get out of hand," he said as levelly as he could manage. "I'm in charge here, and from now on what I say goes. Is that clear?"

Sybilla stared at him without flinching and wondered absently how eyes as blue as a frozen lake could be so full of fire. "Exceptionally." So long as what he said agreed with her wishes, things would be just ducky, she thought. "Trust me, Mr. Devlin. The camels shall make the trek more endurable, and I assure you that the day will come when you will thank me for my farsightedness in retaining them."

"Yeah," he muttered. "And a rattlesnake might get elected governor of the Territory, but don't hold your breath. More likely, the day will come, and pretty damn soon too, when I'll have to wring your pretty neck." Being crossed didn't set well with Hawk, and the quicker she learned it the better off she'd be.

The image of his hard brown hands on her neck, or anywhere else on her for that matter, was not an image Sybilla wished to contemplate. She had dealt with the threat of violence on other junkets. But Devlin was a savage man in a savage land, and all the more dangerous because he seemed uninterested in observing the rules of society.

She dusted her hands dismissively. "Now that we agree about the camels, perhaps we can get under way before too many more hours are lost."

"Not so fast. The camel problem might be settled to your satisfaction, but you ought to know that my price just went up."

"What?"

"You heard me. I don't ride a stinking camel for no lousy ten percent. From here on out, it's fifteen percent or nothing."

"But that's the worst kind of jiggery. Trickery," she explained for the benefit of his limited American vocabulary.

"Hardly. What you did in bringing those camels along after I gave you express orders is the worst kind of *jiggery*. We can call it even on that score."

Sybilla fumed, her fists clenched at her sides, her foot in jeopardy of stamping. She didn't like being blackmailed, but she did need Devlin. "Very well."

"One more thing, Lady Hartford," he said with a mocking emphasis on "lady."

"Please do not address me in that fashion. I am not titled."

He pretended astonishment. "You mean to tell me you're just one of the great unwashed like the rest of us lowly mortals?"

"Hardly," she said with studied indifference. The lip curl, however, was reflexive.

"Maybe I'll call you Billy, how's that?"

"Miss Hartford will do quite nicely."

Hawk had a sudden, appalling urge to kiss that imperious look off her face. He was in no frame of mind to bandy words and badly needed to assert himself in a purely physical manner, to prove that somewhere under that prickly hide she was a woman who had to submit to his superior knowledge and strength. Should he slap her or kiss her? Before he could make up his mind, the urge passed. He'd deal with her later, when he didn't have a headache.

"Who *are* all these people, and what exactly is their function on this trip?" he demanded.

"My, I have neglected introductions, haven't I?" Sybilla knew she sounded like an absentminded hostess at a lawn party, but the way Devlin looked at her made her forget herself at times. Despite the heat, gooseflesh rose up on her arms, and she felt suddenly weak. She didn't much like those feelings and chose the only alternative—talking herself out of them.

"This is Sir John Collings, my kinsman and dear friend," she said when the older gentleman stepped forward. "Uncle John will document our discoveries with his camera and serve as my adviser and chaperone."

Though he was titled, Hawk didn't acknowledge it. "Glad to meet you, Collings," he said in a tone that challenged the older man to dispute the familiarity. "We don't stand on ceremony out here."

"I quite understand, my good man. I gathered as

much from my reading of Western novels—Deadeye Dick is my favorite series. May I call you Hawk?''

"That's my name." Collings's handshake was a tad on the limp side, but the old man seemed harmless enough. His milky blue eyes darted around with the curiosity of a child. His monocle was clamped firmly in place and his walrus mustache neatly trimmed. He didn't look strong enough to stand up in a stout breeze, much less survive the Superstitions, but who was Hawk to judge the frailties of the British upper crust?

Then Sybilla introduced the bowing Persian, Ahmed Mendab, whose primary duty was caring for the camels. His knowledge of the rangy beasts surpassed even Sybilla's, and the dark little man was intimately familiar with their individual personalities; unnaturally familiar, if you asked Hawk.

"I know the little darlings like they are my own children," Ahmed gushed in heavily accented English. "They are mostly sweet girls who require only affection and understanding. Never fear, *effendi*, you will grow to love them, as do I."

The hell he would. Hawk would leave camel worship to the person who smelled most like them. When Ahmed's wife, the dark-haired gypsy, sashayed up, he realized she was younger than he'd originally thought. Zora was probably no older than Sybilla in years, but there was a lifetime of experience in her bold Romany eyes. She was also pretty, in an exotically feral way that appealed to men's baser instincts.

When Hawk extended his hand, Zora grasped it in both of hers and perused it like a book of revelations. "You have a most interesting palm, Mr. Devlin. Your life line is long and your love line is strong." She fluttered her thick lashes and stroked his hand. "I see that you love to live. And," she purred flirtatiously, "you live to love." Except when she said it, it sounded like "leef to luff."

"Yeah, right." The woman was about as subtle as

a widowed coyote, and Hawk made a mental note to stay out of her way. He withdrew his hand with a sidelong look at Ahmed, whose eyes had hardened at his wife's suggestive announcement. Unconsciously Hawk wiped his palm on his thigh, as if to demonstrate to the testy Muslim that he had no designs on his errant wife.

The exchange had apparently gone over Sybilla's head. She explained, "Zora was previously employed as a fortune-teller in the circus where we acquired the camels. As such, she is prone to dwell on the mystical aspects of life. However, her duties are more mundane than arcane. She will be responsible for the cooking and washing and general camp tending."

"What about the Mexicans?" Hawk wanted to know.

"I hired Juan and Miguel as navvies to help with the camels. And we will need extra hands to excavate the mine when the time comes."

Hawk smiled for the first time that day. "Pretty sure of yourself, aren't you?"

"I believe the heart of any venture is optimism," she replied. "Don't you?"

"I believe optimism is nothing more than thinking everything is fine when it's really miserable."

Sybilla studied Hawk curiously. It was an interesting development that a rough cowboy like Devlin even knew of the existence of Voltaire, much less was familiar enough with the great French writer's work to allude to it. Now she knew what he did out there in the desert. He read *Candide*.

"Look, if money's so tight, how're you paying all these people?" he demanded.

"Not that my financial arrangements are any of your concern, but we have an agreement that their pay is contingent upon the eventual success of the venture."

"Which, translated into American," he said with disgust, "means they all get a piece of the pie?"

"More or less," she agreed.

"Well, dammit, which is it? More or less? How much of my gold have you promised away?" He hadn't meant to phrase it exactly like that, and when her eyes flashed furiously, he immediately regretted the slip of tongue.

"Your gold? Just what do you mean by that?"

"My gold, your gold, our gold, the gold. It doesn't matter. What does matter is just what these arrangements of yours are going to cost me."

"On the contrary, I think it matters very much. This is my expedition, and any discoveries made will be mine. Uncle John gets twenty-five percent. Ahmed and Zora will receive two percent each, and Juan and Miguel will receive one percent each. You get a scandalous fifteen percent, and that leaves, if my calculations are correct, fifty-four percent for me. Now that we've clarified exactly who possesses the controlling interest, may we proceed?"

Hawk wanted to tell her to proceed straight to the ramparts of perdition, if she so desired. He didn't like her feudal attitude, her irritating superiority, her overbearing manner, or her damn camels. "I'll be the one to say when we *proceed*. You may have the controlling interest, but if this little body of lost souls is going to be ruled by a dictator, that dictator's going to be me. Savvy?"

The last thing Sybilla wanted to do was waste time on a ridiculous struggle for power. "Yes, my lord." She compounded the disdainful remark with a mocking curtsy.

To say Hawk was unhappy with the arrangements was grossly to understate the issue. "Look, lady, you don't seem to have a firm grip on the situation. Not only are there too many cuts in the pie, there are too many amateurs to nursemaid. I don't need the aggravation. And I don't need their deaths on my conscience."

The Muslim muttered a prayer to Allah, the gypsy crossed herself, and even though he didn't understand what was being said, the Mexican followed suit, as if to be on the safe side.

John blanched. "Now see here, Devlin—" he began before Sybilla cut him off.

"We are all aware of the dangers involved in this venture, and my people have agreed that a share in the riches is worth the risk."

"Well, that's just dandy. I sure hope to hell it is."

John coughed and sputtered. "I must ask you to refrain from so much unnecessary profanity, Devlin. Do you not respect a lady's sensibilities?"

"Hell, yes. But this particular lady is as crazy as a parrot eating stick candy, and I don't want to have anything to do with this go-to-hell outfit." He threw up his hands and stalked back toward town, all thoughts of gold, Spanish or Apache, temporarily forgotten in his anger.

"So," Sybilla called after him. "Is this an example of the famous American honor? The venerated code of the West? Did we not strike a fair bargain and shake hands on it?"

He whirled around. "That was before I found out what I was getting into," he yelled. "And it was before I found out about the camels."

The sight of his retreating back unnerved her, and she remembered just how badly she needed him. She couldn't allow him to leave, but she didn't know how to ask him to stay. "If you wish to talk to me, you will have to do so in a civilized manner. I do not care to be screeched at."

"I was not screeching." His voice was like a roll of quiet thunder. He didn't even slow down.

"Yes, you were. Like the proverbial banshee."

That did it. Hawk wheeled and strode back to the clearing, stopping mere inches from Sybilla's upturned face. "Is this better?" he asked tightly through clenched teeth.

It wouldn't do at all. She stared up at him, determined not to reveal how his nearness made her heart pound and her pulse race. His muscles were tensed in controlled fury, and his blue eyes glittered like diamond chips. She was acutely aware of the heat emanating from his body and was shocked when she found herself straining toward him. Her heaving chest threatened to touch his rock-hard one, and she took a careful step backward. For self-protection.

"Look here, lady. I get a little jumpy at the idea of sharing the location of my gold mine with Muslims and palm-reading gypsies and knighted photographers," he explained grimly. "To say nothing of Mexicans. And when I get jumpy, I get mad as a peeled rattler."

"I accept your apology," Sybilla said formally.

"You *what*?" It might have been an explanation. It might have been an excuse. But it sure as hell wasn't an apology.

"However, I must ask why you persist in referring to the Montoya gold as *your* gold mine. One should be precise, even in matters of semantics."

No way was Hawk going to share the details of what he knew of the mine's existence. Not yet, anyhow. "Look, I've been hunting for it a long time, and it occupies a warm place in my heart. All right?"

Sybilla could debate the existence of that particular organ, but she refused to be sidetracked. "And are you willing to forfeit a chance to find it because of simple male pride?"

He bit back a sharp reply. Was it pride that had worked him into such a lather? Hawk considered her words and when he conceded that she had a point, his temper cooled. This was a chance he didn't want to give up. Not just yet. Not until he'd seen that map. Anyhow, a deal was a deal, and as much as he wanted to, he couldn't back out now. It wouldn't be right.

"One thing you need to learn, Billy. There is nothing simple about a man's pride." Without giving her a chance to reply, he turned to Ahmed. "While we're waiting for Miss Hartford's navvy to

get back, why don't you tell me everything I need
to know about riding the queen of the desert there?''

''Most certainly, *effendi*.'' The small brown man
scuttled forward and bowed. ''I have reserved Delilah for your pleasure.''

Some pleasure. Hawk approached the camel
warily and could have sworn she sneered at him.

The others went about their business, but Sybilla
stayed to observe Devlin's first camel-riding lesson.
She'd heard of his almost legendary prowess at tam-
ing what the locals called wild broncs, and if there
was anything that could humble the churlish cowboy, Delilah would be it.

''The camels are outfitted with Arabian saddles,''
Ahmed explained.

Hawk inspected the contraption. ''Looks like a box
to me.''

''A box? Oh yes, very so. Not like the saddles for
horses. It is a padded frame that fits around the
hump.''

''So where do I sit?'' Hawk was having misgivings, but his pride would not let him say so.

''Atop the frame so that your weight is evenly bal-
anced.''

''Sounds simple enough. How come there's only
one rein?''

''Camels are guided with a single rein and a driving stick. Thus.'' He held out a slender rod. ''Tap
Delilah gently with the stick to tell her in which direction you wish to go. When she falls in love with
you, she will respond to your voice.''

''That'll be the day,'' Hawk grumbled. He approached the kneeling camel with purpose and determination, but without a shred of affection.

Sybilla looked on in amusement. Once again,
Devlin was overestimating himself. She had come to
suspect that was one of his greatest personal fail-
ings.

''And so? Are we ready?'' asked Ahmed.

''Do camels stink?'' Hawk answered rhetorically.

At Ahmed's offended look, he clarified, "I'm ready."

Since there were no stirrups, Hawk wasn't sure where to put his feet. At the moment he didn't give a barrel of shucks about form or camel etiquette and simply leaped into the saddle. His rear end scarcely touched the camel's back before she straightened her hind legs and jerked up her front legs. The movement was so sudden and unexpected that Hawk was propelled over her head and into the dust.

He lay there a moment with his eyes closed, the breath knocked out of him, and tried to figure out what had happened. When he looked up, Delilah's smirking face was only inches from his own. All he could see were bulging eyes, narrow slitted nostrils, and acres of ugly yellow teeth. The animal's hot, fetid breath was as strong as a sheepherder's socks.

Sybilla called out a bit of encouragement. "Good show, Mr. Devlin."

Before Hawk knew what she had in mind, Delilah spit through her cleft upper lip, hitting him in the eye with deadly accuracy. "Shit!" he bellowed. He shoved the camel out of his face, and she nipped at his hand.

"The damn thing tried to bite me," he yelled as he regained his feet.

"Like most animals, camels can sense when one is afraid of them," Sybilla offered sagely.

"Afraid, hell. I just don't like being slobbered on." Embracing the philosophy that there was no shame in being thrown, only in staying thrown, Hawk ordered the Persian, "Knock 'er down again, Ahmed."

Ahmed tapped the standing camel with his stick, and she bent her front legs, kneeled, folded up her hind legs, and fell with a long-suffering grunt.

Sybilla was enjoying Devlin's comeuppance. "Amazing creatures, aren't they?" she asked cheerfully.

"Mind-boggling," he said dryly. "What did I do

wrong?'' he asked Ahmed before trying to mount again.

"Perhaps you failed to hold on, *effendi?*''

"Yeah, that must have been it. Stand aside, Ahmed.'' Hawk was beginning to like the funny little man. At least he showed some respect and a sense of humor.

This time all went well. Almost. Hawk managed to stay in the saddle while Delilah staggered to her feet. He pitched forward and backward violently but didn't fall off. He felt a strong sense of accomplishment. "It's not so bad once you get the hang of it,'' he announced from atop his lofty mount.

"Standing still rarely is.'' Sybilla knew the entertainment was far from over. Devlin still had to make the camel move.

"Apply the driving stick, *effendi*, and sweet little Delilah will be as putty in your hands,'' Ahmed assured him.

Hawk complied and the camel lurched into action, both legs on one side of her body moving forward at the same time. This movement, so unlike a horse's smooth gait, combined with the camel's lack of grace, resulted in a swaying motion from side to side. Given his weakened condition, Hawk considered himself lucky to navigate the grove twice before a distinctly ill feeling overcame him.

No one was more surprised than he when Delilah obeyed his command to stop and kneel. He dismounted quickly, only sheer willpower preventing him from embarrassing himself by chucking up in front of the assemblage.

"Very well done, *effendi*. You have an aptitude for camels,'' Ahmed pronounced proudly.

"Not hardly.''

"It is so,'' Ahmed insisted. "Now that you have demonstrated who is to be boss, she will be like the gentle lamb.''

"Ugliest lamb I ever saw.'' Hawk glared at Sybilla, who was making a bad job of containing her amusement. "Why didn't you warn me?" he demanded while his stomach attempted to settle itself.

"About what?" she asked innocently.

"You know about what. Riding a goddamn camel is like being on a small boat in a choppy ocean. I think I'm seasick."

"Why do you think they are called the ships of the desert? It's not only because of their ability to carry goods across great distances."

"Believe it or not," he muttered, "up until a few hours ago, I rarely spared a minute's time thinking about camels one way or another."

"I think new experiences are the foundation of growth, don't you?" Sybilla's lips hovered on the near side of a smile.

Experience was just another name for mistakes, and Hawk began to sense he'd made a big one. Just as he expected obedience from others, he demanded it of his own body. In a few moments, after he'd gotten himself under control, he swept his hat off in a mock bow. "Miss Hartford, I think you're full of—"

"Mr. Devlin!" she reproached.

"Interesting ideas, I was going to say."

He smiled, and she was taken aback by the ripple of pleasure it gave her. He didn't seem nearly so sinister now. In fact, he cut quite a dashing figure. "Don't worry about Delilah," she said to cover her loss of composure. "She was just testing you."

"Nah, we have an understanding. That camel hates me as much as I hate her."

"The strength of a man lies in his ability to overlook the shortcomings of others. Surely you can allow a poor dumb beast her eccentricities."

"You have an answer for everything, don't you, Billy." Exasperated beyond belief by her arrogance and fancy verbal footwork, Hawk was still intrigued by the stubborn, honey-haired woman. He hadn't figured out what it was about her that made him suffer such indignities and hang around for more,

but before this ill-fated trip was over he was going
to find out.

"A well-read person usually does," she said
pointedly.

"Do you have any other little secrets you're keeping from me, Billy?"

She smiled archly. "Oh yes, quite a few. In fact,
they number in the thousands."

"You going to let me in on any of them?"

"Not hardly," she answered in a tinkling imitation of his own pet phrase.

His gaze raked over her, from her bright, intelligent eyes down to the tips of her shiny boots. She
was a damn efficient female, cool and confident as
any he'd ever come across. She didn't resort to tears
or guile to get her way, and she wouldn't admit to
belonging to the weaker sex if she was staked out
naked on a cactus flat. If she'd been born a man, he
might have admired her, Hawk admitted grudgingly. Maybe even liked her a little.

He noted the gentle swell of her buttoned-up
bosom, the soft curve of her hips, the pale translu-
cence of her skin. She was definitely a woman even
if she hadn't yet learned how to use the equipment.
While it was hard to imagine the bristly Miss Iron
Britches letting down her hair, or her defenses, it
wasn't impossible. Even the inhospitable cholla cactus put out a flower when the time was right.

It would take a mighty patient man to coax a
bloom from such a brittle and unwilling little seed,
and while he'd never had much patience, Hawk was
always ready for a challenge. Maybe that was what
he found so seductive about her.

Then again, maybe it was her treasure map.

"Remember this," he warned before mounting
Delilah. "At the first sign of trouble, I'm hauling ass
back to Tucson."

"Of course, Mr. Devlin." Sybilla smiled smugly
at his back. "After all, you *are* in charge here."

She could afford to be magnanimous. So far she'd

maintained the control she thrived on, and Devlin didn't seem nearly as dangerous as his reputation had made her believe. In fact, he was not at all what she'd expected.

Oh, he was rough, but no rougher than a man from such an untamed land would have to be by necessity. She sensed that he was equal to any task the wilderness could set. And there was depth to him as well. Probing that depth would only make the trip more interesting.

His audacity was maddening, his brashness frustrating, his boldness confounding—to say nothing of his disrespectful attentions that created within Sybilla a wayward excitement that constantly threatened her carefully cultivated control. He brought her untried senses to life, and she had to pinch back the flowering of emotion that, if left unchecked, could tangle and choke her good sense.

Sybilla watched with a secret smile as Hawk maneuvered his camel to the head of the line. Despite the problems she knew he would cause her, she had to admit that he did indeed cut a dashing figure as he led the caravan north toward the Superstition Mountains and adventure.

Hawk felt Sybilla's gaze on his back and turned. Their eyes met and held for a long, unsettling moment. "And stop calling me Mr. Devlin," he muttered peevishly from atop Delilah.

Chapter 5

The caravan lumbered out of Tucson at a slow but steady pace. Despite the late start, the camels' long legs covered fifteen miles before it was time to stop for the night. Hawk chose a spot in a small canyon full of cottonwoods and pinyon pines where hackberry, manzanita, and sotol plants grew abundantly among the rocks. A narrow stream, rushing with winter runoff from the Picacho Mountains, provided the welcome taste and sound of clear running water.

"Enjoy the water, folks," Hawk advised as he dismounted, careful to stay out of biting range of the sneaky camel. "Where we're headed there won't be much of it." He tossed the rein to Ahmed, grateful for the chance to spend a few hours on ground that did not roll beneath him.

As he passed, Delilah curled her lip and spat at him. He sidestepped and cursed himself for allowing Sybilla to talk him into bringing the beasts on the trip. He should have put his foot down, been a little less greedy, and exercised more authority.

That was a lot of "should haves," but Sybilla wasn't the easiest person in the world to deal with, especially when a man was suffering the effects of too much tarantula juice. She was as fastidious as a hundred-dollar whore, as rigid as a rock post, and as demanding as a toothache. But she also pos-

sessed an intolerable combination of beauty,
strength, independence, and capability.

Things would have been a lot easier if she were a
tad less meticulous and a heap more helpless. In her
case, even ugliness would be a desirable quality.
That way he could stop thinking about making love
to her and concentrate on important things—like
finding his gold. *The* gold.

His morning headache had gradually given way
to a qualmy stomach, and his stiff muscles ached
from the unaccustomed motion of the ride. His only
desire at the moment was to soak his head in cool
water and sleep for twenty years, but duty called.
He'd have to get the camp organized first.

God only knew these pilgrims would be as helpless as new-hatched quail. Greenhorns like them
would just stand around waiting for someone more
experienced to tell them what to do.

But before Hawk could decide what needed to be
done and by whom, Sybilla issued a few quiet orders in Spanish to Juan and Miguel. The brothers
Ruiz scrambled off the camel they'd been riding tan-
dem and started setting up camp. They'd been nervous about the camels at first, but having something
useful to do seemed to lift their spirits. Before long
they had a commendable fire going and were jab-
bering excitedly to each other in their Sonoran
dialect.

Her multicolored skirts whirling, the gypsy woman busied herself with a wicked-looking knife, dic-
ing something into a cookpot she set to bubbling
over the fire. As she worked, she glanced around
nervously and rolled her eyes heavenward. She
muttered and clucked in her strange tongue like a
disapproving hen with bad news for the chicken
house.

Hawk rubbed his throbbing temples. What with
Sybilla's dulcet British tones, Ahmed's fractured English, Juan's and Miguel's Spanish, and Zora's

whatever-it-was, the outfit was a regular tower of Babel.

John Collings supervised the Mexicans in the erection of two canvas tents until he was satisfied the boys could complete the task on their own. He waved when he caught Hawk's eye and strolled toward him, blotting his bald pate with a clean handkerchief.

The frail Englishman's unreasonably tidy appearance did nothing to improve Hawk's mood; he was staunch in the belief that anyone who'd just spent eight hours on a camel under a broiling sun should look a little the worse for wear.

"Beastly hot, this." John folded the linen square neatly and pocketed it in his twill jacket.

"It's early yet. Hang around until August," Hawk advised. "It gets so hot that if you die and go to hell, you'll wire home for blankets."

John laughed and slapped his knee. "I do so enjoy Western humor. I'm quite a fan of Deadeye Dick's. Have you ever met him?"

"Can't say as I have." Hawk wondered if the old man really believed the dime-novel character existed. "I did meet Geronimo once, though."

Sir John seemed duly impressed. "You must tell me about it sometime, old boy. Say, are the Superstitions as dangerous as we've heard, or is their reputation founded mostly upon, well, superstition?"

Hawk took a long swig from his canteen and wiped his mouth on his sleeve. The Englishman had a softness about him that blurred the hard edges required for survival. Hawk's instincts told him John wouldn't be much help in a tight situation. "They're twice as dangerous as you've heard and whatever reputation they have, they earned fair and square."

"Do you think they contain gold?"

"Some think so," Hawk answered evasively.

"I've observed the hills in this part of the country and find them composed primarily of igneous materials. Anyone with a rudimentary knowledge of geology knows that gold is rarely found in the presence of volcanic matter.''

"So your niece told me. Her ancestor's story seems to contradict that theory.''

John harrumphed. "Yes, well, her ancestor was completely deluded, if not downright insane.''

The vehemence in John's voice contrasted with his mild personality. "We're all a little crazy, I guess,'' Hawk commented dryly, "or we wouldn't be here. Stories about the gold in that big pile of rocks were circulating long before any Spaniards showed up looking for a share.''

"And which are you inclined to believe, my good man? Wild notions or scientific fact?''

"Neither one. I trust my instincts. I figure today's wild notions might just be tomorrow's scientific facts.''

"A very wise point of view. Still, searching for gold in such a nonmineralized area scarcely seems logical.''

"Nobody ever found gold with his head,'' Hawk pointed out. "You find gold with your heart. If I wanted to follow reason and logic, I'd be a banker in Virginia.''

"I realize you stand to gain a great deal if this venture is successful. However, what if it fails? What will you have to show for your time?''

Hawk wasn't sure what direction the conversation was taking. "Time's about the cheapest thing on today's market. I figure I'll get a holiday out of it. And the pleasure of your company.''

John glanced around and spotted Sybilla conferring with Zora at the campfire. Lowering his voice, he said, "I'm prepared to make this trip worth your while, Hawk. Provided it *is* unsuccessful.''

Suddenly wary, Hawk stated, "I'm listening.''

"What I propose is this. You escort us into the fringes of the Superstitions, make a cursory attempt to locate the gold, and declare the expedition a failure. Upon which we all leave posthaste.''

"Why would I want to do that?"

"Because I'll pay you, that's why."

"That's a good reason. However, I was given to believe this outfit wasn't exactly flush with funds. You holding out on Sybilla?"

John looked affronted. "Of course not. My cameras are worth a handsome sum, and I would be willing to part with them if it meant an end to this trip."

"Why?"

"It's not turning out at all as I expected from my reading."

"Deadeye Dick again?" Hawk smiled at the old man's forlorn expression. "It's not as romantic out here as the dime novelists paint it, is it?"

"It certainly is not. But my real concern is for Sybilla's well-being, of course."

"Of course."

"A lot of things could happen. From what I've seen of this territory so far, no offense intended, all of them are bad."

Far from taking offense, Hawk concurred with the old man's assessment. Arizona wasn't exactly the vacation capital of the world.

"As the last of Sybilla's kin," John went on, "I am responsible for her. I fear the dear girl is becoming obsessed with finding the Montoya gold. Just like her poor father. I shouldn't wish to see her come to harm."

"You're sure it doesn't exist?"

"Come now," John scoffed. "Spanish gold, stacked like cordwood in a cave, protected by some ancient Apache curse? You don't really believe that, do you?"

"You're forgetting one thing. I'm part Apache and I've heard similar stories told around tribal campfires since I was a boy."

"So you think it's there?" John asked with a worried frown.

"Maybe. But being there and being found are two different propositions."

"And what of the curse? Do you also believe all the tales of death and destruction?"

Hawk shrugged. "Maybe. Personally, I think putting a curse on a place like that is a little like salting the ocean. There's enough danger from old Mother Nature herself without calling for the help of spirits."

Just then Sybilla called to them from the other side of the camp. As she approached, picking her way delicately through the dappled shade of early evening, Hawk was struck anew by how tiny and perfect she was, how thoroughly civilized, and how totally out of place.

There was little in her appearance, aside from the stubborn tilt of her chin, to indicate the strength he knew she possessed. But competent or not, such a lady was no match for the wild, uncivilized place he was taking her to. Maybe John was right to be concerned.

John shot Hawk a desperate look. "I'd rather you did not mention my offer to Sybilla."

"What offer? Oh, you mean your bribe?" Hawk flicked imaginary dust from the older man's lapel. "Of course not. That'll just be between us old chaps. For now." Until he could get a better handle on the man's motives.

"Smashing spot, this," Sybilla enthused as she looked around. "Considering our less than auspicious start, I think we did rather splendidly today. Don't you agree, Mr. Devlin?"

She had removed her headgear, and her sleek hair was still secure in its pins. Only a telltale dampness on her forehead where her hairline swooped into a gentle vee indicated she felt the heat at all. Delicate, feminine tendrils curled around her cameo face, and Hawk felt a sudden and shocking urge to kiss his way across it, slowly and unfalteringly.

That unbidden desire, plus her crisp cheerfulness,

aggravated him for reasons that didn't bear thinking about. As did the fact that the whole troop had survived the first day on the trail with maddening good humor and no complaints. He should have been happy, but he wasn't.

On top of it all, John had just offered to pay him to sabotage an expedition that seemed to be faring better than he'd dared to hope. It was enough to spoil a man's day.

"Don't you agree?" Sybilla insisted.

"With all my heart," he grumbled before stalking away to see to his bedroll.

"What a contentious man!" she exclaimed. "What do you suppose is wrong with him now, Uncle?"

"I'm sure I don't know, dear." John watched Hawk's retreating back speculatively, as if wondering if he could trust him to keep their secret. "Like linen suits, some people simply do not travel well."

Things continued to go smoothly. So smoothly, in fact, that Hawk began to be seriously irritated. After all his dire admonitions, he was apparently the only one suffering from the rigors of the trip. Everyone else in the band seemed to understand his role, and camp was made when he called a halt, then struck the next morning with an economy of effort. When Sybilla Hartford demanded efficiency from her people, she got it.

Juan was a far better hand than Hawk had given him credit for, and although Miguel was a little slow-witted, he was able to follow directions well enough. The brothers kept mostly to themselves, eating and sleeping as far from the others, especially the gypsy and her fortune-telling cards, as they considered safe.

Ahmed pitched the gaily striped tent he shared with Zora where he could keep an eye and ear on the hobbled camels. When the couple, who seemed to have little in common, disappeared into their tent, their voices inevitably rose in a highly audible, yet untranslatable, domestic quarrel. Hawk was always amazed when the hot-tempered twosome emerged the next morning as if nothing had happened.

Sybilla and John had separate tents to which they retired as soon as the fire was banked for the night. She read poetry by lantern light when she should have been sleeping, and Hawk surmised that habit was part of her problem. The woman read too much, thought too much, and, most of all, talked too much.

The third night out, he lay awake on his bedroll on the ground, thinking about John's proposition. John hadn't said any more about it, and Hawk had decided the old fellow was probably just what he appeared to be—an elderly uncle concerned for his young niece's welfare.

The shadow play on the side of Sybilla's tent captured Hawk's attention and, feeling only slightly guilty, he watched as she unbound her hair and shook it loose. The long tresses whipped around her head like a silken banner before settling slowly onto her back. Twisting it into a thick coil, she draped it over her shoulder and began brushing it. The slow, sensuous motions were silhouetted clearly on the broadside of the tent, a private show for an appreciative audience of one.

Wrapped in his blankets against the chill desert night, Hawk observed her until she doused the light. If she undressed, she did so in the dark. Disgruntled by the longing she aroused in him, he muttered to himself that she'd probably been born fully dressed and booted, every newborn hair in place.

Despite his fatigue, he lay awake listening to the canyon frogs croak and watching the stars shimmer in the wide night sky. One thought led naturally to another, and he was soon entertaining himself with wild, improbable imaginings.

In his mind, he tried to picture Billy with her fine hair in tumbled disarray, not from its regimen of brushing but from lovemaking. He imagined how her pale skin, soft and untouched by any man's hand, would reflect the moonlight like a creamy saguaro blossom; how she would yield to him. He wondered how her soft, needy lips would feel against his as she cried out his name at the height of passion.

He tried to imagine all that, but didn't quite succeed. Reality had a way of interfering, even in fantasies, and it was hard to picture Miss Iron Britches caught up in the throes of any emotion, especially passion. She kept her feelings snubbed like a green colt to the post she called propriety.

He tossed in his blankets and chided himself for thinking of trying to change the distant Sybilla into the sweet Billy of his dreams. No doubt stronger men had gone loco attempting less impossible deeds.

Before he drifted off to sleep, he heard the faint tinkling of a music box coming from her tent. The melody, borne like a sigh on the desert wind, was "The Blue Danube" waltz, and it brought back memories he'd thought long forgotten . . . of the shining world of Williamsburg. Of gliding around a holly-strewn ballroom with the girl he loved in his arms. Of the refracted light of a dozen chandeliers sparkling overhead. Of merry laughter behind a coquettishly held fan. Of long, fluttering lashes and a lush pink mouth promising to love him forever. The orchestra had played that waltz at the Christmas cotillion the night he'd asked the woman he loved to marry him, so many years ago.

His overworked imagination conjured up her image with ease. Mariel Davenport, all green eyes and yellow curls and innocence. She'd been as blind to the gulf between them as he had been. But, unlike him, she hadn't tumbled willingly into the abyss; her parents had pulled her back from the brink of disaster just in time by pointing out that she hadn't really fallen in love with him but with the man she wanted him to be.

He could hardly blame the Davenports for wanting to save their pure and virtuous daughter from social ostracism. It was his fault the storybook courtship had ended in pain. He was to blame for trying to be something he wasn't, for aspiring to ambitious goals that were unattainable to a man of mixed blood.

He'd been reminded painfully of his place by those who considered themselves his betters, and he wouldn't overstep those bounds again.

A coyote wailed at the rising moon, and Hawk's thoughts snapped back to the present. Determined to forget the past while remembering its hard-learned lessons, he soon fell into a troubled sleep.

The next morning Hawk approached Delilah, who was chewing contentedly with her eyes closed, as peaceful as any Guernsey cow. As Sybilla had predicted, he'd gotten used to the smell of the camels and after only three days was no longer plagued by queasiness. But Delilah had not become ''like the gentle lamb,'' and he had to be on constant guard against her sneaky spitting and nipping.

Having ridden Diablo for three years, Hawk was more or less resigned to having a difficult mount. But such diligence was not only mentally tiresome, it was also downright time consuming. And dammit, he was the boss around here, and he had better things to do.

Like watching for signs of trouble, which in this country could come from any direction, at any time. Just because things had been quiet so far didn't mean they would stay that way. In fact, it almost guaranteed that they wouldn't. Luck, like water, had a way of running out unexpectedly.

As he was tying on his bedroll, Delilah suddenly swung her scrawny neck around, rocky teeth bared to bite. Hawk had spent years busting wilder and more agile creatures, though none with a more vengeful mean streak. His finely honed reflexes allowed him to dance away in time to prevent a nasty wound.

The sum of the insults he'd accumulated during the last few days made him swell up like a poisoned pup. He tugged his hat low over his eyes, tightened the chin strap, and backed a few feet away, his hands clenched into fists.

Anger, as sudden and devastating as a mountain flood, roiled up inside him and he focused all his frustrations on the beast who'd been sent from the middle pits of hell to make his life one long misery.

Wasn't it bad enough that Sybilla had practically taken over, usurping his authority and undermining any confidence the others might have had in him at the beginning? Ever gracious, she pretended to defer to his judgment. "Yes, Mr. Devlin. You're in charge, Mr. Devlin," she assured him at every turn.

He'd heard it a hundred times, but that didn't make it true. The stubborn little baggage listened patiently to what he told her and then did exactly as she'd planned to do all along.

No wonder John wanted the venture to fail so he could get back to the safety of civilization. What kind of scout would let a woman, even one as pushy as Sybilla, take over? Why should the others trust him with their lives? He couldn't lead an expedition if he couldn't even manage his own mangy mount.

There wasn't much he could do about the woman, not yet anyhow, but there *was* something he could do about this camel. He'd have some respect from one damn female or another. The mood he was in, it didn't matter which. After all, he did have a reputation to maintain.

"Listen to me, you shaggy pile of moulting carpet," he railed at Delilah. "You are not going to get the best of me. I'm here and I'm going to stay, so you might as well get your empty head used to the idea."

Delilah ignored him, closed her eyes again, and went back to her mindless chewing. He stepped for-

ward to finish tying down his pack. He knew better
than to relax his guard and, as anticipated, she struck
again, as quick as a rattler and just as deadly. Barely
managing to dodge the bite, he drew back his booted
foot to administer a little long overdue discipline.

"No, no, no, *effendi!*" Ahmed's alarm was obvious as he scurried up to protect his "child" from
her infidel molester. "Begging your pardon, but
force must never be used against a camel. It is bad
luck."

"That backbiting bag of bones is going to learn the
true meaning of bad luck if she tries that again."

"Very so, *effendi*. I shall talk to her."

"You do that. But I think a whack on the head
with a medium-sized stick of firewood would be
more effective. I should have shot her the first day.
Would have, if I didn't prefer riding to walking. Putting a critter like that out of its misery is the only
truly humane thing to do."

"No, no, no." Ahmed looked horrified. "I will
use the gentle art of persuasion."

Hawk watched the Persian whisper into the camel's hairy ear and resisted the temptation to point
out that in Arizona the gentle art of pistol whipping
was the preferred method of getting someone, or
some*thing*, to share your views.

For all his bowing and scraping and talking to
camels, Ahmed, a native desert dweller himself, had
turned out to be the most entertaining of the bunch.
He'd told Hawk stories of his early life in Persia and
of the time he spent with the circus.

Ahmed's father had been recruited as a camel
driver for the U.S. Army, and the two had come to
the country in 1856, when Ahmed was a lad of nine.
Congress had approved the importation of camels
the year before, to carry supplies to the army's
southwestern outposts and to units surveying possible wagon routes to California.

When the Civil War ended, the camels had out-
lived their usefulness. Railroads opened up the West

and provided a much faster method of travel and transit. The Mendabs found themselves out of a job. When the order came to dispose of the camels, some were sold to zoos, some to private citizens, still others set free in the desert to fend for themselves.

Ahmed Senior offered to take some of them off the army's hands and, by negotiating a deal with a traveling circus, had ensured a livelihood for himself and his son. Ahmed Junior had inherited the act after his father's death and had successfully maintained the small herd ever since. Delilah, nearly thirty years old, was all that remained of that original group of mustered-out government-issue camels.

Hawk also respected Ahmed for his religious fervor. He wasn't at all sure he could recall all ten of the Christian Commandments in rote order. He never got much past 'Thou shalt not commit adultery.' But Ahmed could recite all ninety-nine names of Allah, counting them off on a string of beads fashioned from camel bones.

Hawk speculated that if the man showed half as much interest in his wife as he did in his camels and his god, Zora wouldn't be such a nuisance. A little connubial bliss would go a long way toward keeping her away from those ominous cards of hers, and maybe she'd cut out all the sooty glances, hip-swaying, and lip-licking whenever she was around him. As it was, Hawk had almost as much trouble staying out of pinching range of the gypsy as he did avoiding Delilah's well-timed kicks and nips.

No doubt about it. The females of the world were involved in a conspiracy against him.

Ahmed had finished palavering. "Delilah, she is a naughty little girl sometime," he admitted sadly. "Allowance must be made for her advanced years and uncheerful temperament."

"Uncheerful temperament?" Hawk spat derisively in the dust. "That's like calling that villain Maloche a misunderstood delinquent."

"Please, *effendi*." Ahmed covered his ears with his hands. "Do not mention that infidel's name in my hearing. That too is bad luck. By calling a demon's name you can conjure him out of the desert sand."

Hawk didn't believe such nonsense, but the renegade Maloche and his band of cutthroats had a reputation for striking suddenly and unexpectedly, then slipping away as swiftly and silently as bronze ghosts, leaving death and destruction in their wake.

Whites called him a coward, but Hawk knew the Mexican-Yaqui-Comanche Maloche shared the Apache belief that it was wiser to strike and run and live to fight another day. His practice of avoiding open conflict when badly outnumbered or when the terrain was against him was what had kept the undeserving bastard alive for so long—not the sacred amulet that was said to protect him in battle and render him indestructible.

The merciless killer had been a thorn in the army's side for years, and now that Geronimo and the others had been subdued, the army had made it their number one priority to bring in Maloche. So far, they'd failed.

Hawk apologized to the superstitious Muslim whose fear of bad luck was no less heartfelt than his wife's malevolent predictions of it. "I'll try to avoid mentioning demons in the future," he told Ahmed.

"I shall be most thankful, *effendi*."

"But I can't promise that me and that camel won't come to a showdown sooner or later. I can try to live with the highfalutin ways of the duke and duchess over there." He inclined his head toward Sybilla and John, who were sharing a final cup of tea. "But I draw the line at having this misbegotten dinosaur sneer at me."

Ahmed frowned, then his swarthy face suddenly brightened. "Ah ha!"

"Ah ha, what?"

"I have surely discovered the problem. In your

attempts to control Delilah's impulses, you are not acknowledging her natural superiority.

"Her what?"

"Take no offense, *effendi*, but camels have good reason to look at their masters with so much disdain. According to Islamic lore, the prophet Mohammed confided the Secret of Secrets—the hundredth name of Allah—to the faithful camel that carried him safely into exile when his life was endangered. From that time to this, the Secret of Secrets has been handed down from one camel to another."

"So?" Hawk asked suspiciously.

"Just so. When a camel looks at a human who lacks such perfect knowledge, the animal feels superior and its face cannot but help twisting into a sneer."

Hawk glanced at Delilah doubtfully. Her eyes narrowed and her lips curled, looking for all the world as if she not only understood Ahmed, but also agreed with him.

"Tell her you understand now, *effendi*," Ahmed urged.

"I've already lowered my standards considerably by riding the damn thing. I won't sink so low as to talk to it too."

"But you must. You have gravely wounded Delilah's tender sensibilities, and only the most abject apology will do."

Hawk's jaw tightened. He couldn't believe he was in such a position. Little more than a week ago, he'd been one of the most feared and respected men in Arizona. Then he'd met Sybilla Hartford, and she'd knocked him right out of the comfortable niche he'd clawed out for himself. She was to blame for his coming to such a sorry pass as having to beg pardon of a stupid camel. Just one more item to tote up against her on the mental tally he was keeping.

He glanced at Ahmed, whose wide white smile

was meant to encourage, and then at Delilah, who appeared to be chewing up a nice wad with which to bathe his face. He looked around, making sure no one was near enough to overhear, then cautiously sidled up to the camel.

Hawk thought Ahmed was pretty full of it, and what he was about to do went against every principle he held dear. But if he was to enjoy any peace at all on this trip, he'd have to mend fences with his fractious mount.

"Sorry," he whispered grudgingly out of the side of his mouth.

"I do not think she heard you, *effendi*."

"Sorry," he muttered, a little louder.

"Now say 'Excuse me for my ignorance.' "

"The hell you say."

"You must," Ahmed implored.

Although they nearly choked him, Hawk repeated Ahmed's words.

"Now say 'I defer to your superior knowledge in all of Allah's ways.' "

That wasn't hard to do since Hawk had no desire to undertake a religious education. Especially not at the feet of a stinking camel.

When Ahmed was satisfied that Hawk was properly penitent, he said softly, "Now bow."

Hawk whirled around. "I will not!"

"Delilah will not accept your apology without the proper display of respect, *effendi*."

"Goddammit!" If anyone ever found out about this, his hard-earned reputation wouldn't be worth a bucket of hot spit. But then again, nothing in the events of the past few days had exactly enhanced his reputation.

Hawk's bow, when he finally made it, was little more than a slight forward motion, but Delilah seemed satisfied. She rolled her eyes at him and fluttered her long lashes. Then her lips puckered, and she spat with deadeyed aim—into the dust at Hawk's feet.

Ahmed was beside himself with joy at the camel's change of heart. "Praise Allah, she accepts you, *effendi.*"

"That's a relief," Hawk muttered without enthusiasm as he called for the caravan to fall in behind him. "Now I can die a happy man."

Chapter 6

They pulled into Apache Junction late on the fourth day. Hawk planned to replenish their water supplies at the wells there before taking the eastern trail into the Superstitions. To Sybilla, the dusty collection of sunbaked adobe buildings squatting among the mesquite and chapparal barely qualified as a town.

"Do the inhabitants actually *choose* to live here?" she asked Hawk incredulously as they rode side by side down the one and only street.

"I reckon so." The fact that the street was strangely empty made Hawk wary and alerted his senses to the possibility of trouble. Something was wrong. There were no horses at the hitching posts, no men lounging in front of the cantina, no dusky children playing in the waning sunlight. The air was still and silent. The only sound was the dull drone of heat-enervated insects, the only movement that of a skinny brown dog slinking into the alley between two empty storefronts.

Hawk had expected their arrival to elicit the same kind of interest Sybilla's entourage had received in Tucson, but the citizens of Apache Junction were staying behind closed doors. Apparently their curiosity about the caravan was not as great as their fear of something else, something more threatening than the Hartford Traveling Camel Show.

"They weren't sent here as punishment for a

103

crime against man or God?'' Sybilla persisted, unaware of the deadly implications of the silence.

"I reckon not."

If she had thought Tucson devoid of redeeming features, this hot, forlorn place of tumbleweeds and dust devils had even less to offer. "It is amazing that anyone would choose to expend the years God gave them in this unappealing place when there are so many other, greener ones in the world."

"They probably never heard of them," Hawk replied absently as he scanned both sides of the street.

"But what possible interest could such a godforsaken place hold for anyone?"

He shrugged. "Like they say, there's no accounting for taste. Even a cowchip is paradise for a fly." A couple of faces peered cautiously through the dirty windows, but since neither seemed to belong to the welcoming committee, Hawk led the caravan to the wells on the edge of town. While the others refilled the water bags, he strode back toward the cantina, determined to find out what was going on.

"Did we interrupt a siesta?" Sybilla asked when he rejoined the group twenty minutes later.

"Not hardly." He started to tell them what he'd learned, but one look at the nervous Mexicans and the superstitious Muslim, and he thought better of it. No point giving Zora more grist for her disaster mill either. He motioned for John and Sybilla to follow him until they were out of earshot.

"Maloche has been reported in the area, and the townspeople are being careful," he told them.

"I believe I have heard the name before," John ventured.

"It's hard to spend any time at all in the Territory and not hear Maloche's name mentioned," Hawk informed them. "Bad news travels fast, as they say."

"He's just another desperado," Sybilla put in.

"He was a desperado when he was a suckling child," Hawk said grimly. "He's a full-fledged cutthroat now. With Geronimo and Nachez out of the way, Maloche may be the most dangerous man in the Territory."

Sybilla supposed it was too much to hope that their good fortune would continue. "What do you know about him?"

"That he's a renegade, part white, part Yaqui, part Comanche. And mean enough to have a reserved seat in hell. He and his band of misfits raid on both sides of the border and hide out in the territory when the Federales go after them. When the army's on his trail, he heads for the Mexican Highlands.

"Unlike Geronimo, Maloche isn't fighting for his people or his land or any other cause. He rapes and tortures and murders because he enjoys it."

John shivered in fear. "Have you ever encountered him?"

"No, but I've seen his handiwork. I've seen men tied to a giant cactus with green rawhide cords. When the rawhide tightens in the sun, the sharp thorns pierce their bodies in a thousand places. Death comes slow. I've seen others hanged head down over a slow fire and roasted alive. Maloche is nothing short of creative."

"Enough, Devlin!" John pleaded. "Must you be so bloody graphic?"

"Thought you might like to know what you're up against. We can turn around right now and head back to Tucson, if you don't want to risk it. Or we could go west to Phoenix. Of course, who knows where Maloche is headed? Anything could happen on the trip back."

Sybilla shuddered at the images her mind conjured up from Hawk's gruesome remarks. "No. We shall go on."

"Really, Sybilla." John's sun-flushed face blanched white. "We are ill equipped to deal with such a scoundrel. Perhaps we should consider giving up."

"No." Sybilla could not turn back now, it was

unthinkable. There was nothing to go back to, anyway. "We're going on," she repeated resolutely.

"You're in charge here, Devlin." John was visibly shaken, and the look he turned on Hawk was pleading. "What do you propose we do?"

"Well, I don't think we should hole up here like a prairie dog cowering from a coyote." His eyes narrowed as they swept across the flats dotted with cholla thickets and sparse stands of saguaro. He noticed Juan and Miguel standing nearby, watching fearfully.

The boys' English was not good enough for them to understand much of the eavesdropped conversation, but it was clear from the expressions on their faces that they had picked up the name of every border child's bogeyman. Their eyes met Hawk's in alarm before they scurried back to the camels.

"No place to hide out there," Hawk commented. "The sooner we get to those mountains, the better off we'll be."

Sybilla followed his gaze. Ten miles away, through the lavender haze of evening, the Superstition Mountains loomed stark and unearthly, more like the ancient crumbling ruins of a Babylonian fortress than a work of nature. They appeared suddenly, like a mirage in the desert, a compelling specter from a long-forgotten age, older than human imagination could comprehend.

The western end of the range rose vertically from the desert floor, naked cliffs a thousand feet high. They were surmounted by talus slopes, terraces, and, farther away, tiers of ridges that merged with the main body of the range. The summit comprised fairy-tale pinnacles, boulder-strewn battlements, and eerie domes, thrusting out of their own eroded debris.

"Then that shall remain our destination," Sybilla pronounced firmly. "I refuse to give up."

Hawk agreed with her decision. He didn't think they should let rumors scare them off, but gold or no gold, he would have turned back if she'd said the word. The Superstitions were a place a person had to *want* to go to.

The water bags were filled and, despite John's objections, everyone remounted and the camels ambled away from Apache Junction and its frightened inhabitants. Those barricaded behind their doors were no less anxious than those departing.

John's fear communicated itself to the others, and Ahmed gripped the handle of the knife in his sash as his raisin-dark eyes scoured the horizon. Zora moaned that they were riding to their deaths—her sixth sense told her so. Juan and Miguel, who stared longingly over their shoulders at the receding but dubious safety of the town, screamed when a jackrabbit jumped out of the brush along the trail.

A little fear was a healthy thing in this part of the country, but Hawk worried that the whole party had just taken a dangerous overdose.

Instead of falling in behind Hawk, Sybilla guided her camel, Jezebel, abreast of him. The nervous way she kept glancing around made him wish he'd kept the stories of Maloche's foul deeds to himself. But if she was frightened, she didn't say so. Hawk admired that. They rode for several miles in silence before he directed her attention to a towering rock formation that crouched on the horizon like a hulking beast.

"That was the original Superstition Mountain. Over the years, people generalized the name to the other peaks in the range."

"Why is it called Superstition?"

He shrugged. "No one knows for sure. I guess it was only natural. There were legends told about it before the white man came."

"Among your people—the Apaches?" she asked tentatively.

The question made him look up sharply. His people? While it was true that some diluted Apache blood flowed through his veins, he no longer belonged among them. Since his mother's death, he'd stayed away from the reservation and its painful memories; away from his distant cousins who were the conquered remnants of a once-proud race. His people? No, not anymore.

"Yeah, among the Apaches."

"I have heard that the Superstitions are home to the Apaches' gods, and that is why they were ever ready to slay whites who defiled them."

"I've heard that one too," he admitted wryly. "I hate to disillusion you, but the mountain spirits the Apaches believe in inhabit every mountain. They don't pay any special attention to the Superstitions. Besides, Apaches never needed to invent religious reasons to kill white men. The whites gave them plenty."

Sybilla glanced at the man riding beside her. His words were tinged with bitterness, but in profile his face was a perfect mask of chiseled bone and taut skin, revealing little of his true feelings. That he had feelings, and powerful ones, she had no doubt, but she detected a cynicism in him that was wholly unlike the jaded worldliness of the young men of position she'd known in England. She sensed that Hawk's misanthropy was born of genuine pain and loss and disenchantment with mankind.

A surge of undisciplined curiosity fueled her need to understand this strange young man whose eyes possessed the knowledge and experience of one twice his age. Life had hurt him and, although his tanned, sinewy body bore no visible scars, she could only wonder at the severity of the scars he carried in his troubled heart.

As they rode along, Sybilla tried to worry about the bandit Maloche, but her errant thoughts held fast to the man beside her, leading her down paths far more dangerous than any in the haunted mountains.

She well remembered the symmetry of Hawk's long-limbed body as it had been revealed to her the day she went to his hotel room. When she closed her eyes she could almost see again the breadth of his shoulders with their endless expanse of rippling bronze muscles the smooth hairless chest marked by dark male nipples.

She had tried that day to prevent her eyes from straying below his chest, but they had betrayed her and she'd gotten a tantalizing glimpse of his lower body. Of narrow hips and flat stomach. Of legs as long and brown and softly furred as his arms. But it was that other appendage, the one she'd tried not to notice, that had had the greatest impact on her imagination.

It had created a heat that put the desert sun to shame, and on that day she had learned exactly what the term "sexual arousal" really meant. It was a frightening discovery.

Over the years there had been young men who had sought her favor, but only one had dared to kiss her. They'd seemed intimidated by her independent nature and, although her feminine vanity had been injured, she had been almost glad when they turned to meeker-minded ladies to cosset their fragile egos.

But Hawk was different, as rough as a bucket of ore and yet as beautiful and finely made as any classic statue in a museum. She had seen many examples of masculine beauty in art, but never had a sculptor captured in cold stone the vitality and sheer virility that made a flesh and blood man like Hawk so threatening to a woman who questioned her own appeal.

He was a man who took what he wanted. His failure to make any untoward advances troubled Sybilla as much as it relieved her. After all, how much more difficult would the journey be if she continually had to fend off the unwanted attentions of her guide? And yet how painful to think that she was so unappealing that the only emotion she aroused in him was anger.

Using simple Socratic logic, she arrived at a devastating conclusion. Hawk took what he wanted, damning all rules. He had made no advances toward her. Ergo, he did not want her. And since he obviously had the traditional male needs, the failing must be in her womanhood. Simple deductive reasoning.

Sybilla shook off such thoughts and watched his slim brown hand deftly control Delilah's rein. She imagined his skilled touch on her own body and wondered what her response would be.

Outrage? Indignation? Terror? Or any of the many other fainthearted reactions at a gentlewoman's disposal? She thought not. There was no question that Hawk was capable of igniting fierce and frightening emotions, even in her, but she doubted if she would swoon in distress.

What would it be like to be held in his strong arms, to be pressed against his virile length and kissed? No, not kissed—that was too mild a word for what she was sure his lips would do to hers. Ravish, that was it. Hawk was not a man to waste time with courtly gestures like parlor kissing.

Years of training and denial prevented her thoughts from taking her any further in their wild journey, and she was embarrassed by the indelicacy of her indulgences. Perhaps she had been out in the sun too long.

Hawk caught her watching him, and the way his eyes burned boldly into hers, she feared he could read her wayward mind. She could not look away and felt an unnamed but powerful force crackle between them like summer lightning. Suddenly she was suffused with a yearning of both body and spirit that was so new and powerful it threatened to destroy her cool control.

Such feelings were out of the question. She and Hawk had nothing in common; not experience, not values, not background. Nothing. Yet when she looked into his eyes, she sensed they were on a collision course set by fate. She felt as if she'd been caught naked, stripped of the comforting layers of pretension, propriety, and convention. She clutched those layers about her—they were her only protection.

Not only did Hawk seem to know what she was thinking, he obviously approved. His slow smile challenged her, warmed her, reassured and aroused her, all at the same time.

"Penny for your thoughts, Billy," he drawled.

Startled by the amusement in his tone, she blushed. "I fear you've made a bad bargain."

"Let me be the judge of that."

"I was thinking about the Indians," she improvised.

"The noble savage, huh? The race in general, or anyone in particular?"

"Oh, in general," she said evasively. "You know, in my studies of the native southwestern peoples I've come to sympathize with their desire to keep the white invaders out of their lands."

"Is that a fact?"

"I don't approve of their methods, of course." Both her sensibilities and her stomach revolted at the thought of a fellow human being burned alive. "Violence is never a viable solution."

Hawk glanced at her thoughtfully. "Maybe not in theory, but out here, sometimes it's the only answer."

"I quite disagree. There are always other ways of solving problems. Rational discussion and pacts of nonaggression are the cornerstones of civilization." Sybilla resorted to debate to cover the discomfort of her previous thoughts.

"Pacts of nonaggression? You mean treaties?" Hawk asked grimly, thinking that her words only served to delineate the differences between them. While she viewed the Indian "problem" with the detachment of a scholar, his role was that of unwilling participant.

"I believe that is what they are called."

He smiled mirthlessly. For all her uniqueness, in some ways she was like all the other Easterners he'd known, including the Davenports. Despite Billy's so-called adventures up and down the Amazon, she was still an innocent who found refuge in intellectualizing the struggle between the whites and Indians.

It was easy to be liberal in thought, if not in deed, when she'd never confronted the realities of warfare fueled by the desperation of a dispossessed people. Maybe she wasn't familiar with the white man's belief that the only good Indian was a dead one.

Those who'd never seen the bloody results of "solutions" gone awry could not understand it. He'd learned about the white man's solutions firsthand when, at twelve years old, he'd accompanied his mother to the site of the Camp Grant massacre—the day after a group of well-heeled Tucson businessmen and their Papago scouts transformed over a hundred Apaches, mostly old men, women, and children, into "good" Indians. His own grandfather had been among those slain. It was only a twist of fate that he and his mother had been absent from the camp that day.

No, gently reared Sybilla could never truly comprehend the atrocities that men, white and red, could inflict on each other or what it was like to be caught in the middle. There was much he could tell her, but far be it from him to enlighten her on the profligacy of broken treaties. "How long did you say you've been in this country?"

"Several weeks now, why?"

"Spend a few lifetimes here and let me know if your views change any after you've tried to have a rational discussion with a bullet."

"But history has shown—"

"History?" he said contemptuously. "A smart woman like you ought to know what history really is. After the smoke clears the victors get together and decide on a set of lies. In case you never noticed, the losers—Indians, mostly—don't write history books.''

Unable to respond to that hard truth, Sybilla was struck by the fact that, while she had read extensively about the tribes in her study, she had no first-hand experience of them and their problems. Perhaps if she could get Hawk to talk about his own life, she would understand her larger subject better. But she had learned that it was difficult to engage him in *any* extended conversation, and getting him to talk about himself would be next to impossible.

She wondered if she would ever really know him, a stranger into whose hands she had placed not only the fate of the expedition, but also her life and those of the others. Success or failure, life or death. In large measure, everything depended on him.

Being in such a vulnerable position should have frightened Sybilla, but it did not. If ever there was a man she would trust with her life, it was Hawk Devlin. Trusting her heart to him was another matter.

When he looked at her earlier, she imagined she had heard the faint creaking of a door opening between them. If there was a way to learn more about him without having that door slammed shut, she would endeavor to find it.

The rumble of distant thunder drew her attention to the western face of Superstition Mountain. At the crest, a bank of menacing dark clouds boiled and churned, and she shivered in the heat. A long ray of sunlight slanted through the tumbling mass of clouds, and the mountain burned red like a terrible altar covered with the blood of gods.

''Are we in for a storm, then?'' she asked Hawk.

''Not this time of year. Clouds like that often roll up where a high range juts up from the lowlands. There could be rain, and lots of it, but it'll stay in the mountains. The runoff could be a problem, though. You ever hear of anyone drowning in the desert?''

"No, have you?" Sybilla stole a sideways glance at him to determine if he were chaffing with her. His expression was serious enough, but then his expression was always serious.

"Sure. Lots of times."

When no further explanation was forthcoming she said uneasily, "I see. Must we worry about that?"

"Maybe. I'll let you know."

In the distance a jagged spear of lightning forked down through the cloud mass and was followed in rapid succession by several more. Nature was wreaking havoc on the mysterious mountain, and the raw power of it stirred the secret depths of Sybilla's imagination. In that instant her fears and doubts became insignificant. In that instant she believed.

The gold was out there just as Ricardo Montoya had insisted, steeped in legend and hidden in the bowels of that great pile of rocks. She'd wanted to believe all along, but sometimes the reasonable, English part of her warned it was folly to invest her dreams in anything so elusive. Now, in the shadow of the very mountains where her Spanish ancestor had toiled, she remembered all the stories her mother had told her.

At the time they had seemed too fantastic, more fairy tale than fact, but now she knew that they had been passed down from Montoya to Montoya for the fulfillment of destiny.

Her destiny.

As she sat on a camel in the middle of a vast American desert watching the fury of a distant storm, Sybilla Antonia Hartford experienced a sudden overwhelming sense of conviction. The tales of fabulous wealth had indeed been handed down for a reason. She was that reason.

She thought about the conquistador Cortes and wondered if he'd had a similar feeling upon greeting the Aztec emissaries who welcomed him to the New

World. "We Spaniards have a disease of the heart," he had told them, "for which the only cure is gold."

Now the part of her that was Spanish felt the grip of that fever, the lure of those mountains. She believed. The gold was there, and as the last of the Montoyas, it was her fate to find it.

She swore silently that with the help of God and Hawk Devlin she would.

Hawk saw the faraway look in Sybilla's eyes and knew she'd fallen under the spell of the mountains. It happened to everyone sooner or later. But because her head was already filled with stories of the treasure they contained, it had happened to her sooner than most.

"We'll camp in the foothills," he told her. "Then in the morning we'll head for the pass that will take us deep into the mountains. I'll need to see the map before we go any farther."

Unable to take her eyes off the craggy lightning-struck buttes, Sybilla nodded in agreement. "Of course."

He hadn't expected it to be that easy.

They were barely two miles from their destination for the night, crossing an ancient dry riverbed, when Delilah stopped suddenly in the middle of the trail. Hawk jerked on the rein and tapped her with the driving stick, but to no avail. She wouldn't budge.

"What the hell's the matter with you?" When he urged her forward with a firm kick, Delilah suddenly folded her legs and settled on the ground. One by one the other camels also dropped down in the sand and proceeded to chew placidly on the cuds they coughed up.

"Ahmed!"

The little Persian swiftly gained his footing beside his mount, but Hawk's own unseating was stiff-legged and clumsy. "What's going on here? I know it's later than we usually stop, but we need to push on. Do what you have to do to get these damn critters on their feet."

Sybilla dismounted Jezebel and approached, tapping her dusty boots with her driving stick. "There is nothing he can do. We will just have to camp here."

Hawk glared at her. They'd actually had a conversation earlier in which neither of them had resorted to cursing. Now she was spoiling the effect by reverting to her high-handed ways. "I'm in charge, and we stop when I say whoa. Not before."

Sybilla was weary of always being at cross purposes with Hawk, especially now that she'd had a brief glimpse into the personality he hid so covetously. "See here, the camels—"

"The camels were your idea, not mine. Mount up, everyone, we're going on."

"*Effendi?*" Ahmed whispered anxiously and tugged at Hawk's sleeve, trying as unobtrusively as possible to get his attention. "*Effendi*, we must please to camp here."

Hawk swatted Ahmed's hand away as if it were a pesky fly, and the man bowed himself backward, out of harm's way. Hawk thought Sybilla understood the importance of getting out of the open, but apparently her desire to have the last word was greater than her perception.

"If you'll just listen to reason, Devlin—"

"There's no time for reason. It'll be dark soon, and I don't want to be sitting out here like the loser in a turkey shoot." His eyes narrowed as he glanced uneasily at the Superstition Mountains. The sky was dark and roiling with clouds. If as much rain fell as he suspected would, a dry riverbed would be the worst possible place to be.

Ahmed stuck up his forefinger. "*Effendi*, may I be so bold as to intervene?"

"Not now," he said crossly. "I've got to set things straight with her highness here."

Sybilla jammed her fists on her hips. "You are an impossible man."

"Maybe so. But before I signed on for this pitiful pilgrimage, you agreed to my terms, and me being in charge was one of them." Hawk slapped his thigh in frustration. "I know this country a hell of lot better than you do, and we are not going to spend the night here."

"Yes, we are. And if you will be quiet long enough, I shall endeavor to explain why."

Her tone was icy, but it had the opposite effect on Hawk; it ignited his sorely tried temper and snuffed out his desire for explanations. "Don't start with me, woman," he warned.

"And don't you call me that." Her words were measured, but her eyes were bright with the effort to control her own temper.

"What? Woman? Pardon the insult, but it's about time somebody pointed that fact out to you." There were other ways to remind her of her sex, but he couldn't afford to start thinking about those now.

Sybilla drew back as if from a blow. In condemning her lack of feminine virtues, Hawk had inadvertently discovered her Achilles' heel. Fighting the surge of emotion he provoked, she was careful not to reveal the pain he'd caused her. "The way you say it, it is a term of derision. Your contempt for women is obvious."

Hawk saw the flash of passion in her eyes, and although she quickly resumed her cool facade, he was gratified that he'd been right about one thing. If a man could ever break through her barriers, he'd be amply rewarded for his trouble. Such thoughts made it difficult for him to regain his earlier irritation, and he lost most of his enthusiasm for the argument.

"It is exceeded only by your own." Unprepared for the hurt look in her eyes, he was grateful when Ahmed scurried up.

"Please, *effendi*. The camels know the limits of

their endurance and will not move beyond it." He stroked Delilah's scrawny neck and cooed, "Is that not right, my sweet? When she stops, she is stopped, and there is no starting her again."

Hawk looked from Ahmed to Delilah to Sybilla, whose face now bore the signs of triumph. "Do you mean there's no way to get them to move?"

Ahmed and Sybilla shook their heads.

"Well, hell! Why didn't you say so?"

"I tried to tell you," she snapped, "but you were too busy playing know-all, see-all Indian scout to listen. And now, if you have no further need of me, I shall run along and oversee the preparation of our dinner, like a good little *woman* should. I am sure that is the only thing you find a woman useful for."

"On the contrary," he said mockingly. "I can think of several good uses for females that have nothing to do with food." He watched her flounce away, waiting for her to come back with a sassy rejoinder. She didn't even glance in his direction.

Dealing with Billy was a whole lot like tangling with a wildcat, Hawk decided. The fight was over when the cat was finished. He turned to the Persian. "I'll never understand that woman."

Ahmed smiled. "It is a most wise *effendi* who knows when to back up where females are concerned."

Hawk laughed. "I think you mean back *down*."

"Just so, *effendi*. You are a good man. May Allah fill your tent with many sons."

A sudden image of Sybilla, biddable, housewifely, and swollen with the fruit of his seed, scuttled through Hawk's mind and was gone as quickly as it came. He hadn't had such fanciful and impossible notions since the time he'd accidentally ingested some locoweed.

"Not hardly," he said with a laugh.

After the evening meal, Hawk decided to post a guard. Knowing the first watch was the easiest, he drafted Miguel and Juan, gave them loaded rifles, and stationed them on opposite sides of the camp with orders to alert him if anything moved.

Of course, he knew that by the time an enemy's movement was spotted it would probably be too late, but he chose not to further alarm the excitable Ruiz brothers by pointing that out. They already stood a fairly good chance of accidentally shooting each other.

He had mixed feelings about the position of their camp. On the one hand, the riverbed provided needed cover and made their tents nearly invisible to eyes scanning the horizon. On the other hand, if the storm in the mountains dropped very much rain, they would be right in the downward path of a hell of a lot of precipitation.

Many factors had to be considered, including the amount of rainfall, how much of it soaked into the thirsty earth, and how many tributaries diverted the flow. He explained all that to the group, but it only served to create more tension in the camp.

The knowledge that trouble could strike at any moment made everyone edgy and, instead of retiring early as they usually did, the wayfarers gathered around the small smokeless fire, seeking the comfort of one another's company. All except Hawk, who was happier alone and sat apart from the others.

"Mr. Devlin?" Sybilla knew better than to walk up on him unannounced.

He didn't look up from the gun he was cleaning. The lantern provided plenty of light for the job, but he'd performed the task so many times he could do it in the dark.

"Call me Hawk," he said for the hundredth time.

"May I join you—Hawk?" She hadn't stopped thinking about him and had formulated a few questions she wanted to ask.

"Suit yourself."

"Hawk Devlin," she said thoughtfully. "That is an interesting name." Sybilla found a flat stone and sat down on it, smoothing her skirt.

"The first from my mother; the last from my father. She told me that when she saw my blue eyes she knew I would see far—like the hawk. So that is what she called me."

One Apache name, one white, he thought. They symbolized the proximity of the two worlds and his attempt to exist with one foot in each. The names also reminded him of his failure to do so and of each race's contempt for the other.

"Tell me about your parents, Hawk."

He glanced up then and saw that she had changed from her stiff riding skirt into a dirndl of soft cotton. She leaned forward, her chin in her hand, her eyes filled with genuine interest. Her hair was caught up like a living thing, and he fought the sudden impulse to free it, to tumble the tawny curls onto the puffed sleeves of her white shirtwaist. That unbidden image, in which she was more like Billy than Sybilla, momentarily took him aback.

"What do you want to know?" He kept his head down as he plumbed the rifle barrel with a rag-wrapped stick.

"Whatever you wish to share with me."

"Sharing implies a two-way proposition," he pointed out. "Why don't you tell me about yourself?" Years of reticence made Hawk reluctant to reveal his thoughts and motives, but she was a puzzle he'd like to figure out. So long as he didn't sound too eager.

Sybilla interpreted his slight interest as the opportunity she'd been waiting for. "I've already told you about my family and ambitions. What more is there to know?"

"I could have read all of that in an essay entitled 'An English Lady in the Southwest,'" he said dryly. "What I want to know is why a fine-looking woman like you is out here burning herself up on a hopeless quest like this?"

Sybilla had perked up at the unexpected compliment, but when he spoiled it by disparaging her goals, her delight turned to irritation. "You said yourself that you have looked for the gold for years. Obviously you do not think the quest so hopeless."

"I'm a man."

"Ah, yes. And women are not allowed freedoms, or adventure, or even thoughts that did not come first from a man."

"I didn't say that."

"But that is what you meant. I thought you might be different from the other males of my acquaintance, but your attitude is as unenlightened as theirs."

"Just how many male acquaintances have you made, Billy?" It was the real question he'd been longing to ask.

"Enough to ignore my grandmother's advice about learning to be no more than a charming companion to a man. I choose to be a person in my own right."

"But that isn't the way it's usually done. Your grandmother sounds like a smart woman. Maybe you should have taken her advice."

His words made Sybilla lift her foot to stamp in frustration, but she eased it back down in an effort to hold such outward displays of emotion in check. "I have no wish to be a mere complement to a male. I have a brain, and I intend to use it. What is wrong with a woman working and contributing to the world's store of scientific knowledge?"

"Hey, it's no hide off my butt one way or another. I don't care what you do to support yourself. But out here, women have two choices; to become a wife or a whore. Since you don't want to be one, aren't you worried that you'll end up as the other?"

"If you are implying that I can't take care of myself without resorting to selling my . . . my attentions, you are quite mistaken."

"Maybe you could have in England. Maybe you should have stayed there. Out here a woman alone is easy prey."

"I hired you to see to our safety."

"I thought you hired me to help you find the gold."

"That too."

"Bodyguarding will cost you another ten percent. I deserve at least as much as John, who's just taking pictures."

"That's robbery!"

"That's business. Take it or leave it."

"I do not really have a choice, do I?"

"Nope."

Sybilla regretted that she'd let him know just how dependent on him she was and fumed inwardly as he went back to his gun cleaning.

Hawk tried not to show his amusement at the fit of temper Billy was so clearly trying to conceal. It was gratifying to know he aroused her in at least some small way. That nearly stamping foot had told him more about her in an instant than he would have discovered with a hundred careful questions.

He'd already suspected she was a woman capable of passion. Now he also knew that it had yet to be aroused by any man. Her emotions were as innocent as a newborn babe's, and as basic: anger, hurt, self-absorption.

Sybilla sat on the rock and wondered how best to change the subject that had sidetracked her from her original purpose. "I really would like to know about your mother, Hawk. Won't you tell me?"

The sincerity in her voice made him decide that sharing that small bit of his past would be okay. "The whites called her Mirry, but her Apache name was Finds-the-Fawn. She was a half-breed. Her mother was a white captive stolen from a wagon train, her father an Apache warrior. The tribe named my grandmother Cries-a-Lot, which tells you how she felt about the hand fate dealt her."

"What happened to her?"

"She killed herself when Mirry was a baby. My mother's small band eventually settled into one of those pacts of nonaggression you were talking about and set up camp around Fort Lowell. They weren't farmers and they weren't allowed to hunt, so they became dependent on the army for their livelihood. My mother was young and pretty and found work as a post laundress. Of course, post laundresses frequently had other duties."

He knew the instant she understood his innuendo because she blushed pink in the lamplight. "So she was a . . ."

"Whore?" he asked savagely. "No. She was lucky. One of the officers took a fancy to her and claimed her. I guess he saved her from degradation, though not shame." He finished with the rifle, loaded it, and laid it aside. From his shirt pocket he withdrew a harmonica and blew a few experimental notes.

"This officer. Was he your father?"

"Captain Malcolm Devlin, of the Williamsburg Devlins. A West Point graduate fresh from Virginia on his first Western campaign. I guess he was lonely. My mother was fifteen and hungry," he added derisively. He turned his attention to the harmonica and played a few bars of a sad ballad.

Sarcasm did not hide the pain in his words, and Sybilla's heart contracted in its effort to open up a place for him. She longed to gather him to her bosom, to draw his proud head down on her shoulder and tell him she understood. But she was hesitant to lend comfort to a man as hard and self-sufficient as Hawk, and the fear that he would reject such overtures made her do nothing at all.

"Did you know him?" she asked.

He looked into her eyes over the hands cupped around his harmonica and stopped playing "Barbara Allen" to answer. "I was four when he left us. I don't remember much about him except that he had a big mustache and he laughed a lot. He was good to my mother and his little Apache bastard, I'll give him that much. Maybe he even loved her, I don't know. He provided for us so that she didn't

have to sell herself to every trooper on the post just
to buy food."

"He sounds kind. Why did he leave?"

"His tour was up. It was time to go home to his
wife and children in Williamsburg."

Sybilla's eyes widened.

"Does that shock you?" he asked. "It shouldn't.
There's a lot of indiscriminate mingling of blood out
here. It confuses the issues and it damn sure makes
it hard to choose up sides in a war based on racial
prejudice."

"What happened then?"

"My mother returned to her people to wait for
Devlin to come back as he'd promised, and I grew
up knowing I'd never see him again. End of story."

He blew a few strains of "The Blue Danube"
waltz, a selection that startled Sybilla. So he'd heard
her playing the music box. Was this his way of trying to reach out to her? The look in his eyes said he
understood how much the song meant to her.

Hawk played to cover his dismay. He'd revealed
more to her in the last few minutes than he had to
anyone else in a very long time. Something drew
him to her, something he'd never confronted before.
What was it she'd said about sharing? He'd never
had the desire to share his past with anyone, not
even Mariel Davenport.

When he finished the song and looked up he saw
that a mist had gathered in her eyes. Of all the tunes
in the world, why had he picked that particular one?
She was obviously fond of it, and he'd thought to
show her that they had at least one thing in common. He hadn't meant to make her cry.

Not that she was actually crying. Sybilla Hartford
would never sink so low. He quickly changed his
tune, launching into a livelier melody without thinking.

Sybilla wasn't satisfied. The story was far from
over, even though she'd learned more about the man
than she had dared to hope. Before she could speak,

he played the sweet notes of the theme from one of Mozart's sonatas. In the distance a lone coyote howled its appreciation, and the two sounds, blending with surprising harmony in the desert air, made her smile. The humor of the moment was not lost on Hawk, who grinned back at her.

"That's a lovely piece," she said softly. "I don't know why it surprises me. Any man familiar with Voltaire has probably also heard Mozart." She waited for his explanation.

Deciding he'd revealed enough already, Hawk said lightly, "Mozart? I don't know who wrote it, but the words go something like this: 'There was a young lady from Lynn, who was uncommonly thin . . .' "

"Never mind." She laughed. "I don't think I want to hear the rest of it."

Without warning a gunshot exploded, propelling Hawk to his feet. John's terrified squeal followed close upon the report. When another shout arose from the camp, Hawk thrust his freshly loaded rifle into Sybilla's hands, drew his pistol, and ran back to the firelit circle with Sybilla close behind him.

Chapter 7

Sybilla was sure Maloche had found them and was even now taking advantage of their vulnerable position. Tales of what the craven marauder did to his victims sliced through her mind, and her heart raced painfully in her chest. Contemplating her own torturous death and that of her friends was terrifying enough, but fear for Hawk's life clutched her heart like a cold hand.

She had never killed another human being. She had never been confronted with the necessity of doing so. But now, as she hurried along behind Hawk, she knew she would fight to the death for him. She had no reason to think he would do the same for her, but she believed it with equal certainty. That was his job.

Hawk stood in the shadows and gestured for her to keep back. His keen eyes and survival-honed senses quickly determined that the camp was not under siege, not by Maloche or anyone else. The party, all of which was still in one piece, was held hostage by its own fear. Having abandoned their posts, the Mexicans were babbling in Spanish, Ahmed was babbling in Persian, and John Collings was just babbling.

"What's going on here?" Hawk directed his question to the only person babbling in English.

"Ask her." John pointed an imperious finger at Zora.

The gypsy swished into the circle, her fortune-telling cards clutched in her hand. "These fools will not listen. I have consulted the tarot on the matter of this expedition." Her announcement was made without preamble in heavily accented English. Her black eyes narrowed as she looked at each member of the group in turn, challenging them to interrupt her. No one did.

"It looks bad for us. Very, very bad. Some will surely die if we do not turn back before it is too late."

"Superstitious mumbo jumbo," Sybilla declared. "Parlor tricks."

"It is no parlor trick." Zora fanned the cards. "The cards predict the future, and the wise heed their warning."

"She's got the navvies so overwrought they're jumping at their own shadows," John blustered. "I was doing them a good turn, taking them coffee so they wouldn't fall asleep and allow Maloche to steal up on us, and that fool Miguel narrowly missed shooting me."

Miguel looked downcast. And guilty. He said nothing, but his brother attempted to explain in Spanish that they were nervous and frightened about the possibility of Maloche being in the area. He confessed they had heard what Hawk had told John and Sybilla and were not sure they wished to enter the Superstitions under such circumstances.

In Spanish, Hawk assured them there was no need to be alarmed yet, but he could tell they weren't convinced. He should have seen it coming and put an end to Zora's doomsaying and wild predictions before she'd planted the seed of fear and doubt in the others. It was one thing to know that Maloche was out there somewhere, quite another for Zora constantly to remind them of their own mortality.

Ignoring their protests, he sent the brothers back to their posts with the promise that he and Ahmed would relieve them soon. They obeyed reluctantly, their fearful backward glances communicating their belief that there was safety in numbers.

Hawk turned to the gypsy. "Look, Zora, I know you put a lot of stock in those cards, but you're scaring the pants off Juan and Miguel."

Hawk immediately wished he'd phrased his statement differently because Zora flashed him a sizzling look and murmured that it was not Juan and Miguel she wished relieved of their britches. "They are foolish boys. Not a real man like you."

Ahmed took an angry step forward but stopped as if unsure what to do about his wife's outspoken boldness.

Hawk ignored Zora's smoldering look as best he could. "Boys they may be, but I want you to keep your damn fortunes to yourself from here on out."

"No, Mr. Hawk. That I cannot do. I am cursed with the sight and I must use it as I see fit—to save those too blind to know what is good for them."

"That's admirable, but you're not in the circus anymore and you're not in the fortune-telling business. You don't have to impress us with your predictions. Cut it out." Hawk was as exasperated by the woman's refusal to listen to reason as he was by her unwanted overtures. If ever a female needed a firm male hand on her bridle, this one did. But it wasn't going to be his hand.

"No. Never have I seen such a bad prospect, and you would do well to heed my warnings. I asked the cards if we would find the gold and then I dealt ten out. Would you care to know which ones turned up?"

"No!" Sybilla and Hawk called out in unison.

Ignoring them, she waved the cards in the air one at a time. "Le Pendu, the hanged man. It is for sacrifice and abandonment of goals. Le Diable, the devil—violence and bondage. La Mort is the death card." She smiled grimly. "It speaks for itself. La Maison de Dieu, calamity, misery, ruin. La Lune—danger."

Not finished, she continued to read the cards she held. "Le Mat, the fool, tells me this undertaking is folly. L'Ermite, the hermit, indicates caution. This card, La Roue de Fortuen, was dealt upside down. It is very bad luck when that happens."

She had two cards left. "The justice card is for Mr. Hawk's fairness and," she cast a contemptuous look at Sybilla, "for someone's virginity. All in all, not what you call a pretty picture."

John spoke up. "What about the last card? What is it?"

" 'Tis nothing," Zora dismissed.

"Now, see here my good woman. You have subjected us to this nonsense thus far. I demand that you explain the last card." Obviously agitated, John withdrew a snuffbox from his pocket and, using the tiny silver spoon attached to his watch fob, helped himself to a measure of snuff.

"L'Amoureux," she said with a dismissive wave.

"The lovers?" Sybilla asked in surprise, careful to keep her gaze from finding Hawk's.

"This card is for beauty and love. I cannot explain its presence in such an ominous reading." She glanced slyly from Hawk to Sybilla and then at her own husband. "Then again, who understands the folly of fate?"

"This is all a lot of bunkum," John scoffed. But as he polished his monocle, the look on his face said he was afraid he might be wrong.

"You will not think so, Mr. Glass in the Eye," Zora pronounced melodramatically, "if it is you who die."

John spluttered, replaced his monocle, and stomped away without another word.

"That's quite enough, Zora," Sybilla snapped. "I too have endured your pessimism and grow weary of it. This expedition is doomed only if we doubt ourselves and one another. It will fail only if we lose faith in Mr. Devlin's ability to guide us to our destination. We have our wits and our map, and we shall not give up."

"But the cards!" Zora cried. "They are trying to warn us."

"No, woman." Ahmed, who had been silent until then, finally spoke. "The cards have no powers. Imagination is our enemy." With that he snatched the colorful pasteboard cards from her hand and flung them into the fire.

"You godless heathen!" Zora screamed. "What have you done?"

"What I should have done long before now," he answered with quiet authority. "Go to the tent, woman, and wait for me. After we talk you will play your concertina. Perhaps music will lighten the black spell you have cast."

Hawk and Sybilla watched the exchange with interest. To Hawk's way of thinking it was about time Ahmed asserted himself.

"I beg you forgive my wife's indiscretions," Ahmed said. "She is strong in the head, but she has a big heart. Now I have put my foot up, she will give no more trouble." He bowed and followed the muttering Zora into their tent. Before long their voices were raised in an incoherent maelstrom of unintelligible language.

Hawk shook his head. "Beats me what those two see in each other. I think poor old Ahmed bit off a bigger piece of jerky than he could chew when he married that hot-blooded wench."

"Believe it or not, they are quite happy," Sybilla said.

"Could have fooled me."

"Zora says marriage is like a goulash. Without paprika it's just meat and potatoes. Ahmed saved her from the clutches of a very wicked man. She is grateful to him and I think, in her own way, she loves him. Ahmed, on the other hand, is so reserved and formal he does not quite know how to deal with Zora's easily aroused passions."

Hawk grinned. Ahmed wasn't the only reserved one he could name. "Passions? Arousal? I never thought I'd be talking with you on those subjects, Billy."

She blushed. "Must you always endeavor to twist everything I say? It is most difficult to have a decent conversation with you." She walked away from him. The pale glow of the new moon illuminated her figure as she picked her way through the clumps of vegetation clogging the dry riverbed.

"Where do you think you're going?" he called after her.

"For a walk, if you have no objections."

"But I do." When he caught up with her, he reached out and spun her around. He held her, his hands grasping her upper arms. They were alone in the shadows and there was nothing, and no one, to keep him from doing what he'd wanted to do for a long time.

"Have you ever been kissed, Billy?" he asked, his voice a husky whisper.

The warmth of his hands burned through the sleeves of her shirtwaist, and Sybilla's breath caught in her throat. "What a ridiculous question," she croaked.

"Just answer it."

Her mind raced like a snow-blinded mare—headlong into nothing. Did that incident with Basil Heath count? It hadn't been much of a kiss, but technically his lips had touched hers. The callow young man had been a junior museum official in Cairo and blamed his excess of emotion on an utter dearth of eligible Englishwomen. At the time, she hadn't known whether to be honored or insulted by his attentions.

Her thoughts were just as jumbled now. As a man, would Hawk find innocence alluring or would he prefer a woman with experience to match his own?

"Bill-eee," he drawled.

"I am thinking."

"Something you do too much of. Answer me."

"Yes."

"Yes, you have been kissed?"

"I think so."

"You think so?"

"I'm not sure."

Hawk threw back his head and laughed. "Oh, Billy."

"I fail to see the humor in that confession," she said indignantly.

"Honey, if there's any question in your mind, it couldn't have been much of a kiss."

"I assure you it was quite proper." Her mind harked back to the way Basil's thin, dry lips had settled on hers. She remembered she had flinched a bit, and she'd held her breath, not knowing what etiquette demanded. The whole thing had lasted but a moment, and she recalled with acute embarrassment that when it was over she had committed a major faux pas by asking her would-be suitor the one question men apparently did not want women to ask: "Is that all there is to it?"

"Billy?" Hawk saw the faraway look in her eyes, and male pride prompted him to think he had put it there. "If you'd been kissed the way you should have, there wouldn't have been anything proper about it." He breathed deeply, and the soft rose scent of her hair filled his nostrils. "Close your eyes," he commanded softly.

Caught up in the moment, she found it impossible to disobey him. She waited. For what, she wasn't sure. Perhaps ravishment was what Hawk was about, and she wondered if she should kick and scream and call for help before it was too late. But she did none of those things. Prudence and good sense dictated that she await further instructions from a man who obviously knew what he was doing. If she was to be kissed again, this time she wanted to get it right.

Hawk couldn't believe that the soft, pliable young

beauty in his arms was the same starchy female who had started the trip. "There's something I've wanted to do since I first laid eyes on you," he whispered.

Her tawny eyes fluttered open, and she gasped when she saw the ardent look on his face. What he had in mind had nothing to do with genuine feelings but was founded purely upon primitive lust. In spite of her reflexive chagrin, something warm and moist blossomed inside her at the thought that this thrilling man found her desirable. He did not love her, in fact had never indicated he even liked her. But he wanted her, as only a man like him could want a woman.

After years of ignoring and denying her physical needs, she was suddenly engulfed by a startling and breathtaking awareness. The heat Sybilla felt radiating from Hawk's body was carnal in origin, yet she did not care. That worried her.

"And are you about to do that thing to me now? This very moment?" she asked breathlessly.

"I am indeed."

She hoped so. The languid weakness that overwhelmed her pulled down her eyelids and made her fear her limbs might fail to support her. She simply could not swoon; she was not the swooning type. Yet how could she feel as heavy as a cannon ball and as light as goosedown, both at the same time? Shivery and hot. Ice-burned and frosted with fire.

And at the very center of all that was female about her was a painful ache, a yearning that overcame good sense. She waited for the ravishment to begin and, when it didn't, she blinked up at him. "Well?"

"Well, what?" Hawk was enjoying the myriad expressions flitting across Billy's upturned face. The pale moonlight revealed indignation, anger, confusion. He'd seen submission quickly transformed into something remarkably like impatience. Perhaps she even felt a trace of the frustration he'd known since meeting her. Hawk gripped her shoulders. If he didn't kiss her pouty lips soon, he would lose his mind.

This time she gave in to the impulse and stamped her foot. "What was it you wanted to do since the first moment you laid eyes on me?"

"This." He reached out slowly, and one by one, pulled out the pins that confined her hair, freeing the honey-gold mass that flowed to her waist. It was every bit as soft as he'd known it would be, and his fingers tingled as he plunged his hands into the wayward curls. He gently massaged her scalp with his fingertips, fluffed the mane once more, and tossed an errant lock over her shoulder.

"There. That's better." Now she was the Billy of his dreams.

Sybilla quivered with indignation and disappointment. She had practically offered herself up for this man's carnal enjoyment, expecting the worst—or perhaps the best—he had to offer, and all he'd done was muss her hair! "Is that what you've longed to do to me?" she asked.

"Yeah," he teased. "Among other things." A lot of other things. "You bind your hair up so tight it gives you a pinched look."

"A *what?*" she sputtered, feeling an entirely different kind of heat now.

"A pinched look. Like you're suffering from a bad case of chronic dyspepsia."

"Why, you bloody jackass!" She wasn't trembly and submissive now. Her eyes flashed with real passion that was uncannily like the Billy of his dreams. Too bad it was inspired by anger instead of desire, but Hawk would take what he could get.

"I like your hair down," he said simply.

"I don't give a good bloody damn what you like!" she muttered as she tried to repair the damage he'd done.

He pulled her hands away from her hair. "Leave it alone, Billy."

She sent him a scathing look. If he had set out

with the sole purpose of making her feel foolish, he couldn't have been more successful. Why had she thought he wanted to kiss her when humiliation had been his goal? He had just reminded her, painfully, that she wasn't the kind of woman who excited a man's prurient interests.

She was a scholar, not a coy ingenue. Her grandmother had been right and her dear mother wrong. Men did not want women who could think for themselves. The yearning she'd felt was replaced by sadness that Hawk was truly no different from the others.

Hawk knew he had to leave before he lost control. After taking a few steps, he pivoted on his heel as if inspired by an afterthought. "While I'm thinking about it, there is one other thing I've been wanting to do," he said with lazy indifference.

Sybilla could only glare at him in exasperation. "And what might that be, pray tell?"

"I can show you faster than I can tell you." His mouth swooped down and captured hers as suddenly and effortlessly as his namesake captured a field mouse. She put up the equivalent struggle, melting like jam on a hot scone under his practiced manipulations. His lips were softer than she'd ever imagined and, while fierce in their intent, they were also gentle, coaxing, urging.

His hands wound into her hair as his questioning tongue slipped between her lips. When she opened her mouth in surprise, he groaned and plunged deeper. She answered with a mindless sigh, and feelings twitched and stirred inside her like a sinuous animal awakening from a long sleep.

An exquisite warmth, as sweet and slow-running as honey, spread outward into each nerve-tingled limb. She was sure she could never move again, but when Hawk reached down and lifted her arms around his neck, she found it natural to twine her fingers in the long hair at his nape.

One of his hands smoothed its way across her

cheek and nestled in the tumbled curls at her temple, while the other slipped down her back and drew her close to his hardening body.

She was blind and deaf to the world around her, and if Maloche himself had come tearing into camp with a hundred armed banditos, she could not have stirred from Hawk's embrace. She was trapped, a prisoner in his arms, captive to the frightening and powerful feelings his kiss ignited. She tightened her hold on him to keep from falling off the edge of the slowly tilting world, and he moaned again. The sound gave her a sense of power she'd never known before.

So this ravishment of the senses was kissing, she thought dreamily. It was an inadequate word for such a profound act. Small wonder the poets wrote about it with such heart-wrung emotion. No wonder it had been the undoing of so many women. The sensations created when the right set of lips was applied to one's own defied description. Only a poet could do it justice.

Her thoughts flittered about like a manic honeybee drunk from too much nectar, and she wondered irrationally if Basil Heath had ever figured out what he was doing wrong.

Hawk was fighting for control and losing the battle. Who was seducing whom here? He'd expected any number of reactions from Billy, but this sweet, heartbreaking surrender was not one of them. How could he have known that the blood he'd thought made of ice could be so easily brought to the flashpoint? Her tongue flickered timidly across his lips as though seeking shelter from the storm of emotions she was experiencing. He moaned, the sound no more than a tortured sigh. This was all a man could stand without either dying or taking things to the next logical step.

As he placed his hands on her shoulders and set her away from him, their lips were the last part of their bodies to break contact. This time her sigh was one of frustration.

"Billy?"

"Yes?" she murmured, unable to open her weighted eyelids. Her worst fear had just been confirmed, if her pleasure was any indication, she was well and truly on her way to being a wanton woman.

"In the future, if anyone should ask you if you've ever been kissed?"

"Yes?"

"You can say you have been and be sure of it." His rich laughter wrapped around her like a warm cloak.

The insufferable brute was making fun of her. Sybilla's eyes flew open, and realizing she had once again made a complete fool of herself in his presence, she battled an overwhelming urge to slap his face. Never in her life had any man provoked her as much as Hawk did, and she was growing weary of forever quelling her impulses. Resigning herself to doing just that, she assumed an attitude that was as unaffected as she could aspire to. Extending her hand, she grasped his in a firm handshake.

"Thank you," she said tightly, having doused the momentary flash of passionate heat with a liberal application of stiff-necked propriety.

Hawk couldn't believe what he was hearing. "For what?"

"For your assistance, of course. At twenty-three, my first *proper* kiss was somewhat overdue, and I do so appreciate your patience with my ineptitude."

Treating him for all the world as if he'd just unmired her cart from a soggy English roadside, she shook his hand again. He half expected her to offer him a tip.

"May I please have my hairpins back now?" she asked primly.

He nodded in wonder. Here he'd thought to shake her up and loosen her laces, and instead she'd gone and surprised him. He smiled at the irony of that and dropped the tortoiseshell pins into her out-stretched palm.

"My pleasure, ma'am," he said with a hearty laugh at himself for mistaking Miss Iron Britches's virginal quivering for the kind of passion that couldn't be snuffed as quickly and completely as a candle flame. It was a good thing he'd put a stop to it before he'd forgotten himself and given her a real education.

He bowed mockingly and presented his arm. "Shall we?" he asked with false formality. "We'd better get back to camp before we're missed."

Fearful of what might happen if she dared to touch him again, Sybilla ignored Hawk's outstretched arm. "I can manage, thank you very much." With a sweep of her skirt, she preceded him back the way they had come.

Approaching the camp, they heard music and saw Zora dancing around the fire, writhing and twisting and wringing a gay melody out of a wheezy old concertina.

Hawk smiled at the sight. The couple had obviously reached an amicable compromise in that tent of theirs because Ahmed was jumping around happily, fit to shake his turban loose. John sat on a rock, tapping his feet and clapping his hands in time with the music.

Intent on relieving Miguel, Hawk hurried past the revelers, but Zora suddenly snatched at his hand in an effort to pull him into the dance.

Hawk declined with a good-natured grin. "No thanks, that's too fast for me."

"Do as I do, *effendi*." Ahmed demonstrated a few steps and beamed encouragingly.

Hawk shook his head firmly, suddenly remembering other times and other dances. It had been so long, he wondered if he could remember how. He decided he'd rather not even try. "No, thanks."

John took Sybilla's hand. "Come on, old girl, let's give it a go."

Sybilla's feet began tapping out the sprightly rhythm, anxious for the challenge of the movements and she and John danced away. She'd been tempted to go to her tent, never to come out again, so great had been her embarrassment. But that was hardly a viable alternative. She would have had to face Hawk sooner or later.

Rather than allow him the satisfaction of knowing how much pleasure being in his arms had given her, she danced with false gaiety. Difficult as it was, it was better to laugh and carry on with the others than to show how much the experience had affected her. It also shamed her that he had kissed her soundly and then had the audacity to laugh at her.

She'd been such a ninny to think their kiss had meant anything to him. He'd laughed it off as a joke, but she'd loved every exquisite moment of it and would have been unable to deny him anything he demanded while she was under his spell.

It was, upon reflection, no surprise that he'd found her so amusing. She was little more than a shameless spinster succumbing to the calculated attentions of a man bent on humiliating her. She'd played right into his hands, both figuratively and literally.

She had been reared to protect her virtue at all costs, but the first time a man truly kissed her, she'd been ready to offer herself up like a Whitechapel doxy. Perhaps virtue was nothing more than the lack of opportunity. What a frightening thought. She shuddered as the music swelled and John twirled her around in the dust.

Enjoying the freedom of her unbound hair, she tossed her head until the long tresses whipped around her face. Well, she promised herself, it would not happen again. She was on to the scoundrel's tricks now and would not allow herself to be seduced by him again. Fortified with determination, she forced a laugh, as if she were having the time of her life. Let him make of her actions what he would.

Hawk knew he should relieve the Ruiz brothers, but he couldn't turn away from the sight of Billy enjoying herself. Her hair, loose and curling, glinted gold in the firelight. She stepped gracefully through the heel and toe movements. Her face flushed prettily. Looking at her as she was now, he couldn't remember why he'd ever called her Miss Iron Britches.

"Uncle, are you quite all right?" Sybilla's worried tone drew Hawk to her side.

John took his seat on the rock again and fanned his face with his handkerchief. "Fine, dear girl," he wheezed out. "Just a bit old for such frolicking about."

"Too much of a good thing, John?" Hawk asked.

"Rather. I think I shall call it a day and retire to rest these weary old bones." John gave Hawk a beseeching glance. "I say, old boy, would you mind finishing the dance with Sybilla?" He stood up, adding, "That's a good chap."

Sybilla took John's arm. "I'll come with you, Uncle, just to make sure you're not ill."

"Not a bit of it, girl," John blustered too cheerily. "I am not ill, just old. Dancing is for young men," he insisted with a glance at Hawk.

Hawk didn't want to dance, but John made his expectation clear, and to refuse would be a breach of etiquette. This was no formal cotillion, and he was no slave to social rules, but the look on Sybilla's face made him waver. After what had just occurred between them, further rejection would be a slight she didn't deserve.

"Billy, will you dance with me?"

Hawk's offer had been too long in coming to be genuine. "Please do not feel obliged."

"I want to." With sudden clarity he realized that he did want something. If not to dance, then to have a legitimate reason to hold her in his arms again.

John seemed satisfied that things had been ar-

ranged to his liking and bid them good night, then
disappeared into his tent.

Sybilla's hesitation prompted Hawk to say, "Don't
you trust me? Or is it yourself you're worried
about?"

She frowned. How was it that he always seemed
to find her weakest spots? Was she so naive and
transparent? "I simply do not feel like dancing
now," she denied airily. It was an effort to lie. In
spite of her earlier chagrin, she could think of nothing she wanted more than to be held in Hawk's
arms.

He ignored her feeble excuse. "I promise not to
let you take advantage of me. I'll call for help at the
first sign that your animal urges are getting out of
control."

She attempted to hide her smile. "I do not have
animal urges. But in the unlikely event that I did,
you would be the last person on whom I would inflict them."

"Then I guess I'm safe enough." Without giving
her a chance to protest, he grabbed her hand and
pulled her to him. The melody creaking out of
Zora's concertina was faintly reminiscent of a waltz,
and before Sybilla knew what he was doing, Hawk
led her into the dance. Since fighting him was pointless, she allowed him to sweep her around the dusty
circle, once, twice, thrice.

On the fourth turn, she forfeited her inhibitions
and allowed the music and the man to carry her
along. She was amazed. Hawk was a graceful
dancer, as polished as any ballroom partner she'd
ever had.

Her surprise must have been evident because he
teased, "What's wrong, Billy? Did you think savages only knew how to dance the war dance?"

"Considering what you know of Voltaire and Mozart, it is obvious that you are not a savage."

Don't be so sure, Billy," he whispered into her
ear.

She wanted to ask just how he'd come by a sophistication that contrasted with what she knew about him, but he didn't give her a chance. He pulled her close, and again she felt the heat of his body, the hard ridge pressing against her stomach. She was truly shameless! Only minutes before she'd resolved to stay out of Hawk's dangerous clutches and here she was, as close to a man as a woman could get in public.

"Where did you learn to waltz?" She was breathless with the effort to disguise the excitement he provoked.

"In a gilded cage." His evasive answer increased her curiosity, but the firm set of his mouth told her he would suffer no further questions. Then Zora played a tarantella, and Sybilla was too busy keeping up with Hawk in the vivacious dance to say anything else.

When the music stopped Sybilla's heart was pounding, and she looked up to see Hawk grinning down at her. He made a mocking bow and thanked her for the dance. Before she could speak, he added, "I think everyone should turn in. We'll get an early start in the morning and be in the Superstitions before midday."

Ahmed and Zora said good night and turned toward their tent. Hawk walked Sybilla to hers. "We've gone as far as we can without me looking at that map of yours. I know you don't want to reveal all your secrets, but you'll have to let me see it now."

She knew he was right. "Certainly. I'll bring it straight away."

She ducked into her tent and emerged a few moments later with the famous Montoya map. She laid the oilskin-wrapped bundle carefully on a camp table, and Hawk picked up a nearby lantern and held it aloft. This was what he'd been waiting for, Hawk told himself. The chance to look at this map was the real reason he'd agreed to come along in the first place.

Sybilla untied the leather thongs securing the package and carefully unfurled the crackling and faded parchment. Before Hawk had more than a glimpse at the crudely wrought drawings on the paper, she hid a large portion of it with the oilskin.

He supposed he should be hurt by her lack of trust, but in truth, he was secretly amused by her pointless subterfuge. Didn't she realize that if he wanted to look at the entire map, he damn sure would, and nothing she did would stop him? But he'd let her have the bit of mystery she seemed to need. For now.

Sybilla regretted not sharing the entire map with Hawk. She wanted to trust him, but tonight he'd shown just how unpredictable he could be, and she could not afford to take any chances.

Hawk examined the parchment as well as he could in the inadequate light. The drawings were inexpert, and many of the Spanish captions were misspelled. But it was definitely ancient. And, if the quickening of his sixth sense was anything to go by, it might also be authentic. A most alluring development.

As Sybilla had told him at their first meeting, the two wavy lines did indeed seem to indicate the Salt and Gila rivers. That gave him a fair orientation with which to attempt to identify the other landmarks.

"Old Montoya wasn't much of an artist, was he?" he complained so as not to reveal his excitement.

"He drew the map from memory."

"Or from imagination."

She bristled. "Do you still think it is a fake?"

"I don't know yet. I guess we'll find out soon enough. Or die trying, as you so eloquently put it."

"The gold is out there. It has to be," she added soberly.

"Because some half-baked Spaniard said so?"

"Because I feel it, here." She brushed her chest with her hand.

"You're certain, then?"

Sybilla looked abashed and hesitantly admitted her ambiguous feelings. "In the daylight. At night this vast land makes me feel very small and alone. I confess that in the dark, when the coyotes' howls fill the silence, I am plagued by doubts. If only I had a sign. Proof." She laughed, a soft, desperate sound. "But there can be no such thing."

Hawk said nothing.

"I *want* to believe—in the gold as well as in the love story of a dashing Spanish nobleman and a beautiful Indian maiden. It's so romantic, the stuff of epic poems and novels."

"Yeah, it's so romantic I doubt it ever happened."

"Then why are you here?" she demanded.

He hesitated. "Maybe I didn't want to have your death on my conscience."

"Really? You led me to believe you did not possess a conscience."

He grinned. "Some of the details of Montoya's story do coincide with tales my mother told me," he admitted grudgingly. "Tales about a group of bearded white-eyes who stole from the Earth Mother and suffered death for their crimes."

Her gaze widened. "Truly? Then the existence of one story proves the other. Why did you not tell me this before?"

"For the same reason you aren't showing me your goddamn map."

She considered that for a moment. "Very well. We shall each keep our secrets, then. Unless there is something else you wish to tell me."

He could tell her a lot of things. But there was one that would provoke her to no end. He couldn't resist divulging it. "My mother also told me about an amulet, a golden cross."

"The Montoya cross!" She pointed eagerly to a curling corner of the map. "This is supposed to be

a drawing of the one Montoya gave his maiden.
Could it be the same one, do you think?''

"I don't know," said Hawk. "The one in the
Apache legend supposedly belonged to a witch."

"A witch?"

"Apaches believe strongly that witches possess
special power to do evil. They may look like real
people, but their alliance with malignant spirits of
the supernatural world enables them to do things no
mortal being could."

She tried to fit what he told her into the puzzle.
"Is it possible that the Spaniards in Montoya's ex-
pedition were seen as supernatural beings by the
Apaches?''

"Possibly. They possessed firearms and other innovations which would have seemed magical to a
primitive people."

"And what of Ricardo's maiden? Did the Apaches
think she was a witch because she associated with
them?''

"Maybe."

"If Montoya's story is true and he gave this cross
to his lover,"—she tapped the parchment for emphasis—"what happened to it?''

"The cross of legend has been lost for many
years."

"But there *was* an amulet," Sybilla concluded.
"There was a maiden. That means Montoya really
did find the gold."

"Hold on. Don't jump to conclusions. There's a
name for what we're talking about here."

"What?"

"Coincidence. A very convenient coincidence."

"It could also be fate. Can't you believe that it
may be our destiny to recover the lost Montoya
gold?''

"That's a little hard to swallow."

"Not if you believe in the doctrine of predestination. It has been held since the fourteenth century
that God, in His foreknowledge of all events, infal-

libly guides the steps of mortals in the proper direction."

Hawk didn't want to get into that. "It's a little late for a discussion of theology tonight. I need to relieve Juan and Miguel." He turned to leave.

For Sybilla the conversation was far from over. "But you can't just walk away. We must discuss these portentous developments further."

"We can discuss them tomorrow. Juan and Miguel need their rest, and I suggest you get some too."

"Hawk!"

"Good night, Billy."

"In the Apache legend, what happened to the owner of the amulet?" she called to him.

He stopped and turned to regard her thoughtfully. "I suppose she suffered the fate of all witches."

She wasn't sure she wanted to hear his answer, but asked anyway. "Which was?"

"Death. It's never far away in the Superstitions."

Chapter 8

It was a long time before Sybilla fell asleep. She could not stop thinking about Hawk. He was such an enigma. How was it that he seemed to possess more than a passing knowledge of subjects not required for survival in such an untamed land?

She was baffled by his ability to set her pulse pounding and her heart racing with so little effort, when others had tried much harder and failed. Dancing with Hawk had been a revelation in itself. At her father's request, she'd attended a few fancy dress balls in London. She'd danced with the most dashing men and found it pleasant. But nothing quite compared to the thrill she felt when Hawk whirled her around the campfire.

Earlier, when Hawk had kissed her so thoroughly, she'd nearly lost her ability to think. Why, just the memory of that kiss made her skin tingle and her cheeks grow warm. She told herself that, perhaps, it was only because it had been her first *real* kiss, and next time the act would leave her as cold as her experience with Basil had. But, somehow Sybilla doubted that.

She'd always known her flamboyant Montoya blood would cause trouble eventually, but she'd never thought it would happen at a time like this. She tried to remind herself that she had undertaken this journey for one reason: to find the Montoya gold, not to become romantically involved with her guide. That was a distraction she could ill afford.

After what Hawk had told her, she was even more convinced that the gold existed. The story he'd recounted tonight only reaffirmed her belief in the quest. Learning what he knew of the amulet depicted on Ricardo's map was like unearthing the long-lost glass slipper that would prove to cynics forever that Cinderella had really gone to the ball.

On a personal level, the portents were even more disturbing. Was it just lucky happenstance that of all the men she could have selected to guide her expedition, she had chosen Hawk Devlin, a man who possessed a small piece of the puzzle in the stories his mother had told?

Had an unknown force, one even more powerful than her growing attraction for him, pulled them both to this wild place, inexorably linking their fates? And if so, for what purpose?

When it came to uncertain matters like predestination, there were too many unanswerable questions for a logical mind to find rest. However, Sybilla was sure of one thing. She'd been right to dare pursue her father's dream. She had not squandered her meager funds on a hopeless chimera. The money she'd spent might be recovered, many times over.

Ricardo Montoya had not been mad, and he really had reached Pimeria Alta, just as he claimed. If he hadn't, she would not have encountered such striking similarities between his story and those of the Apaches.

If Montoya had indeed befriended the native people, helped them advance their technology, and contributed, however briefly, to their culture, then obtaining the proof would have a profound impact on the scientific world.

She would also possess a fortune. But she was unable to work up much enthusiasm for the wealth involved. Her thoughts kept drifting back to the moments when Hawk had held her in his strong arms, kissing away her good sense.

Her attraction to him defied contemplation, and she was too tired to worry about it now. Sybilla fell asleep confident that fate would take care of everything. It was small wonder that she dreamed of Hawk.

In the dream, Hawk was kissing her lips, her neck, her shoulders. His hands pushed away her clothing, and he touched her in forbidden places as their bodies entwined on a bed of gold.

An hour before dawn, Sybilla was still dreaming when Hawk poked his head in her tent and awakened her with a curt order.

"Get out quick. Grab what you can and get to higher ground."

Befuddled by sleep and confusing dreams of making love with Hawk, Sybilla sat up, too surprised to worry about being seen in her nightclothes. She smiled sleepily.

That smile tempted Hawk to linger, but considering the circumstances, he had to keep his wits about him. "Dammit, Billy, get moving."

She was slow to react. "What is it?"

"A flood's coming. Get out!"

She was awake now. Despite the darkness, she felt his eyes on her and reached for something to cover her thin cotton nightdress. "A flood? In a bone-dry desert? Are you daft, man?"

Hawk grabbed her shoulders and shook her. "I don't have time for your modesty or your arguments, Billy." He thrust a canvas bag into her shaking hands. "Just stuff what you can in this and move. Hurry!" he urged before dashing back outside.

In a moment her thoughts cleared and she recalled what he had told her earlier about drowning in the desert as they'd watched lightning fork down to the buttes. She began packing.

This was his terrible country and if he said a flood

was coming, however improbable it seemed at the moment, one would come. Donning a jacket over her gown, she put on her boots and snatched up the map along with her books, papers, clothing, and other possessions before running outside.

The air was chill, as it always was without the sun, and Sybilla fumbled with the jacket buttons. The sky was like slate, high and wide and marred by only a few late stars that bathed the desert with pale witchlight. Lanterns glowed brightly, and she saw Ahmed and Zora unhobbling the camels while Hawk and John systematically disassembled the camp. Apart from a strangely fragrant odor in the air, nothing seemed the least bit amiss, much less life-threatening.

The she noticed the cryptlike silence. This was not a typical desert dawn, she realized. The ever-present drone of insects was oddly absent, as was the morning trilling of birds.

"Where are Juan and Miguel?" she asked Hawk.

"Gone."

"What do you mean?"

"I mean they're gone. Grab that box, will you?"

She hefted one end of a food storage crate and helped Hawk load it onto one of the pack camels. "Why didn't you stop them?"

"How could I, Billy? They weren't prisoners."

"When did they leave?"

"They lit out shortly after I relieved them at midnight."

"But why?"

"They didn't choose to discuss it with me, and frankly I don't have time to worry about it right now. Any minute a wall of water is going to come flashing down from the hills. It might be two feet high or it might be ten. Do you understand?"

"How do you know that?"

"I just do. Move, dammit."

The grim look on Hawk's face convinced her that their very survival was at risk, and all her energy was suddenly focused on escape. Speaking softly to soothe the nervous beasts, she helped pack the camels for the move to safety.

When she hurried back to her empty tent, she realized with a frustrated sigh that she did not know how to take it down. Someone else had always performed that task for her. She stood trying to decide whether to untie the ropes first or pull up the stakes when Hawk rushed up to her.

"Forget the tent. Get up to that bluff with the others. It's coming."

She heard it then, a sound like a runaway locomotive, but she couldn't see much in the gloom. He grabbed her arm, and together they stumbled out of the arroyo carved by a river that had probably gone dry in the last days of the mastodons.

The others were already on the ridge trying to control the agitated camels. Sensing the impending disaster, the animals bleated and milled around wide-eyed with fear. Thinking Juan and Miguel must have been just as terrified, Sybilla headed back toward the embankment.

Hawk intercepted her and held her arm in a firm grip. "Where the hell do you think you're going?"

She tried to yank free from his grasp, but he wasn't about to let go of her. "I can't allow those poor boys to be swept away. I must find them."

"They're long gone by now. Besides, it's too late. Look!" He had to yell over the roar of the oncoming water. The gray fingers of dawn illuminated the scene with a ghostly light, and as if caught up in a terrible dream, Sybilla watched the drama unfold below.

There was indeed a wall of water just as Hawk had predicted. But it was not two feet high, or even ten. Like a tidal wave born in a stormy sea, a fifteen-foot torrent surged down the dry bed. It gained momentum as it came, a foaming, roiling tumult that destroyed everything in its path in a veritable avalanche of mud and water.

The flotsam included many dead animals and a few that still clung pathetically to life. Uprooted saguaros, their branches outstretched like the arms of drowning men, tumbled along like corks. Large trees, obviously carried a great distance, had been ripped up by the roots and scraped naked of bark by the grinding action of water and rock. It was then that Sybilla recognized the smell she'd noticed earlier. It was the odor of raw green wood.

The thunderous noise precluded speech, and everyone watched the violent display in stunned silence. Sybilla shivered, and Hawk's arm tightened around her, giving her an unexpected feeling of well-being. Thinking of what would have happened to them all had he not sounded the alarm, she turned away from the violence of the flood. Pressing her face into the scratchy comfort of his poncho, she shuddered when she realized how close death had come.

She looked up at him, unable to say all the things she wanted to express, hoping her eyes conveyed some of the gratitude she felt. Gratitude that was all mixed up with a dozen other emotions she was unable to sort out. "How did you know?"

He bent low and spoke close to her ear. "I kept an eye on the mountains during my watch. It's not unusual for a spring storm to dump several inches of rain in a short time. If the creeks and tributaries are already full from the winter runoff, there's no place for it go but down. When I smelled green wood, I knew it was coming."

After what seemed like hours, but in reality was no more than a few minutes, the worst of the flood subsided, taking its roar and destruction with it. By the time the sun was fully up, the thirsty lowland soil had soaked up what was left of the deluge. The only visible sign of the event was the absence of underbrush in the riverbed. It had all been scoured away, swept clean as if by a giant's savage broom.

The weary travelers assessed their losses, which

luckily consisted only of Sybilla's tent; she had saved the contents. John assured her he would be happy to sleep under the stars and kindly offered his tent for her future use. Due to Hawk's early warning, they'd managed to save all the food, the camels, and their personal belongings.

"Did it really happen?" Ahmed's white-knuckled fingers clutched his camel's halter as he surveyed the site. "Or was it just a nightmare?"

"It was no dream, Ahmed," Hawk assured him. "What it was was a close call. We were lucky. We didn't lose much."

"What a violent and totally awful country." John, still wearing a long nightshirt and a sleep cap on his bald head, plopped down on a small crate, his shock at the magnitude of nature's capriciousness apparent on his pale face.

Sybilla turned in a slow circle, one hand shading her eyes from the rising sun as she scanned the empty stretch of horizon. "I hope Juan and Miguel are all right."

"They were pretty scared last night after all that card hocus-pocus," Hawk put in with a sharp look at Zora. "My guess is they struck out for Apache Junction. I suppose the promise of gold wasn't enough to overcome their fear."

"But they were afoot. Do you think they can make it back to safety?" Sybilla felt responsible for the two boys and hoped nothing unfortunate would befall them on their trek across the desert.

Hawk patted her shoulder. "They know this country. They took plenty of food and water. Don't worry, they'll make it."

She sighed as the muted gray-brown landscape changed hues under the searing light of sunrise. "Should we try to find them, do you suppose?"

Hawk was adamant. "No. They don't want to be found and we're not turning back now. We'll have a cold breakfast and get started."

A keening wail, disturbing in the quiet aftermath

of the flood, drew everyone's attention. Zora, who had been silent throughout the ordeal, covered her mouth with her hands. She stared at the forbidding peaks of the Superstitions, her knowing eyes wide with dread, as if witness to something terrible that no one else could see.

"It has begun," she announced in a tight, quiet voice.

Shaken by their brush with death, the group traveled all morning in silence. It was as if recent events weighed too heavily on their minds for idle conversation. Sybilla wanted to speak to Hawk in private—there was so much she needed to ask him—but the opportunity did not present itself.

At midday they halted to rest and eat. John took advantage of the respite to set up his camera and expose a few plates to document the trip. The apparatus, one of the new smaller field cameras, was only ten inches by fourteen inches and used the dry plate process to expose gelatin-coated celluloid negatives.

John motioned for Sybilla to join him. "I should like to photograph you beside these rocks, just there."

Sybilla complied. "How's this?"

He nodded enthusiastically, then hunched down behind the tripod-supported box. "Stand very still, that's a good girl."

When it was over, she moved to his side. "How is the documentation going, Uncle?"

"Jolly good! I'm glad I decided to take up the hobby. Like other amateurs, I never would have considered it before all these newfangled gadgets became popular. When messy collodion-coated wet plates were used, it was best left to professionals."

Sybilla settled herself on a rock. Once started, John could wax enthusiastic on his favorite subject for hours.

She already knew the story, having heard it so

many times before. "Not to mention that the exposure time was slow and tedious."

"Quite. And the plates had to be developed within
ten minutes, no matter what the circumstances,
which made photographers slaves to their dark-
rooms."

"So I have heard," she murmured.

"I have immense respect for frontier photographers such as William H. Jackson and Timothy
O'Sullivan. Those intrepid men, working with fragile glass plates and portable darkroom tents, traversed the wildest territories, and still produced
striking high-quality photographs of America's wilderness areas."

"You are a good photographer too," Sybilla reminded him.

"Only fair," John replied modestly. "The new
innovations make my task simple by comparison.
Recently I've heard rumors that a man in New York
is trying to make photography accessible to the
masses by perfecting a small box camera that uses
rolls of flexible gelatin-coated paper to capture images."

"It sounds too good to be true," Sybilla told him.
"But if it does come to be, we shall buy you that
wondrous camera when we find the gold."

"I am quite content with my current equipment.
Exposure time for the dry plates is much faster and,
though large, my own camera can be held in hand
to facilitate complicated shots. Since the plates can
be developed later, there is no need for the portable
darkroom nowadays. I shall develop and print my
plates when we return to civilization."

Checking the angle of the light, John positioned
Sybilla beside a giant cactus for another photograph.

"I've composed the image with the horizon low
in the shot to suggest the vastness of the land," he
explained. "The saguaro in the foreground is perfectly symbolic of the desert, but I need a compara-
tive human figure to indicate its enormous size. You

don't mind, do you, my girl?'' Without waiting for
a reply, he disappeared behind the camera again.

"Amazing, isn't it?" he asked as he worked.
"That cactus was probably already several feet tall
when Marie Antoinette lost her pretty head."

Sybilla held her breath while he exposed the plate.
It was indeed ironic that a country which enabled
individual cacti, century plants, and Joshua trees to
live for several generations could be so hard on its
human trespassers. At their first meeting, Hawk had
told her that there were a thousand ways to die in
the desert. She sincerely hoped she would not have
to learn each and every one of them firsthand.

When John was finished he trained his lens on
Hawk, who was leading Delilah into position at the
head of the camel line. Hawk didn't like to stay in
one place for very long and always seemed eager for
the rest periods to end.

"How about you, Devlin?" John called out cheerfully as he passed. "Would you mind posing for me?
You and that beast would make a most interesting
composition. I could call it 'Cowboy on Camel
Back.' ''

Sybilla fully expected Hawk to refuse the request
and was surprised when he halted Delilah. She was
even more surprised by his answer. He looked
straight into the camera's lens as he spoke, his visage dark and unsmiling. "Go ahead, shadow
catcher, shoot before I change my mind."

A few minutes later, Sybilla approached him while
John was packing his equipment. "What did you
call my uncle just then?"

"Shadow catcher. That's what the Indians call
photographers. They believe the black and white images are shadows captured on paper. When the paper is taken away, so is the spirit. They also believe
that whoever controls their shadows controls their
destiny."

She started at his use of the word "destiny," for
it had figured so prominently in her thoughts. Look-

ing deep into his blue eyes, she asked, "What about you, Hawk?"

He adjusted Delilah's halter, and her necklet of tiny bells and blue beads jingled merrily. Each of the camels wore a similar necklace because Ahmed insisted the charms thwarted the unearthly fiends that plagued all camels. Hawk grinned, his smile lighting his face and lifting Sybilla's spirits.

"I vaguely understand the chemical and optical processes involved in photography."

She looked abashed. "Of course you do. I didn't mean that."

"What did you mean, Billy?"

"Do you believe in destiny?"

He tapped Delilah with the driving stick, and when she knelt he mounted with lithe grace. "The Spanish have a saying. *Que sera, sera*. What will be, will be."

He still hadn't answered her question, but because he rode away, she was unable to press the issue.

They traveled for hours under the sweltering sun, the landscape gradually changing to a rockscape as the flat lowlands gave way to the *bajadas*, or rocky slopes, preferred by the saguaro forests. The dense chaparral of greasewood and burrobush was nearly impenetrable in places, but the sturdy camels barreled along at a steady pace, pausing now and then to snatch up a mouthful of the prickly pear cactus they seemed to favor.

Neither daunted by the rubble underfoot nor deterred by the inhospitable vegetation, the camels had gained Hawk's gradual, if grudging, respect. After a week on the trail, he had to admit that Sybilla had been right. The camels were supremely well suited to this rugged country in ways horses and mules never would be.

The camels drank when water was available, but didn't seem to miss it if it wasn't. Because of their horny dental structure and the thick coarse hair that protected their lips, they feasted on the thorniest bushes and relished the alkaline plants that other animals found unpalatable.

It was easy to understand why, in some countries, they had been the transportation of choice for thousands of years. But camel-packing would never catch on out here, as the government's ill-fated experiment had proved. The West had a romance with the horse, and as much as it would hurt Delilah's feelings to be told so, she and her kind would never make a satisfactory "other woman."

Now that he'd learned the idiosyncrasies of camel driving and made his peace with Delilah, Hawk was able to concentrate on more important things—like finding the gold. Once they located the unidentified landmarks on the map, it would be only a matter of time, diligence, and luck . . .

Unconsciously he fingered the leather bag around his neck. Whenever he thought of luck, he thought of the medicine bag his mother had made for him as a child. She'd filled it with tokens and herbs and other symbols of a mother's hope that her son would grow up strong and good.

Most of his belief in the power of its contents had died with his mother, but he wore it still, out of respect. He never touched the bag without thinking of Mirry, dead four years now but very much alive in his memory. It linked him to his mother's disappearing people and separated him from his father's.

Whenever he found himself thinking of Williamsburg and the life he'd led there, or feeling sorry for himself for leaving it, the medicine bag was there. A symbol of his Indian-ness, it reminded him each time he touched it that the doors of upper-class white society were forever closed to him.

However, if he found the gold, none of that would matter. Wealth spoke louder than background, education, or family connections, or the lack of them. The gold would give him freedom.

As he rode along, he thought about what he

would do with the riches he found. In each of his
fanciful scenarios, Billy figured prominently. He
tried to rid his thoughts of her, but it was no use;
they were continually interrupted by memories of
their kiss. She'd been soft and sweet and as yielding
as a ripe guayaba, her innocence inflamed by a
passion she didn't even know she possessed. For a
moment she'd been his.

How he longed to claim her—to undress her, button by button, layer by layer, until she stood pale
and pure before him. She was like a desert flower,
the seeds of which lay tiny and hard and dormant
for years. But, given the proper nurturing, that seed
would produce a bloom so beautiful it would break
the heart of those who saw it.

He wanted to liberate her, the part that was buck-
led down and corseted and contained by pins. He
was sure that if given an opportunity, her desire
would spark like dry tinder. Once aflame, it would
rage unchecked, a wildfire whose heat would consume any man fool enough to ignite it.

He'd never been a slave to his physical needs and
unlike many men did not spend much time thinking
of ways to satisfy them. But since he'd kissed Billy,
and especially since she'd kissed him back so hungrily, he'd been able to think of little else. He also
found himself beginning to like her. That liking,
coupled with the needing and the wanting, was
dangerous for any man, but even more so for one
who'd sworn to learn from his mistakes.

As though summoned by his thoughts, Sybilla appeared beside him, nudging her mount into line with
his as they passed through a small canyon created
by towering masses of rock.

Sybilla guided Jezebel through the silent pass and
was startled by a hawk wheeling and shrieking overhead. The caravan wound in and out of deep rock
shadows. They were in the Superstition Mountains
now and the terrain was more treacherous, the way
more difficult.

Apparently lost in thought, Hawk did not acknowledge Sybilla until she spoke. "I've been thinking about the gold."

"It's been on my mind, too."

"I think fate means us to have it."

"I'm glad fate and I agree—"

A rifle shot cracked suddenly over their heads, and Hawk reached for his weapon. But what he heard next discouraged him from completing such a rash action.

"Sigue y hazlo, hombre camello, si puedes."

Cursing the inattention that had put him in such a position, Hawk turned slowly toward the lazy voice that urged him to go on and do it if he could. With a sinking feeling, he saw several gunmen positioned in the rocks around them.

The men, with cold eyes and droopy mustaches, wore the sombreros and huaraches of Mexican peasants. Cartridge belts crisscrossed their chests, and assorted machetes, shivs, and knives supplied extra deterrents. Hawk didn't know where they came from or how they had materialized so suddenly, but the bandoleros sure as hell had them outmanned, outarmed, and outflanked.

"Is it Maloche?" Sybilla whispered frantically.

"They haven't seen fit to introduce themselves."

"What do they want?"

"They haven't said, dammit," Hawk snapped at her, but it was himself he was angry with. If he hadn't been daydreaming like a horny coyote, the banditos never would have gotten the drop on him.

"Then I'll ask him," Sybilla said resolutely. Before Hawk could stop her, she spoke to the gaunt man who'd questioned them. The way he had taunted Hawk made her presume he was the leader. *"¿Que desea usted?"*

The man's hooded gaze traveled slowly up and down Sybilla's small frame; apparently he liked what he saw. He licked his lips and sneered.

Hawk recognized the libidinous look in the bandit's eyes, and the mental picture it conjured up was disgusting. Hawk itched to knock the leer off his face, and the thought of those dirty hands touching Billy was enough to make him go foolishly for his gun. That move was met swiftly and unerringly with the sudden cocking of several rifles and the drawing of even more knives.

Hawk obeyed the order to drop his weapons on the ground and, watching as Ahmed and Zora followed suit, he felt utterly helpless. His frantic mind churned up—and immediately discarded as futile— a number of possible escape plans. He'd just have to wait and see what happened next.

The leader's mirthless grin revealed a lot of big yellow teeth when he finally answered Sybilla's question "*¿Que tiene usted, senorita?*" What do you have?

"*Que tiene es sin valor.*"

The bandits must have found her answer amusing because it elicted a rumble of lascivious laughter from the rank and file, who clearly thought she had plenty they would value.

Hawk glanced back at the others and saw John paralyzed with fear. His lips were moving, but nothing was coming out. No help from that quarter. Ahmed looked as ferocious as a small cornered fox but kept glancing skyward, as if praying for divine intervention.

Two of the men approached Zora and flicked her colorful costume with their rifle barrels. She boldly stared them down and cursed them in her native tongue, her black eyes filled with the contempt her words expressed. She was convincing, even in a language they didn't understand, and the bandits backed off nervously.

Though he didn't know what the famed desperado Maloche looked like, Hawk had ruled out the possibility that this was he. After all, it had been five minutes and they weren't dead yet. A good clue.

"What are you, anyway?" the leader asked,

switching to English. "Some kind of traveling circus?"

"Let me handle this," Sybilla said out of the corner of her mouth.

"Be my guest," Hawk obliged. If she were afraid, and he was sure she was, she was hiding it well. Her exchanges with the now amiable bandit gave him time to think about more important things, like how to save their hides. If anyone could talk them out this mess, it was Billy.

"We are a scientific expedition, and we travel under the auspices and protection of the British Bureau of Ethnology. Perhaps you have heard of it?" Most of that was fabricated, but under the circumstances Sybilla didn't think the bureau would mind if she invoked its name.

Hawk coughed to hide his amusement as the leader grimly translated for the rest of his band. Leave it to the English to try such intimidation on a bunch of illiterate desperadoes.

The dangerous-looking men shook their heads and whispered among themselves, as if ethnologists were beings they knew and feared from reputation alone.

Sybilla glared at Hawk. "How dare you laugh, you idiot," she muttered. "These men could choose, at any moment, to reduce us all to dust."

"Sorry."

"*Cientificos*, eh? What do you seek?" the leader asked suspiciously.

"Lost civilizations," she improvised. "We study them."

He translated again, and the group looked long and hard at Sybilla and John, the camels, and Ahmed and Zora. Leveling his rifle at Hawk's midsection, he asked, "Him too?"

"No, he is our guide," she told him. "May I inquire as to your business in this area, sir?"

The man was silent for so long that she feared he was planning a painful way to kill them. When he answered, his tone was serious and proud. "Despite what you may think, we are not evil men. I am Donado and these are my *companeros*. There is much political strife in our country and the people are very poor."

It was then that Sybilla noticed how old the men's weapons were, how ill fed the *revolucionarios* appeared. She wondered how often they'd been sustained by zeal rather than meat.

"We have heard tales of gold in the Superstitions," he went on. "We wish to find it so that our people can arm themselves with more than pitchforks and stones when the Federales harass our villages."

"A noble cause, sir." Sybilla wasn't sure they were out of danger yet, but her heart had ceased its furious pounding, and she felt optimistic enough to venture a question. "Would it trouble you too much to stop pointing those guns at us?"

Donado barked an order in Spanish, and the men lowered their rifles. Hearing Sybilla's sigh of relief, Hawk seized that moment to regain control of the situation. "If it's gold you're after, maybe I can help you."

She looked at him furiously, but he ignored her. "Two nights ago, we camped in a canyon about thirty miles east of here. I saw color in the stream there, and if you have panning equipment, it shouldn't be too hard for you to get yourself a stake."

Donado translated for his band, and an argument broke out. It seemed some of the bandits were for killing the Yanquis in the name of the cause, taking what they had and going home. Another faction wanted to hear more about the gold; Hawk was relieved that Donado was among that group.

"If this story is true, why did you not take the gold yourself?" he asked.

"Like the lady said, this is a scientific expedition. We're not all that interested in gold," he lied. "But if you know where we can find some old bones and broken pots, we'd be much obliged." He wasn't sure Donado was buying his story, but the leader gestured for his disagreeable *companeros* to join him.

After conferring in a barrage of Spanish, Donado said simply, "I believe you, senor. A man on a camel can only be taken seriously."

"I'm glad to hear that."

"If you will direct us to this golden stream, we will leave you in peace." He brandished the rifle again, this time sighting it between Hawk's eyes. "But if you are lying, we will hunt you down and kill you like dogs."

Sybilla shot an I-hope-you-are-satisfied look at Hawk. "I quite understand your reservations, sir, but my guide has a reputation for honesty." She couldn't believe Hawk had made up such a stupid story. Maybe he had bought them a little time, but they'd soon have these *pistoleros* after them.

Weren't Maloche and all the malignant spirits of the Superstitions enough to contend with?

"Shut up, Billy. Let me handle this."

"I say!" she sputtered indignantly.

"No, you don't. Shut up."

She opened her mouth for a further rebuke, but Hawk's murderous look made her close it. She kept quiet while he dismounted and drew a map in the dust with a pointed stick.

"Good luck," he told Donado. "May you find much gold for your people."

Before leading his men away, Donado doffed his sombrero in a gallant gesture. "And may you find many old bones, *senor y senorita.*"

When they were but a cloud of dust in the distance, Sybilla rounded on Hawk. "Bloody, hell! I thought they were going to kill us."

"Or worse."

"What could be worse than death?"

"Many things," he said cryptically.

"I shudder to contemplate them."

"As well you should. You know, my opinion of you just went up a few notches, Billy. You had those men shaking in their huaraches at the thought that they might have the British Bureau of Ethnology people after them. I didn't know you were such an accomplished *mentirosa.*"

"That wasn't lying, that was bluffing," she defended.

"Call it what you will."

"We just looked down a dozen rifle barrels and saw the eye of death. And you have the nerve to shrug it off. I didn't see you doing anything heroic."

"I didn't have to. You had 'em by the . . . where they lived," he amended.

Infuriated by his calm, she snapped, "If anyone is a liar, it is you. Really, Hawk, that fellow seemed like a man of his word to me."

"He was convincing, wasn't he?"

"I suppose we'll have those ruffians on our trail when they discover you lied to them about the gold."

"I wasn't lying."

"You mean you really did see gold in that stream? Why didn't you say so?"

"What was I supposed to say? I told you before that if a man's patient enough he can find placer gold in just about every stream in the Territory."

Sybilla recalled that earlier conversation and backed down. "So you did. As scary as they were, I felt a little sorry for them. Do you think Donado and his men will find gold?"

"Sure. But several revolutions will come and go before they get enough to go home and arm theirs."

John rode up and fell into line beside them. "I've been talking to Ahmed and Zora," he said. "I think the gypsy may be right."

"*Et tu, Brute?*" Hawk mocked.

The reference to Caesar made Sybilla look sharply at him, but she didn't have time to question his knowledge of Shakespeare. ''Oh, Uncle. Do you propose to defect like poor Juan and Miguel?''

''Of course not. It's just that we have had the deuce of luck, and it might be time to reconsider going on before anything worse befalls us.''

''I warned you this wasn't going to be a picnic,'' Hawk reminded him.

''We are not going to turn back, so please let's not have any further discussion of that.'' Sybilla told John about the similarities between the Montoya story and the stories Hawk's mother told him.

He shook his head in disbelief. ''Surely you don't think that proves anything?''

''I do.'' Sybilla was not about to let John's skepticism undermine her confidence. ''Don't you see? It is our destiny to find the gold.''

''Or get killed,'' John muttered.

''Or worse,'' Hawk put in, just to hear a non-British voice.

''What could possibly be worse than being killed?'' John asked with a tremor.

''Oh, many things,'' Sybilla snapped.

Hawk just smiled.

Chapter 9

The encounter with the revolutionaries prompted Hawk to select a campsite that was even less vulnerable to attack than what he might otherwise have chosen. Located at the bottom of a steep slope of loose rock, richly studded with cholla and prickly pear, the position was easily defensible.

After the evening meal of Dutch oven quail and dumplings, the three men worked out a plan by which they would post a guard from their depleted ranks.

"Why can't the women take a turn at sentry duty?" Sybilla wanted to know.

Hawk looked intrigued by the idea. "It never occurred to me that you might want to."

It had never occurred to her either. Until now. "With the Ruiz brothers gone, I see no reason why Zora and I cannot take up their duties. By dividing the watch among the five of us, everyone can get more sleep."

"Don't be silly, my dear," John said in a patronizing tone. "Despite what the suffragists would have us believe, there are some roles for which women are simply not suited."

"I wasn't aware that special skills were required for standing watch. The primary requisite is staying awake, is it not? That and sounding an alarm should we be attacked?"

"You sure you know what you're getting into?" Hawk asked.

She smiled smugly. Sooner or later he would have to admit that she was a capable human being and not some useless female to be wrapped in wool and stored until needed. "I insist Zora and I be allowed to stand watch. There is no place on this expedition for gender-based inequality."

"Wait." Zora's sharp gaze pierced Sybilla's aplomb. "Insist for yourself, missy. I am not opposed to what you call gender-based inequalities. In fact, they are what make life most interesting. As you would agree if you knew anything about a gender other than your own," she added with a sniff.

"Zora!" Ahmed volubly scolded his wife's impertinence and Sybilla was, for once, left speechless.

Hawk used the pretext of pouring himself another cup of coffee to hide his amusement. Zora might not be a genuine fortune-teller, but she had uncanny insight in some matters.

The gypsy was not to be hushed. "I will not sit alone out here in the dark, with a gun about which I know nothing, and wait for a massacre to happen."

"Zora votes no," Hawk pointed out. "Do you still want to take your turn?"

"I most certainly do," Sybilla professed with more enthusiasm than she felt. Though she stood firm on the principle, it was a hollow victory. She did not relish the thought of being the only one in camp awake, nor did she like the heavy burden of responsibility her speech had imposed on her.

An hour after sundown, as the party discussed their plans for the next day, a strange rumbling sound rolled down from the escarpments above. The camels bleated and Zora screamed.

Ahmed jumped to his feet. "What is that terrible noise, *effendi*?"

"Hawk?" Sybilla had at first thought an earthquake was impending, but she felt none of the accompanying tremors. No, the noise was like a game of primitive ninepins being played with boulders for balls.

"Don't worry. We're not under siege. That's just the wailing of the Lost Tribe." Hawk dashed the last cold dregs from the coffeepot into the dirt.

John's monocle popped out. "The wailing of the what?"

"The Lost Tribe." Hawk warmed up to his story. "A long time ago a bunch of Pima Indians displeased their god, Elder Brother. No one remembers what it was they did wrong, but it must have been something pretty terrible, because the gods don't normally take much notice of mere mortals.

"Anyway, Elder Brother banished the tribe deep into the Superstitions to wander homeless forever. That sound is just their sobs and moans."

Zora crossed herself and Ahmed looked around furtively, as if expecting to encounter the refugees in person. "Are they dangerous, these Losts?"

"There have been rumors of human sacrifices and ritual cannibalism, but I don't put much store in those," Hawk said with mock seriousness.

The rumbling continued for several more seconds and then stopped as abruptly as it had started. "That's a fine story," Sybilla snapped, "but a ridiculous one. That noise was nothing more than igneous material reacting to extremes of temperature."

The others looked to her expectantly, wanting to believe her explanation.

"It was over one hundred degrees today and now it must be near fifty. The contraction and expansion of rocks would certainly account for such rumblings."

"I'm inclined to agree with Sybilla," John asserted. "I climbed the slope earlier to take pictures, and those rocks were hot enough to annoy a stoker."

"Then it isn't the Losts out there wailing?" Ahmed asked.

"Of course not," Sybilla assured him. "Remember, for every seemingly supernatural occurrence, there is a perfectly logical scientific explanation. Primitive people do not have such knowledge and so make up lurid tales to explain what they cannot understand.''

"I have relief that what you say is true," Ahmed said with a sigh. "However, in my homeland it is one's lot to contend regularly with evil spirits and demons and diabolical beings. My father told me of one truly hideous fiend who disguises himself as a poor camel and preys upon weary travelers. He eats them," he confided with a shudder.

"Sounds like the Phantom Camel to me," Hawk put in casually.

"The what?" John and Ahmed chorused.

"Really, Hawk. Must you fill their heads with another of your prehistoric tales?" Sybilla was disgusted with the way his storytelling fed the others' already vivid imaginations.

"This one's of more recent origin," he told them. "Back during the days of the cavalry's camel experiment, there was a soldier in one of the camel troops who refused to ride his assigned mount. Personally, I can understand the man's objections, but his commanding officer did not. Being a little crueler than the ordinary officer, but not much, he ordered the man tied to his camel's back as punishment for disobeying an order."

"And did this change the chap's mind about camels?" John ventured.

"No one will ever know." Hawk shook his head. "Seems the critter bolted into the desert. Since the trooper's hands were tied, he couldn't stop it. No one ever saw him alive again."

Sybilla groaned. As annoyed as she was by Hawk's tall tales, she had to admire his way with words. He had his audience's rapt attention. "Oh, please, let me guess. The poor wretch died under the broiling sun," she intoned melodramatically, "And to this very day the Phantom Camel gallops across the desert with the soldier's bleached bones still strapped to his back."

"Oh, shucks, you heard it already." Hawk's disappointment was far from authentic.

"Is that how it happened, *effendi?*"

"More or less. I talked to an old prospector once who swore he saw the Phantom Camel with his own eyes. Said it was as black as the devil's heart."

Ahmed sent up a few hasty prayers to Allah. "There is an old proverb which says 'Death is a black camel which kneels at everyone's gate.' "

On that bright note, Hawk sent everyone to bed. "Billy, you have first watch. Don't shoot yourself or any of us by mistake. Oh, and if we're attacked? Don't try to talk them out of it. Just yell."

"Thank you, Mr. Devlin, for that bit of unnecessary advice," she clipped out as she grabbed up her rifle and strode away. She made herself as comfortable as possible on the outcropping of rock that served as a sentry post. The easily accessible ledge was about ten feet up the slope and provided a clear view of the surrounding area. At least it would have if it weren't so dark.

"Don't shoot any of us by mistake," she mimicked under her breath as she tossed a piece of ironwood on the small, smokeless fire. The smoldering embers provided a measure of warmth against the cool night air. "Don't try to talk them out of it. Just yell." If she had ever met a more arrogant man than Hawk Devlin she certainly didn't remember him.

She almost wished they would be attacked so that she could rise to the occasion and save Devlin's insufferable hide. Then, thinking how dangerous it was to make wishes, lest they be granted, she quickly negated that thought.

She soon grew impatient with the job she'd talked herself into. She listened to every little squeak and rustle in the desert night and wondered about its source. A bit of brush moved nearby. What was that? A kangaroo rat scuttling through the chaparral? Or was it Maloche, intent on murder, slithering on his belly toward her, a gory knife gripped between his teeth? She had to do something to take her mind off the endless night sounds so she started fantasizing about the Montoya gold.

What would a fortune in gold look like? If it had indeed been melted down into bars as Montoya claimed, how high would the stack be? How wide? Would it be a dazzling, glittering display, or had time tarnished it to dullness? Never having seen gold outside of coins and jewelry settings, she had no idea what to expect.

The wail of a lone coyote brought her back to reality, and she stretched her hands toward the fire. Only hours before, she'd been ready to perish from the heat and now she was shivering. Phantom camels and lost tribes notwithstanding, this was indeed a strange part of the planet.

Later, she grabbed up her rifle when someone called out to her from below her vantage point. "Sybilla?" came John's familiar voice. "It's me. I'm coming up."

He joined her in a few moments, huffing from the exertion of the climb. "Are you ready to retire?"

"Are you taking the next watch?"

"Yes. Ahmed after me. Hawk says the hardest sleep to lose is that just before dawn, so he volunteered for that duty."

"How very thoughtful of him."

"He seems a capable man."

"He is that."

"I suppose if anyone can get us out of here alive, it is Hawk." John didn't sound very confident of their chances of survival.

"Don't be such an old worrier," she chided.

"Given the events of the past few days, how can I be otherwise?"

"We've just had a run of bad luck, that's all. One must expect such things to happen in the wilderness."

"Are you quite sure, Sybilla? Perhaps we should turn back while we still can. I don't feel good about this at all. You are my responsibility now that your father and dear mother are both gone. I shouldn't want to meet them on Judgment Day if you come to harm because of my inability to protect you."

"Nothing is going to happen to me." She grasped her uncle's hands in hers and was startled by their frailness. His skin, as thin as parchment, was criss-crossed by a network of nubby blue veins. "Uncle John, I know you don't understand what this trip is all about, but you do trust me, don't you?"

"Of course I do, my dear." He appeared reluctant to say more. When he did, the words came out in a nervous rush. "It's just that . . . well, are you never afraid? I'm frightened all the time, ready to jump out of my skin at every turn. When those men appeared today, I thought my heart would fail. As much as I hate to admit it, I am worthless to you. I could not have done a thing to protect you and yet that is what I live for."

"Oh, Uncle. Of course I'm frightened. Only a fool is unafraid. But I'm doing what I must. You read the letter Dr. Handelman sent me after father died. It was full of sympathy for my loss, but he couldn't wait to rescind the grant. Even after I'd sent him my credentials, his letter was so patronizing it made me want to scream."

"I know, dear."

"I am a qualified ethnologist, and by finding the Montoya gold and the evidence that the diaries are authentic, I can prove it."

"But thumbing your nose at authority isn't worth risking your life for, is it?" he asked gently.

"What kind of life would I have if I didn't?" she countered.

He looked away. "I had hoped you might con-sider returning to Chelmsford with me, find some suitable young man to marry, and settle down to the country life. Is that such a terrible prospect?"

"No, Uncle, it isn't terrible at all. But it is not for me. I don't want to settle down. I like adventure and excitement. I can't explain it, but I just know that my future lies far away from Chelmsford. And as for those suitable young men you have in mind for me, I fear they would bore me to distraction."

"Not so Hawk Devlin, I suppose?" he asked.

"What do you mean? I have no feelings for him." She did indeed have feelings, but not of the sort she wished to discuss with her aging relative.

"Don't deny what is clearly there. I see it in your eyes every time you look at him. It's the same thing I saw in your mother's gaze when she looked at your father. You are very like Vittoria, you know. She was an orphan with no one but a few nuns in a convent school to call family, when Thomas met her in Mexico City."

"It must have been hard for her to leave everything familiar and travel to a foreign country."

"True love overcomes all difficulties, if we are to believe the poets. Your mother worshipped your father," he added wistfully. "Love that blind and unwavering is rare."

"Extremely rare."

"You must have gotten your love of adventure from Thomas. You got your beauty and goodness from Vittoria. She was the only totally selfless person I ever met. Thomas recognized her strength at once. I know that he came to depend on it."

"How so?"

"His long absences nearly broke her heart, but your mother never complained. She grieved for him when he was out of the country, always worried about his safety. A lesser woman might have turned to other men for comfort and admiration. After all, she was young and very beautiful. But not Vittoria. She was completely faithful to a husband who took her goodness for granted."

"Uncle John!"

"I'm sorry, my dear. I've said too much."

If her proud, arrogant father had been less than the man she remembered, she did not want to know about it now. "Uncle John, do try not to be afraid. Hawk knows this country and he will protect us."

"It is not the country I fear, nor the uncivilized people who inhabit it. No, my dear, my greatest fear is that somehow I shall fail you. That when you need me most, I will not be up to the task."

"Don't worry, Uncle. Nothing you could do would make me love you any less. Nothing."

She hugged him then and turned to return to her tent. She thought she heard him whisper something, but it could have been a trick of the wind whistling down from above. It sounded as if he said, "It is doing nothing that I fear."

Two hours before dawn Sybilla was jarred from sleep by a terrible nightmare. In it she was tied onto the back of an enormous black camel with evil yellow eyes. Fighting the dream bonds that held her, she kicked and thrashed until she fell off her narrow cot. She awoke then and the dream broke up, splintering into cracks of darkness, leaving a premonition of danger.

She found herself on the ground, clutching her twisted blanket in a death grip. Feeling like a child who had heard too many ghost stories before bedtime, she climbed onto her cot. She tried to sleep, but it eluded her and she stared up at the peaked ceiling of the tent. She smiled in the darkness when she heard the unlikely melody of a Chopin etude lilting through the desert night.

Hawk was quite accomplished on the harmonica. She wondered if his skill extended to any other instruments. She lay listening while he worked through his extensive repertoire. Since she couldn't sleep, perhaps this would be a good time to speak to him privately.

She got up and slipped into her boots. Pulling her jacket on over her nightdress, she picked her way across the campsite, stepping lightly around her uncle's blanket-wrapped figure. She was careful to avoid the cacti that created an obstacle course between the camp at the base of a rocky sentinel and the slope where the lookout station was located. The whole area was part of an upthrust mass of dacite rock that was one of the many bizarre formations protruding out of the desert. The plugs and dikes created a miniature mountain range filled with a maze of chapparal-choked canyons. The slope leading up to the vantage point was littered with loose rock and the debris of thousands of years of erosion.

She called softly to Hawk to announce her approach, and the music stopped abruptly. She wanted to tell him to continue, but she sensed his playing was something he preferred to do in private.

"What are you doing up?" he asked.

"I couldn't sleep." She decided not to tell him about the nightmare. She didn't want him to know she was susceptible to such silly flights of fancy. "I felt like having company. May I join you?"

Hawk tapped the harmonica on his palm before dropping it into his pocket. "No one's ever accused me of being good company, but be my guest."

She settled down on the opposite side of the fire that was no more than a few smoldering embers now. "Have you seen anything tonight?"

"Like phantom camels or lost souls, you mean?"

She smiled at the teasing note in his voice. "I was thinking more in terms of knife-wielding renegades."

"None of those either. It's been as quiet as a grave out here."

"Really, Hawk. In light of recent events, I do wish you would choose your words more carefully."

"Sorry. It's been so quiet you can hear daylight coming."

"That's better."

"What do you want to talk about?"

What indeed? She couldn't reveal the real reason she'd come. How could she tell him she was drawn to him in spite of herself? That the differences between them only made him more irresistible? "How long do you think it will take to locate the landmarks on the map and find the gold?"

"I don't know . . . kind of depends on old Ricardo's mapmaking ability. This is a mighty big country, and it all looks pretty much the same. I've got to tell you, Billy, we've got about as much chance of finding that gold as a wax cat has in hell."

"That's an appalling attitude."

Hawk saw how his words hurt her and softened his tone. "Maybe, but it's realistic. After all, you haven't let me see much of the map."

"I realize that we have gone as far as we can without allowing you to see the rest of it. Now that we are in the mountains, you may examine it in the morning."

"So you trust me now, do you?"

"As much as possible," she admitted. "I know that a guide is next to worthless unless he knows the geographical goal of the expedition."

"While we're on the subject, what exactly is that goal?"

Sybilla decided there was no disadvantage in telling him tonight what he would plainly see for himself tomorrow. "The gold is hidden in a mountain that looks like a half-buried heart."

Hawk considered the interior landmarks of the region, landmarks he was familiar with from his own searches. He knew of none that fit that description. "I've been all over these mountains and I've never seen anything like that."

"But it is there. Ricardo's drawing is most definite. We will find it," she insisted. However, his words, along with the bad luck they'd encountered, cast a shadow of doubt over her own thoughts.

"If you say so."

"You aren't sure?"

"Nothing's certain in this life, Billy. I stopped counting on sure things a long time ago."

"How is it that you know how to waltz and quote Shakespeare and play classical music on your harmonica?" She wouldn't have asked the blunt question if her desire to know more about the man beside her hadn't been so strong. She watched anxiously to see if the question displeased him.

He didn't speak for a several moments, and she wondered if he were trying to decide whether to answer truthfully or to invent a suitable deception.

"The advantages of a liberal education are many," he said. "Those are just a few of the things I learned."

"Where did you go to school?" She knew he couldn't have been educated in a one-room territorial schoolhouse, but she was unprepared for his answer.

"The College of William and Mary. Class of '81."

Her eyebrows rose. "That explains many things." She couldn't resist another question. "How is it that the son of a mixed-blood laundress from Arizona ends up graduating from a prestigious school like that?"

"It helps if he's also the bastard of the scion of one of Virginia's wealthiest families," he said bitterly. "My father died when I was thirteen, and his will provided for my schooling. I was sent to boarding schools and then college. It was all a big surprise to me. My mother and I hadn't heard from him for nine years."

He paused as if deciding how much to tell her. "I didn't want to take anything from him, even after he was dead, because I'd convinced myself I hated him. But my mother made me go back East and get an education. She thought racial prejudice wouldn't be as strong there as it is here. She thought things would be different."

"And were they different, Hawk?"

"Hell yes. They were worse."

He stared out at the moon-washed buttes, his blue eyes unblinking, his thoughts dragged back to the day he had left for Virginia. The post commander had bought him a new suit of clothes, but they were a size too small, and he remembered how he'd had to pull at the scratchy collar and cuffs. His mother had taken away the soft deerskin moccasins she'd made for him and forced him to wear white-man shoes of stiff leather. His shoulder-length hair had been cut off, leaving him feeling naked and vulnerable.

And scared.

He told Sybilla about the clothes. He didn't mention the fears.

When he didn't go on, she said, "You must have felt as I did when my father insisted upon a grand ball for my coming out. I thought it a rather old-fashioned and silly idea to be primed and primped as if the sole purpose of my life was being presented to society."

"But you went along with it?" he asked incredulously.

"I am a female, I had no choice in the matter. My father sold precious antiques to pay for my coming out."

Sybilla chuckled at the memory of how her grandmother had tried to reform her into a perfect lady. She raised her voice and pretended to fan her face the way the older woman always did when Sybilla shocked her sensibilities. "A lady mustn't talk to a gentleman caller about horses, dear. She must speak only when spoken to and must never ever, under any circumstances, express a different point of view."

Hawk laughed. "I'll bet you shocked more than a few of your gentleman callers."

Sybilla smiled. "That I did. And I kept on doing so, until most of them gave up and went off in search of simpering half-wits who appreciated them."

"What did you do for fun?"

"I studied. I loved learning about my father's work, and his library was extensive. When he was forced to retire due to ill health, I nursed him and convinced him we could work and travel together to exotic places.''

''Doesn't seem like much of a life for a young girl,'' Hawk said thoughtfully.

''Oh, but it was. I was very happy. Before that time I barely knew my father. We became quite close, and I am so thankful for that, as well as for the knowledge I gained while working at his side.''

Hawk remembered from their first conversation that she'd been young when her mother died. ''You must have missed your mother very much during your youth.''

''Yes, I did. But I remember her quite well. She was young and vibrant, and she taught me to be my own person.''

''So we have her to thank for your bossiness, huh?''

Sybilla peered up at him and, realizing he was teasing, she smiled and ventured another question. ''Who taught you to be the kind of man you are, Hawk?'' she asked boldly.

''My mother gave me good advice, but I'm afraid any blame for what I turned out to be is mostly my own.''

''What kind of advice?''

''When I left for Virginia, she told me not to be afraid and reminded me that I was a brave young man. She said the trip into the white man's world of education would be as nothing to one of my courage.''

''You didn't want to go to Williamsburg?'' Sybilla guessed.

''No. I couldn't shame my mother with tears and pleading, so I climbed onto the supply wagon that took me to Tucson and the stage. At that moment I hated my father more than ever. Even in death he had managed to reach across the miles and yank me away from the only person who had ever really loved me.''

"Your father must have had some good in him, if a woman like Mirry loved him," Sybilla suggested tentatively.

"She did love him, and that's something I've never understood. Mother swore that someday I'd find a soul mate, and then I would know the depth of her feelings." Hawk shrugged. "I suppose he saved her from some of life's degradations, but I'll never forgive him for abandoning her."

"Why do you suppose she sent you away?"

"The world as we knew it was changing, the old ways dying. She wanted me to learn to live in the white world because she knew there would soon be no other. I argued that I was descended from a long line of Apache warriors. Even if the blood link was watered down, the cultural link was strong."

"And what did she say to that?"

"She argued in her quiet way that I was also a Devlin, and she told me, 'Go and be the best among them. Show them that Hawk Devlin is the smartest, the strongest, the bravest of all to bear the Devlin name.' I resisted, told her that I wasn't sure I could find a place there, that I would run away if she made me go."

When he stopped talking, Sybilla encouraged him. "But that didn't change her mind, did it?"

"No, she simply reminded me there was no honor in running from what one fears. Sometimes a man has to do things he doesn't want to do."

He recalled that his mother had not cried when Malcolm Devlin left her, so confident had she been of his return. But Hawk had seen tears in her eyes as the supply wagon rumbled away with him perched precariously on an empty barrel. He realized that she feared he might not come back and was just as afraid of being alone as he was.

"She thought she was making my life better," Hawk said softly. "She had no idea that having something and then losing it is much worse than never knowing it at all. But I never told her that."

Sybilla was touched by the unhappiness Hawk
had known and was suddenly overcome by feelings
so powerful and tender that she quite forgot herself.
She felt compelled to undo the injustices that had
been heaped on him. Without thinking where her
rash action would lead, she moved to his side, put
her arm around his waist, and rested her head on
his shoulder.

"You are quite a man, Hawk Devlin," she whispered. "Your mother would be proud of you."

Hawk was surprised by her offer of comfort. It
had been a long time since he'd felt such total peace.
His lips brushed against her temple when he spoke.
"And you are quite a woman, Billy."

He hesitated for only a heartbeat, then his lips
found hers as surely as a bee finds waiting honey.
It was the embrace he'd dreamed about, longed for,
and he pulled her closer.

Despite her recent vow not to succumb to Hawk,
she wrapped her arms around his neck and lost herself to the feel of his warm lips on hers. She melted
against him, yearning for something more, something only he could give her.

Spurred by her response, Hawk slipped one hand
inside her jacket to caress the breast that quivered
beneath the thin fabric of her nightgown. The other
hand skimmed her hip, and she trembled in his
arms. He was nearly crazy from holding back the
surge of desire that threatened his carefully maintained control. He'd never known such sweet torture.

Sybilla was barely aware of the hard rock where
they sat, of the stars winking overhead, or of the
mournful cry of her old friend the coyote. Her world
was suddenly reduced to the feel of Hawk's lips, hot
and insistent upon hers. She strained toward him,
still unsure of what she wanted, but knowing she
craved it with the very essence of her being.

Then his lips trailed down her throat and one of
his hands pushed up her nightgown, exposing her

pale, slender legs to his hungry eyes and the moon's silvery kiss. Sybilla gasped and pushed his hand away, remembering she was naked beneath her nightclothes.

Hawk groaned with frustration. "Don't shut me out, Billy. Won't you let me love you?"

Sybilla was amazed at how much she wanted to do just that. But she felt guilty that her reaction to this man could be so strong. Where was her respectable British reserve when she needed it?

She had been raised to respect virtue and the sanctity of marriage. But Hawk's request showed clearly that he did not. Maybe out here such things weren't so important. She didn't know how to respond.

Hawk feared the moment had been lost and was torn between relief and disappointment. As much as he wanted Billy—and he did want her—he knew she was not the kind of woman he was accustomed to having. Her growing arousal told him he could seduce her. But seduction wasn't what he needed; he wanted her to give herself to him because she desired him and no other. She'd have to make a conscious decision. Her commitment was as important as his own.

"Billy?" he asked.

"Yes?" she replied dreamily.

"Are you still thinking about it?" he teased.

She had no time to respond because at that moment they heard the skittering of falling rocks high above their heads. Seconds later the first shower of small stones fell, striking them with such force that they cried out from the pain.

Hawk reacted immediately by grabbing Sybilla's arm and pulling her to her feet. He jumped off the ledge, taking her with him, and unceremoniously stuffed her under its puny overhang. He scrambled in beside her just as several large boulders crashed down the slope. They crouched in the small dark space, choking on dust and clinging together while the rockslide unleashed its fury.

Hawk tossed his poncho over their heads to shield their faces from the hail of small, deadly stones. The larger rocks and boulders crashed down around them. Hawk and Sybilla hugged their arms and legs close to their bodies and tucked in their heads for protection.

The bombardment seemed to go on for a small slice of eternity, but when the slide was over, Hawk pulled Sybilla to her feet and searched her frantically for injuries. His hands were no longer gentle as they'd been only minutes before, but brusque and determined.

"I'm not hurt," she sputtered, spitting out a mouthful of dirt.

"Thank God. Damn, that was close. Too close." Assured that she wasn't injured, he became tender once more, wiping dust from her face and picking small pebbles from her long, tangled hair. Her jacket was ripped and dirty, and her eyes were wide with fear. She coughed and backhanded tears from her irritated eyes.

She looked up at Hawk and saw blood trickling from a small cut on his temple. "You're hurt."

He wiped the blood away. "It's nothing." The pain from that small injury could not compare with the stab of cold fear he'd felt when he'd thought her in peril. He had been so caught up in his feelings for her that he had been oblivious to their surroundings. When he kissed her, it was as if they were the only two people in the world.

He'd never known such consuming desire, and the intensity of his reactions shook his so much that he retreated behind his old, familiar barriers. Guiltily he reminded himself that Billy was paying him to do a job, not to seduce her. What kind of bodyguard got so wrapped up in kisses that he failed to hear impending danger? His inattention was nothing but softness, and he hated that. If Maloche had attacked, they'd all be dead.

"I'm sorry," he said curtly. "That won't happen again."

Sybilla saw Hawk's eyes harden and, with an acute sense of loss, concluded that he was apologizing for kissing her. Now that the danger was past, her fear receded, leaving her weak and vulnerable to his sudden withdrawal. She wasn't sure which hurt more, the battering stones or Hawk's rejection.

Vying for acknowledgment among her swirling emotions was shame. But it wasn't shame for what she'd done. No, that would be too simple. She was ashamed because she didn't feel more guilt about the liberties she had allowed Hawk to take.

Finding comfort in the familiar, she straightened her back and assumed an impersonal manner. "What happened?"

Hawk stared up the rocky face of the canyon wall, his gaze piercing the darkness. "Something, or someone, started a slide from about halfway up that slope."

"Someone? Who?"

"I don't know, but I'm going to find out. Wake up the others. It's nearly sunrise anyway." He started climbing before he finished issuing the order.

She hurried back to camp, still shaking from the random nature of the unexpected violence. Would they never be safe again? So many things had happened to them, she felt as though some force was trying to drive them away. She squared her chin resolutely, determined not to give in to fear.

She would arm herself by always expecting the worst, by never letting down her guard. Disaster seemed to be waiting for them at every turn. If vigilance would protect her from Hawk's dangerous advances, it should also serve to protect her from that hoary old reaper, Death.

She charged into camp and was surprised to find

Uncle John already up and fully dressed, poking incompetently at the cookfire and setting water to boil. He gasped when he saw her bedraggled appearance. "Sybilla, my dear, what happened to you?"

"I was in a rockslide. Bloody horrible it was too."

"A rockslide?" His shock was apparent. "Weren't you in your tent?"

"No, I was talking to Hawk." She flushed when she thought of what else they had been doing and hoped the pale rays of early light would not reveal her embarrassment. "What are you doing about so early?"

"Uh . . . well . . . I thought I'd get a jump on breakfast, as they say out here. Where is Hawk?" he asked anxiously. "Was he hurt?"

"No. He'll be along. He wanted to see if he could find any clues as to how the slide started."

John looked concerned and glanced nervously up the slope. "Perhaps it was caused by the same contraction and expansion as the rumbling last night."

"Not very damn likely." Hawk strode toward them, wearing a lot of dirt and a grim expression.

Sybilla had never seen him so angry. "It was an accident, a freak of nature."

"Somebody wanted it to look that way. Unfortunately he made one mistake."

"What was that?" John whispered, his strained voice barely audible.

"He left his calling card behind." Hawk held out his hand, and the bright rays of dawn glinted off the object in his palm.

A little silver snuff spoon.

Chapter 10

Sybilla held her breath for several moments. When no one spoke, she pointed out rather unnecessarily, "That's your spoon, Uncle John."

"Indeed it is," concurred the ashen-faced old man. He seemed as surprised as anyone else to see it in Hawk's hand.

"Would you care to explain how it got up on that slope?" Hawk's voice was tight.

"I . . . I might have lost it yesterday when I was up there to take photographs."

"Strange you didn't mention it," Hawk said.

"I hadn't missed it yet. I'm running low on snuff and put myself on a strict ration."

"Are you sure you didn't drop it while you were up there early this morning?"

John looked uneasily from Hawk to Sybilla. "Well . . . uh . . . I—"

"You cannot mean to accuse Uncle John of starting that rockslide," Sybilla snapped.

"I'm not accusing anyone of anything. I just want some answers."

"I would never do something like that intentionally." John withdrew a handkerchief from his pocket and patted his face. "I'll have you know I am a man who abhors violence."

Hawk wiped at his face with a dirty sleeve. "Can you prove you were up there yesterday?"

"He doesn't have to," Sybilla interceded coolly.

189

She was dismayed by Hawk's insinuation and looked at him as though she had never seen him before. "Uncle John is the gentlest man I know, and you have no right to accuse him. Besides, he stands to gain as much as I do if we find the gold, so why would he want to sabotage the expedition?"

Hawk felt betrayed by the reproachful look in Sybilla's eyes. An hour ago she'd been kissing him and enjoying it thoroughly. But doubt had surfaced again. What was implicit, what hung thick in the air between them, was the fact that she didn't trust him. And that hurt.

He sealed it up in that secret place in his heart where he stored pain and folded his arms across his chest. He hesitated before adding, "Since your uncle already tried to bribe me into sabotaging the trip, I was naturally suspicious."

Sybilla was shocked, but not too surprised to glimpse a flicker of emotion in Hawk's eyes before he had a chance to hide it. She turned tentatively to John. "Is it true, Uncle? Did you try to bribe him?"

"Dear girl, I can explain that."

"You mean you did?" she asked weakly.

"I confess I offered him money. But that was at the outset, before I knew how much finding the gold means to you. We really didn't know much about his character then, and I thought to test his loyalties. That's all. It was all quite innocent, I assure you."

"Uncle John," she said quietly, disappointment in her shaky voice. "How could you?"

"Sybilla, dear, you must forgive my foolishness."

"You said you wanted me to return to Chelmsford. Would you go so far as to start a rockslide? We could have been killed."

John looked genuinely indignant. "Of course not! I'd never stoop to anything so heinous. You must believe me."

She looked at Hawk, then to John in confusion. "I'm quite sure I don't know who to believe." With that she walked away from the two men.

"Come back, Sybilla," John pleaded. "Let me explain."

Hawk didn't want her to leave before he could clear the air, yet he didn't know what to say. He glanced at John, saw how stricken the old man was, and immediately regretted his hasty words.

"I must think," Sybilla called over her shoulder. "I'll be in my tent." But when she reached it, she knew the shelter was far too small to contain the magnitude of her feelings. She knew in her heart that Uncle John could not have intentionally done anything violent. Yet he had petitioned her time and again to abandon the expedition and return to England. In his desperation had he done something foolish?

No. She could not believe it of him. But Hawk did, and that only made the chasm between them more difficult to bridge. The evidence Hawk possessed, the snuff spoon, did raise a question in her mind. It was the question that caused her turmoil. She had handled the situation badly, and instead of calmly insisting on facts, she had allowed her emotions to rule. That was something that had never happened to her before.

Her feelings for Hawk had clouded her good judgment. She had vowed not to let that happen, but with each passing day she became more dangerously vulnerable to him. He owed her nothing, and she knew better than to expect anything from him. Yet when he kissed her, she wanted everything. It was the difference between what she knew in her mind and what she felt in her heart that made the conflict so difficult to resolve.

After a few minutes of claustrophobic pacing back and forth, she slipped from the back of her tent and made her way out of the canyon. She set off at a quick pace, hoping the physical exercise might help put things back into perspective. She needed some distance between herself and Hawk, even if it was only temporary.

If she hadn't been so overwrought, she never would have stormed out of camp alone, unarmed, and in her nightgown, without informing anyone of her whereabouts. Although it was a foolhardy thing to do, she felt better for having taken those defiant steps and she walked on, determined to think the situation through in solitude.

All around her, the rising sun smeared the landscape with broad strokes of glorious but unlikely colors: violet, lavender, and mauve. The area, with its craggy buttes and ghostly peaks, was as vast and raw and silent as an imagined moonscape. It beckoned to Sybilla's senses, and soon she fell under its spell.

The land looked barren and empty, but it hummed with secret life. For all its wide openness, it teemed with activity that was hidden from the casual eye.

She might have felt alone in the universe as she stalked away, but a million insects buzzed in the chaparral and scuttled under every stone. She felt the lethal presence of reptiles that slept by day and slithered in the cool of the evening. She sidestepped eccentric arachnids who crept out their lives among the rocky crevices.

She saw the evidence of tiny cactus wrens who built their nests in the only available space. Her movement roused flickers, ravens, an occasional hawk. In the underbrush a covey of pretty quail scattered before her, and she kept her eyes open for the comical chapparal cock, a strange bird who preferred running to flying.

The larger mammals—mountain lion, bobcat, coyote, deer, and antelope—were not so visible. But they were out there, just the same, going about the business of life in an unforgiving land.

Above it all, the loathsome and patient turkey buzzards drifted in the endless sky. With lidless eyes and voracious appetites they circled in the distance, the power of flight lending them an awkward grace as they waited. It seemed they were always waiting for something, somewhere, to die. They knew their vigilance would be rewarded, for here the battle for survival often fell in death's favor.

But for all its harshness, the desert possessed a savage beauty. The bright green paloverde, with its tiny, timid leaves, waved in the breeze like a giant land-locked seaweed. The ocotillo, an unusual tree that she'd first mistaken for a cactus, was like a lighted candelabrum with its single cone of red flowers flaming at the tip of each tall branch.

As if to make up for their homeliness during the rest of the year, the true cacti—the prickly pear, barrel, pincushion, and others—had burst forth with an immodest display of wild spring flowers. Red, purple, yellow, orange, magenta, and pink dotted the landscape: paintbox bright on a burnt umber canvas.

For sheer splendid majesty, nothing rivaled the saguaro. The giants grew to forty feet and towered over the landscape like a titan's lost children. Hawk had told her that the spines were cored with a flammable resin and caught fire easily. Once the lower spines were ignited, the flame passed upward, burning off the spines all the way to the top. Such living flares were sometimes used by Indians to send messages at night.

The quiet and solitude soothed her, and Sybilla felt better soon. She looked around to find her bearings. It would be easy to lose her way when every cactus and rocky outcrop looked exactly the same. As she gazed at the rugged splendor around her she understood why Hawk felt so at home here. Like him, the land was a study of blatant contrasts.

She had made the mistake of thinking he was a simple man, composed in equal parts of survival instinct and nerve, held together by sheer stubborn will. But she now knew he was much more complex than that. He didn't fit easily into any category she could name, and he was just as much an enigma to her as he had ever been.

Her questions had given her little relief from her

curiosity; in fact, his answers had only whetted her need to know more. Now that she knew about the time he had spent in Virginia, she understood him a little better. But, she did not understand why a man with his education and abilities had returned to a place as forsaken and unrelenting as Arizona.

Despite the influence of college, Hawk was definitely a Westerner, strong and sparing of words, like the men described in the dime novels Uncle John read so voraciously. Since leaving Tucson, she'd had fleeting glimpses of a side of Hawk that she was sure he rarely showed. And then only unintentionally. Despite all the rough edges, there was a pure, shining center to him. If only she could touch it, she knew she'd find it as bright as a diamond and twice as hard.

The contrast between what he was and what he seemed to be captured her imagination. Philosophical quotes rolled off his tongue as effortlessly as muted curses, and he was equally familiar with Mozart's sonatas and with bawdy barroom ditties. The night they'd danced, he'd been as at ease waltzing as he had ever been squatting along the trail, reading animal spoor.

Neither a gentleman turned renegade nor a wild woolly taking on airs, Hawk was unlike any man she'd ever met, as amazing and inscrutable as an ancient puzzle that was not meant to be understood by mere mortals. But she would certainly undertake to comprehend him, or her name was not Sybilla Antonia Hartford.

Billy. Every time Hawk called her that it reminded her of her mother and the happy days they'd spent together before Vittoria's death. Her mother had called her Billy also. Except when she said it, in her lilting Spanish accent, it had sounded like "Beelee." The pet name had been a secret between them. Grandmother Sybilla would never have approved of such lack of formality.

But formality was the furthest thing from Sybilla's

mind when she thought of Hawk. Although in her actions she must remain chaste, in her thoughts she could be bold. While it was dangerous to allow her imagination the freedom to conceive of being Hawk's lover, it was a joy she could not deny herself.

Had they not been interrupted by that rockslide, she would have been tempted to let Hawk do things she could not even consider in the cold light of day. But his kisses had weakened her resolve, and for a few moments she had longed to know what came next, what all the mystery was about. Maybe the rockslide had been neither accidental nor deliberate. Perhaps it was fate working again, giving her a sign that such thoughts and actions were better left unexplored. Frustrated, she didn't know whether to curse her misfortune or thank her lucky stars.

When she realized she had been moonraking, she gazed around in confusion. Nothing looked familiar. Rocky slopes rose in every direction. Lost in thoughts of Hawk, she'd forgotten to pick out landmarks and now had no idea which way the camp lay. She noted with alarm that the sun was climbing in the pale sky. She had no time to lose.

Dressed as she was, in a nightgown and jacket, without so much as a hat to protect her from the broiling sun, heat prostration was a very real threat. She ripped several inches of cotton from the bottom of her gown and fashioned the cloth into a turban with a Foreign Legion flap in the back.

Striking out in what she hoped was the right direction, she hiked into a small arroyo she didn't recall having passed through earlier. She knelt to look for footprints, but the wind-blown dust gave no sign of her passing. She yanked her nightdress free from the prickly pear spines snagging it, and the ragged hem ripped as though made of tissue paper, creating a rent that exposed her pale leg when she walked.

"Drat it all!" she exclaimed for the benefit of the

desert tortoise making its unhurried escape. At the rate she was going, it wouldn't be long before she was completely naked. She didn't know where she was or how far she'd wandered from camp, but pride made her refuse to admit she was lost.

"Just wait until the bureau hears about this," she muttered. "Sybilla Hartford, novice ethnologist, disappears in the Arizona desert in a snit! Wearing her nightgown!" She looked down at the thin garment that was definitely the worse for wear. "How they will laugh then."

She scooped up a stone and flung it into a thorny thicket of catclaw acacia, known locally by the colorful name of wait-a-minute bush. The act gave her a sense of satisfaction, but she regretted it immediately when she heard the snuffling, scrabbling sound that emanated suddenly from the brush. Not knowing what desert creature she might have disturbed, she backed away warily.

Before she'd gone three steps, a dozen sharp-tusked javelinas emerged and locked onto her with their small piggy eyes. She surmised the ill-gauged rock had interrupted their morning browsing. She took another step backward, and the herd, composed of both adults and their young, evidently interpreted the action as threatening. They tensed en masse, their moist snouts quivering in excitement. They raised their bristles, and her own nostrils flared at the pungent odor exuded from the musk glands on their hindquarters.

The beasts were as large as foxhounds and quite gruesome-looking. She'd once seen a native porter nearly ripped apart by the brutes' South American cousins, and the memory made a cold shiver of dread slither down her spine.

Having flounced out of camp without a weapon, she was defenseless. She groaned at the realization. Uncertain what her next move should be, she pondered how she'd managed to come to such a foolish end. Here she was, in a shredded nightdress, in imminent danger of becoming breakfast for a bunch of pigs!

One thing was certain. She had to keep her wits about her. With a minimum of movement and a maximum of anxiety, she glanced around for possible escape routes. Her only hope was a small, scrubby tree growing out of the rocks at an almost horizontal angle.

The lowest branches were at least three feet above her head, but if she could jump high enough to grasp them, she could pull herself out of the path of the wary pigs before they reached her. She dared not contemplate what would happen if she made the dash and missed, for she knew any action on her part would signal the beasts to charge.

Nor did she want to think about what she would do once she attained such a lofty position. At this point her plan didn't extend much beyond hanging on and screaming for help.

One pig, the leader judging from its size and aggressive attitude, made a tentative charge that sent her scurrying for the tree. She propelled herself upward with all her strength and closed her fingers around the slender trunk. Just as the grunting javelina overtook her, she swung her feet off the ground and struggled up the face of the rock until she could wrap her legs around the tree trunk. Her gown swept nearly to the ground, baring her legs to the thighs, and she yanked it up with one hand while holding on to the tree with the other.

Following the example set by their fearless leader, the rest of the wild pigs charged forward and milled just below her in a snorting, squealing, stinking mass of porcine frenzy. Sybilla would not allow herself to think about what other, smaller, but no less deadly creatures she might have vexed in the course of her climb. She forced her thoughts away from rattlesnakes and scorpions and tarantulas. Better to concentrate on the disagreeable javelinas and leave the rest to fate.

Unfamiliar with piggy persistence, she had no idea
how long it would take them to give up and go
away. But she did know her own limitations and
realized that she wouldn't be able to maintain her
tenuous hold indefinitely, even assuming the tree
didn't give way first.

Loosened from its precarious niche in the dust-
filled crevice, the little tree dipped alarmingly with
every breath she took. She could only guess which
would succumb first: the tree's roots, the javelinas,
or her tender hands.

"Surely you must realize I pose no threat to you
now," she muttered to the bristly throng below her.
"Go away like good little piggies."

They rooted around and grunted, but they didn't
go away, and she decided it was time to implement
the second stage of her strategy. Gathering as much
air as possible into her lungs, she screamed. "Hawk!
Help!"

Shortly after Sybilla stalked off to her tent, John
explained to Hawk what had happened up in the
rocks. "I didn't like saying so in front of my niece,
but I seem to be plagued with dysentery this morning."

"Why'd you climb up in the rocks?"

"I wanted to get as far from the camp as possible,
but I was afraid to venture a long distance for fear
of getting lost. One pile of rocks looks much like
another," he ended lamely.

"Well, that explains things."

"Frightfully embarrassing, this." John shook his
head. "I wanted to explain sooner, but I didn't know
how. I knocked against a rock, and before I quite
knew what was happening, it was over. I rushed
down to make certain the camp wasn't in the path.
I would have called out a warning, but I didn't think
anyone would ever know. I thought your watch had
already ended."

"Yeah, it should have." Hawk grinned sheepishly when he remembered why he'd lingered.

"I couldn't explain to Sybilla without mentioning my condition, and I am reluctant to do so even now. She worries about me and if she suspected I was ill, she might want to abandon the search. You understand, don't you?"

"I understand." Hawk knew now that the attempted bribe really *had* been a test of sorts. It had been all the old man could come up with at the time. He also knew why John had wanted to keep the indelicate nature of his problem from Billy, even at the risk of his health. Sometimes too much propriety could be dangerous.

"I'm sorry I overreacted," Hawk told him, "but I was concerned for Billy's safety. I lost control when I realized she could have been badly hurt."

"That's quite all right, old boy," John said. "I am glad she has you to look after her welfare. Lord knows, I made a bad job of it by starting that slide."

"It was an accident,"Hawk commiserated. "I just hope the two of us looking after her will be enough. But dysentery should be taken seriously. I know an Indian remedy. I'll brew a tea for you."

Hawk went to Sybilla's tent to explain and apologize for whatever it was had made her angry this time. He was furious when he found she wasn't there. He struck out after her, and for a man who could track a whisper in a big wind, following her careless trail was easy. Maybe he'd been wrong to accuse John before hearing him out, but even John admitted he'd had good reason.

Hawk ran around a spire of rock when he heard Sybilla's frantic shout. He sized up the situation immediately. Billy, long hair streaming and bare legs flashing, was clinging to a tree like a possum. The terrified look on her face changed to one of relief when she saw him. He drew his pistol and fired two shots at the largest javelina, and it dropped into the dust with a noisy thud. The rest of the herd scattered. He grinned smugly, thinking about the tasty pork chops they'd have for supper.

"Don't just stand there with that bloody stupid grin on your face," Sybilla yelled at him as she tried to quell her joy at seeing him. It disturbed her that even in her precarious situation, she couldn't help noticing how handsome he was. She tried to school her features into a properly indignant expression, but he was too attractive for such self-delusion.

"No, ma'am," he agreed amiably.

He made no move to help her, and his nonchalance grated on her nerves. "What are you doing?"

"Just enjoying the scenery." His grin prompted her to yank down the revealing nightgown, and she almost lost her grip on the tree in the process.

"Stop ogling and help me," she commanded. The tree slipped another inch and she glanced down, judging the distance to the ground. She realized with dismay that just below her perch an amazing and wholly unnecessary variety of cacti grew unchecked. Her eyes widened with alarm. "Now! If it isn't too much trouble for you."

Hawk took his own sweet time holstering his gun. "Do I detect a rebuke?" He shook his head and clucked his tongue. "I just saved your pretty hide, Billy. At the very least I deserve a proper thank you."

She took a deep breath and swallowed the curses vying for release. "Thank you," she muttered. "Now get me down from here."

"That sounds suspiciously like an order instead of a request, and I thought we agreed I give the orders around here," he reminded her.

"Bloody hell!" she screeched, and the tree gave another inch. "Do you want me to beg? Very well, Devlin, I'm begging. Please, get me down."

"Hell, Billy. All you had to do was ask." He started forward, but it was too late.

The tree roots gave up their tenuous hold, and Sybilla dropped to the ground like a rock, her night-

dress billowing around her in a most unladylike
fashion. The frightening sensation of falling quickly
gave way to a horrible pain in her backside, a pain
so intense it brought tears to her eyes.

"I'm sorry, Billy, I really was coming after you."
Feeling more than a little guilty, Hawk held out a
helping hand and tried not to look at the tempting
display of pale skin. As he yanked her to her feet,
her nightgown snagged on the cacti, shredding it
even more.

"Bloody hell!" she muttered, trying to tug the tattered gown over her bare legs. Unfortunately, there
wasn't enough of it left to provide much coverage.
Her bottom was stinging, but not unbearably so, and
she tried to ignore it.

"Are you all right?" he asked innocently.

"Am I all right?" she screamed. "Since meeting
you I've been nearly washed away in a flood, narrowly escaped being murdered by revolutionaries,
and been bashed about the head in a rockslide. Just
when I think nothing worse could possibly happen,
I'm set upon by wild pigs and then fall nearly naked
into a bed of prickly flora."

"A bit of a sticky wicket, that," he said, mimick-
ing her carefully enunciated syllables perfectly.

She glared at him. "What's worse, I must suffer
your fatuous attempts at humor, and you have the
audacity to inquire if I am all right."

"Jesus, I was just asking."

"The answer is no, I am not all right. I am full of
cactus spines, you dolt!" She winced at the re-
minder of her pain.

"Let me see." He tried to turn her around, but
she whipped away from him, covering her backside
with her hands. "Stay away from me. You've done
quite enough." Oh, how she longed to kick and
scream like an angry child at the indignities that had
been heaped upon her.

Hawk was perplexed by the lone tear spilling

down her cheek. Gently he wiped it away. "Is anything broken?"

She moaned. "Would that it were that simple."

He glanced at the ground. "That's a nasty pile of cholla there. The damn things stick like crazy."

She attempted to look at her posterior by craning her head over her shoulder. Touching the affected area was too painful for words. "Thank you for that astute observation. Do you have any equally brilliant ideas about how to remove them?"

"Hell, what are you mad at me for?" he demanded.

"I'm not mad at you," she admitted as another tear rolled free. She was angry with herself for thinking about how compelling he was when she had far more pressing matters at hand. "I am upset for getting into this ridiculous position. It's difficult not having a scapegoat, I assure you."

Somehow he managed to keep a straight face. It wasn't every day that Sybilla Hartford admitted to being human. "Turn around and let me see."

"Not in a million years."

This time he couldn't help grinning. "Come on, Billy, no one will know. And those cholla needles do need to come out. They can cause problems if they're embedded too long."

"If you will be so kind as to look away, I shall take care of them myself."

"You can't do it yourself. The needles will just restick themselves in your hand. Besides, you can't see what you're doing and you'll only make things worse. You'll have to grant me the dubious honor of picking your stickers."

She gave him a glance meant to put an end to such foolishness. "When hell freezes over. Now turn around," she commanded.

"Yes, ma'am." Hawk complied, knowing he was right and she'd soon have to admit it.

She yanked up her gown, twisted to an uncomfortable angle, and reached tentatively for an isolated needle. The culprit quickly embedded itself in her finger. "Ouch." Reflexively, she pulled at it with her other hand and the trophy was instantly transferred. "The bloody little devil's alive."

Hawk took her hand in his, pulled the needle out with his teeth, and spat it onto the ground. He had the strength of character not to say I told you so. "Doesn't that feel better?" he asked softly. He brushed his lips across her finger and let them linger on her palm.

"Is that how it's done?" she asked as she smoothed down her nightgown with her free hand. The fabric dragged painfully on the embedded spines.

"It's the most effective method."

Sybilla jerked her hand from his. "If you think I am fool enough to submit to your removing these spines from my . . . my . . . " She faltered, completely shaken by the indelicacy of the situation. "From my . . . anatomy with your teeth, you are indeed mad."

"There're other ways," he said.

"I shall wait and ask Zora for assistance."

"We're at least thirty minutes from camp. Can you walk that far? In that condition?"

"Of course." She took three excruciating steps before admitting defeat. She'd expected discomfort, but this was much worse than she would have thought possible. The skin around the stickers throbbed, the pain radiating up her back with each step. As much as she hated to admit it, Hawk was right. The stickers had to come out. Now. And only he could take them out.

"What other ways?"

"I can remove the cholla joints by grasping them between two sticks. The prickly pear spines will have to come out one at a time." He grinned. "But no teeth, I promise."

"It would not be at all proper."

"This is one time, Billy, when comfort is more important than propriety."

Suddenly she felt as if she'd been out in the desert sun too long. Hawk was right, but the very idea of his viewing such a private part of her person made the pit of her stomach quiver. Her trembly knees only made her more determined to put on a strong facade and prove to him that such a delicate operation did not unnerve her.

She squared her shoulders and pushed her nose up a little higher. "Very well, I have no choice. But—"

"Are you spelling that with one *t* or two?" he teased.

"There are stipulations," she intoned imperiously.

"I just love stipulations." Hawk bent down on one knee and searched through an assortment of brush and stones until he found two small, sturdy twigs. He sat down on a flat rock and gestured at his lap. "Stretch your . . . uh . . . sticky wicket across here and make yourself comfortable. I'll get rid of those nasty little varmints in no time."

Lie across his lap? Her derriere exposed to his scrutiny? To his touch? Unthinkable! The very idea. "The stipulations are," she said haughtily, "that no one, absolutely no one, is to hear of this incident."

Hawk winked. "The better part of valor always has been discretion."

"And I won't have you leering at me with that asinine grin."

He arranged his features into a suitably serious expression.

"And under no circumstances whatsoever are you to touch my . . . my person."

"Well," he hedged, "that might be difficult when you consider the task at hand. But I'll be careful not to do so unless it's absolutely necessary."

"See that it isn't." Instead of reclining across his legs, she marched painfully over to another rock.

She bent over it with all the drama of Marie Antoinette at the guillotine. Truly mortified by what she was about to do, she commanded him with as much hauteur as she could manage. "Get on with it."

The cotton nightgown did little to conceal her shapely bottom, and Hawk swallowed hard at the ideas a lesser man might have acted upon. "You'd better lie across my lap," he said as he wrangled her into position, despite her protests. "It makes the job easier."

Hoping to spare her as much dignity as possible, he removed his poncho and, gingerly lifting her tattered nightgown, arranged the clothing to expose only the affected area. Her pale, soft skin was brutally pierced by a number of vicious needles.

She gasped when he bent her over his hard thighs, but she nearly fainted when she felt his hands on her. Much to her shame, her entire body began to tremble. "Please," she implored. "Get it over with."

Hawk wasn't totally insensitive. He knew what this little maneuver was costing her. He had a sudden overwhelming urge to protect her—especially from himself.

How many times had he dreamed of coming upon her in a state of undress? How many nights had he dreamed of seducing her until she succumbed to his mastery? Now all he could feel was guilt. If he had helped her out of that tree immediately and skipped the teasing, she would not now be in pain.

Sybilla waited for what seemed hours, but was really only a moment. Bracing her hands on his knees, she peered over her shoulder. "What is taking so long? Are you trying to decide how best to make me suffer?"

He gazed at her longingly before answering. "Believe me, Billy, suffering is the last thing I want you to do."

"Do get on with it."

"Oh yes, let's," he mocked enthusiastically in an

effort to detach himself from the blatant intimacy of their positions.

"Try not to sound so thrilled about it."

Given the painful frustration he was experiencing at the moment, Hawk wasn't too thrilled about anything. "Believe me, this is going to hurt me much more than it hurts you."

"Somehow I rather doubt that."

Still he hesitated. He'd seen his share of bare-bottomed women, so why did this one arouse him to unheard of levels of tenderness?

"You have done this before, haven't you?" she asked.

"No, ma'am. I don't believe I've ever plucked cactus from a pretty woman's backside. The opportunity never arose."

"I would have to get stuck with an inexperienced lout!" she complained.

He chose that moment to extract a rather stubborn quill.

"Ouch!" she cried indignantly.

"Sorry. Be careful how you talk to the sticker puller, Billy. You're in a vulnerable position, you know."

She sighed and braced herself for his next attempt. "I have been from the moment I made your acquaintance. I do not understand it at all."

Hawk extracted another needle from her tender flesh and she squirmed. "What don't you understand?"

She tried to concentrate on the conversation instead of the peril she was in—both physical and moral. "I am beginning to think Zora's superstitious mumbo jumbo is having a strange effect on me."

"Zora has a strange effect on everyone, but I suspect that's because Zora's so strange herself."

Everything about this trip was strange, Sybilla thought. And her predicament was funny in a perverse way. Sybilla wouldn't have thought she was capable of it, but she giggled. Recklessly, girlishly, and out of control. She peeked over her shoulder, knowing her gaze would collide with Hawk's.

When their eyes met, Hawk laughed with her. The joy of it set her free, and she felt happier than she'd felt in a long time. Suddenly, she wanted to be Billy and do all the wild, uninhibited things a woman named Billy would do.

"It isn't funny," Hawk spluttered.

"Then why are you laughing?" She wiped tears from her eyes.

"Because you sounded so happy. Laughter like that is contagious. You should do it more often." He eased out another sticker.

"It must get lonely for a man out here. Do you ever get lonely, Hawk?"

"Sometimes."

"You should marry. Then you could bring your wife along on these trips of yours."

"I don't want a wife, and even if I did, I'd never bring her out here. This is no place for women."

"Women belong wherever they wish to be. Am I not here?"

"Yes, you are. And with a backside full of stickers to prove it," he teased.

"But don't you ever want to have children?"

"I never thought much about it. Besides, women are usually the ones who want children. What about you?"

"I should love to have some, but I'd need a husband for that. Like you, most men don't like their wives to have any adventure, and I, for one, could not be happy without it."

"What would you do with your children while you were out adventuring?" he asked her.

She thought about that. She'd been left behind so many times as a child. She had secretly resented her father for going away and leaving her. She couldn't do that to her own children. "I would keep them with me," she told him.

Hawk smiled. "Wouldn't an infant be a bit uncomfortable on camel back?"

Sybilla propped her chin thoughtfully on her hand. "Not my child. He would love excitement as much as I do."

"That's assuming a lot," Hawk pointed out.

"What about Indian women? Do they not strap their children on cradle boards and take them everywhere? Do the children not thrive in the most primitive conditions?"

The picture she presented amused Hawk to no end. "What about propriety? Didn't you tell me it must be maintained at all costs? How do you reconcile rearing a perfect English gentleman by hanging his cradle board in a tree?"

She grinned back at him. "Who said anything about wanting a perfect English gentlemen? There are plenty of those in England and, as you recall, I left them all behind."

Hawk eased out the last of the stickers and noted that the injured area had taken on an unhealthy redness. He scooped up a handful of powdery sand and rubbed it briskly over her delicate skin.

Sybilla's head snapped up at the liberties he took, but his firm hand on her back pressed her down. "I thought it was understood there would be no touching!"

"Unless it was absolutely necessary," he repeated in an unusually husky voice. "It was necessary. The tiny hair spines of the prickly pear are impossible to get out and they can cause a hell of a lot of discomfort when rubbed or touched. Since you're most likely planning to sit on your injuries, the only solution was to rub sand on them and break them off at the skin."

"What about the part that's in me?"

"You won't be able to feel them now and they'll dissolve gradually. Don't worry about them." He smoothed down her nightgown and gave her a gentle pat on the bottom for good measure. "There you are, good as new."

Not really. Now that she'd felt his hands on her flesh, she would never be the same. She feared her spinsterish imagination would fire up at the most unlikely moments, causing no end of trouble.

Hawk turned her around and placed her limp arms around his neck. "Now say thank you," he instructed.

"Thank you, Hawk," she said softly, leaving her arms where he'd put them, but knowing she shouldn't. "I feel much better now."

"Glad to oblige." He planned to move away from her, but discovered at the last moment that he could not. Before every hard lesson he'd ever learned came back to remind him that he was making a big mistake, he kissed her. Thoroughly, soundly. As though kissing would be outlawed starting tomorrow. Desire spread through him, arousing him to dangerous levels.

Sybilla melted in Hawk's arms, overwhelmed by a powerful, consuming need. What could it hurt? Just one more kiss. She refused to admit, even to herself, that there was only one way to satisfy the hunger his touch created. She felt her breasts strain wantonly toward him and kissed him back, reveling in the searing heat of his skin upon hers. She found delicious excitement in his manly scent and thrilled to the way his eyes burned her with their blue fire.

Forgetting prudence, she knew that if he wanted to possess her here, now, she would be his. She feared she would be unable to deny him.

Hawk felt her surrender, and it jarred him back to reality. He had promised himself that he wouldn't seduce her, and as she kissed him he realized it *would* be seduction. As soft and pliable as she was right now, she still wasn't fully willing to give herself to him. She would only allow him to take her, absolving herself of responsibility. To her, their

heated kisses probably seemed the epitome of de-
bauchery.

To him, they were only a prelude to what he
hoped would follow. Since nothing could, he tore
his lips from hers and stood her away from him.

"What is it, Hawk?" she whispered, wondering
why he'd put an end to the pleasurable kisses.

He brought himself under control before answering. Walking stiffly back to the dead javelina, he
tossed it over his shoulder. "I almost forgot the pork
chops."

Chapter 11

~~~~~~~~

Riding was painful for Sybilla, but with the help of a little extra padding she managed well enough. By neither word nor deed did she reveal what had happened between her and Hawk in the desert, and she was grateful to Hawk for keeping quiet about it as well. He had explained the circumstances surrounding the rock slide, and though she tried not to worry, Sybilla was more attentive than ever to Uncle John's declining health.

They traveled through the pale glare of afternoon. Butterflies flitted around the orange blooms of globe mallow, and armor-plated geckos sunned themselves on rocks. The terrain was craggier now, the trail steeper as they climbed among the buttes and mesas. They camped just before sundown in a canyon with a spring, and everyone enjoyed the fresh meat Hawk had provided.

Although nothing unusual had happened, the tension around the campfire that night was as thick as the eerie mist that had settled unexpectedly upon them. Sybilla knew the vapor was the result of uncommon weather conditions, yet as it obscured their surroundings, she was filled with a sense of foreboding.

The others were even more deeply affected, and Zora's doomsaying reached a fever pitch. This was no ordinary fog, she claimed. It was a cover for evil, a forerunner to disaster.

Hawk, sensing that ghost stories would not be met with much enthusiasm tonight, tried to diffuse the mood by recounting the Apache creation myth. When the story was over, Zora made another pot of strong coffee, and the party passed it around glumly, waiting for the worst the haunted mountains had to offer.

Nerves stretched as taut as bowstrings, everyone jumped when Zora screamed and pointed to the fire. "Look!" She crossed herself and hid her eyes. "The ghosts have come," she wailed. "The ghosts of the lost souls."

To everyone's startled surprise, the mist was suddenly churning around them like a living thing. Seeming to take on human forms, it was like an evil miasma unloosed on the earth. The spectral figures gyrated and danced through the flames of the wildly flickering campfire.

"Egad!" John sputtered. "The woman's right for once."

Sybilla gasped. A chill chased down her back as a moist, heavy coldness settled over her. A steadily rising wind keened and swirled the dreadful apparitions around the fire. The muteness of the startled travelers was proof of the fear that became another presence among them. Somewhere in the back of her mind, in the part that wasn't totally involved in trying to understand what was happening, Sybilla sensed menace in the wind-torn darkness.

Her morbid fascination made her unable to think rationally. Hawk's strong hand briefly touched her own, comforting her. "Calm your wife, Ahmed," he instructed quietly.

"Yes, *effendi*, I shall try. But who can calm those demons in the fire?"

The smoky phantoms hovered, then swooped above the heads of the party. In a mysterious instant they disappeared as quickly and as unexpectedly as they'd come. The fog grew so dense it was impossible to see anything except the fire, which burned through the mist like a lantern-eyed cyclops.

No one moved. No one breathed.

The wind howled and the fog purled around the small knot of humans, touching them with cold fingers. Then a miniature cyclone twisted down the mouth of the canyon, loosing a terrible vacuum that aspirated the remaining fog, sucking it and their very breaths away. Immediately all was quiet again.

Sybilla tried to find a rational explanation for the occurrence, but this time she could not. Momentarily speechless, she stared at Hawk, doubt and wonder in her eyes.

Hawk waited for her scientific explanation, but none was forthcoming. Judging from the shocked expressions on the faces of the others, it was clear that it wouldn't take much to send most of them running screaming into the desert. "Calm down, everyone," he said authoritatively. "There's nothing to be alarmed about. Because of the rock formations, these hidden canyons are subject to all kinds of strange phenomenon."

Sybilla, who was normally the first to explain things away, glanced at him skeptically. The others looked relieved, clearly wanting to believe what he told them.

"My father related many strange tales of the desert," Ahmed put in. "Some things are beyond human understanding."

"It was naught but a trick of the wind," Sybilla said with regained composure.

"Indeed," John said uneasily. "I am sure that was all it was."

"No," Zora denied. "It was the spirits of this place. They do not want us here. They want us to leave. We are intruding, and death shall be our fate."

"Do not be absurd." Sybilla would sanction no such talk. "Fog is nothing but the collision of cool and hot air."

"Deny the truth," Zora told her. "Our deaths shall be on your conscience."

John glanced from one strong-willed woman to the other. "I believe I shall turn in," he blustered. "Will you wake me for my watch, Hawk?"

"Sure thing."

Claiming that a young woman needed privacy more than an old man, John had insisted Sybilla take his tent after hers was lost in the flood. He got up, his joints creaking, and retrieved his bedroll. Placing it near the fire, he crawled between the blankets and covered up his head as though that action would protect him from whatever hovered nearby.

The four remaining travelers sat around the fire without speaking. The way Ahmed and Zora glared at each other wasn't conducive to conversation, and Hawk had no desire to be drawn into one of their domestic disputes.

Sybilla was tired, and the pain in her backside made her irritable as well. She'd already dismissed the eerie fog incident as not worth contemplation and instead kept thinking about what had happened in the desert. About the way Hawk had kissed her, then turned his back on her, more interested in pork chops than in her. What was wrong with her?

Since coming West she'd seen a lot of plain, raw-boned, and downright homely married women, many of them with stairstep children. Some man had obviously found them attractive, so why couldn't *she* hold Hawk Devlin's attention long enough for more than a kiss to transpire?

Perhaps he'd decided to take her at her word when she professed to disdain his advances. Or, worse thought, maybe she was such a poor kisser that her untutored attempts left him cold. She couldn't help it if she was inexperienced in such matters. Before Hawk, she had felt no desire to experiment.

Hawk felt Sybilla's gaze on him and assumed she was angry about something. What now? He'd held back his desire that morning. He hadn't debased or misused her, or done anything to her. Women! Civilized women! He'd be damned if he could figure them out.

When he chanced another glance in her direction, her moody stare made him doubt his ability to judge the situation. Was she really angry? Or sad? It was impossible to tell from the mixed messages she sent.

Or had he offended her tender sensibilities by having the effrontery to pull those damn stickers out of her butt? Was she upset because he'd kissed her? Or was she mad because he hadn't tried more? As he watched, she stuck her haughty nose into the air, excused herself, and left the fire. He got up and, after a quick detour to his saddlebags, caught up with her at her tent.

"Wait up a minute, Billy."

"Yes?" Sybilla turned hopefully to him.

"I need to talk to you." He motioned for her to follow him. He stepped into the shadows on the far side of the tent, away from prying eyes.

She didn't know what to expect, but she followed him anyway. The memory of his kiss made her steps falter and her heart quicken. She attempted to hide her nervousness with diffidence. He must not know how deeply affected she was by his nearness. "What is it you wish to speak to me about?"

Hawk noticed Billy's flushed face and reminded himself that the feverish glow might be a result of her run-in with the cholla. He touched her cheek with the back of his fingers and found her skin warm. "Lord, Billy, you're burning up."

She ducked shyly away from him. "Am I?" she whispered, trying not to want his caress. Recalling the intimacy with which he had already touched her, she said, "I should think it is no more than well-deserved embarrassment."

"There's no need to be embarrassed. I didn't tell anyone about your accident."

"I thank you for that. You are indeed a gentleman."

Hawk didn't feel like a gentleman. All he wanted was to kiss her again, but she was oblivious to his need. "Yeah, well, I'm sure my old deportment teacher would be gratified to hear that. Are you sure you're all right?"

"Quite all right." Being near him evoked such feelings of euphoria in her, that Sybilla could do little more than echo his words. She was suffused by a languid warmth, and her eyelids grew heavy. A soft smile touched her lips.

Was there ever a more innocent temptress, Hawk wondered as he fought the urge to take advantage of the moment. He reminded himself why he'd brought her back here in the first place. Reaching into his pocket, he took out a small tin. The salve was an old Apache recipe, and it would not only dull the residual pain she must be feeling but also prevent infection.

"Take this," he said as he dropped the tin into her hand.

Sybilla frowned when she realized that the object she held had been his reason for this rendezvous. How foolish she was to hope he'd had other things on his mind. Once more, she had almost revealed her true feelings. "What is it?"

"It's a salve and it's good for what ails you." For his own ailment, a bucket of cold water would serve best.

She opened the tin, and a pungent odor assailed her. She tried not to wrinkle her nose in distaste. "What is it made of?"

"Mostly medicinal plants and deer fat. It's not prettied up like you're used to, and it doesn't smell like flowers, but it works."

"No, thank you." Driven by the need to retreat before he discovered her disappointment, she thrust the tin back at him and whirled around.

Hawk caught her arm and slapped the tin of salve

back into her ungrateful hand. "Look, I don't know what's wrong with you, but you'll take this salve and use it, or I'll put it on you myself. Infection can be an ugly thing."

"Why do you care?" she asked stiffly. "My demise could only make your life easier."

"That's a valid point," he agreed. "But your uncle would probably want to bury your remains in merry old England. And I'd have to haul your smelly carcass to the nearest depot, fighting off buzzards all the way."

"You really can be a brute," she said quietly. "And to think I had actually entertained thoughts of allowing you to kiss me." Realizing what she'd admitted, she clasped her palm over her mouth, threw the tin to the ground, and bolted into her tent.

Stunned into inaction by her words, Hawk stood for a few long moments, considering them. She had actually been *thinking* about kissing him? Well, hell! How was he supposed to know that? She hadn't acted as though she'd had anything even remotely resembling kissing on her mind. She was a confounding woman, one that he might never understand. After all, he had little experience figuring out difficult females.

The women of his acquaintance had let him know right away what they wanted from him. The problem was, Billy was so mulish she didn't know herself what she wanted. A man could go crazy! He picked up the salve and tossed it in the tent after her, uncaring if he beaned her in the process. He didn't believe in mistreating women, but this one surely needed a good whack on the head.

He stomped back to the campfire in frustration. Zora and Ahmed were arguing, but when they saw him they retreated into stony silence. Hawk squatted by the fire and poked it with a stick, hoping they would go away and leave him alone to think in peace.

Zora's expression was angry, and sarcasm lined

her tone when she turned to him. "You waste your time with that one." She tipped her head toward Sybilla's tent. "She fights you as hard as she fights her own desires."

Hawk added wood to the fire and said nothing. Zora seemed inclined to carry on all by herself. "If you want her, take her. It is what she needs." She kicked the sand. "You call yourself a man, but you do not act like a man."

Hawk had the feeling she was addressing Ahmed as well as himself. "She's not my problem."

"She is a problem for us all. Because of her lust for gold we will die, and because of your lust for her you will allow it." Zora spat in the sand.

Ahmed jumped up, a fierce look on his face. "Go to bed, Zora," he commanded.

She laughed mirthlessly, but she didn't defy her husband. With a toss of her head and a swish of her skirt, she stalked off and disappeared into the striped tent.

Ahmed's expression was sad as he watched his wife fling herself away. He sat down across from Hawk. "I should go to the camels," he said without moving to do so.

Hawk reached for the coffeepot and poured them both a fresh cup. Women!

Ahmed took a sip, studied the contents of his cup, then blurted, "A thousand pardons, *effendi*, but you are most wise in all things, and I have need of your wisdom."

Hawk looked at him over the rim of his cup. "I'm not wise in all things, Ahmed." He could read a trail with ease, but he couldn't read Billy at all.

"I need your help, *effendi*. It is Zora. She shames me."

Hawk stirred uncomfortably. Women were hardly his area of expertise, so how could he help Ahmed with his vixen wife? "I'm afraid I'm fresh out of ideas where women are concerned, friend."

"There is no one else I can turn to, and as you

see, Zora grows more and more unruly each day. I am saddened by her bad behavior, but know not how to change it."

Hawk shifted his gaze to Billy's silhouette in the lighted tent and watched as she brushed her hair. When Ahmed sighed beside him, Hawk clapped him on the shoulder. "Friend, women are one of life's biggest mysteries. I don't think men are meant to understand the rules they operate by."

"But you must help me. I have nowhere else to turn, and I am just about to reach the top of my rope."

"The end of your rope," Hawk supplied helpfully.

"Just so." Ahmed's dark eyes peered at him eagerly, as if he expected Hawk to supply solutions as easily.

Recalling how devoted Ahmed was to his camels, Hawk made a suggestion. "Maybe you should try to spend more time with her."

"No! She kicks and bites and snarls worse than Delilah."

He sympathized with Ahmed's plight. Billy was too refined to kick and snarl, but she was no less unapproachable. "It could be she just wants you to notice her."

"I notice her. I watch her with the eagle eye every minute, *effendi*, and still she is difficult." Ahmed hung his head. "Should I beat her?"

"I don't think that would solve anything." Hawk shook his head, wishing Ahmed had asked for advice on something he knew more about. Like horses. He had a sudden inspiration.

He mentally dug up some horse lore and generalized it to cover Ahmed's problem. "Overguidance distracts a woman, makes her rebellious, nervous." Ahmed nodded expectantly, so Hawk continued his lesson on horsebreaking. At least he was giving the man a direction. "Use gentle pressure and apply it delicately. Spend as much time near her as possible and don't let anyone else take care of her or feed her.''

Ahmed looked puzzled. "Feed her, *effendi?*"

Warming to his subject, Hawk kept one eye on the silhouette outlined on the tent. ''Put your hands on her every chance you get. Let her get used to you.''

"But that is not possible.''

"Why not?'' he asked tentatively, making himself look away from Billy's delectable form.

"She refuses my advances.''

"She does?''

Ahmed hung his head. "She scorned me once. That was when I swore never to touch her again unless she got down on her knees and begged. That is her punishment.''

It sounded as if Ahmed had punished himself. "That's a problem, friend.''

"Yes,'' he agreed sadly. "I have great difficulty to stay away from her pallet. I cannot go on this way much longer. Just when I think she is about to beg for my favor, she flashes her eyes.''

"Does she?'' Hawk didn't point out that she'd been flashing more than her eyes. "Why don't you try tempting her, Ahmed? Gentle her, tease her. You know what to do.''

Ahmed looked skeptical. "Do you think she will beg if I do this?''

"Why is that so important? Lovemaking should be a mutual decision. No one should have to beg for love. It should be given freely.'' Every word of advice he spouted to Ahmed inspired Hawk to try harder to solve the puzzle that was Billy.

"Yes, yes, you are right of course. Thank you, Wise One.'' A look of immense relief flooded Ahmed's dark face as he gazed hopefully toward his tent. "You have turned my darkness into dawn, my misery into hope. May Allah bestow upon you a thousand blessings for your benevolence.'' He jumped up and made his exit in the usual manner, by bowing obeisance.

Hawk had an idea that when Ahmed's watch was over, he'd make a beeline to that tent to settle things with his errant wife. Hawk was still grinning when he caught sight of Billy's silhouette again. His smile faded as he watched her moving around inside the tent.

Maybe it was all that talk of touching and teasing, but he felt a heat rise up in him. He'd never been in such an unlikely position before, so jumpy he didn't know "Come here" from "Sic 'im." He stood up, tossed what was left of his coffee onto the ground, and strode purposefully toward Billy's tent.

He was determined to find out what she wanted from him, once and for all. When he got there, he was so intent on his mission, he overlooked etiquette. Shoving back the flap, he stepped inside unannounced. He'd planned to use the salve as a pretext, but he could only stand in the door, stunned.

She was kneeling on a towel, her frilly, knee-length drawers and camisole a delightful contrast to her normally tailored attire. The filmy garments could not conceal the perfection of her small body as she bent over a washbasin and pushed the wild mane of hair over her head. She lifted a sopping rag and squeezed cool water over the back of her soapy neck.

She flung her head back, eyes closed, and slid the rag slowly over the slim column of her neck. The soapy water trickled down between her breasts, and her small nipples were clearly revealed as they thrust against the thin damp fabric.

He had no right to be here like this. Billy was a lady and deserved better. He should turn around and leave before she realized he was there, but he was so entranced by the sight of her sweet beauty, by her vulnerability, that he just stood there, staring. What was he thinking of?

Sybilla heard a rustle and opened her eyes. She ceased breathing when she saw Hawk standing in her tent, watching her intently, an expression of heart-rending tenderness on his face. His eyes, dark and heavy-lidded, raked over her.

He stood tall, his proud, powerful body filling the small tent. His breathing was quick and shallow, and a muscle jumped in his jaw. She was fully aware of his arousal and knew she should cover herself immediately.

But knowing and doing were two different things, and Sybilla was too mesmerized to move. She gave herself up to the moment and indulged some of her more disquieting fantasies. She remembered a very naked and bronzed Hawk, and unexpectedly wanton images laid siege to her common sense. This man wanted her.

And she wanted him.

It was several long moments before Hawk could speak. "I'll leave if you tell me to," he said softly.

Sybilla panicked when she thought he might go. With all the dangerous things that had happened on this trip, it was possible she might not survive. Did she want to die without ever experiencing the wonders of lovemaking? Hawk's eyes promised so much, and for the first time in her life she wanted to know all the secrets between men and women.

He made no move toward her as he waited for her decision. Once made, there would be no turning back. If she denied this moment, it would be lost forever. If she gave herself to him without reservation, would she not be lost?

No. Love was part of life, and it was time to stop denying the powerful attraction between them. "Don't go," she whispered.

Her whole being was filled with waiting as his well-muscled body moved toward her with the easy grace of a desert cat. He stopped in front of her. "Do you know what will happen if I stay?"

She trembled expectantly, well aware of the commitment made by her invitation. "I want you to make love to me," she admitted shyly, still uncomfortable speaking the words aloud. "But I confess an appalling lack of experience."

Hawk sank down on his knees in front of her, anxious to make things as easy as possible for her. It took strength to keep his hands at his sides when all he wanted to do was wrap her in his arms. But he would have to move slowly, reassuring her every step of the way.

"I was afraid of what might happen if I came here tonight, Billy."

"You afraid, Hawk? Why, you are the bravest man I've ever met."

"My fear came from not knowing if you would accept me. I don't understand you, and I don't know what you expect from me."

She stroked his cheek. "Always the gentleman. Were you so reluctant to compromise me? Or to be compromised by me?" she asked.

"I don't know. Both, I guess." Hawk had seldom felt at ease with Billy. She had always maintained a distance that enforced rational behavior. The times he'd kissed her, daring to push those limits, he'd expected her to observe them and she had. The fact that she was ignoring them now prompted him to ask, "Why are you doing this?"

"That fog tonight made me realize something I've been trying to deny since this trip began. Things *are* different out here. Even time is different, and we cannot always behave as we would in a more civilized place. Events are shaped by needs, not by convention. I never felt those needs—until now.

"Tonight, when I realized I wanted you to kiss me but was too afraid to do anything about it, I knew I was trying to live by rules that have no meaning on the frontier. Rules dictated by a society that I had already turned away from. I do not want to let rules keep me from experiencing life."

"I'd assumed rules were important to you."

"So they have been. Because by allowing those

rules to dictate my behavior, I didn't have to take responsibility for my actions."

"What do you want from me?"

"I want to experience everything you can teach me."

"Are you sure?"

Her hesitation was so brief, it was almost nonexistent. "I am certain."

His need precluded further speech. He pulled her to him, and her lips parted in surprise. He covered them with his own, his sigh a deeply felt echo of hers. His mouth slanted over hers with slow, sensuous intent as he held her close.

Sybilla was rocked by emotions so powerful that they threatened to consume her. He leaned back, and she immediately felt the loss of his warmth. She framed his face with her hands tentatively, unsure if her actions were too bold or perhaps not bold enough. She didn't know how to please him. "Tell me what to do, Hawk," she murmured.

"Listen to your feelings, Billy. Don't think about it and don't worry about whether it is right or wrong. Tonight, in this tent, there can be no wrong between us." He leaned over and extinguished the lantern.

Emboldened by his encouragement and the darkness, Sybilla brushed her lips over his and felt the delightful, coarse skin of his cheek. There were such wonderful differences between men and women, so much to explore. But uncertainty prevented her from acting on her awakening impulses.

She shivered when he cupped her breasts through the fabric of her camisole and toyed with the taut nipples. The pleasure she felt was stronger than her inhibitions, and she let them slip away, unheeded and unwanted.

Hawk's voice vibrated with emotion when he said, "You're so beautiful, Billy." He slid his hands around her waist and pulled her against him until she could feel his arousal. Slowly he tugged the ribbon closures on her camisole and gently slipped it off her shoulders. She gasped, whether in shock or delight he couldn't tell. When she made no protest, he touched her lightly, reverently. Her breasts were lavish with their intimate and welcoming warmth.

Sybilla's heart raced so fast, she felt dizzy. When Hawk trembled, she realized she possessed the same power over him as he did over her. It gave her the self-assurance she needed to unbutton his shirt with shaky fingers. She wanted no barriers between them now that she'd made her decision. She wanted it all.

Hawk held his breath as she slowly undid the buttons. His hands slid down her back, and his fingers spread across her flaring hips. She groaned and curled herself against his body, as if unable to get close enough.

He curved his hands under her bottom and lifted her until she straddled his hips. He fully expected her to protest such intimacy, but she only twined her arms around his neck. This newly aggressive Billy was exciting beyond all his expectations.

Sybilla slipped Hawk's shirt down his arms. Tentatively she placed her hands on his bare, nearly smooth chest. At his ragged intake of breath, her confidence grew, and she allowed her palms to drift downward until they rested on his hips.

She leaned forward until her breasts brushed his chest lightly, and the shock of feeling her skin against his made her gasp with forbidden pleasure.

Hawk dragged her bedroll down from her cot and spread it on the sandy floor of the tent. Gently he eased her onto her back and out of her pantalets, his hands lingering on the insides of her slim thighs. He shed his own clothes and stretched out beside her.

"You're so sweet." His words were a shaky whisper against her cheek as he sought her earlobe and nibbled it gently. He pulled away slightly, his eyes shadowed with desire. "The thought of making you

soft with passion and pleasure is almost more than
I can bear.''

Sybilla sighed. She'd overheard married women
whispering about their connubial relations, but they
had made it seem so disagreeable that she was unprepared for the wonderful sensations Hawk awoke
in her.

He slid his hands up and down her ribs, and her
heart beat faster. His fingers kneaded her trembling
breasts, scorching her flesh like fire. Lightly he
grasped her shoulders and drew her to him, his lips
brushing hers in a feathery kiss.

Once, twice, he repeated the delicate caress, then
his mouth hardened and his lips sank hungrily onto
hers. His tongue explored the warmth of her mouth.

She was caught in a sensual storm. His touch set
her body ablaze and she trembled, longing for more.
She didn't know what to expect, but she possessed
an emptiness that cried out to be filled by the man
who held her. She kissed him back, pressing her
mouth hard against his, reveling in the taste of him.

Hawk's hand slipped between her legs and teased
them apart. She stiffened, and he knew that what
he did in the next few moments was critical. It would
make this experience either pleasurable or painful
for her. The responsibility made him tremble.
''Don't worry, Billy. Like I said, there can be nothing wrong between us. Relax and let me show you.''

She had placed herself in his hands, and now she
had to demonstrate her trust. It took a great effort,
but she turned away all thoughts and fears and
opened up to his touch. She reached for him blindly,
running her hands across the smooth strength of his
shoulders and back, entwining her fingers in his
hair. Hawk's gentle massage sent fresh currents of
yearning through her.

She surrendered to his magic, the taste of his
kisses, the sleek hardness of his body, the sorcery
of his touch as he discovered her most intimate secrets. It was a wonder that this strong, tough man

was capable of such exquisite gentleness. Not an inch of her body escaped his loving attention, and she luxuriated in the new and marvelous sensations.

"Do I please you, Billy? Talk to me."

"Oh yes." Her words came in panting bursts.

Nothing could stop him after that. He groaned hoarsely, wrapped her in his arms, then curled his body around and over hers.

Sybilla hadn't guessed at the power she was unleashing when she asked Hawk to love her. His mouth devoured hers from every conceivable angle, and his hungry body covered her blossoming one. As inexperienced as she was, she gloried in the sheer, blinding intensity of his passion. A passion that inflamed him and drove him toward one end.

To possess her.

The force of his desire left no room for thought or reason. It invaded her senses and reduced the sum of her world to a single need—her need for Hawk.

His desire was her desire, his need her need. She felt a fleeting moment of pain when Hawk penetrated the last barrier between them. He kissed her gently and whispered sweet assurances in her ear. Fear was gone, pain unimportant. As Hawk moved rhythmically inside her, pleasure overwhelmed everything else.

The weight of his damp, powerful body atop hers, the scent of him, the earthy words he spoke, all of it was wildly exciting. He rocked against her, and intuitively she locked her legs around him. Time seemed to stand still and suspend the long moments in ever closing spirals of ecstasy.

Each movement brought him deeper inside her, creating exquisite harmonies and a joy she had never guessed existed. Hawk's lips traced a sensuous path down her neck, and she burned with an innocent desire. Her answering moan inspired him to push them both toward the apex of desire until a burst of white-hot heat made them one in a sudden, spasmodic passion.

Sybilla's breath came in frantic pants and she gripped Hawk desperately, lest she float away completely on a cloud of joy. She had never known such satisfaction of body and spirit was possible. Tears of happiness overflowed her eyes and trailed down her cheeks. Was this love?

Hawk collapsed beside her, and noticing her tears, wiped them away with his thumb. Nuzzling her neck, he asked softly, "Billy? Are you all right?"

"I am better than all right," she murmured.

"No regrets?" he prompted, fearful of her answer.

"I am not a woman who makes decisions lightly, Hawk. You should realize that I do not regret them either."

He had never met a woman like Billy, so how should he judge her reaction? "I just thought that since we—"

She looked at him nervously, wondering if her words had been too bold. "Should I feel guilty, Hawk?" she asked with simple honesty. "Is it wrong that I do not feel the bite of conscience? I apologize if I'm supposed to bemoan the loss of my virginity." Leaning over him, she cupped his face in her hands and kissed him. "But I did not lose it. I gave it to you."

"It was a wonderful gift."

"But nothing compared to what you gave me."

"What was that, Billy?"

"My womanhood, Hawk. You've given me a new maturity, an understanding I never had before."

He longed for the light so he could see her face, but knew it would break the spell. He pulled her to him in the darkness and settled her head on his shoulder, stroking the tangled hair from her face. When he'd come in here tonight, he'd thought to settle matters between them, to discover what she wanted from him. Now she'd given herself to him completely and without reservation. But nothing was settled. If anything, he was more confused than before.

She hadn't asked him for promises, and neither had she offered any. What would the future hold for them? They had bound themselves together by actions, but not by words. Now was the time to speak them, but he didn't know the right ones. Even if he did, he wasn't sure Billy would want to hear them.

It was better to say nothing than to say the wrong thing, so he remained silent and held her as if he'd never let her go.

Chapter 12

For the sake of appearances, Hawk and Sybilla tried to conceal from the others the strong new feelings they shared. After that first hesitant night, through his gentle tutoring and her eagerness to learn, they discovered all the joys of lovemaking. Hawk slipped into her tent between watches and as the nights went by, they came to live for those stolen hours.

They didn't waste their brief time together talking about the future or what it would bring, but each seemed to know that no matter how much they denied it, tomorrow would come. They would have to confront it eventually.

Love, even love as wondrous as what they found in each other's arms, was not blind, and both realized that this idyll in the desert could not last forever. There was an unspoken understanding that someday they would have to go back to their own lives, lives as different as any two could be.

Hawk felt he couldn't ask Billy to share his. What could he offer her? He owned no property, no assets. For the first time, he examined the life he'd willingly chosen and found it lacking. Maybe roughing it on a gold claim in an uncivilized territory suited him, but it was not good enough for a lady like Billy. He was accustomed to the solitude, the hostility, the unexpected violence of this country.

For all her love of adventure, Billy was a gentle girl. His land would not be good to her.

Of course, he didn't have to remain a prospecting bronc buster. He possessed plenty of totally useless knowledge. But what good was a classical education out here? He could stand on the corner in Tucson, reciting Shakespeare and passing the hat, but he didn't think there would be much call for that skill. He was qualified to be a schoolmaster, but considering his reputation, he didn't think local parents would be too thrilled about entrusting the care of their precious children to him.

The gold was another option. If they found it, he would be a man of independent means. With his share he could give Billy all she deserved. A perverse part of him chided that if they found the gold, Billy would be a woman of means, even more independent. Once she had her share she wouldn't need him at all.

For the next few days, their search for the landmarks on the map filled Hawk with mixed feelings. He wanted to find the treasure because he knew how much success meant to Billy. Yet every step put them one step closer to an inevitable parting.

Sybilla, for the first time in her life, tried not to think. What she was doing with Hawk in her tent at night did not bear close examination by light of day. According to everything she had ever been taught, it was wrong. But it did not feel wrong when he kissed her. When he made sweet love to her and held her close afterward, she felt no guilt or remorse, only joy. What kind of woman was she that she could not ask for the promises she needed so desperately? What kind of man was Hawk that he couldn't give them?

After a particularly rigorous day of riding through the relentlessly unchanging landscape, looking for clues that might no longer be there, Uncle John suffered an attack of heat stroke. Sybilla questioned the practicality of pushing themselves so hard as she nursed him. That evening the group camped in the shadow of a towering mesa, and as they sat around the campfire discussing the next day's travel plans, she spoke her mind.

"Sometimes I think we could wander around out here for the rest of our lives and never find the gold."

"That does not sound like you, Sybilla dear," John put in. "You are ever the one to trudge onward." The old man's dysentery had been arrested by Hawk's medicine, but the heat prostration had left him weak and pale.

"It's these rocks," Hawk said. "They all look alike." He and Billy had spent hours poring over the map, searching for clues that would lead them to the mountain that looked like a half-buried heart. His gaze traveled up the face of the craggy mesa. "Tomorrow I'll climb to the top and take a look around. I want all of you to rest and renew your strength."

He was especially concerned about John. He was a game old guy, but he wouldn't last much longer without rest. If he continued the way he was going, he'd be dead from apoplexy within a week.

Smiling at each other, Ahmed and Zora agreed that Hawk's plan was a good one. Since the night Hawk had talked to Ahmed, their battles had dwindled down to occasional mild disagreements.

"I shall go with you," Sybilla said. Maybe if she and Hawk had some real time alone, they could discuss the problems they faced. Maybe if they could be frank, they could come up with solutions.

"No." Hawk sipped his coffee.

"Whyever not? I've met every task you have set me, have I not?"

He did look up then, and smile that curved his lips told her just what tasks he was thinking of. "Oh, you've been an avid student, all right."

She flushed and hoped the gathering gloom hid her embarrassment. "I am going with you."

Hawk was proud of the way Billy had adapted to

life in the desert. She was strong and capable. But she was still a woman, and she didn't have any business doing something as dangerous as climbing a mountain. "It's too risky, and you'll only slow me down."

She didn't like his explanation and refused to give up so easily. "This is my expedition," she reminded him. "I'm going and that's that."

The next morning Hawk and Sybilla set off on their arduous climb before the sun was fully up. When they stopped to rest, she took out her father's compass, a large silver-plated model nearly three inches in diameter, and shaded the glass top with her hand. Thomas Hartford had relied on this same instrument on many of his field trips, and it had saved his life more than once by unerringly pointing north. But now as she held it, watching in disbelieving fascination, the shiny black needle whirled, stopped, pointed east, then west, then whirled again. Crazily. Impossibly.

"I can't understand it," she remarked uneasily. "It seems unable to find north."

Hawk glanced over her shoulder and shrugged. He was still miffed because she'd insisted on accompanying him after he'd explained how dangerous the climb might be. "Stranger things have happened. There may be forces at work here that don't want us to intrude in this area."

She looked up sharply. It always surprised her when Hawk alluded to the supernatural, although by this time she supposed she should expect such nonsense from him. If nothing else, he possessed a vivid imagination and a natural storyteller's enthusiasm for the bizarre.

"Save your tall tales for Ahmed and Zora," she said disdainfully. "There must be a simple explanation."

He stood still, his head cocked to one side as

though listening to something impossible to hear. "They're near."

"Who is it this time?" she asked impatiently. "The Phantom Camel? The Lost Tribe? The Ghost of Christmas Past?"

"The shadow spirits of the long dead."

"Oh, *them*." She feigned relief. "For a moment there you had me worried."

"Don't you feel their presence?" Hawk asked reasonably, as though inquiring if she'd read the morning news.

"I feel hot and tired." It disturbed her that such an earthy man could entertain such unearthly thoughts. Dropping the sarcasm, she added, "You don't really expect me to believe that Indian ghosts are making my compass act crazy? That's impossible."

"Nothing is impossible in these mountains. You should know that by now."

She could not accept the sudden failure of the compass any more than she could accept Hawk's preposterous theory. Her logical mind grappled for a rational explanation as she watched the erratic twirling of the needle. She was seized by the unreasonable thought that there might not be a rational explanation and shivered in spite of the heat. What kind of place was this where one could not depend on something as infallible as a compass?

"Of course, there could be mineral deposits in the area that interfere with the magnetic field," Hawk offered belatedly with a grin.

"Of course. A mineral deposit," she repeated, latching on to that alternative because it made more sense than any other. "Why didn't I think of that? And why didn't you say so in the first place and leave the spirits of your hapless ancestors out of it?"

It was a rhetorical question that required no answer. "Think what you want, if it makes you comfortable. I'd hate for you to tax your scientific mind with such unscientific thoughts." Hawk took a swig from his canteen and wiped his mouth with the back of his hand.

"Is it wrong to believe only in reality?"

"Ah, but in whose perception of reality? My mother's people believed in a spirit world which co-existed with their own. For them that was reality. One of these days maybe you'll open your mind to other possibilities."

"Are you accusing me of being narrow-minded?" she demanded.

"Right now your mind is so narrow, a gnat would have to turn sideways to walk through it. But someday maybe you'll admit that there are things in the world that defy rational explanation." He extended the canteen. "We have a hard climb ahead of us. The trail goes straight up for a ways before it gets steep."

The tepid water tasted unpleasantly tinny, but it served to clear her head. She put away the compass, confident that Hawk was right about the mineral deposits—and absurdly wrong about the ghosts. He just said those things to poke fun at her, to remind her of the differences between them so that she would not get too smug or secure in his attentions.

As though she needed such reminders. Not once during the past week had she completely forgotten that he came from a world very unlike her own.

The climb was all Hawk had promised, and more. The sun was a merciless hammer that beat them down at every step. Since her last encounter with a cholla, Sybilla was careful to avoid the ornery cactus, but such caution made it difficult to maintain the grinding pace Hawk set. She cursed the prickly underbrush that she had long since decided had been created as one of God's jokes on mankind.

Hot, tired, and wholly out of sorts, she struggled against the temptation to act like Delilah and plop down, refusing to go on. But she knew that it was best to plod onward, slowly and steadily. It was all right to pause at times to catch her breath, but it was a mistake to sit down. Climbing relied on heart and will as much as on legs and lungs.

The sky was like a vast pale bowl turned upside down over the earth. It prevented even the slightest relief-bringing breezes to reach the parched land, and not even a shredded cloud offered respite from the unrelenting sun.

Perspiration trickled down Sybilla's back, and her hands were slick inside the heavy gloves she dared not remove. Her legs ached from the unaccustomed exertion, and she wished she'd agreed to stay behind with the others to tend Uncle John.

Surely this grueling climb was her punishment for trying to prove she was every bit as stout-hearted as Hawk. If only he weren't so hard to talk to and would give her the opening she needed, she would challenge his reluctance to commit himself to her in some small way.

"How much farther?" she called to the tireless man ahead of her. He leaned forward as he climbed, his well-defined leg muscles straining the thick fabric of his trousers. She was reminded that, despite his strength and blatant masculinity, he was a gentle lover. She knew from his taciturnity today that he was displeased by her presence. After all they'd shared, she was still too proud to ask why.

"Getting tired?" His voice was maddeningly cheerful.

"No!"

"Then it doesn't matter how much farther it is, does it?"

Sybilla swatted a buzzing insect away from her face. Bloody hell, but he could be insufferable. It made it even more intolerable that the real reason she'd set herself up for this Herculean effort was so that she could talk to him privately. She was frustrated by her inability to understand him. He behaved one way in her tent at night, and quite another by day. She realized the necessity of his actions; it was the ease with which he made the transition that made her seethe.

She watched his ascent, not unlike that of a surefooted mountain goat, and realized with a disconcerting start that she was dangerously close to falling in love with him.

What would become of her when the journey was over? What role could she play in his life? These questions pressed upon her as heavily as the heat.

She glanced down the way they'd come, down the narrow trail that was hemmed in on both sides by steep, rocky walls, down farther to where the thin ribbon of the Salt River flowed lazily through a maze of long-forgotten canyons. The place was eerie in its rock-bound silence, which was somehow full of the voices of the past.

But they weren't the voices of spirits, as Hawk would have her believe. No, what spoke to her was the voice of prehistory. Her scholar's curiosity aroused, she wondered about the feet that had beaten out this path so many centuries before. Had they first crossed the Bering Strait land bridge in a migrant wave from Asia, as some ethnologists believed?

Whatever their origins, those first people had eventually evolved into a fairly sophisticated race. They had settled in this harsh land, digging a network of canals from the Salt River to irrigate their fields of corn, squash, and beans. This much she knew from her studies. That and the fact that they built extensive cliff dwellings, cremated their dead, and disappeared sometime in the fifteenth century.

By the time Montoya and his fellow Spaniards arrived, the land between the Salt and Gila rivers was occupied by the Pimas, who spoke of those ancient peoples as the Hohokam, ''the ones who went away.'' What she didn't know, nor did anyone else for that matter, was why they had left.

She looked up the trail, expecting to see Hawk's steadily ascending figure, and was startled to find

that he had disappeared from view. Walled in as
they were, there was no place for him to have fallen,
and he could not have simply vanished into thin air.
The fact that he seemed to have done just that sent
a chill down her spine.

"Hawk!" Her voice quivered in the heat-
shimmered air, but there was no answer. She called
again and again. The only reply was a hollow echo,
the taunting replica of her own voice. She didn't
know where he had gone, but the thought that she
was suddenly, inexplicably alone in this place gave
her new energy. She redoubled her efforts, sending
down a shower of pebbles as she scrambled frantically up the trail.

It took her several minutes to reach the cliff where
she had last seen Hawk. She panted and clutched
the painful stitch in her side. She leaned against the
hot rock wall, her head down, trying to catch her
breath, then glanced around to see where he might
have gone.

Narrowing slightly, the trail curved around a large
outcropping of hanging rock. Loose rubble from a
landslide littered the way. Maybe if she climbed up
on the largest of the boulders in the path, she could
see where he'd gone.

Before she had time to put that thought into action, she felt, rather than saw, another possibility.
A draft of chill air, like a demon's breath, pricked
her skin into gooseflesh and she was drawn to its
source. A cave. Partially hidden by rubble and further obscured by overgrown vegetation, it had almost escaped her attention.

She approached it warily, a yawning black hole
slashed out of the rock. "Hawk?" she called tentatively. The entrance was no more than a couple of
meters across. The inside—as far as she could tell—
was much wider, perhaps as much as five times the
width of the opening. It was too dark to see very far
into it, but her voice ricocheted off the interior walls,

giving an impression of immense emptiness.
"Hawk, where are you?"

He did not answer.

She inched her way into the cave, amazed at how
fast the darkness swallowed up the light that seeped
through the opening. Those weak rays of sunlight,
fractured by the walls of surrounding rock, had little
chance of penetrating such immutable emptiness.
She stopped at the edge of that light and called to
Hawk again.

The void seemed to swell and groan around her,
touching her with its icy fingers and devouring her
words. Had Hawk ventured into the recesses of this
dark place, only to fall into an unseen abyss? Was
he even now lying broken and injured and beyond
her help? The thought clutched at her heart.

"If you can hear me, Hawk Devlin, I would advise
you to answer." In the tomblike silence, her voice
was edged with panic. "Don't make me come in after you." She started in before the warning left her
lips, driven by the notion that she could somehow
help Hawk, if he needed it.

"Gad, it's darker than a wolf's mouth in here."
She fumbled in her pocket for the packet of lucifers
and struck one to dispel the gloom. "There, that's
better. Now we can see what we have here."

She turned in a slow circle, her breath catching in
her throat as the feeble light from the match illuminated a scene so macabre that at first her mind refused to accept it. But it *was* real. Strewn about the
interior of the cave, which may have extended as far
as fifteen meters into the mountain, were piles of
human corpses, all of which were in varying, and
grisly, stages of decomposition.

The close, dry air of the cave had slowed the process so that some of the skeletons were still covered
with a tight, mummified skin that had shrunk and
pulled back from the mandibles, baring yellowed
teeth in grotesque grins. Dozens of empty eye sock-

ets stared back at her, as if reproaching her for disturbing this unholy resting place.

Some of the bodies had been crushed by the avalanche of rocks she'd first noted outside, but most of them had been riddled by a barrage of bullets. The dusty, ragged clothing of the bodies bore the coppery stains of incredible blood loss. Bony fingers were still clamped over wounds from which life had long since drained out.

Seconds slogged by like hours, and Sybilla's shocked gaze snagged on a knot of much smaller skeletons, children who'd obviously huddled in fear from their attackers. Several of the tiny skulls, serrated by gunfire, had crumbled and fallen away. Shards of splintered bone littered the floor.

Caught in the unshakable grip of horror and revulsion, she could not move or utter a sound until the match burned down to her fingers and she let out a yelp of pain. Reflexively, she extinguished the light, plunging herself, and the corpses, back into darkness.

With death in its grimmest form all around her, she bolted for the entrance. But her senses were confused by terror and she stumbled backward, tripping and falling into a musty bundle of rattling bones, spidery hair, and rotting cloth. She screamed as she struggled out of the skeleton's embrace and crawled across the dusty floor on her hands and knees, bumping into corpse after corpse in her panic.

God, what was this place? What unthinkable thing had happened here? She struggled against the urge to retch and forced herself to stop and take a deep draft of the musty air. What was the matter with her? She had seen mummies and skeletons before; had, in fact, helped to excavate ancient burial sites.

As great as her revulsion was the shame that she had reacted with primitive fear instead of the scientific detachment on which she prided herself. These poor people were dead and could not harm her. But she could hurt herself by letting her terror dictate her actions.

She closed her eyes in an effort to block out the image made even more horrific by the knowledge that this was no ancient burial ground. It was the site of a massacre. From the sickening glimpses she'd had of the Indians' bodies—for she was sure that they were Indian—it was evident that they had all died violently.

She closed her eyes so tightly that scintillas of light pricked her retinas. Her heartbeat filled the cave with its erratic tattoo, and the blood coursed through her veins so fast she feared they would burst.

She pressed her fists to her chest, calling back the composure that had deserted her. When she opened her eyes, she would look for the light from the entrance and make her way carefully toward that. Though she still clutched the oilskin-wrapped packet of matches in her hand, she could not bring herself to strike another one. She wasn't willing to view the nightmare again. Not yet.

A sudden tug on her arm made her scream. And scream. And scream. Despite her earlier resolve, she was sure one of the skeletons had reanimated and was about to punish her for blundering in where she didn't belong.

"Billy! It's me. Open your eyes, dammit."

The sound of Hawk's voice made her tremble with relief. He was not hurt, he was safe, and he was here. Thank God. She opened her eyes cautiously and saw him kneeling beside her, shaking her with one hand. The cave was illuminated by a bright torch he held overhead.

"What the hell are you doing in here?" he demanded.

"Looking for you." She shuddered when she saw the bodies again and turned her gaze to his. "I thought you might have fallen in here . . . that you might be hurt."

"Only a fool would stumble blindly into a cave. I

was looking for creosote to make a torch. I didn't think you'd get up here so fast. Last time I looked you were struggling up the trail at a snail's pace."

"What is this place?" she asked with a shudder.

"A playground for death." Hawk pulled her to her feet and held her close. She clung to him, shivering, and pressed her face into his chest. His nearness gave her back a sense of security.

When her heartbeat returned to normal, they explored the cave, its contents now garishly illuminated by the torch he'd fashioned by lighting a twisted bundle of resinous creosote bush.

"They were mostly Apache," he deduced. "That one was a Yavapai from the looks of him, as were a few others. Allies." He examined the weapons, of a fairly recent manufacture. "They've been dead ten, fifteen years, I'd say. That means they were probably hiding from the cavalry. There was a big push to exterminate the Apaches during the early seventies," he explained in a grim footnote.

"But why?"

"I guess the army wanted to save face. A major at Fort Lowell told me once that the government was embarrassed that it had spent nearly forty million dollars fighting the Apaches—and that just between 1864 and 1873. They didn't have much luck killing warriors, so they resorted to slaughtering women and children. As far as their reports were concerned, a dead Apache was a dead Apache."

He led her back toward the entrance, reconstructing, as best as he could, what must have happened. "It was winter. They're dressed for cold weather. They were fleeing the cavalry, but this was no war party. It was a fairly large band, over a hundred in all, made up mostly of old people, women, and children." He pointed to a young female who had collapsed with an infant still clutched in her arms. "One bullet killed both of them. It must have passed through the baby and into the mother."

As Sybilla stared at the pathetic sight, she felt all

the helpless terror the mother must have known when she realized their situation was hopeless and there was no way to save her child.

"The people must have thought this was an impregnable fortress, that they could hold off the troops indefinitely. Firing directly into the cave would have been impossible because of the right angle turn of the trail."

He waved the torch high overhead and pointed to a sloping granite slab overhanging the entrance. It had been pockmarked by bullets. "The soldiers, or their scouts, must have figured out that if they directed their fire at the rock, the bullets would deflect into the cave."

"But that's all speculation. How can you be so sure that soldiers did this? It's unthinkable that trained military men could perpetrate a crime like this, murdering indiscriminately, women and children as well as warriors."

Sybilla's naivete didn't surprise him, for like most people she could not comprehend the frenzy of blood lust that overcame even civilized men during battle. "Like I said, when it came to the Apaches, the army never made much distinction between combatants and noncombatants. But if you need proof, I found these down the trail."

He dug into his pocket and displayed a handful of fifty-caliber shell casings. "Army issue," he said with distaste as he tossed them aside. "From the looks of these rocks and the number of casings I found, they must have gone through hundreds of rounds."

"The Indians didn't stand a chance."

"No. If they hadn't had so many women and children in tow, the men might have tried to make a stand somehow. As it was, the whole thing was probably over before they had a chance to consider alternatives."

"It's gruesome," she pronounced, deeply disturbed by the heaps of dead bodies. But what really sickened her was what she had discovered about the nature of man. No wonder Hawk had turned away from so-called civilization. Early in life he'd seen beneath the thin veneer of society.

"Maybe you were right about the spirits protecting this place," she said. "Let's leave the poor souls in peace."

He led her outside, and together they rolled several large boulders against the entrance and covered it with chapparal. It seemed the least they could do. Sybilla wondered how long it would be before this gory bit of American military history was rediscovered. The massacre would, undoubtedly, go unpunished. At least in this life.

"Come on," Hawk told her as he urged her away from the cave. "I found something while I was looking for the creosote. I think you should see it."

What he had discovered was a series of small *tinajas*, or natural basins, scoured from the rocks by powerful summer rains. They were located in a small canyon not far from the cave. Shaded at all times by overhanging rocks that prevented rapid evaporation, they were filled with cool, stagnant, but potable water. There were four basins in all. The smallest wasn't much bigger than a china washbowl, but the largest was three or four times the depth and size of a copper bathtub.

"Heavenly," Sybilla exclaimed. The cool, inviting beauty of the setting and the welcome sight of so much water in one place went a long way toward dispelling the gloom that had settled over her after her experience in the cave. She desperately needed the purifying effects of a complete bath. She longed to wash away the taint of death, although she knew the memory of what she'd seen could not be gotten rid of so easily.

She could almost feel the water against her skin, but knowing what she did of the paucity of water, she hesitated to suggest using the precious commodity for something as frivolous as a bath.

Hawk, however, had brought her here for just that purpose. He knew how disturbed she was and felt that a good soak, her first since leaving Tucson, was just what she needed. He found a small amole plant and dug into the soil around it until he had freed the bulbous root.

"Soap plant," he explained as he peeled the root with his knife. "It lathers up pretty good. Indian women use it to wash their hair. I thought you might want to take a bath."

The thought of submerging herself in cool water was a dream come true. "Do you mean it? I thought water was sacred out here."

"It is. Use the biggest basin for your bath. In a few days the amole will dissolve and the water will be clear again. No harm done."

Smiling gratefully at Hawk, she wondered if this was the right time to question him about his intentions. Before she could formulate a query, he plopped down on a flat rock and began to remove his boots and socks.

"What are you doing?" she asked.

"I'm going to take a bath."

"You are?"

"We Americans like to be clean as much as you English," he chided.

"Of course you do, but you can hardly bathe with me."

"As I recall, you didn't hesitate to join me in the bathhouse back in Tucson. And that was before we had much more than a passing acquaintance." Hawk enjoyed watching Billy's reaction to his suggestion. Even though they had been together several times in much more intimate ways, she still clung to an unreasonable sense of propriety. He was determined to awaken all her senses.

"How very boorish of you to point that out."

"Boorish maybe, but true."

"It would not be at all proper."

"Proper? After all we've shared, how can anything be improper?" he asked curiously.

She blushed. "Have you no sensitivity? No gentleman would speak of such things."

"There you go." He shrugged and turned his palms up. "I guess I'm no gentleman. Look, Billy, I've seen all your womanly charms. I've taken a full inventory, you might say. That is, of course, unless you've been holding out on me."

"That was different."

"How so?"

"It was dark. You can't expect me to disrobe in front of you in broad daylight."

He looked up innocently as he unbuttoned and removed his shirt. "Why not?"

"It just wouldn't be proper."

"There you go again, worried about propriety. Who would know? Who are you being modest for, Billy?"

"I would know, and I can't do it."

He unbuckled his belt and worked the buttons on his trousers. Women had such funny ideas. Especially *civilized* women. "Suit yourself, but you're missing out on the treat of your life."

"I beg your pardon?"

"The bath, Billy, the bath." He slipped out of his pants and kicked them to one side. Before she could avert her eyes, he skinned out of his longjohns, and she had a glimpse of the lithe, tan body that had given her so much pleasure.

Apparently unencumbered by common decency, Hawk picked his barefoot way to the largest of the *tinajas* and lowered himself into the water, looking for all the world like a primitive god of myth.

"Are you sure you won't join me?" he cajoled as he worked the amole root over his upper body. Just as predicted, it burst into a luxurious lather. Sybilla sighed with longing.

"Positive." She sat down on the rock he'd vacated and forced her gaze away from his bronzed body, concentrating on the blossom of a prickly pear growing out of a crevice. She enjoyed only limited success.

"Ahhh, ooohhh." Hawk splashed about like a child in a puddle. "This is the second best feeling in the world."

She didn't need to ask what was the first. Thanks to him she already knew, and it was all she could think of at the moment. She sat in the shadows of ancient monoliths and cursed the fact that none of the other pools was large enough to immerse herself.

Envying Hawk his lack of inhibitions, she wanted desperately to be in that water, but she could not undress brazenly in front of him. All she could think about was the way her Grandmother Sybilla had made her wear her shift in the bath so that she would not be too overstimulated by the sight of her own developing body. Old habits were hard to break.

She could only imagine the kind of wantonness the sight of Hawk's virile body might provoke her to. She longed to touch and be touched in the erotic manner he had shown her. She remembered the delicious pleasure he gave her, the steady rhythmic joining of their bodies and the tension that grew to intolerable proportions before the shattering peak of ecstasy released her from its grip.

But that pleasure was a private, nighttime activity. She had already relented enough to concede that marriage was not as necessary for carnal enjoyment as she had been taught. But in this strange land that challenged even her most basic concepts of reality, she could not give up all of her inhibitions. She simply could not disrobe while under Hawk's scrutiny.

Despite the shady niche in which she sat, she felt the heat of the sun as keenly as the secret fire that smoldered inside her. She tapped her foot to release her frustration. God, it was hot.

As if reading her thoughts, Hawk called out, "Sure is cool in here."

"Perhaps I'll bathe when you're finished."

"Nah." He floated on his back, his arms at his sides. The greenish water did nothing to hide his nudity, and after a brief glance in his direction, she looked at a point beyond him. "We've got to be shoving on when I get through here."

She removed her hat and fanned the perspiration from her face. Her hair was sticky with dust and sweat and badly in need of a wash. She removed her gloves, which suddenly felt as heavy as lead. There, that was better already.

Maybe if she just removed her boots and stockings, she could at least bathe her tired feet. As Hawk had pointed out, he'd already seen all of her, so what harm would come of exposing her feet? The possibility was so enticing that she wasted little time and was soon dangling her toes in the basin.

It was cool beyond belief and she kicked delightedly. She closed her eyes and savored the feeling, but it wasn't enough. While moderately refreshing, it wasn't at all satisfying—it only tempted her more.

Hawk watched but said nothing. She looked so cute struggling with her ideas of right and wrong that he had to be careful not to show his amusement. He had suspected Billy was a passionate woman. She just wouldn't admit it.

"I'm just cooling off a bit," she told him.

"Be my guest."

Discreetly she unbuttoned the top buttons of her shirt and splashed water onto her bosom. It was indeed heaven, and her envy of Hawk's freedom soon dissolved into resentment.

"It isn't fair for you to enjoy what is denied to me, simply because you're a man and I'm a woman," she said with an unfamiliar note of petulance.

"I thought you didn't hold with gender-based inequalities," he pointed out.

"I don't." When he closed his eyes, she eased up her split skirt, nudged up her pantalets, and splashed water on her limbs. Her frustration grew. She'd worked just as hard climbing this stupid mountain as he had. And she'd had a much worse fright in the cave, so, in short, she had earned a bath.

Boldly she finished unbuttoning her shirt, although she knew the thin cotton camisole under it was damp and transparent. She removed her shirt and felt the cooling breeze on her skin. "If I join you in there, will you promise not to look?" she asked warily.

Hawk grinned. "Sure. But you have to promise not to look at me either." He wouldn't remind her that she already had.

"You needn't worry in that regard."

"Oh, I shan't," he teased.

"Will you turn your back until I get in?"

"Will that satisfy your misplaced sense of modesty?"

"It will." Barely.

"Very well, then." He turned around, but she thought she saw his shoulders shaking with restrained laughter.

She quickly discarded her skirt but kept on her delicate underthings. They were sadly lacking as a bathing costume, but at least she wouldn't be totally naked and exposed. Feeling every bit as self-conscious as she would have had she disrobed in the middle of Piccadilly Circus, she walked to the edge of the basin and stepped in.

It was as blessedly refreshing as she had anticipated, and she sighed audibly as she lowered herself into the water. She seated herself on a narrow rock ledge, the water reaching her chest.

"Nice, huh?" Hawk asked lazily when he heard her sigh. The basin was less than six feet in diameter and she was near, but not close enough to touch. "Can I turn around now?"

"If you must."

He tossed her the amole root. It was surprisingly fragrant, and she quickly worked up a lather to wash her hair. When she was ready to rinse, she lowered herself under the surface and came up coughing as she parted the curtain of hair covering her face.

"You're supposed to keep your mouth shut when you go under water," he pointed out.

"I'll try to remember in future." At the moment she was having a hard enough time trying to forget that he was only a few feet away and that all she need do was wade a step in his direction. One step, possibly two, and she could touch his smooth brown skin. One step and she could enfold him in a fierce embrace, kiss him the way he'd taught her he liked to be kissed, deeply, urgently.

It was difficult to think rationally when her mind was filled with such wayward images. That had been her problem ever since she'd met Hawk. They operated under different sets of rules. Because of his experiences, he had developed his own code of behavior which blurred the thin line between right and wrong.

The Commandments condemned killing, yet in this country it was sometimes necessary for survival. Hawk realized that and viewed each situation individually, applying his own moral interpretations.

On the other hand, she had been taught from earliest childhood to respect the line between good and bad. In her society, one was either a good person who followed the rules or a bad person who broke them. A hero or a villain. You could not be both and survive with your conscience intact.

But she wasn't in that world any more and might never be again. If she wanted to have any kind of life outside England, she would have to decide which set of rules she wanted to live by. No matter where she ended up in the future, she must change her outmoded ideas. Hawk had told her that when in Rome, do as the Romans did. It had been a good piece of advice.

With sudden clarity, she realized her father had been wrong about maintaining decorum in all situations, at all costs. Proper drawing room behavior was out of place and burdensome here. She would have to take the first step in proving to Hawk that she could adapt to his way of life.

She stood in the water and folded her arms across her chest. "I suppose I have been rather silly, haven't I?"

"Silly about what?"

"About rules. They really don't apply now, do they?"

"I wondered when you were going to figure that out." His grin showed her how happy he was about it. "Want me to scrub your back?"

Sybilla glanced around. Despite the privacy of their location, she still didn't know if she could handle so much, so soon. Not without darkness to shield their secrets. "I realize I've been silly, but I do not know how long it will take me to get over it. Could we work up to it gradually?"

"We can try." Hawk attempted not to notice that Billy's underwear might as well have been made out of gauze for all the coverage it provided. The fabric clung to her small, upturned breasts, outlining and accentuating the rosy smudges of the areolas, the pebblelike hardness of her nipples.

They stood there for several moments, more aware of each other than ever. Sybilla knew the next move was hers. "Perhaps you could wash my back." She passed him the soap root, presented her back, and hiked up her hair with one hand.

He made no move to touch her. "What's wrong?" she asked.

"Is it the custom in England to bathe in your underwear? If it is, you people are a lot worse off than I thought."

She smiled when she recalled her grandmother's

bath policy. "As a matter of fact, it is." Now she realized how foolish it was to cling to any standard of modesty with Hawk. They'd made love, touched and tasted and explored each other's bodies with shameless abandon.

"Then I'll just have to work around it." His rough hands, slick with lather, massaged first her shoulders and then her back through the flimsy fabric, slowly, sensuously, thrumming her taut nerves like a mandolin's strings.

She gasped when his hands kneaded her buttocks, but she immediately gave herself over to his touch. He stroked and massaged, under the pretext of washing her, and his actions set up an unbearable longing.

As he rubbed the sweet-smelling lather over her back, she turned slowly until he was soaping her breasts.

"Need your front washed too?" Hawk's murmured question expressed his thrill of anticipation. He'd waited for the moment when Billy would shed her final inhibitions and come to him as the passionate woman he knew her to be.

Sybilla looked deep into his eyes while she slowly untied her camisole. "I need more than that."

He spread the edges wide and stroked her nipples. "Tell me what you need, Billy."

"You'd make me say it?" she asked, lowering her gaze. She watched his lean brown hands play upon her pale skin, and the inner fires caught, surged, and immolated her.

"I'd make you spell it out in Morse code if I could, Billy. I need to hear you say it."

"Kiss me."

What he did next surprised her, for she had expected his lips to slant over hers in the mind-shattering way she remembered. Instead, he gripped her waist and raised her effortlessly from the water until her breasts were level with his mouth. He licked droplets of water from her skin, his tongue flicking her nipples with studied concentration. Her hands gripped his shoulders, and her head dropped back until her long hair trailed into the water.

She cried out in erotic pleasure as he drew a dusky areola into his mouth and suckled, first at one and then at the other, as though trying to extract the essence of her being. She went limp as his mouth worked its magic on her, kissing, licking, flicking, sucking, until she was sure she would go mad. ''Hawk,'' she cried.

''What else, Billy? What else do you need?''

''More.'' She was breathless from the sensations sweeping through her.

Slowly he lifted her higher, and his lips left her breasts in an agonizing trail down the center of her chest, to her stomach, her abdomen, and lower. He pressed his lips to the pale brown mound beneath the sheer pantalets and she gasped at his boldness, at the warmth of his tongue and lips through the fabric that now seemed as thick as canvas. Her hands left his shoulders and grappled with the knotted silk ribbon that held the garment in place.

''Help me, Hawk,'' she murmured.

He couldn't without releasing her, and that was one thing he would not do. So, succumbing to the primitive passion boiling inside him, he used his teeth to bite through the narrow ribbon and tear the thin material.

The savagery with which he ripped off her clinging pantalets both shocked and thrilled her, but she was unable to act. It was as though the heat she felt radiating from his body had melted her bones, dissolved her muscles, leaving nothing but tingling raw nerves in their place.

His rock-hard arms quivered as he held her up, but she knew it was not because of her weight. She sensed his need, recognized it as her own.

''Billy?'' he whispered.

''Yes, yes, yes.'' She closed her eyes as his mouth sought her intimate secrets. His lips caressed her, and his tongue worked its magic. She cried out again when he found the nub of her desire, and her fingers knotted into his hair as he used tongue and teeth and lips to build her to a crescendo of need so powerful that it must surely be unquenchable. It built, stretching and pulling her in a thousand directions at once, into an ocean of erotic sensation. Wave after wave crashed over her until she thought she would drown in the wake of so much pleasure.

She felt herself coming apart, rent into a million pieces by the passion that finally released her.

But not for long. Hawk allowed her to slide through his hands, down his slick body until her soft breasts flattened against his chest. Until her silky thighs pressed into his hard, hair-roughened ones. Until her sweet, warm sheath welcomed the rigid length of him. He settled her against the side of the *tinaja*, grasped her thighs, and lifted her onto him. He entered her slowly, and cool water filled her before being displaced by his impossible heat.

"Do you want me, Billy?" he asked before his lips met hers in a kiss that had nothing to do with tenderness.

"Yes, oh yes." Weak with the pleasure he'd already demanded of her, she could do no more than whisper. "Please."

That was all he needed. He plunged in, finding a steady rhythm that seized and held her as surely as did his strong hands. There was no time for gentleness, no time for sweet words. He was driven by an urgency as strong as that which he sensed in her.

He lost control, swept away by the same storm of desire that had rocked Billy moments before. The same one that made her clutch his shoulders, dig her nails into his back, and moan with ecstasy, all the while writhing atop him, pulling him deeper and deeper inside until he thought he could touch her heart.

This was what he had wanted, the passion he had sensed in her the first time they'd made love. This unbridled desire, this wildly primitive mating that tore away restraints, removed all vestiges of civilization, and made them realize that they were destined to fulfill needs that no others could.

She wrapped her legs around him as he rocked into her, crying out his name at the moment of their simultaneous release. They clung together, the trembling flotsam of a brutally erotic storm, until they were washed up, too soon, on the shore of satiation.

Chapter 13

The shadows in the canyon grew longer and darker as Hawk and Billy, caught up in the mystery they discovered in each other's arms, made love again. They lay together on flat sun-warmed rocks, and this time their coupling was gentle, giving, loving, without a trace of the wild taking of before. She had not known it was possible to love and be loved in such different ways, and she reveled in her new knowledge.

They bathed again, and afterward she gathered up her scattered clothing. She dressed in silence, knowing they needed to talk, but unsure how to get Hawk to open up. She now knew the depth of her love for him, but in order to reconcile herself to it, she needed to know how he felt about her.

She was more Billy than Sybilla now and always would be, no matter how their future and fortunes turned out. She was reluctant to leave this secret place, to resume a role that was no longer clear.

Hawk pulled on his boots and observed Billy donning her clothes like a protective armor. She had mentioned the word "gradual" when discussing their lovemaking, and what they'd just done must have shocked her in ways he hadn't suspected. After several moments, he could stand the silence no longer.

"Did I overstep some boundary?" he asked.

She looked up from buttoning her shirt. "No. I have been thinking, is all."

"I hate it when you think," he teased. "It puts the starch back into you."

She grinned to show she understood the gentle jibe. "I was thinking about what you told me once. You said women could only be one of two things out here—wives or whores. Since I have chosen not to be a wife, should I consider myself a whore?"

Her question stunned him. "Of all the things I've told you, and all the things you've chosen to ignore, why on earth you would latch on to something as ridiculous as that, is beyond me."

"A woman likes to know these things."

"You are definitely no whore," he said vehemently. It hurt him that just when he'd decided he was falling in love and there might be hope for them, she declared she didn't want to marry. She hadn't even given him a chance to offer. "I care about you, Billy. Whatever you think of yourself, you'll always be a lady to me."

"Thank you for that," she said softly. "And I care about you too." She tucked her shirt into her skirt neatly and turned away from him so he wouldn't see the emotion she could hide no longer. She had given him the opportunity to mention marriage and he hadn't. Which only proved that he had no plans to ask her to be his wife. She would have to make the best of the situation while it lasted, taking from her time with Hawk what she would need to sustain her throughout the rest of her long, empty life.

They left the *tinajas* and continued their climb to the top of the peak. They would have to push themselves if they wanted to return to camp before nightfall. Their plan was to survey the surrounding area from one of the tall peaks in hopes of locating the mountain depicted on the map as a half-buried heart. According to Montoya, it was in that mountain that the gold was hidden.

It took an uneventful hour of steady climbing,

during which they seemed to be alone in a vast empty world. The only other creatures they saw were scuttling lizards, darting birds, and once, an enormous diamondback rattler coiled sleepily in a shady niche under a rock.

"Aren't you going to kill it?" Billy asked Hawk, who regarded the reptile with interest and respect but without fear.

"Why? It was here first. Rattlers are the landlords of the desert. We humans are the trespassers." He stepped carefully around it and advised her to do the same.

With a safe distance between her and the somnolent viper, she turned back for a last look. Its head, sleek and beautifully detailed, raised up. Its flat dark eyes stared into hers. The snake's mouth stretched open, slowly, deliberately. The large hollow fangs swung forward from their folded, resting position— ready to stab and inject venom in one rapid, deft move.

But it was disinclined to attack. Perhaps it was the heat that stayed it. Or maybe it was waiting for a better opportunity. The hooded eyes and dripping fangs were like a warning, and she was transfixed by the reptile's silent malediction. If it was speaking to her, she couldn't hear. If it was urging caution, she didn't understand.

When they finally reached the top of the mesa, they could see for miles in every direction. Just as Hawk had predicted, they had a clear view of all the neighboring peaks. Sawtooth monoclines, boulder battlements, goblin rocks. Here and there a few scrubby-looking plants crept cautiously out of the cracks, but their muted gray-green color was swallowed up in the endless wasteland.

"What have we gotten ourselves into?" Billy whispered as she scanned the sun-soaked horizon. "It's as forbidding as the gates of hell." Mesmerized and repelled, she stared at the arid land, the lifeless, dreary, ugly, empty land that spread out for miles like a vicious wound in the earth.

Again she felt the almost imperceptible pull and tug of whatever nameless force had drawn her here.

Stronger now was the quickening of blood and spirit that told her she was one step nearer her destination. From this eagle's aerie, with all the Superstition Mountains spread out around them, the resting place of the gold was visible. If only they knew where to look.

They unrolled Montoya's map and compared the mountain in the drawing to the surrounding terrain. "The two rivers are right where they should be," she remarked eagerly. "Montoya rendered their meandering paths with remarkable skill."

"Yeah," Hawk agreed with frustrated curtness. "But nothing else matches."

Refusing to accept defeat, she searched the map, but was soon forced to admit that his observation was true. Had they made this tortuous climb for nothing? Was it all to end here? Without a clear indication of which direction to take, they could wander these hills and hidden canyons for a lifetime, walking over and around the gold, and never know it.

After a long moment Hawk's eyes narrowed, and he jabbed the map with a slim finger. "Wait a minute. Maybe we're going about this all wrong."

"What do you mean?"

"On the map, a two-humped mountain looks like a half-buried heart, right?"

"Right. Unfortunately, there's nothing that even remotely resembles such a mountain," she said dismally.

Transferring his gaze to a distant rock formation, Hawk looked long and hard at the majestic spire known as Weaver's Needle. The five-thousand-foot-high formation, named after an early-day trapper, figured prominently in many of the tales he'd heard about lost gold. That wasn't surprising, considering it was the most visible and impressive piece of rock in the interior of the Superstitions. What was surprising was the fact that such an outstanding landmark was not included on Ricardo Montoya's map.

Or was it?

Using the almost forgotten skills his mother had taught him, Hawk became his namesake in his mind, soaring across the miles to circle around the volcanic needle. In his mental flight he saw, and recognized, the changing faces of the rock.

"It's not a needle on the other side," he said quietly.

"What?" Billy had seen the faraway look in Hawk's eyes, and for a moment it was as though he had somehow left her. "I don't understand."

"What would the heart look like if you viewed it from another angle? If you could see not two humps, but only one?"

Immediately following his train of thought, she riveted her gaze on the boulder-strewn monolith that had been the object of his intense concentration. "Yes," she cried. "It could very well have another hump that isn't visible from here. That's it. It must be. Montoya drew his map from a different perspective, that's all."

"It's about the right size and distance from the river," he allowed. "Of course, things could have changed since Montoya's day. Earthquakes, landslides, floods. Any number of natural disasters could have changed the geography."

"But none of those could have changed a peak that size. That's why it has to be the right one." Renewed excitement underlined her words. "Let's get back to camp and tell the others how close we are. The news will give Uncle John the encouragement he needs so badly. How long will it take us to reach that mountain?"

"Distance is deceptive in the desert. It could be fifty miles from here. Maybe more."

"Fifty miles? Two days, then. Three at most." She

grabbed Hawk's hand. "Just think, in a few days we'll be in the general vicinity of the mine. Then we can start searching seriously for the other clues on the map. Hawk! This is what we've been waiting for," she said breathlessly.

He was strangely quiet. "Maybe. Maybe not."

"Don't be so pessimistic," she chided. "We're closer now than ever. I feel it."

Hawk felt something too, but it wasn't Billy's certainty. He couldn't explain the strange sensation that came over him as he gazed into the sun-shimmering distance. His whole being quivered like a tuning fork picking up psychic vibrations of throbbing menace.

There was nothing of darkness in the bright, cloudless day, but he felt a sudden and inexplicable shadow fall across him, across his soul. A shadow whose cold, probing fingers made him question seriously, for the first time, the wisdom of going on.

The excitement had brought a pretty flush to Billy's smooth skin and an eager glitter to her eyes, reminding him of the way she looked when they made love. They had shared something magical back there at the *tinajas*, but it was foolish to think it could go on forever. Since she didn't want marriage, once the gold was found, his role in her life would come to an end.

"Hawk? What's wrong?"

He shook his head to clear it of morbid thoughts. "Nothing." His half smile was meant to reassure her and to prevent her from probing further. He'd been only too glad to tell her about the Lost Tribe and to enlighten her about the Phantom Camel. But he could not tell her about the shadow.

The climb down the mountain took less than half the time it had taken them to climb up it. They hiked back through the long canyon of the *tinajas* and slipped quickly past the cave, reaching the campsite just as the lavender light of dusk began casting its own shadows. As soon as they were greeted, Zora dished up plates of savory rabbit stew, and Hawk and Billy ate ravenously.

The gypsy woman kept her eyes downcast when she served Hawk and displayed none of her old wiles. He was relieved and curious about this change until he saw her beam with undisguised pleasure when she handed Ahmed his plate. She curtsied before her husband, demurely submissive, and flashed a secret smile.

Apparently, the two had reached an understanding of sorts and Hawk could only hope his unorthodox advice to Ahmed had helped. He'd been worried that it might backfire in the anxious husband's face.

The three who had stayed behind reported that the day had passed quietly. As they ate, Hawk and Billy recounted what they had discovered about the landmarks on the map. By unspoken agreement, neither mentioned the cave full of skeletons or the *tinajas*.

"Does this mean we may actually be on the right trail?" John asked. He was recovering from his bout of heat prostration, but his appetite had not improved and he only picked at his food.

"I think it's just a matter of time," Hawk told him. The older man's skin was still a sickly shade of gray, and Hawk doubted his ability to go on. "But there's no real hurry. We can stay here for a few days so you can rest up."

"That's right, Uncle." Billy too was concerned about John and smiled at Hawk to let him know she appreciated the offer.

"No, no," he said in a weak imitation of his normally hale manner. "I am determined to see this through. By all means let's push on. The sooner we find the blighted gold, the sooner we can get out of this hellish place."

"Good enough," Hawk said. "We'll leave at dawn, then. Barring further difficulties we should reach Weaver's Needle in two or three days."

None among them was inclined to question what

difficulties he might be referring to. The possibilities, as they had already learned, were not only endless, but disturbing.

Ahmed approached Hawk while the women were cleaning up and asked to speak privately to him. Hawk suggested they take a walk, and they were scarcely out of earshot of the camp when Ahmed spoke.

"I do not wish to kitty-foot around the bush."

"No," Hawk agreed with a smile. "Let's not do that. Get straight to the point."

"Yes, the point. I have been following your excellent advice these past days and it has worked. Have you not noticed a change in my little jewel of late?"

"Zora does seem a mite calmer."

"Changed for the better, would you agree?"

"Yes."

"I told Zora that I wanted to get to the end of her problem."

"To the bottom of it, you mean?"

"Just so. What she told me shook me to my very boots."

"What was that?"

"It is true that my Zora has been acting crazy. But not because she was unhappy with me and desired other men."

"I didn't think so, Ahmed. You're a good man. Any woman worth her salt would recognize that."

"My Zora is with child," he announced proudly. "I am to be a papa."

The unexpected news caught Hawk completely by surprise. It took a moment for it to sink in, and then he clapped the man soundly on the back. "Congratulations, old man." He thought fleetingly that Zora's pregnancy was mighty inconvenient, but the happy look on Ahmed's face made Hawk keep his doubts to himself.

"Thank you for your well wishes, but surely you must see that our position has changed."

"I reckon so. A baby changes a lot of things."

"Fatherhood is a most serious responsibility."

"Indeed it is."

"I feel I must take Zora back to Tucson. It is not wise for a woman in her condition to be traveling in such dangerous places as these. Already it may be too late. The child may be marked by one of her frightening experiences. I cannot take more chances with my eldest son."

Hawk regarded the little man seriously. "You've discussed this with Zora?"

"Oh yes. You know how she fears these mountains. She very much wants to return to Tucson." He shuddered. "I do not wish to speak of bad things, *effendi*, but my Zora is most certain that disaster will befall us if we continue."

Hawk rubbed his chin and thought of recent events. Floods, landslides, revolutionaries, a cave full of dead Indians. It had been an eventful journey to say the least. "What do you propose?"

Ahmed quickly sketched out his plan. He and Zora would take two of the camels and a share of the supplies and water, leaving the rest. They would find temporary lodgings in Tucson and await the return of the gold-seekers. He discussed his plans to start up his own circus as a legacy to pass on to his yet unborn son.

"Have you thought about what it means to take off across country alone? That's a lot of miles to cover."

"That was my worry, *effendi*. But Zora has consulted the tea leaves, and they say there is much more danger in going on than in going back. I must believe her."

"What about Maloche?"

Ahmed shuddered. "That infidel villain does not figure in her prediction. Zora is determined that he is ahead of us, not behind us."

Hawk didn't hold much with fortune-telling, but this time he was inclined to agree with Zora's assessment of the situation. Maloche, in all probability, was indeed ahead of them somewhere, a thought guaranteed to disturb the most careful man's sleep.

"Are you sure this is what you want to do?"

Ahmed clasped Hawk's hand in his. "I count you among my friends, *effendi*. Ahmed Mendab has never been a stopper, but now I must think of Zora and the child."

"No one will accuse you of being a quitter, Ahmed Mendab." Hawk would miss him, but he sympathized with the man's feelings. If he had a son to think about he might even share them.

It suddenly occurred to him that Billy could be carrying his child. It was improbable, but certainly the possibility existed. He hadn't considered the consequences of their lovemaking before and wondered if she had. If so, what did she think?"

Turning back to Ahmed, he asked, "When do you want to leave?"

"At dawn, *effendi*. We must not delay."

More than a few tears were shed the next morning, all of them Ahmed's, as Ahmed and Zora prepared to depart. He was torn between loyalty to his employer and concern for his family. Billy did her best to set his mind at ease, explaining that she understood how necessary it was for him to put his wife's wishes and welfare first. She assured him that the party would meet them in Tucson before they knew it, heavily laden with gold.

Although Ahmed protested, she promised him and Zora their agreed upon share of the gold in exchange for the continued use of the camels. This time Hawk said nothing about her generosity.

He did, however, suggest that John return to Tucson with Ahmed and Zora. For once Billy concurred with him.

"No," John protested. "I will not abandon you, Sybilla."

"You won't be abandoning me, Uncle. You'll be sparing me a great deal of worry because I would know that you are safe. You really must think of your health.''

''Billy, dear,'' John appealed to her, using Hawk's name for her. ''Don't send me away. I know I am just a useless old fool, but do give me this chance for adventure. It could very well be my last. As for my health, I've suffered a temporary setback, that's all. I'll be fine. You shall see.''

She didn't like the fatalistic tone of his words, but she did recognize the urgent need in his eyes. It was the desperation of a man who, because of society's expectations, had never before had the freedom to do as he pleased.

In the face of such need, Billy could only relent. In truth, she didn't like the idea of her uncle going back without her. For some reason she did not fully understand, it was essential that they see this trek through to its conclusion together. But she made him promise he would rest as much as possible and regain his strength. He agreed and the matter was settled, despite Hawk's reservations.

Hawk did not understand why John was so determined, but he was glad John had turned down the offer. He'd come to admire the older man and enjoyed his company.

Billy watched Ahmed and Zora until they were out of sight as the two groups traveled in opposite directions. She would miss them. She'd come to rely on Ahmed's flashing smile and good humor. Despite her stormy moods Zora had been an excellent cook, and Billy had come to depend on her skills to provide nourishing and pleasant meals on the trail.

At the noon stop, Sybilla, Hawk, and John shared a cold meal of dried venison and leftover biscuits. As they ate the tasteless food, Hawk bemoaned the fact that with Zora gone, the culinary level of the outfit was sure to decline. He could cook what he caught or killed, but he had neither the imagination nor the flair with which Zora had prepared even the simplest dishes.

Referring to the quote about an army marching on its stomach, he wondered aloud if that also held for gold-seeking expeditions. If it did, in his opinion they were doomed.

Billy argued with him briefly about whether the quote should be rightfully attributed to Alexander the Great or Napoleon, and then in an effort to stop his complaining snapped, "For God's sake, *I'll* do the cooking."

"You mean you can?" he asked incredulously.

"Of course I can. Any half-wit can cook." That statement and a piercing look had brought an end to his complaints, but when the party stopped that evening to camp, she had second thoughts. Despite her waspish assurances, cooking was not a chore she was particularly qualified to perform. All her life, servants had dealt with the basics of survival.

As soon as they unpacked the camels, Hawk went out to scout the area and hunt for meat. Billy convinced John to rest, and he was soon dozing fitfully in her tent, which though swelteringly hot at least provided a modicum of shade. She was worried about his steadily declining health and wondered if perhaps the trip wouldn't be his undoing after all.

In an effort to dispel such thoughts, she busied herself building a fire and then sat down on the cooler side of a big rock and opened a book of Mr. Shelley's verses.

She wasn't sure if it was by accident or design that the volume fell open at the poem "Love's Philosophy." Billy had read it before, dozens of times, but never had she felt the poet was speaking to her; never had she understood his yearning. Never had she felt the thrill she experienced as she read those heartfelt lines now. By the time she reached the second verse she was reading aloud.

" 'See the mountains kiss high heaven,
    And the waves clasp one another;
No sister-flower would be forgiven

If it disdained its brother:
And the sunlight clasps the earth,
    And the moonbeams kiss the sea—' ''

'' 'What are all these kissings worth, If thou kiss
not me?' '' Appearing as quietly as a mist, Hawk
finished the poem in his gruff voice. ''Ah, the poet's
everlasting quest for understanding,'' he mocked.

She looked up and saw him standing a few feet
away, as implacable as a mountain, his big rifle resting in his arms. His wide hat brim was tilted down,
adding its own shadows to the bristly day-old
growth of whiskers on his face. His hunting trek in
the desert had left him covered with a thin layer of
dust, and he was chewing on the burned-out stub
of a cigar. His visage was, without a doubt, the most
unpoetic and uncavalier she had ever seen.

Although she was no longer surprised by his endless store of knowledge, hearing Mr. Shelley's lilting
words tripping from Hawk's sardonic mouth was an
unsettling experience. As was his amused commen-
tary.

She snapped the book shut. ''I wish you would
not take such great pleasure in sneaking up on me
like that.''

''That's hardly what I take great pleasure in doing
to you,'' he said with the trace of a sly smile.

Reading the poem had elicted certain ethereal desires, but Hawk's words released a torrent of more
earthly memories. She flushed scarlet at his re-
minder of the intimate activities in which they had
recently engaged. Afraid Uncle John might overhear
their conversation, she changed the subject.

''Do you admire Shelley's work?'' she asked with
dinner-party formality.

''Not particularly.''

''Yet you have committed his words to memory.''

''That was Professor Dalrymple's idea. It sure
wasn't mine. Did you have any trouble getting the
cookfire started?''

"Of course not." With undisguised disappointment, she glanced pointedly at the canvas game bag tied to his belt. "I see we must suffer the dreaded rabbit stew yet again."

"Oh, contraire," he mocked. "Tonight you're in for a real dining experience." He reached into the bag and withdrew the looped coils of a rattlesnake and dropped it at her feet. He turned and strode several steps away before saying, "Call me when supper's ready."

Billy just managed not to scream. Her strange encounter with a similar snake made her susceptible to unreasonable fears, but she fought back her revulsion. "Very funny. Now that you've had your little joke, what did you bring for dinner?"

Hawk leaned against a rock and pulled his hat brim down. "No joke. I had a hankering for some rattler."

"Why is it you never got a *hankering* for rattlesnake when Zora was doing the cooking?" she demanded.

"I don't know." He shrugged expressively. "I guess seeing that big fellow up in the rocks yesterday got my taste buds all worked up or something."

"Do you mean to tell me you are serious about eating that . . . that thing?"

"Oh, dead serious."

"I can't eat a reptile."

"Why not?"

"It's disgusting. Rather like eating a worm."

"Worms aren't reptiles," he pointed out. "But if you've eaten worm, snake'll be a pleasant surprise."

"I didn't mean to say that I've eaten worms. Merely, that . . . oh, never mind." She saw the look in Hawk's eyes. He wanted her to squirm and dissemble and beg him to take over for her. Well, she wouldn't do it. Pride wouldn't let her.

She stalked over to the cooking utensils and snatched up the largest frying pan she could find. It didn't look big enough to contain the snake, but she wasn't about to let that minor detail deter her.

Using a long stick to fork the snake into the pan, Billy held it under his nose. "How do you like your reptile, Mr. Devlin? Boiled, sauteed, or fricasseed?"

"None of those. Don't you know how to cook a rattler?"

Standing over him as she was, Billy was obliged to look down her nose at him. "Alas, I fear I do not. Despite my vast travels, I have never been reduced to eating such a delicacy."

"I thought not. Here, let me show you this time." He scooped up the snake, which was at least five feet long, and carried it to a flat rock. She followed him, reluctant to learn this particular bit of desert lore.

"First, you have to cut the head off and bury it in a hole at least a foot deep." He proceeded to do just that.

"Why? Is it some primitive Indian ceremony? Does this prepare the creature for the happy here-after?"

"Nah. It's just common sense. Plenty of people have been bitten by dead rattlers."

"I beg your pardon?"

"Snakes have certain reflexes that allow them to inject poison for a while even after they're dead. If you handle the head you could accidentally stab yourself on the fangs. Better safe than sorry."

With Billy looking on in disgust, he made a two-inch slit in the skin, starting at the wound from the severed head, and peeled it back. Next, he tied a length of heavy cord around the area where the skin had been peeled and hung it from a scrubby tree, leaving his hands free to remove the rest of the skin. Working down the body, he loosened the skin from the flesh until it had been completely removed.

Billy averted her eyes when he slit the belly and removed the viscera, but he noticed and chided her.

"Better pay attention. Next time you'll have to do it."

She made a face behind his back and muttered something about the probability of that happening being about equal to that of the icecap melting.

He rinsed the meat in salted water and cut it into serving sized pieces, then dropped it into a pail and handed it to her. "Now, all you have to do is roll it in flour and fry it up in grease. Tastes just like chicken. You'll see."

He left her to stare at the bucket of shiny reptilian flesh with distaste. How was she going to make this more palatable? Then she remembered that Zora had seasoned all her dishes with herbs she found in the desert. Unfortunately, Billy hadn't paid much attention to the gypsy's herbal lectures, but she did recall a basil-like groundcover that grew in abundance in the desert. She'd find a bit of that, use it to flavor the meat, and surprise Hawk with her culinary efforts.

While the meat cooked, she prepared gruel for John because he claimed his stomach would not tolerate such exotic fare. He ate only a bit of it, despite Billy's insistence. Her uncle was growing thinner right before her eyes, and she was very worried about him. He was still pale and subject to cold sweats.

He assured her that he was fine, only tired, and spread his bedroll in a protected area near her tent. He was asleep by the time the meal was ready.

Billy was surprised when she forced herself to eat a bite of the meat. It was tender, white, and delicious, and she was soon eating with gusto. But it didn't really taste like chicken. No, she thought it faintly reminiscent of frog legs.

"It's got a funny whang to it," Hawk muttered.

"What do you mean, a funny whang?"

"It tastes . . . different. What did you season it with?"

"Flour, salt, pepper and—"

"And?"

"And a secret herb." She didn't really know what the desert plant was called, and she had no intention of admitting her ignorance.

"A secret herb, huh?" Hawk ate another piece of meat and licked his fingers. "Call me old-fashioned, but I like my snake plain. Next time, keep your secret herbs to yourself."

She clattered around, clearing up the pans and plates, grumbling all the while about some people's ungracious behavior and lack of gratitude.

Chapter 14

Later Hawk and Billy sat in companionable silence by the small fire as night stole through the canyon. It came quickly, after a fleeting twilight, and it came completely. The high indigo sky was vacant except for the gauzy ribbon of the Milky Way and a cold sliver of moon. Dense underbrush choked the protected niches in the ancient, tumbled rocks whose towering shadows added another dimension to the darkness.

They didn't speak, but the night was alive with sounds orchestrated by nature itself. Unseen scores of insects chirked and creaked a treble undersong to the strident crescendo of the crickets and grasshoppers. The canyon frogs croaked a basso profundo accompaniment and, as if on cue from some cosmic conductor, a lone coyote added its ululating yowl to the dissonant wilderness symphony.

The howl pierced the night like a cold blade. Once that call had sent primordial shivers of dread skittering down Billy's spine. Now, free of gooseflesh, she smiled at the familiar sound. "There goes friend coyote. The old boy's canine tenor is in fine form tonight."

"He's calling for a mate." Hawk always reduced things to their most elemental form.

"Would that such things were so simple for the rest of us." She'd been intensely aware of Hawk all day and wondered—no, hoped—he would come to her in the night. Aside from his snake-skinning lesson today, they'd had no time together, and she missed that.

He had said he cared. That was something. But it wasn't enough. It was possible that he viewed their lovemaking as just a way to satisfy a need. Like the need for food, water, and warmth. What had he really meant? He had hankerings for rattlesnake, but would he want to eat it exclusively? Maybe he did care for her, but did that mean he would want to spend the rest of his life with her?

Hawk didn't respond to her remark, and when she turned to him she found him staring at the moon-washed ridge above them. His gaze was so intent that she thought he must surely see something that her own eyes couldn't. "Hawk? What is it?"

"There." He pointed. "Do you see a man on horseback?"

"Nooo." Her eyes strained against the inhibiting darkness, but she saw nothing.

"He's in the cutbank." Hawk reached for his rifle and had it pointed at the lone horseman before all the words were out of his mouth. He had no idea why anyone would approach a camp at night, but he wanted to be ready.

Billy saw Hawk tense, every nerve cued to respond to approaching danger. But she still didn't know what that danger was.

"Here he comes," he whispered. "He's behind that chapparal. Move behind me."

She did as ordered, and when she peered from around his broad back she saw their visitor for the first time. "An Indian," she squeaked.

"Yes, but what kind of Indian?" Hawk asked. He'd never seen a warrior such as the one who rode slowly toward them. As the Indian approached, the air around him seemed to hum, and the scant glow from the fire grew more brilliant until the figure was surrounded by a nimbus of light that made even the smallest detail of his person stand out in bas-relief.

His horse was a magnificent prancing paint, decked out in full war regalia. A bloodred handprint was stamped on the animal's rump, and its mane and tail were decorated with strips of dyed buckskin and feathers. The saddle was made of two rolls of stuffed rawhide covered with a brightly patterned blanket. The bridle was braided horsetail hair, and the rider carried a fringed quirt.

He also carried a shield painted with a large sun symbol and decorated with eagle feathers. He possessed no firearms; his weapons consisted of a knife in a sheath and a hardwood bow and coyote-skin quiver full of arrows. He wore only a broadskin breechclout and high, buckskin moccasins, the toes of which were turned up in a distinctive tip. In the middle of his bronzed chest hung a heavy golden cross, and turquoise stones hung from his ears. His thick, shoulder-length hair was slick with deer fat and tied out of his eyes with a rawhide thong.

Billy's amazement overcame her fear, and her awe of the mysterious warrior precluded speech. He was neither young nor old, but he was magnificent. He had a broad forehead, a large straight nose, intelligent black eyes, and an immobile mouth that looked as if it had been carved from granite. Or from a dream of what the Indian had once been, before the white man had broken and banished him.

Hawk had reached the same conclusion. This was no ordinary reservation Apache. Nothing about him had been borrowed from the whites: he had no leather saddle or bridle, no cotton trousers, no gun. Although he was silent, he spoke of an earlier time, a time Hawk knew only through his mother's stories. Hawk called out a greeting in the Apache language, but the warrior did not heed it. Instead he sat impassively on his high-spirited horse and gazed at Hawk and Billy.

"Is it Maloche?" she whispered.

"No. You can be sure it isn't."

"What does he want?"

"I don't think he wants anything." Hawk had no sooner spoken than the dream warrior slid from his horse in a lithe, graceful movement. Hawk's hand tensed on his rifle, but he didn't use it. A gun would not be proof against this man who was not a man.

Billy's gaze was captured by the warrior's movements, by the unusual amulet swinging upon his chest, an amulet that seemed somehow familiar. The silence was broken only by the soft brush of his moccasins in the sand. There was no wind this still-born night, but an inexplicable breeze sifted his hair and ruffled the fringe on his breechclout. He stopped at the outer edge of firelight and then started circling slowly, deliberately, silently.

Although she saw it with her own eyes, Billy's shocked senses refused to accept what happened next. The warrior metamorphosed abruptly and fluidly into an enormous wolf that paced the circle. His growl was the distant thunder, and the earth trembled beneath his heavily clawed paws. Pale light reflected off bone-white fangs as the wolf circled the campfire, all the while keeping its huge yellow eyes fixed upon her, looking through her.

She trembled, her heart pounding with unnameable fear. As she watched in disbelief the wolf shimmered and turned silver. Fur and muscle, fangs and claws, dissolved into vapor, then vanished as suddenly as a wind-blown cloud.

She could not move, or scream, or cry out. She could only witness in silence what her rational mind told her could not possibly be happening.

Hawk saw the transformation take place, and even though his mind was open to such improbable things, he found it hard to believe. The warrior stole close to camp, and with a heart-stopping thunder of wings, he changed into a gigantic hawk that took flight, and soared into the sky high above the campfire, circling, dipping, shrieking.

The wind stirred by its gigantic wings was colder than a mountain blizzard and chilled Hawk to the bone. The giant bird swooped down, diving straight for Hawk's eyes. The horny hooked beak was open, the mighty talons poised. It came at him faster than any airborne missile, but he couldn't move. He stared upward as the hawk loomed over him, his eyes refusing to obey his mind's command.

He could not close them, could not even blink. He could only watch as the monster bird zeroed in on him with deadly accuracy, preparing to take him home to hell.

At the last possible second, when it was so close Hawk could feel the bird's hot breath upon his face, it disappeared. It was there one moment, and the next it was gone. The icy wind retreated and the horrible shrieking stopped. And there were only he and Billy, clutching each other beside a dying campfire in the middle of the Superstition Mountains.

When the shock that had held him motionless receded, Hawk turned his attention to the trembling woman beside him. Her eyes were wide and she gripped his arm so hard the circulation was impaired. "Billy?" he said softly, unsure of his ability to speak. "Are you all right?"

Her lips moved, but the words were frozen in her throat. He pried her fingers off his arm and clutched her shoulders. "Billy! Talk to me!" He shook her hard and in doing so loosened her tongue.

She began to scream and babble incoherently, all the fear of the past few minutes erupting in hysteria. "Stop it, Billy! Stop it!" He slapped her then, and the dazed look slowly left her eyes, which filled with tears.

"Oh, Hawk!" She flung herself into his arms and hid her face against his chest. "Dear merciful God, please explain what just happened."

"I can't explain it."

"You saw it too?" she asked incredulously. "I'm not losing my mind?"

"I saw it. If you're going crazy, so am I."

They made enough noise to rouse John from sleep, and the old man stumbled toward them from the shadows, rubbing his eyes. "I say, what's going on here?" he wanted to know.

"Oh, Uncle," Billy gasped. "You won't believe me if I tell you." She proceeded to describe in amazing detail what she had just seen. When she was finished, she turned to Hawk for corroboration. "Isn't that right?"

His breath caught in his throat. "Not exactly."

"What do you mean, 'not exactly'? You told me you saw it as well."

"I did, but I didn't see any wolf." He told her about the giant hawk.

"I say, this is a strange phenomenon." John wiped his brow, his eyes owlish without the monocle. "In most cases of mass hysteria the subjects experience the same hallucination."

"It was no hallucination, Uncle." For once, Billy eschewed logic. "I know what I saw. It was very real. I felt it with all my senses. I smelled the wolf," she emphasized.

"The hawk was every bit as real to me." Hawk still didn't understand what had happened, but he could not accept John's theory about mass hysteria. Two people didn't constitute a mass, and they had nothing to be hysterical about.

"Perhaps it was an optical illusion," John suggested hopefully. Apparently the need to explain away the unexplainable was a family trait.

"Then why didn't we see the same thing?" she demanded.

"I don't know, my dear. I do wish I had an answer."

"Maybe it was a hallucination." That was something Hawk understood. The Apache often experienced fast-induced as well as drug-induced hallucinations. They called them visions. Since they had not fasted, it had to be a drug. "Billy, what was that secret herb you seasoned the meat with tonight?"

"I don't know its Latin name, but it's similiar to basil."

"Do you have any left?"

"I think so." She fetched the plant and handed it to Hawk, whose laugh filled her with indignation. "What's so funny?"

"This is locoweed, Billy."

"Locoweed? You mean the herb caused the hallucinations?"

"You sound disappointed. I thought you'd be happy to find out that there was a perfectly logical, scientific explanation for what happened tonight."

"Oh, I am," she said recovering quickly. "I'm quite relieved, actually. I really did fear for my sanity. I was almost ready to start believing in ghosts and shape-changers. I'm much more comfortable blaming the incident on locoweed."

"Is it a temporary condition, do you think?" John asked.

"Most assuredly." Billy was back in control now. "A chemical in the plant must have caused a temporary disorder of our perceptions by interfering with impulses to our nervous systems. It has been medically proven."

"Then I guess we can all get some sleep without having to worry about ghost warriors," Hawk said.

"What about posting a guard?" she asked.

"I've seen no signs of Maloche or anyone else for several days, and after tonight I need a good night's sleep. Deep as we are in this canyon, a trained bloodhound couldn't find us."

Billy retired to her tent, sure that she wouldn't be able to sleep a wink. However, the locoweed also had a tranquilizing effect, and she was lost to sleep as soon as she put down her head.

She rose early the next morning, after a sound night's sleep undisturbed by nightmares or dreams. She dressed and stepped out of her tent to find Hawk squatting on his heels a few feet from the cold fire. He was sifting through the sand, a worried look on his face.

"Good morning." She supposed that brief nod was his idea of a greeting. She started toward him when something on the ground caught her eye. She stooped to pick it up and examined it with mounting excitement, her heart pounding erratically. Hawk looked up then, and she thrust the hand holding the object behind her back. She went to him and peered over his shoulder. "What's so interesting?"

"Nothing." Hawk stood up and scuffed the sand hurriedly with his boot. He wasn't sure how Billy would take the news that he had found the campfire completely surrounded by a scattering of large animal tracks—wolf tracks. Telling her would shoot the locoweed theory clean to hell, and he didn't have an explanation to offer in its place. He thought about the vacant terror he'd seen in her eyes last night and decided to keep this little bit of news to himself for the time being.

"Don't tell me it's nothing when it is obviously something." She elbowed her way around him, but could see nothing in the sand to merit such attention.

"Has anyone ever told you you're a pushy woman, Sybilla Hartford?" he asked huskily as he drew her into his arms, using the most effective form of distraction at his disposal.

"Only you, Hawk Devlin," she whispered as his lips descended to hers and she lost herself in his kiss. One hand stole up to encircle his neck, but she kept the other, along with the thing she'd found, out of sight. She didn't know what to make of it, and she was afraid to ask Hawk's advice. She didn't think she would like his answer.

So much for scientific explanations, she thought. As she clutched in her hand the biggest damn hawk feather she had ever seen, she wondered what other surprises these mountains had in store for them.

Chapter 15

⌒◯◯⌒

They soon left behind the canyon where they'd seen the Ghost Warrior, but Billy could not get the incident out of her mind. She packed the hawk feather away and told herself that what they'd experienced was nothing more than a hallucination caused by the locoweed.

Still, she believed there was a purpose behind the strange occurrence. It was an omen, a portent. There had to be a greater meaning to what they'd seen. As she swayed along on Jezebel, under the brilliant midday sun, she suddenly realized what that meaning was.

Urging her mount alongside Hawk's she tested her theory. "That was no ordinary warrior we saw last night," she said.

"Yeah, I'd just about figured that out."

"Did you notice what he was wearing around his neck?"

Hawk considered her question. His mind replayed details of the Indian's appearance and formed an impossibly clear image of the talisman. "A cross."

"A golden cross," she clarified. "Possibly the same one Montoya gave his maiden."

He frowned. "What makes you think that?"

"Remember the drawing on the map? The cross the warrior wore resembled it so closely, it has to be the same one," she insisted.

Hawk was still doubtful. "We can't be sure of that, Billy. The Spaniards took Catholic friars along on all their expeditions to convert the Indians to Christianity. I'm sure they were free with their crosses, and hundreds of them probably fell into Indian hands."

Sybilla was obstinate. "I know the warrior had the Montoya cross for a purpose, just as I know he visited us for a purpose."

Hawk was willing to concede her point. The cross hanging around the Ghost Warrior's neck was indeed remarkably similar to the one depicted on the map. "If it was the same cross, what purpose could he possibly have had in appearing to us?"

"To let us know we're on the right trail."

"According to legend, the spirits don't want anyone to find the gold. They protect it, in fact. Why would one come down from the happy hunting ground and offer encouragement?"

"Because he was your ancestor. And I don't mean just because he was an Apache. There is a blood connection between you."

Her conclusions disturbed him, and he didn't know why. Was it because he'd felt an undeniable yet inexplicable connection to the apparition? "I should have come to your tent last night and made love to you," he grumbled. "You've had entirely too much time on your hands. That's the wildest thing you've come up with yet."

"I know I'm right. We're going to find the gold. Do you not think it significant that the apparition changed into a hawk right before your eyes? He became you, because you come from his blood."

Hawk realized that what she said made sense in a strange Apache way. It was not unknown for ancestors to appear in visions, and it was common for them to take an active role in their descendants' destinies. "I'll give you that much for the sake of argument. Why did he appear as a wolf to you?"

Billy's brow furrowed prettily. "I've been thinking about that. I believe he appeared as a wolf to warn me about Maloche."

Despite the hot day, Hawk felt a chill when he heard that name on Billy's lips.

"You see, Maloche is really a corruption of two Spanish words, *mal* and *noche*. Evil night. And what creature stalks the blackest night in the folklore of every culture from ancient Greece to present-day Europe?"

"The wolf?" he ventured.

"Exactly." Billy was proud of her deductions and couldn't understand why Hawk wasn't more eager to agree with them. "What do you think?"

He smiled suggestively to cover his dread. "I still think you have too much time on your hands." He didn't want to frighten her with the information that in Mexico, Maloche was known as El Lobo.

The wolf.

A startled cry interrupted them and they turned as one to see John staring at a mesa running parallel to the one they were crossing. His monocle had dropped from his eye, and he wore a shocked expression on his face.

"What is it?" Billy called.

"I saw it. There." He pointed, but they saw nothing except the usual scrub vegetation and saguaro.

"You saw what?" Hawk asked.

"The Phantom Camel. It was monstrously big and as black as the devil's teapot."

"There is nothing there now, Uncle," Billy pointed out.

"But it was a moment ago. Don't look at me like that. I'm not suffering from another bout of heat stroke. I saw it, I tell you."

"We believe you." Hawk said it to calm the old man, who was more likely suffering from apoplexy.

"It was right there," he insisted.

"Of course it was, dear," Billy put in.

"Don't humor me, I know what I saw. If you can see savage Indians turning into wolves and birds, and we all can see ghostly figures dancing around the fire, I daresay I can see the Phantom Camel.'' He retreated into a huffy silence, glancing nervously at the nearby ridge from time to time.

Hawk looked at Billy, and they both shrugged and smiled. In this strange country, they were willing to indulge an old man's fancy. As John pointed out, what was one more weird happening between friends?

That evening the camels seemed agitated but were finally hobbled for the night. Hawk, Billy, and John were just finishing supper when across the still air came a loud gurgling sound like running water. The camels struggled frantically against their hobbles, and Hawk was immediately on his feet, his rifle poised to fire.

''Don't shoot, Hawk,'' Billy said. ''It's a camel.''

''Shoot, man,'' John implored. ''It's the phantom.''

Hawk eyed the shaggy black beast standing some hundred feet away. ''To shoot or not to shoot,'' he paraphrased drolly. ''That is the question.''

''It's a male,'' Billy said.

Hawk cocked a brow. ''Yeah, I can tell.''

The creature gurgled again, more desperately this time, and Delilah answered, her response clearly an invitation for romance. Hawk figured anything having to do with camel love had to be loud and exceedingly messy, so he fired a warning shot over the black camel's head, and the startled beast loped away.

''I bet we haven't seen the last of him.'' Hawk quieted the camels, all of whom were females. According to Ahmed, very few male calves were allowed to live to maturity because they were so difficult to handle. Considering his past experiences with Delilah, Hawk figured that black son of a bitch had to be trouble with a capital T.

''Where do you suppose he came from?'' Billy asked.

"Well, he wasn't any phantom, that's for sure," Hawk said. "He's either a survivor of the cavalry camels that were set loose in the desert or one of their offspring. From the looks of him, he hasn't had any female companionship in a long time."

"A perceptive observation," Billy allowed. "Of course, it takes one to know one."

The look in his eyes told her to expect a late-night visitor to her tent that evening. "I think I'd rather contend with a phantom camel than with a lustful one."

Billy hid her amusement behind an embarrassed cough and wondered if her uncle had noticed what had transpired between them. "Perhaps he'll be back."

"You can bank on it."

All the next day the black camel dogged their trail, keeping just out of rifle range.

That night when they camped in another secluded canyon, this one with a natural spring, Hawk and Billy discussed what they should do about the camel. She claimed that, considering theirs were probably the first females he'd seen in while, he was being a respectful suitor. Hawk held that he was as cagey as he was ugly.

The lone camel proved to have a nasty, stubborn disposition, and Hawk dredged up every bit of camel lore he'd heard from Ahmed in the hope of persuading the animal to give up and go away. Nothing worked. Delilah was obviously primed for the experience the shaggy male offered.

"Get the hell out of here, you mangy, flea-bitten bag of bones." Hawk flapped his arms wildly.

The camel stared at him, cocked his head over his shoulder, then turned back.

Hawk gave the beast what he hoped was a fearsome glare. "Yeah, you. Get on out of here, you contrary varmint. You're causing trouble. Go on."

The camel blinked twice.

"Damn!" Hawk took off his hat and wiped his

forehead with his shirtsleeve. "If I have to," he threatened, "I'll blow your damn brains out."

A smiling Billy stood at the campfire, her hands on her hips. Hawk was glad someone was enjoying the show.

"Please," he whispered grudgingly, desperate enough to stoop to begging to win this standoff. "Please, dammit."

The stupid camel seemed determined not to go anywhere until it got what it came for. He couldn't really shoot the damn thing—Billy would think him gutless if he killed a defenseless animal—so he picked up some small stones and got ready to fire those instead.

"Wait." Billy unhobbled Delilah and led her by the halter. "I have a plan. Let's play matchmaker for these two."

Hawk grumbled, "It could only improve his attitude."

"Perhaps Delilah can domesticate him."

"Females do tend to have that effect on males," he allowed.

"If he becomes tame enough, we may be able to use him later. We might need an extra pack animal."

Hawk shook his head. "I'm no camel expert, but it seems to me that getting a taste of what he's been missing all this time might make the old buzzard worse."

"Oh, I don't know," Billy said breezily as she led Delilah toward the far end of the box canyon. "Female companionship hasn't done you any harm."

They gathered brush and closed off an area of the canyon, erecting a honeymoon corral well away from the camp so that the humans wouldn't have to endure the animals' amorous overtures. Hawk and Billy watched the lovestruck camels as they got acquainted.

"I think I'll call him Samson," Billy announced.

"It's fitting, don't you think? Look, he's flirting with her."

The newly christened Samson stuck out his long tongue, inflating it like a big pink balloon until it seemed in danger of bursting.

Hawk took Billy's hand in his, running his thumb lightly over the back of her knuckles. "I know what it takes to make your knees wobbly, and it has nothing to do with gurgling or tongue inflation."

She pretended to be interested in the animals. "I wouldn't say that. I quite adore the little choky sound you make just before you—" Shocked by her own boldness, she broke off in embarrassment. When she looked into his eyes, she knew there was no reason to be ashamed about what they'd shared.

Some might consider it wrong, but to her their loving was beautiful. She had discovered a new freedom of expression after relinquishing her out-of-place inhibitions, and the part of her that reveled in that freedom prompted her to add, "And being noninflatable does not make your tongue any less skilled."

Hawk lowered his lips slowly and kissed her. There was nothing tentative about the way she opened her mouth for him, nothing restrained about the way her tongue sought and parried with his. There was nothing reserved about the insistence of her desire as she pressed brazenly against him. She was a woman with wants and needs as powerful as his own.

Her response excited Hawk. And scared him, too. His lips slid over hers with more ferocity, and every whispered gasp of pleasure he provoked from her stoked his own desires.

Because he feared he'd end up taking her in the sand with as little finesse as Samson was now taking Delilah, he ended the kiss. He held her and leaned back to gaze into her eyes. With sudden realization, he knew he'd never before needed a woman to need him, and the feeling left him shaken.

With Mariel Davenport, he had been more smitten than in love. He'd placed her on a pedestal, and any physical desire he might have felt had been uncertain and adolescent. He had wanted to marry her because he had thought it was time he wed. His peers were all announcing their engagements, and settling down seemed to be the next logical step after graduation.

He'd chosen Mariel because, at the time, she'd represented everything he thought he wanted in a wife. She was sweet and innocent, refined and vapid. Had he elected to stay in Williamsburg and work in her father's bank, she would have made a perfectly suitable wife. But he hadn't really loved her or needed her. When he'd returned to Arizona, he'd gained sexual experience from women who had been employed to give it. He had not expected, or received, any tender emotion from them, and he'd certainly never met one he'd want to stay with. In fact, he'd never really thought about them once he'd left their beds.

But Billy was different. He'd heard men talking about wanting a woman to be a wildcat in bed and a lady in the parlor, but he'd never thought such a creature could exist. Now he knew that a woman could have needs and desires as powerful as any man's.

He respected Billy for her tenacity which he'd thought was stubbornness. He admired her dignity which he'd assumed was haughtiness; her independence which he'd mistaken for pride. She had a good mind and the strength of character to use it, but what made her special was her essential goodness.

He understood what his mother had meant about loving someone unconditionally. The revelation was startling, but suddenly Hawk knew that he did love Billy. He wanted her strength and goodness in his life. He wanted her.

Unsure how she would react to such a confession,

he said nothing. He took her hand, and they walked back to camp, met halfway by a clearly frightened John. "What is it, Uncle?" Billy asked.

The old man's chest heaved with the effort to get the words out. "I was up on the bluff above the water hole taking pictures and I saw something. Hurry."

They followed John to the vantage point on the bluff and watched a cloud of dust coming steadily closer.

"Damn," Hawk swore quietly.

"What does it mean?" Billy asked, knowing from Hawk's reaction that it wasn't good.

"Riders, and they're headed this way. Twelve, maybe more."

"Indians?" She cursed herself for jumping immediately to that conclusion.

"Could be, but I doubt it. There hasn't been much Indian trouble in these parts since Geronimo surrendered. More than likely it's a band of outlaws. If we're lucky, it might be a posse chasing some."

Billy tried to think positive thoughts. "Which do you suppose it is?"

"Probably Maloche. He's about due. It doesn't much matter, because when that many men ride together in this country it usually means trouble."

"For us?"

"For whoever gets in their way. Men don't ride in this area of the desert unless they have a desperate reason."

"What can we do?" John asked.

"They're probably headed for the water hole. Since we wouldn't stand a chance if we ran for it, our best bet is to stay here and keep them from the spring. If it's Maloche's band they can last longer than most without water, but they can't live without it forever."

"What are they doing way out here?" The dust cloud now seemed as dangerous to Billy as a tor-

nado. Like that storm, it was also unavoidable and
deadly.

"They've probably been raiding across the border. One of Maloche's sidelines, besides murdering
and stealing, is slave trading. He steals white women
and children and sells them in Mexico. If that's what
he's been up to, they're probably hoping to lose
themselves in the desert. There sure as hell isn't
anything out here to steal . . ."

His words trailed off when he saw the frightened
look on Billy's face. It occurred to him that she herself was very valuable, a woman Maloche would
want as soon as he saw her. A woman as beautiful
as Billy would bring a good price across the border.

Interpreting his thoughts correctly, Billy shivered.
She would rather die than be at the mercy of such
an unscrupulous monster as Maloche was rumored
to be. She sent up a silent prayer that the rapidly
approaching riders were just a posse. "What should
we do to secure our position?"

Hawk issued instructions and worked alongside
the other two to set up points of observation. John
hid the rest of the camels in the brush corral to protect them from wayward bullets. There was little
more they could do, except wait for whatever danger darkness would bring.

Restless, Hawk prowled the perimeter of their
camp, checking its defenses. The spring emerged
from its red rock source near the mouth of the canyon. The pool supported relatively lush vegetation
and a teeming colony of skimming insects, a sure
sign that it was safe to drink.

There was only one way into their canyon stronghold. The steep, rocky trail made it easily defended
by a few guns, but the dense brush below provided
plenty of cover for potential attackers. Cover that
Maloche knew all too well how to use.

The shadows lengthened as Billy prepared a hasty
meal. She'd had qualms about lighting a fire, but
Hawk had assured her that if it was Maloche, eating

a cold meal wouldn't deter him. Besides, he probably already knew their position. Using ironwood, Hawk showed her how to make a nearly smokeless fire.

As she dished up the food, Hawk joined her. Her voice was a tense whisper when she spoke. "Are they close?"

"We still have a while."

"Hungry?"

"Always."

"Then you shan't mind eating beans again."

"Not at all." Hawk took a bite but stopped in mid-chew when a birdcall carried on the still air. He turned toward the sound.

"Was that a quail?" Billy asked nervously.

Hawk shook his head and swallowed. "It was meant to sound like one, but it wasn't."

"How do you know?" John was badly shaken, had been since he'd first sighted the approaching riders.

"It's just something a man learns when he lives out here. It won't be much longer now."

"Are you sure it wasn't a posse and they simply bedded down somewhere for the night?" John gave up any pretense of eating and leaned forward anxiously.

"What we saw earlier was no posse. They'd have ridden in here as bold as brass. And they'd have ridden in tonight. It's Maloche all right."

Billy didn't ask how he knew, she simply accepted that he did. "Will they attack?"

Hawk thought about it as he finished eating. "Maybe not. Any man who believes an amulet can make him immortal must be pretty superstitious. He's a mongrel, but most tribes have war taboos, like not eating certain foods before a battle and staying away from women. There's an especially strong taboo against fighting at night."

Billy jumped when the distant birdcall sounded again. "Why?"

''Many believe that warriors slain in the dark get lost in the blackness between the world of the living and the world of the dead.''

''Then we shall have a brief respite?'' John wanted to know.

Hawk nodded. ''It'll end at dawn.''

''You're sure?'' Billy wished they could spend this night differently, in each other's arms instead of contemplating their own deaths.

Hawk shook his head again. ''Nothing's sure with Maloche. We'll keep watch. There may be skeptics among his men who ignore the old superstitions. Many men have died in the desert without ever knowing an Indian was near. Maloche is part devil, but he's mostly Indian.''

John picked up his rifle and his cup of coffee. ''I shall take up my watch now. It will be dark soon.'' He was obviously trying to put on a brave front for Billy's sake, but Hawk could see what it was costing him. His estimation of the Englishman rose several notches. John might be old and he might be scared, but he seemed determined to do his part.

Once they were alone, Hawk disposed of his plate and took Billy's hand in his. He was troubled, fearing what might happen to her if he got himself killed. Despite his courage, John would be less than useless as a protector against a man as ruthless as the wolf.

Hawk removed a sheathed knife from his boot and placed it in Billy's palm. ''This belonged to my mother. I want you to have it. Use it if you have to.''

She asked no questions, but withdrew the small, pearl-handled dagger from its scabbard. It was wickedly sharp, and the thought of using it made her stomach lurch. She replaced it in its sheath and slipped it into her own boot. ''Thank you.'' She hoped she wouldn't have to use the weapon, but knew exactly what to do if the need arose.

It was nearly dark now so Hawk doused the fire,

careful not to look directly into the flames. A man who gazed into the bright flames was temporarily blinded and out here if he turned quickly into the darkness, it might cost him his life.

Billy stood next to Hawk, gazing deep into his eyes before pressing against him, then urgently seeking his lips. He responded hungrily, and she momentarily forgot the threat all around them.

She forgot everything except the feel of his warm lips as they caressed hers and the gentle strength of his arms as they tightened around her waist. She delighted in the way her breasts flattened against his muscled chest and in the pulsating ache between her thighs that demanded so much more.

Hawk's heartbeat thundered when her arms folded around his neck and her fingers massaged his nape. He took her mouth completely, passionately. The soft scent of amole came from her silky hair, and she moaned softly.

Instantly he was hot and hard and hungry. Only with great reluctance did he manage to force himself to end the kiss. He wasn't so caught up that he could forget the danger.

"We'll continue this another time."

"Will we?" Her voice trembled as she faced the fact that this might be their last night together.

"I'll get you out of this, Billy. That's a promise."

The night passed quickly. By the time dawn filled the canyon with its pale gray light, Hawk's eyes were red-rimmed from staring for hours into the darkness. He could almost feel the evil presence of Maloche. He knew from the soft calls which were not of nature that many men had slipped silently into position. They lay in wait, listening to the morning sounds, waiting for the signal to attack.

He remembered the stories he'd heard of Maloche. The man was aptly named. He was as cunning as the wolf, shrewd and untiring, not a man to be taken lightly.

A shot came suddenly out of nowhere and struck

a rock close to Hawk's head. It ricocheted with an angry whine before silence once again filled the canyon. Silence and the rising sun.

Billy scrabbled up the rocks, being sure to keep her head down. "Are you all right?" she cried.

Hawk nodded and flashed a cocky grin. He touched a finger to his lips to quiet her. Gently he traced the line of her jaw, then gestured for her to stay low.

Billy had never been so frightened as when she'd heard that shot. Her heart had nearly pounded out of her chest as she'd raced to his side, fearing what she might find. But her fear was for Hawk, not herself. She'd had lots of time to think during the long, tense night, and she knew that Hawk meant more to her than anyone else. Part of her died each time she thought of losing him. The gold, and the fame of finding it, now seemed unimportant.

If they got out of this alive, she was determined to risk everything, even her pride, by telling Hawk how much she loved him. All that mattered, all she wanted, was for him to be safe. She couldn't even consider a world without Hawk Devlin in it.

Hawk took off his hat and raised up slowly to stare hard into the rubble and brush at the bottom of the trail. A cluster of rocks didn't look quite natural. He lifted his Winchester and sighted. Drawing a bead on the flat surface of a rock slightly behind the grouping, he steadied himself and blinked the sweat from his eyes. He concentrated, then squeezed off a shot.

From behind the rocks came a startled yelp, and he fired into the rocks again and again. There was silence once more.

When Hawk slid down to safety, Billy breathed a sigh of relief. She stared into his eyes, made as blue as a stormy sky by his fervor, and tried to convey her feelings without words. She wanted to tell him she loved him, but this was not the tender moment a woman longed for. Turning suddenly away, she raised her rifle and fired at a moving bush.

Their eyes met over her rifle and briefly, lightly, he touched his lips to hers. "You're quite a woman. A woman any man would be proud to ride the river with. I want you to know that."

She cocked the gun and fired again, then grinned happily. Coming from Hawk, those words meant a lot. "I shall take that as a compliment."

"It was meant as one." Hawk squeezed off another shot.

"Does that mean we haven't a hope of getting out of here alive?"

"Hell no!" Hawk grinned. "I'm just a man who likes to cover his ass."

Soon the fight became fast and fierce. The attackers hid in the thick underbrush, as hard to hit as bronzed ghosts. Within moments they rushed onward, moving quickly on a silent signal. Hawk and Billy fired and two fell to the ground, then the area was empty again, as if the whole movement had been no more than an illusion caused by sunlight on the sand.

Hawk searched the brush and jumble of rocks for a target he didn't expect to find. He glanced at Billy and found her staring at him in a peculiar way. "Are you all right?" he asked.

She mopped perspiration from her forehead. "I'd feel better if we had something to shoot at. This is spooky."

"Perhaps we should have gotten out of here when we had a chance," John said in a low voice. "We're no more than prisoners in this bloody canyon."

"Not hardly. We've got plenty of food and water, and we're armed." Hawk figured their ammunition would last several days. Time was their only hope. Maloche's band would eventually look elsewhere for water, but just how long that might take was anybody's guess.

John fired two shots that furrowed the crest of a

sand hill a short distance away, a crest where an instant before a half-naked Indian had showed himself. "Missed the bugger."

"I think you made him pretty unhappy by coming so close," Hawk replied. "Good shot."

John beamed. "Not exactly Deadeye Dick, but not bad for an old scudder like myself."

The hours passed slowly. Heat waves shimmered over the desert floor, imbuing the landscape with an unreal quality. Finally the shadows lengthened. Hawk knew that under cover of darkness Maloche and his men would creep closer and closer.

Hawk moved around their stronghold, scanning the desert from every vantage point. His main concern was to keep the enemy away from the spring and the rocks bordering it. Feeling as secure as the deepening twilight allowed, he sank down beside Billy.

"Will we really make it?" she whispered.

"Yes," he replied, determined.

"This waiting is unbearable. I do not want to experience many more days like today. It makes me nervous the way those savages appear suddenly and then melt into the rocks when we return their fire."

"They're trying to get us to waste our ammunition. Eventually they'll grow desperate for water and be forced to make a move."

John paced, then snapped his fingers. "I remember reading a novel in which Deadeye Dick found himself in a similar situation. Perhaps we should do as he did—rush them and force their hand, as it were."

"We wait," Hawk insisted stubbornly.

"I could jump on our fastest camel and draw them out, then you and Sybilla could pick them off. What do you say?"

"I say that's the most ridiculous thing I've ever heard and does not bear consideration," Billy snapped.

John sank onto the nearest rock, his face more forlorn than that of any lost hound Hawk had ever seen. Poor John. Hawk knew how difficult it was to be Billy's hero and exactly what it felt like to be on the receiving end of her haughty lectures. Lowering his voice, he asked, "Weren't you a little rough on the old guy? He was only trying to help in his own way."

Billy realized her rebuke had been caused by frayed nerves. She didn't have a lot of patience even under normal circumstances. "I apologize for barking at you, Uncle John. I love you, and I wouldn't want to lose you."

"Quite all right. I had not contemplated the possible consequences of such an act." John took out his handkerchief and mopped his brow before scooting into the shade of a boulder to do just that.

No one spoke for several moments, and Billy found the silence more oppressive than a volley of gunfire. "If something does not happen soon, I fear I may explode and do something quite foolish."

Before Hawk could ask what she had in mind, John leaped to his feet. "By George, that is a bully idea, Sybilla."

Hawk stared at him, and Billy frowned. "At the danger of sounding obtuse, Uncle, I must ask what you have in mind."

"Exploding, my dear," John explained patiently. "Are we not in the possession of a quantity of dynamite? Quite a bit if memory serves me."

"Yes," she exclaimed, clapping her forehead with the heel of her hand. "I'd quite forgotten about that. We can use the dynamite to get rid of these cutthroats once and for all."

"Whoa there," Hawk said. "I think you'd better hear me out before you go blowing up that mountain. You run the risk of blocking the trail. We might not be able to get out of here unless you handle the explosives very carefully."

Billy hadn't considered that, but she placed her trust in the man she loved. "Can you do it?"

"I don't know," he admitted.

A barrage of shots filled the canyon, and he made a quick decision, scuttling over to the packs and retrieving the dynamite they'd brought to help excavate the gold.

John's shout warned him that Maloche and his band had slithered out of the rocks and were coming at them, boldly and from several different directions.

"Looks like they're in a hurry to die. Well, let 'em come." Hawk grabbed three sticks of dynamite, lit the long fuses with his cheroot, and handed one each to John and Billy. "Don't get nervous and throw before I say. Now, on the count of three."

They watched the renegades come up the mountain. When no answering gunfire drove them back, they became a brazen, screaming, terrifying wave.

"One, two, three. Now!" Hawk and John threw their explosives, but Billy froze at the sight of the mauraders and held fast to hers. Even though they were still some distance away, she saw the murderous looks on the faces of the men moving toward her. She saw the glint of knives and rifles, felt the terror in her blood. Time seemed to stand still as she clutched the stick of dynamite and watched the enemy advance.

"Goddammit!" Hawk jerked the stick out of her hand and threw it as hard as he could. The blasts came almost simultaneously, filling the small canyon with deafening roars that cracked and rumbled like thunder gone crazy. The explosions lit the bright sky with an eerie glow, and upflung boulders burst into fragments, showering down a rain of debris. An avalanche of rocks tumbled down the rocky side of the mountain, making the ground tremble.

It was several moments before the blinding dust cleared enough for Hawk, Billy, and John to see that the damage was devastatingly complete.

Billy was still mute with fear, and Hawk hugged her to him while keeping one eye on the trail. The men who hadn't been blown to bits were being bombarded by falling rocks that crushed the life out of them. Down below, nothing moved, but he was even more pleased by the fact that the rubble hadn't blocked the trail completely.

Billy felt numb, as if the blast had blown away her feelings. She observed Hawk, who surveyed the destruction with grim satisfaction. Her uncle's eyes, on the other hand, fairly glinted with elation.

"I say, that was bloody exciting! Three people doing in all those cutthroats." He paced nervously, talking faster. "I don't mind telling you, for a moment there I thought we were doomed."

"We might have been if you hadn't thought of the dynamite, John." Hawk patted him on the back. "I'd forgotten all about it. You probably saved our lives." He checked his rifle and headed down the trail.

Billy found her voice. "Hawk! Where are you going?"

"To look for survivors."

Chapter 16

Hawk picked his way carefully over the tumbled debris, his rifle cocked and ready, his every nerve tuned to detect threats from enemies who might have lived through the explosion. He swung his gaze from side to side, from crumpled unmoving bodes to half-buried unmoving bodies. The destruction was even more complete than he had dared to presume. The wall of rock loosened by the explosion had crashed down on the renegades without mercy. Hawk counted eleven dead men before he climbed the rocks to search higher.

Back at the camp Billy gathered firewood while trying to cope with her own shock and her uncle's unexpected exuberance over the annihilation of their attackers. "I cannot believe you are so happy," she said with tired incredulity.

"Happy? Well, I suppose I am happy. We just trounced those hostiles, did we not?"

"Trounced, Uncle? Trounced is what one does to cricket opponents. I believe the correct term for what we did is *killed*."

"Yes, as it were."

"I find it hard to accept that I just slaughtered my fellow man."

"They were our enemies. Those fellow men of yours would have butchered us, and gladly, if we'd given them half a chance. In this wild land it is kill or be killed. Surely you understand that by now."

She understood, but she couldn't accept how cheaply life was held in this country. The violence she'd witnessed had made her more aware than ever of the differences between the quiet, civilized world she had grown up in and the savage one that had spawned Hawk. It also pointed out her unsuitability for such a life.

She'd thought herself strong, capable of surviving, but when the crucial moment came she'd been unable to act. She'd frozen like a doe in a hunter's gunsight. Her background and innate civility had worked against her. In the moment of truth, she'd found that she could not kill to save her life. She had fooled herself. She was no adventuress.

John climbed onto a pile of rocks and peered into the deepening shadows for a sign of Hawk. He pulled out his pocket watch. "He's been gone half an hour," he said uneasily. "I hope he did not run into difficulties."

She sat morosely in the flickering shade of a paloverde tree. "I shouldn't worry too much about Hawk Devlin if I were you. It will take more than a few bloodthirsty savages to stop him."

"Oh, blast it all," John said suddenly.

"What is it, Uncle?" She watched as he knelt on the rocks and peered into a crevice.

"It's this benighted snuff spoon. I thought I'd reattached it adequately to the chain, but it's come loose and fallen into this dark crack. The infernal thing is more trouble than it's worth, I'm sure."

"Perhaps you should consider giving up the snuff habit."

"I might at that." He thrust his hand between the rocks and withdrew it a moment later with a shriek. "I've been bitten," he pronounced in a surprised voice, his eyes wide, his face white.

Billy ran to his side. She heard the ominous rattle at the same moment that she saw two distinctive fang marks on the inside of her uncle's right wrist.

The skin surrounding the injured area was already swelling and becoming discolored, a clear indication of the seriousness of the bite. "Diamondback," she breathed. "Move slowly away from the rocks."

Hoping Hawk was within earshot, she cupped her hands around her mouth and called to him. "Hawk! Hurry!" She wanted to scream, but such panic would only frighten John unnecessarily and cause his heart to race, the venom to spread faster.

"Of all the bloody rotten luck." John seemed unable to believe such a thing had happened to him. "Got the blasted spoon, though."

The giddy note in his voice alarmed her. "Don't worry. You'll be all right." Billy spoke the words to calm him; she did not really believe them. The diamondback rattler's venom was deadly, and as she led her uncle into her tent she tried frantically to recall what first aid measures were necessary.

"Hawk will be here soon," she said, making him comfortable on the narrow cot. "He'll know what to do."

Even as she spoke, she grappled with the frightening possibility that her beloved uncle might die because of her own fear and ignorance. She couldn't let that happen and knew she had to act. She unbuttoned his cuff and rolled up his sleeve. The swelling had already advanced several inches.

"How do you feel?" she asked gently as she tore a rag into narrow strips, glancing frantically at the raised tent flap. If only Hawk would get here.

"My wrist hurts like Hades. I know it sounds silly, but my lips feel numb as well."

"I'm going to apply a tourniquet to restrict the blood flow while I incise the wound," she explained in an effort to keep his mind off the pain. "I'll remove the venom by suction." She sounded much more confident than she felt.

"Now, my dear, I don't know if you should do that. It might be dangerous."

"Rattlesnake venom isn't poisonous if swallowed." She remembered that much from the reading she'd done to prepare for the journey.

"Perhaps we should wait until Hawk returns.
He'll know . . ."

A bout of violent retching convinced Billy that the
venom was already spreading dangerously and that
she had no time to lose. Moving quickly, she ster-
ilized a knife over the flame of a match and washed
the wound as best she could with soap and water.
She would have preferred the antiseptic properties
of alcohol, but Hawk had been adamant about not
allowing any on the trip. As she made a small inci-
sion over each fang mark, she was appalled by the
amount of blood that flowed from the cuts.

She wiped her forehead with the back of her hand
and, after cleaning away the blood, sucked at the
wound and spat into the dirt. She had no idea how
much of the venom she could remove that way, but
she went on, sucking and spitting, until she heard
Hawk's voice behind her.

"What happened?"

"Uncle John was bitten by a rattlesnake," she said
between breaths.

"Here, let me do that." Hawk nudged her aside.
"Are you sure it was a rattler?"

"I heard it," she pronounced grimly. "I'll never
forget that sound."

Hawk loosened the tourniquet and, taking turns,
they continued the suction for nearly an hour. Even
so, he knew they had probably removed no more
than fifty percent of the venom. He noticed that the
swelling had progressed nearly to the elbow.

John's breathing was shallow, and he drifted in
and out of delirium. Hawk tucked a blanket around
the old man and led Billy outside.

"Will he be all right?" she asked, worry and concern dragging at her words just as fatigue dragged
at her body.

"I don't know. We'll have to wait and see. We did the best we could. The next twenty-four hours will be critical."

"Is there anything else we can do? Anything to improve his chances?"

Hawk took a good look at her for the first time since the siege. The day-long battle, combined with her uncle's accident, had taken their toll, and she showed signs of imminent collapse. Because of her strength and courage, he sometimes forgot that she was a gently reared Englishwoman. She really wasn't equipped to deal with the emotional and physical stress this country regularly imposed on those audacious enough to challenge it.

"There is something," he said.

Her eyes brightened. "What is it?"

"The Pimas make a poultice out of a desert plant. They claim it cures snakebite, but I don't want to give you false hope."

"False hope is better than no hope at all," she cried.

"Are you willing to put your belief in something as unscientific as an Indian remedy?"

"After what I've seen and heard and been through in the past few weeks, I'm able to believe anything. Do you know how to prepare this poultice?"

"I've seen it done."

"Do the plants grow in this area?"

"I don't know. I'd have to go look." He glanced at the tent. "It could take a while and I don't want to leave you alone."

"Why not? Maloche and his men died in the explosion, didn't they?"

"I'm assuming they did. But I've never seen Maloche, and like I said before, it's a mistake to assume anything where he's concerned. I found a lot bodies, but with all the debris, I can't say for sure that there weren't any survivors."

Hawk didn't see how anyone could have lived

through the blast and falling rock, but if only half of the stories he'd heard about Maloche were true, the man had as many lives as a cat.

Billy gripped his arm. "You must go after the plant, Hawk. Uncle John might die if you don't. Please!"

The desperate note in her voice made him agree despite his reservations. "All right. I'll leave first thing in the morning."

"No! You must go immediately. We can't waste another moment. Tomorrow might be too late."

Hawk knew she was right, but the day was nearly gone. "I can't find it in the dark. I have to wait until morning." That way, if Maloche or anyone else showed up for revenge, he'd be on hand to greet them, up close and in person.

"You can go now and be back before dark. I know you can! Please, Hawk. You have never mentioned love, and I suppose the future can hold nothing for two such as us. But if the intimacies we shared meant anything to you, you must do this for me."

Sensing that she was near hysteria, Hawk pulled her into his arms and held her tight. He did care about her deeply. He wanted her, needed her, but feared they had no chance. Two people couldn't exist only in the world of their love for each other.

He yearned to tell her just how much she meant to him. But not now, when he was about to leave her. He didn't know the words to bridge their differences. Words, he'd learned, were sometimes the tenderest form of torment.

"Please, Hawk." Billy looked up at him, tears running down her cheeks. "I've never begged anyone for anything, but I am begging you now. After my mother died, my father traveled more than ever and left me in the care of my Grandmother Sybilla and Uncle John. That dour old lady never loved me. I think she held my Spanish blood against me. But none of that mattered to my uncle. He never had a wife, never had a child of his own. He lavished his affection on me.

"He made me feel like a worthy person in the face of Grandmother's disapproval. He was always there, gentle and loving, ever ready to step between me and her sharp tongue. Looking back, I don't know why I thought my father was the brave one. Running away from responsibility isn't the mark of courage. Taking on those who are not your own, is."

"Billy, don't cry."

She wiped her tears away. "I'm sorry. I didn't mean to. It's just that Uncle John means so much to me."

"If I go, you have to promise to stay awake and keep your guard up until I get back."

"I can do that," she agreed staunchly.

"But can you use the rifle? Can you use it against a real flesh and blood man if one shows up while I'm gone?"

After what had happened with the dynamite, she doubted her ability to do just that, but she didn't waver in front of Hawk. "If I have to, yes."

He gave her last-minute instructions as he saddled Delilah. He didn't know how long it would take him to find the plant with the spotted leaves, or even if he could. "If John dies while I'm gone, I want you to take the rifle and hide out in the rocks. Don't show yourself to anyone but me. You got that?"

"I won't let him die, Hawk. I know you'll find the plant quickly. Don't worry about us, we'll be fine."

He kissed her briefly before mounting up. If anyone could will the old man out of death's clutches, it was Billy.

She couldn't bring herself to watch Hawk ride away. What if something happened to him and he didn't come back? The thought filled her with a sense of loneliness so strong it was almost a tangible thing. He had to come back to her! She couldn't go on without him. She couldn't save John alone or even ensure her own survival.

The crushing acceptance of her own fragility in this hostile land frightened her more than any real or imagined threat ever had. Clutching her rifle in her hand, she hurried back into the tent to check on her uncle.

John seemed to be having even more difficulty breathing than before, and she feared the venom had poisoned his nerves. She knew it killed by causing a complete shutdown of respiration and circulation, but she refused to consider such a possibility.

"Hold on, Uncle. Hawk has gone for a cure and when he returns he'll make you as right as rain. Never fear." She sat by his side for long minutes, listening to every sound, praying for Hawk to return soon.

After a while, John patted her arm with his good hand. "It doesn't matter anymore, my dear. I fear I am, as they say so colorfully out here, a goner."

"Don't be silly," she said, dashing away a sudden tear.

"I'm not afraid to die, you know. I've lived a long time. Of course," he amended, "much of my life was spent in unrelieved tedium, but the past few weeks have been most exciting. My only regret is that I won't live to see you and Hawk find the gold. That would be a sight to behold."

"There isn't any gold," she denied softly.

"What's this, you say? Of course there's gold."

"Ricardo Montoya was a deluded man who probably drew that map and made up the legend for his own self-aggrandizement. We have no proof that he was even here."

"What about Weaver's Needle? You're so close now. And what about the amulet the Ghost Warrior wore?"

"I wanted them to be significant, so I convinced myself they were. Perhaps I'm as deluded as Montoya." She'd certainly fooled herself about other things.

"This doesn't sound like my Sybilla Hartford talking." John winced with pain when he waved his hand at her. "Are you giving up, then?"

"Not giving up. Admitting at last that coming here was a fool's errand from the very beginning. As soon as Hawk returns and you're fit again, we're going home."

"And where might that be? Hartsmoor doesn't belong to us anymore," he reminded her. "We have burned all our bridges."

"Then we'll go back to Tucson."

"And do what, pray tell?"

"Any number of things." She smiled, recalling the dearth of culture and entertainment in the town. "Perhaps we can take to the stage. You can learn to pull rabbits from a hat, and I can recite poetry while performing cartwheels. I fear neither of us is much qualified for anything else."

"Don't make me laugh, my dear. It hurts too much."

She planted a soft kiss on his forehead and tucked the blanket around him. "Can you ever forgive me for dragging you all the way out here for nothing?"

"Hardly for nothing! And as I recall, I had to fight for the right to come along. As for forgiveness, it is I who should be begging it of you."

"What do you mean?"

"You made it possible for me to have some adventure in my dreary life, to see a part of the world I'd only read about in Deadeye Dick novels. I, on the other hand, have contributed nothing. Then I up and get snakebit, for God's sake. Such a doltish thing to do."

"What do you mean, you contributed nothing? Why, you are the one who thought of using the dynamite. Most likely that single act saved all our lives. You've been most brave."

"God bless you for trying to ease an old man's last hour, but I wish my death could have been less ignominious and more worthy of recounting to your children and grandchildren."

"Don't speak so. It's bad luck to dwell on such things."

"Bad luck?" He smiled weakly and lightly tweaked her nose. "Has the logical Miss Hartford turned superstitious at last?"

"It's these infernal mountains. The sooner we get out of here the better for all of us."

"But what of Hawk?"

"What about him?"

"Do you think he will be willing to call off the search?"

"He is in my employ and will do as I say." But she wasn't at all convinced he would. As stubborn as he was, he would most likely challenge her decision, but she would deal with that once her uncle was out of danger.

John struggled to sit up and gripped her hand. "Don't give up! Not on the gold or on Hawk Devlin. Even if you find the former, it won't be worth as much as the treasure to be found in the latter."

She gave him a gentle hug and eased him back down on the cot. "Hawk and I could never have a life together. I can't find a place in his world and he has rejected mine."

"Then make a place where you can be together. This is an untamed land—make of it what you can. You and he are more alike than either of you is willing to admit." His excitement brought on a wracking cough, which induced another bout of violent retching. He apologized for the mess as Billy cleaned it up.

"See what I mean by ignominious? Nothing noble or heroic about sicking up oneself to death, eh?"

"Just rest. Hawk will be back soon."

"I do have one small request."

"What's that, Uncle?"

"Since dead artists always have a better chance for fame than living ones, will you promise to take my photographic plates back to civilization? Perhaps you can interest a publisher in them, and I can have that bit of immortality.''

''Of course. That's why you must get well. You'll want to see your work compared to that of other famous frontier photographers, won't you?'' She was alarmed by how unfocused his gaze had become.

''I can't see you very well, my dear,'' John said weakly.

''I'll light a lantern.'' Night had crept into the tent as they spoke, filling it with cool shadows. Far away a coyote howled.

''It's not the darkness. Is double vision a symptom of snakebite, do you suppose?''

It was a very bad sign. She held his left hand, which was cold to the touch, while his right was swollen and mottled and hot. ''I'm sure it's only temporary.''

''My whole face is numb. I think I am well and truly a goner. And so quickly, too.'' Though weak, he spoke as calmly as though discussing a change in the weather. ''It's really quite ironically fitting that a man who escaped his fear of the country churchyard by reading Wild West novels should have only a pile of rocks for a grave marker and a baleful coyote as an eulogist,'' he said.

''You won't die,'' Billy whispered. But even as she said them, she knew the words were a feeble defense against the Superstitions' most powerful inhabitant—the bright angel of death.

''We had a grand time, didn't we, old girl?'' he asked softly.

''Indeed we did, Uncle, and shall have many more.''

''No, love,'' he demurred. ''But you and Hawk will.'' His breathing became ragged, and he closed his eyes, whether to sleep or unconsciousness, Billy could not tell.

Caught up in her fear and grief, she forgot all about Hawk's warning. She forgot the rifle leaning against the tent wall, well out of reach. Kneeling on the ground, her head still resting at her uncle's side, she whispered, ''I love you,'' before succumbing to fatigue and drifting off to her own haunted sleep.

Chapter 17

"**M**aloche is not an easy man to kill, eh?" The menacing voice was hard-edged and dangerous.

When she first awoke, Billy thought that what she was witnessing was part of a bad dream. But when her eyes finally focused she realized the gruesome scene being played out in the tent was all too real. Poor Uncle John was locked in mortal combat with a dirt-caked, blood-soaked madman. The old man struggled gamely, but even wounded, Maloche, was a far stronger man.

Shock slowed her ability to react, and when she made a grab for the rifle, it was too late. Maloche yanked her back brutally by the hair and stuffed a dirty rag into her mouth to stifle her scream. He slammed her onto her stomach on the ground and, digging his knee into her back, knelt and tied her hands behind her with a leather thong.

In the lantern's dim light, her frantic glance sought John. A horrified sob swelled in her throat when she found him slumped at her side, a knife in his chest. His sightless eyes stared back at her as if apologizing for his weakness. Her heart broke. Dear old John had died a hero's death after all.

Before the tears could roll down her cheeks, before she could mourn her uncle, Maloche grabbed her hair and jerked her painfully to her feet. Her physical discomforts scarcely registered, so great was her grief for John. But in moments fear for her own life took priority. Maloche was the embodiment of savageness.

Their gazes caught and held briefly, but Billy looked away, unable to bear the cruelty in his flat, black eyes. Eyes that were cold and empty—reflecting nothing of the soul within.

His weathered face was dark and broad, with a flat nose and blunt jaw. He was as tall as Hawk, but heavier, his bunched muscles straining the thin fabric of his baggy cotton shirt. He wore a loose-fitting black vest and heavy trousers stuffed into knee-high moccasins. Lank black hair hung below his shoulders and was tied away from his face with a dirty red rag. He wore a leather thong around his neck, but whatever was attached to it was hidden under his shirt.

"Come," he commanded with a kick.

She made a sudden decision that whatever sinister plans this animal had for her, he would carry out without her help. She knew she would die sooner or later, but she would not be a party to her own demise. She shook her head and refused to move.

The legendary killer's eyes narrowed menacingly as he advanced on her. "You will pay for your stubbornness, *perra*. When the time comes for you to die, you will pay a dear price." He slapped her hard, and Billy reeled before he slung her over his shoulder and loped down the moonlit trail. He moved effortlessly over tumbled boulders, slipping quickly past the bodies of his slain men.

When he reached the seclusion of the chapparal-choked arroyo below, he rolled her off his shoulder. Unable to catch herself, Billy fell to the ground hard enough to knock the breath out of her. For a blessed moment she teetered on the brink of unconsciousness. She willed herself over the edge. It was the anguished, pain-filled scream of a horse that dragged her back to horrible reality.

Pale moonlight illuminated the grisly scene with

haunting clarity. Terror slithered down her throat as she watched Maloche move among his men's tied ponies with deadly purpose. He plunged his knife deep into the neck of a spotted pony bearing Indian markings on its rump and neck. With blood flowing from its wound, the pitiful creature crashed to the ground in the throes of death.

He moved on to the next and the next and the next, and in her shock Billy could not determine his motive. Was he killing the horses for some ritual purpose, or was he destroying them so they could not benefit either herself or Hawk? Each moment that passed magnified her dread until she had a clear vision of Maloche's terrible power. That was his purpose, to show her how utterly helpless she was.

The screams of the horses left alive rent the still night. Maloche was so intent on the slaughter that he didn't notice two of the animals rearing and plunging, yanking at the ropes that held them. But Billy did, and she prayed they would escape. When the limb they were tied to broke free, they milled blindly in the brush, unable to find their way out.

Refusing to let the hopelessness of her situation paralyze her, Billy gathered her wits about her and stumbled to her feet. Making as much noise as possible with the gag in her mouth, she managed to save at least one of the horses by scaring it out into the desert. Watching the nervous horse race away was a small victory over Maloche, but a decisive one.

She didn't have long to savor it because a strong arm caught her around the throat. Her captor threw her to the ground, dropped down to straddle her body, and slapped her repeatedly until she lost count.

She fought him, but her struggles were ineffective against one as strong and filled with hatred as her captor. When his fingers closed tightly around her neck, she tried to tell him with her eyes that she was ready for death. But it seemed Maloche had another, more horrible end in mind. His choking hold made her gasp, but was not quite tight enough to put an end to the nightmare.

"I will take great pleasure in your torture and that of the mestizo who will follow us." With his thumb he applied pressure to her larynx, and his ugly, leering face was the last thing Billy saw before giving herself over to howling darkness.

Hawk's pulse quickened when he came upon the Indian pony a short distance from camp. Something was wrong. His first instinct was to rush up the mountainside to see what it was. If anything had happened to Billy and John he'd never forgive himself for leaving them alone.

Sensing that he might need the pony, but praying he wouldn't, he dismounted Delilah and tried to catch it. It took several minutes to calm the spooked animal. He tossed his poncho over its head and led it and the camel through the chapparal thicket where he was horrified to find the slaughtered horses. Pushing down his overwhelming revulsion, he tied the animals as far from the smell of blood as possible and crept up the rubble-strewn trail.

He was filled with fear for what he might find when he reached the camp. When he entered the mouth of the canyon near the spring, he was met by silence. Silence and a sense of death.

He found John immediately. The condition of the body told him the old man had died no more than two or three hours ago. Billy was gone.

Frantic, he searched the area. Despite the darkness, he read the signs in the sand. One man had stolen into the tent. One man had murdered John and struggled with Billy. One man had carried her down the mountain. One man.

Maloche.

He'd heard the legends of Maloche's so-called immortality, but he hadn't really believed them. Now he had to wonder. Hawk cursed himself for a fool for not finding the renegade after the explosion and making sure he was dead. John's emergency had taken precedence.

Outrage and pain clutched at his heart, squeezing until all that remained was a great black anger. Hawk groaned and rose to his feet. Thrusting his fists into the air, he threw back his head.

"Maaalooche," he bellowed to the heavens. "You will die for this."

Something sinister awoke in him, fanning the flames of his hatred as his vow echoed through the hollow hills of the Superstitions. The blood pounded thickly in his temples and his throat tightened. He fought to control the hatred, knowing he would need all his faculties to rescue Billy before it was too late. If it wasn't already too late.

He refused to acknowledge that possibility. He would save Billy from the evil that was Maloche. They had made no promises to each other, and their future together was still in question. But when he found her, he would risk the pain of repudiation and confess his true feelings. He'd tried to voice them that day at the *tinajas*, but instead of saying "I love you," as he'd wanted, he'd only been able to admit to "caring" about her. Now, realizing she might be lost to him forever, he cursed himself.

He had feared she could never return his feelings. He, who had faced death and danger many times, had been scared of Billy's rejection. But none of that mattered now. The important thing, the only thing, was that he loved her. He would save her if it was the last thing he did.

He rebuilt the fire and sat before it, concentrating the formidable power of his thoughts on Maloche. Carefully he assembled all the information he possessed, all the fragments heard and overheard about the man. Everything that happened from now on, any chance of survival Billy had, would be based on how he used that knowledge.

Maloche had been the scourge of the desert for twenty years and was now in the prime of manhood. He'd eluded posses and patrols and platoons of trained soldiers. He'd ridden fearlessly into battle, his sacred amulet reportedly deflecting bullets like magic. He showed no mercy, had no heart. He was untiring, unwavering, driven by the evil that possessed him.

These things Hawk had heard. But at the bottom of all the myths and stories was a simple truth. Maloche was not protected by mystical powers. He was not immortal. He was a man. A very lucky man perhaps, but a man nonetheless.

The bastard's luck was about to run out.

Hawk rummaged through his pack and found the bootlike moccasins made of soft buckskin with rawhide soles. The hard soles extended well beyond the toes and turned upward in a disklike tip. He also found the buckskin shirt, breechclout, and leggings, and the rawhide belt with attached knife sheath that his mother had made him. Filled with a sense of destiny, he changed into the Indian garments and tied a blue cloth headband around his head.

Although he had not practiced the Apache customs for many years, some were so deeply ingrained they'd become habits. He never used wood from a tree struck by lightning to make a fire. He never drank water from a creek in which a bear had been swimming. When hunting, he turned the head of the deer toward the east—the sacred direction where the life-giving sun arose and whence would come new life for other game.

He sat cross-legged on the ground and opened the leather pouch he wore around his neck. He drew a circle in the sand and spilled the contents into the circle, sifting among them until he found the hawk's talon. It was good medicine in battle. The eagle feather would ensure swiftness. The quartz crystals would bring victory. The petrified wood would help him endure.

He withdrew the war necklace that had belonged to his grandfather. It was decorated with chalcedony, obsidian, red beans, feathers, and a yellow bird's head. He slipped it over his right shoulder and under his left arm as a charm to ward off enemy blows. It hadn't saved the old warrior during the Camp Grant massacre, but Hawk had to trust in its power now.

If he was to outsmart the most cunning enemy he'd ever faced, he had to think like him, act like him, and believe in the things that enemy believed in. His mother had taught him that everything in the world around him was filled with spirits and held a power that controlled or affected the destinies of all men. He called on those spirits now.

He had already asked his father's God to help him find Billy alive. But it was his mother's gods he asked for help in killing Maloche.

By the time he was finished, the sun was burning over the horizon. Hawk stood, bowed to the east, then to the south, the west, and finally to the north. He then scattered sacred pollen from his pouch to the four winds. He was ready.

He dug John's grave and buried him. In Billy's tent he found her trunk. He opened it in hopes of finding a Bible from which to read a few verses to commend the dead man's soul to heaven. He found the book, but he also found a giant hawk feather. Where had it come from? And why hadn't she mentioned it?

Recalling her theory about the Ghost Warrior, Hawk slipped the feather beneath his headband, letting it hang down over his left ear.

He struck the tent and hid their belongings beneath a small escarpment and covered them with the canvas weighted down by rocks. He found the other camels, including Samson, unharmed in the corral he and Billy had erected. Retrieving Delilah and the pony, he turned the camels loose to fend for themselves. He had no idea how long it would be before he returned. If he returned.

"The girls are your responsibility now, Samson,"

he told the big-eyed black camel. "Take good care of them."

The animals batted their eyes questioningly until he shooed them down the trail.

The sun was up now. It didn't take long for Hawk to locate the tracks Maloche had made no effort to conceal. So that was the game, was it? The devil wanted him to follow. At least they wanted the same thing. Hawk cursed Maloche and whispered Billy's name into the wind before swinging easily onto the Indian pony and galloping off in pursuit.

When Billy regained consciousness, she had no idea how long or how far they had traveled. She knew only that the sun beat down on her like an anvil. Maloche had thrown her onto the heavy Mexican saddle, tied her hands around the horse's neck and her feet beneath its belly. Her horse was snubbed to his by a short rope. How would she ever escape?

Her throat was as dry as dust, and every muscle in her body cried out in pain. The thong binding her wrists had rubbed them raw, and it took a concerted effort not to choke on the coarse gag in her mouth. But Billy refused to beg Maloche for mercy. As the sun rose higher and hotter, it became harder and harder to ignore her body's needs. She managed by thinking of Hawk.

Hawk. Oh God, would she ever see him again? In her heart she knew he would come for her, and she was torn between wishing he would hurry and praying he would not come at all. Maloche's maniacal taunts made her fear for his life.

Finally they stopped and Maloche dismounted. He untied her, pushed her toward the shade of a scrawny cottonwood, and shoved her down, promptly retying her hands and feet.

"I will remove the *hilacho*, but I do not like women who chatter," he warned.

When he reached to remove the gag, Billy instinctively jerked away from his touch. Maloche snorted his amusement and yanked it from her mouth, then deliberately grabbed the delicate material of her shirt and ripped it from her. Billy crossed her arms over the flimsy camisole, her heart beating in her breast like the wings of a tiny wild bird trying to escape.

Maloche slapped her hands away and leered. "Such skin, so very white. Let us see how the sun likes it. Do not be afraid, little *puta*. I cannot touch you. Yet."

He reached inside his shirt and pulled out the object secured to the leather thong. As he fingered the golden cross, Billy started in recognition and almost cried out. It was the same cross the Ghost Warrior had worn, the cross Montoya had given his lover. How had it tumbled down through the centuries only to find its way around this monster's neck?

Maloche caught her staring. "You like my amulet? It protects me," he boasted. "The medicine man who gave it to me promised me immortality as long as I do not break the taboos. That is why I must wait. Spilling my seed into a woman without first killing her man would destroy its magic."

Billy glared at him. What an ignorant fool the great Maloche had turned out to be. Hawk had suspected he was superstitious, and he was right. Maybe she could use those primitive beliefs against him when the time came.

"If ever you spill your seed into me, you filthy heathen," she promised, "it will indeed be bad for your immortality. For I shall kill you." She showed her contempt for him by spitting, and he kicked dirt into her face as he walked by.

"I will enjoy putting out your fire," he said as he fished in his saddlebags and pulled out two pieces of dried meat. He ate one before thrusting the other into her face. She turned her head away.

"There are many ways to die, white woman. Will you choose to starve?"

Billy wanted to refuse the meat, but she knew she

would need strength for the ordeal ahead. She tore off a piece with her teeth and chewed the tough meat before venturing a question. "Will the choice of how I am to die be left to me, then?"

"Only if it amuses me."

"Does killing amuse you?"

Maloche smirked. "At times."

Billy scowled, but cringed inwardly at his cruelty. "You are crazy," she taunted. "Loco."

"*Perra!* Bitch." Maloche backhanded her and spat on the ground. He held up the dirty rag in a threatening gesture. "I am no longer amused by this conversation. Do you want the gag?"

She shuddered at the thought of the filthy rag in her mouth again. What if Hawk came charging in and she needed to warn him? She shook her head, but held it erect lest he comprehend her terror.

Maloche offered her nothing to drink but held the waterskin high so the water ran into his upturned mouth and overflowed. Billy guessed he meant it as a form of torture. An effective one, considering how her thirst had been increased by the salty meat. When he finished he turned on her. "So you are not afraid, eh?"

Her first reaction was to show him true Sybilla-like disdain and ask him why she should be afraid of a filthy savage. But she hid her true feelings beneath a cloak of false humility. If there was one thing she'd learned on this trip, it was that one had to do what one had to do. Survival was all, and if she antagonized this madman now, before she learned his purpose, she would only further endanger herself.

If she allowed herself to be murdered because of haughtiness, all the lessons she'd learned from Hawk would be for naught. She wouldn't answer and ducked her head in silence, refusing to meet Maloche's cruel eyes.

Apparently he wasn't satisfied with her response because he bared his teeth and growled. "So you think yourself so far above me that you will not answer, eh? I shall show you why you should be afraid of me." His fist connected with her delicate jaw, and she fell backward.

Maloche climbed onto her, his fingertips gouging into her breasts. The pain was excruciating and although she tried, Billy could no longer hold back her screams. He clamped one powerful hand over her mouth and with the other grabbed a handful of flesh between her thighs.

When she whimpered and curled into a ball, he finally released her. "Do not anger me again, *puta*. That is only a little taste of why you should fear Maloche." He tied a length of rope around her neck and the other end around his waist. Soon he fell asleep.

She didn't move. She made no sound that might wake him or rile him again. She wanted to curse him, spit at him, tell him that it did indeed take a brave man to attack a woman who could not defend herself. But she said nothing. She did not sleep.

He woke as the sun was setting. He ate again, but this time offered her nothing. He drank and allowed her to have a scant mouthful of water. He untied her feet so that she could relieve herself, but he kept her hands tied, the neck rope taut.

He threw her back onto her horse and retied her feet beneath its belly. This time he bound her hands together in front of her so that she could hang onto the pony's shaggy mane. Mounting his own horse, he led her away from their hiding place and back onto the rocky trail.

Billy had spent the night thinking. She concluded that as far as maniacs went, Maloche was none too stable. She decided to watch him carefully, looking for his weaknesses. That he had them, she had no doubt. Anyone as mad as Maloche had a weakness.

She sat erect on her horse, refusing to look beaten or cowed, and she could tell her attitude angered him. But he did not kill her and, although he seemed to delight in her suffering, she knew he had a plan. They were traveling toward a particular destination and if she bided her time, perhaps she would learn what it was.

During the next two days, in which they traveled only at night, she made an interesting discovery. Anger made Maloche less effective. This was the fatal flaw she would turn against him.

She did that by taking advantage of every opportunity to ruffle his feathers, to goad him into rash action. Although this meant she was slapped about as a result, it also meant Maloche was not functioning at full capacity. By keeping him constantly agitated and always preoccupied with his unpredictable captive, his keen-eyed vigilance was diminished. As would be his chances in the final showdown.

For a showdown would surely come. She did not require the skills of a master tracker to realize Maloche was luring Hawk into a trap. She was frightened, because a trap devised by one as twisted and devious as Maloche was sure to be deadly. She knew that under normal circumstances, Hawk would not be tricked. But Maloche was smart. He was using her for bait.

If he needed her for bait in the final confrontation, he would not kill her just yet. That was why she felt confident enough to continue her badgering tactics.

Billy couldn't be sure how far they'd traveled. Half the time they seemed to be going in circles and the other half she was either too hungry or thirsty to care. Although he didn't abuse her sexually, his cruelty was unrelenting, and she felt the veneer of civilization slipping away from her.

Tied to Maloche day and night, she had no privacy. When the sun burned her pale skin, she coated her face, arms, and shoulders with a mudpack of urine-soaked dirt. Her hair was tangled and dirty, her clothing foul-smelling, her skin raw.

She prayed that she would die, that God would

deliver her from the misery she endured. But dying was not so easy.

After two days, she was still alive and her prayers changed. After suffering unheard-of indignities at Maloche's hands, she now asked for the strength to kill him. She was at first shocked by her change of attitude, but that dismay was soon overcome by a strong desire to live.

She was not the same person who'd been taken captive. She was stronger now, tempered by her experiences. It was her responsibility to see that justice was accomplished.

Maloche had murdered many people in his long and bloody career. Innocent people like Uncle John. He had caused endless suffering and reveled in it. Like a mad dog that had to be destroyed before it inflicted pain on others, Maloche deserved to die. She vowed to end his reign of terror, and that vow gave her the strength to persevere.

They were deep in the Superstitions now, but because they traveled only at night, she was unable to pick out landmarks recalled from the map she had left behind. They crossed moonlit ridges, traversed shadowy canyons, and ranged through dark arroyos.

On the third morning of her captivity, they reached their destination. Dawn lit the landscape with gray light, and the rising sun burned away the last of the morning mist. Billy recognized the majestic spire at once.

Weaver's Needle.

Now she knew why Maloche had doggedly dragged her onward when he could have waited anywhere along the trail for Hawk to catch up. The five-thousand-foot-tall monolith figured somehow in his superstitions and plans. Her speculations were confirmed a little later when they stopped at the base of the peak.

"We leave the horses here," he said. "We must climb the sacred rock. I will call upon the spirits of the amulet and the spirits of the mountains in my battle with the mestizo who follows.''

When he untied her feet, Billy slid to the ground in an exhausted heap. She was tired and sore, hungry and thirsty, and so dirty she barely recognized herself. And she was mad as bloody hell.

She didn't think she had the strength left to struggle up the rocky face of the mountain, but with Maloche behind her, shoving, cursing, and prodding her every step of the way, she managed. Climbing to the top would have been impossible without grappling irons and ropes, but she soon discovered the top was not his destination.

Several hundred feet up, the rough talus rock formed a sizable shelf, a plateau roughly forty feet by thirty feet surrounded on two sides by rocky walls. It was here that Maloche stopped. He pushed her down on the sandy rock in order to bind her. Before he could grab her hands, Billy summoned what little strength she had left and raked her nails into his cheek, drawing a bloody furrow along the length of his jaw.

Maloche bellowed a few choice words in Spanish and quickly tied her hands and feet together. He rolled her to her back and slapped her until her head felt loose and detached. With a feral gleam in his eye, he ripped her split skirt at the waist and yanked it off. Now her only protection was a pair of cotton pantalets and the ragged camisole.

She tried not to think what her fate might be now, but the Montoya cross swung into her line of vision, and the sight of it gave her courage. It did not belong to this horrible man; it belonged to the Montoyas. She was the last of that noble family. Would she die here in the dirt?

No.

In a voice made as calm as she could manage, she said, "Take me now, Maloche. Give me your immortality, for I very much want you to die.''

Fury twisted his features, and Billy almost wished

she had not been so brave. When she felt him tense and harden against her, she knew she'd gone too far. Moments crawled by, and finally he shoved off her. "Soon, white woman. Soon."

Without another word he began climbing the sheer rock wall of the Needle. Like a human fly, using tenuous finger and toe holds, he worked his way upward and out of sight. She was alone.

"Oh God," she prayed aloud, "Let Hawk come now while that monster is communing with his spirits." She tamped down on her fear, refusing to doubt that Hawk would rescue her, hanging on to her faith that this nightmare would have a happy ending.

Weakened by hunger and fatigue, she lay there for hours, drifting in and out of an almost delirious sleep. She woke up with a start when late afternoon shadows filled the rocky niche.

Maloche had not returned.

Hawk had not come, either.

Maybe he was already dead, she thought with despair. She shook her head as tears spilled down her cheeks. No. If anything had happened to him, she would have felt it. He was alive and he would be here soon.

Despite her dizziness, Billy tried to organize her thoughts. Maloche was going to great lengths to trap Hawk. Did revenge burn so hot in his heart that he would stage such an elaborate confrontation? Yes. She knew without a doubt that the man was insane. There was no understanding the demons that dictated his actions.

And what chance did Hawk have against such a wicked man? Hawk, for all his roughness, was not the savage Maloche was. Hawk was sensitive and caring. He felt compassion for others and was driven by his emotions and senses. Maloche was driven by base instincts and a psychotic hatred for anyone who thwarted him. If Maloche wanted vengeance, he would have it.

He'd left her here not because she was too weak to climb farther, but to lure Hawk. When Hawk came to save her, Maloche would swoop down and kill him. She couldn't let that happen.

Summoning her depleted reserves of energy, she struggled against the hastily tied bonds and felt the knot slacken. Squirming in excitement and frustration, she worked the stringy rawhide and ignored her bleeding wrists. She concentrated on making her hands as small as possible so they would slip out of the bonds. One hand broke free, and with it she reached into her boot for the knife Hawk had given her.

Since her capture, knowing that the knife was there, so close and yet out of reach, had driven her nearly mad. If she had been able to get to it, she would have used it. But Maloche had kept her tied at all times, and she had avoided trying to retrieve it for fear of betraying its existence. She used it now, to cut the thongs.

"I did it," she exclaimed triumphantly as she replaced the knife in its leather sheath and slipped it back into her boot. She was about to start the rocky descent when a scuffle of falling rocks below told her someone was coming up. She backed into a narrow defile and hid behind the scattered boulders. She didn't know what she would do, but she would think of something.

Hawk left his pony with the others at the base of the Needle. He made his way up the steep, rock-strewn, cactus-studded incline much as Maloche and Billy had done before him. He thanked God that she was still alive and marveled that she possessed enough strength to climb after everything she must have suffered. He'd barely slept since setting out, and exhaustion dragged at him as he willed his way up and over the battlements of rock.

When he reached the plateau he looked around cautiously. He approached the edge of the cliff and leaned out, peering over the edge. On this side, the mountain dropped straight down into a deep ravine. A narrow brush-clogged ledge jutted out from the sheer rock wall about forty feet down.

Before he could move away from the edge, he was struck from behind by a blow so forceful that he nearly toppled over. Something clung to his back, and he barely managed to recover as he swayed near the brink. Stumbling away from the edge, he shook the burden off, turned and crouched, pistol drawn. He was ready to shoot before he realized the dirty, wild-eyed, knife-wielding hellcat was Billy.

He'd never been so happy to see anyone in his life. His first thought was to sweep her into his arms and tell her how much he loved her, to promise never to leave her. But he didn't know if she would welcome his embrace after what she'd been through. The last thing she probably wanted to hear right now were tender words of love.

Rubbing the back of his head where she'd hit him, he grumbled, "Hell, woman, I thought you'd be glad to see me. You nearly shoved me off that cliff."

"Hawk?" she asked, disbelief in her tone. She rubbed her eyes to make sure he was no mirage.

"Who the hell did you think it was?" he asked, lowering his gun.

Billy got up and brushed the seat of her pantalets. "I thought you were an Indian." She took in the breechclout, the leggings, the moccasins, the buckskin shirt. "You look like an Indian," she pointed out.

"Are you in the habit of dry gulching every Indian you see?"

"I'm sorry," she sobbed. "I thought you were Maloche. That murdering bastard killed Uncle John." A fresh torrent of misery flowed out of her. "He's dead. Dear Uncle John died trying to save me."

Hawk pulled her into his arms and held her, comforted her. "I know, Billy. I buried him. Don't cry, you're safe now." Ever alert, he kept his eyes and ears open for danger.

Aware of her wretched appearance and state of undress, she whispered, "Aren't you going to ask me where my clothes are?"

Hawk smoothed the hair away from her face. "I don't care about that."

"You don't?" Billy backed away.

"I didn't mean it that way." Hawk stroked her poor sunburned shoulders gently, lovingly. "What I'm trying to say is, it doesn't matter. Nothing Maloche could do would ever change the way I feel about you."

She shrugged his hands off and spun away from him. "You don't know all the terrible things he did."

He was forced to converse with her back. "I have a fair idea. And I'm sorry. I would have done anything to save you that."

"I don't want your pity." She wanted his love. Why couldn't he tell her he loved her? Was that so much to ask after all she'd endured?

Hawk sensed she was waiting for something. Maybe she was upset because it had taken him so long to rescue her. "What did I do wrong here? What do you want me to say?"

"Why don't you say you're glad I didn't kill myself before that savage could defile my body and leave you with damaged goods."

"The idea of you killing yourself for such a stupid reason never even crossed my mind."

"Then why in bloody hell did you give me your mother's knife?"

"Because I wanted you to protect yourself. Not kill yourself."

Billy sighed hopefully. Maybe he did care what happened to her. She turned and placed her palms on his chest. "What does that mean?"

"It means I love you, goddammit."

"Oh, Hawk, do you?"

"Yes," he answered softly, surprised at how easy it was to say the words. "Yes!" he repeated. "I love you, Billy."

"I love you too."

Her lips were welcoming in the first instant of contact, and Hawk kissed them with warming insistence. Her hungry response almost made him forget what lay ahead of them, and some of his feverish longings tore loose, making him rough with her when he wanted to be gentle. He held nothing back as they strained against each other, locked in each other's arms as their lips and tongues sought refuge from harsh reality.

When Hawk finally pulled away from her, Billy was breathing hard and was as shaken as he by his heartfelt confession. The sensation of being held by him was still with her, the press of his long legs, the strength of his arms, the thrill of his hands moving over her back.

"Oh, Hawk," she whispered urgently. "We must get out of here before Maloche crawls back down the mountain. I'm the bait to trap you."

"I know." He touched her bruised and swollen face, and his hatred for the man who had abused her was complete. "He hurt you."

"It doesn't matter anymore. We must hurry. I'm afraid Maloche will kill you."

"Not without a fight, he won't."

"No, we must run."

"We wouldn't get far and even if we did he'd only come after us. I must fight him or he will chase us forever. That's how things are done."

"But what if he kills you? What happens to me then?"

"I don't plan to die."

"Hawk, I love you." She couldn't say the words enough.

"Go back the way you came. The horses are tied below. Take two and head west. Ride one as far and as fast as you can and, when it gets tired, change to the other.''

"You want me to leave you?"

"You have to get away from here." He pulled off his fringed shirt and slipped it over her head. It fell to her knees. "This will protect you from the sun and the cool nights."

"No, I won't go!"

"Listen to me, Billy." He cupped her face in his hands. "For once in your life, don't argue."

"I won't go without you." How could she leave him now? He loved her. She loved him.

"One of us will follow you soon, and hopefully it will be me."

"But Hawk . . ."

"I can't afford to worry about you while I'm fighting Maloche. And I don't want you to see it. It won't be pleasant."

"But I want to stay with you . . ."

"If he kills me . . ."

"Then I'll die with you . . ."

"Please, Billy, don't argue. Will you just go?"

She looked deep into his blue eyes and saw the pain and fear there. Fear not for himself but for her. She gave in reluctantly. "As you wish."

"Thank you," he said.

"Hawk, there's something you need to know about Maloche's magic amulet. It's the Montoya cross. We found it after all." Before he could respond, she kissed him again. "I love you," she whispered, needing to leave him with that.

"And I love you," he said softly as she started down the rocky trail.

Chapter 18

Halfway down the mountain, Billy changed her mind.

Leave? Decamp? Desert? Or in the immortal words of Willie Shakespeare, "Show it a fair pair of heels and run for it"? Not bloody likely. How could Hawk expect her to leave him now that he'd finally told her he loved her?

If he thought Sybilla Hartford was one to run out on a fight, he had a lot to learn. Besides, what kind of woman fled to dubious safety and left the man she loved to face the enemy alone? For she did love Hawk, with all her heart. Her brief but highly enlightening captivity had taught her what life without him would be.

In a word, unbearable. And certainly not worth living. It had also taught her a thing or two about the occasional shedding of civilization and the relative merits thereof. Because she had survived captivity, she knew she could make a place for herself in Hawk's world.

As long as he was at her side.

It didn't matter that she still knew little about him; she knew enough for now and would have a lifetime in which to learn more. Nor did it matter that they were so different. As Uncle John had so astutely pointed out, they were alike in the ways that counted. Now that she and Hawk had been reunited, nothing, not even Maloche, was going to separate them.

Furtively she retraced her steps back up the mountain and slipped behind a scratchy barricade of mesquite. Moving cautiously, she ducked behind the boulders in the same narrow defile that had hidden her from Hawk before. She waited, breath held and knife in her sweaty hand, for further developments. It would not be in her best interest to show herself too soon, she decided, for Hawk would certainly disapprove of her flagrant disobedience.

She knew he'd take her to task, belaboring the fact of her insubordination with total disregard for the matter at hand. And since that matter was Maloche, who was sure to show up at any moment, it was best to postpone the discussion. If there was one thing Hawk did not need while dispatching that villain, it was additional distractions.

A small green lizard scuttled over her foot, and the movement startled her, making her gasp. She looked up quickly, fearing Hawk had heard the sound, but he was so intent on gathering brush that he didn't notice.

The fire Hawk built blazed brightly, a clear signal to Maloche. He drew a large circle in the sand and stood tensely in its center. He waited. He did not look forward to the coming fight, but he had to draw Maloche into a hand-to-hand, fight-to-the-death battle.

He hoped that Billy had a considerable head start by now, but what good was a little time and distance against a relentless killer like Maloche? Besides, she'd never survive in these mountains alone, and the thought of her suffering any more at that devil's hands filled him with anger so intense that it blocked out all other emotions. He was ready.

The sun was just settling behind the ridge when Maloche materialized like a malignant puff of smoke and strode boldly into the firelit circle. His cold eyes raked contemptuously over Hawk."So, the white-eye Apache does not fear facing Maloche in a *torneo* of strength? *Mano a mano*?" he taunted in a guttural combination of English and Spanish.

Hawk stared down the man whose very name struck terror into the hearts of Arizona's hardiest citizens and tried not to flinch from the venomous hatred in his eyes. "I do not fear any man."

"But I am not just any man. I am Maloche." Dressed in only soft knee boots, buckskin breech-clout, and paint, he was an imposing figure. A large golden cross swung upon his bare chest as he strutted arrogantly around Hawk.

Hawk's gaze was momentarily transfixed by the cross, and when he recognized it, he was filled with a profound sense of destiny. Billy was right; it was the same one worn by the Ghost Warrior. It also matched the drawing on the map. Montoya had been here. The gold was here. Somewhere. With Maloche out of the way, he would find it.

He loved Billy, and they would be together. He couldn't let Maloche win.

"You killed my *companeros*, white-eye Apache," said Maloche, "and you tried to kill me. Now you will die."

"Not hardly." Hawk freed his mind of all thoughts except survival. He lunged first, his big dagger slicing through the air a few inches in front of Maloche's leering face. The renegade laughed and charged, but Hawk danced away from the slashing blade. He circled, crouching low to present the smallest possible target, and looked for an opening while simultaneously trying not to provide one.

The adversaries were well matched, not just in strength and endurance but also in the will to win. As evening advanced, the fight dragged on, both grunting, thrusting, plunging, gaining and losing advantage in turn. Both drew and lost enough blood to make the arena satisfactorily gory, but neither lost or drew quite enough to end the battle.

Billy's hiding place did not afford much of a view, so she hunched down and crawled to a boulder only a few feet from the battle. From that vantage point, she could see that Hawk was bleeding from an angry-looking cut on his shoulder, and at least three other superficial wounds bloodied his chest.

She would have gone to his aid but for the fact that Hawk managed to inflict a serious wound on his opponent. A profusely bleeding cut on Maloche's right thigh made him limp. He circled Hawk, his eyes wild, yowling with the fury of an injured animal. Neither man paid heed to the wounds. They were beyond their pain.

The men stalked each other like wary wolves, and when Maloche slashed a thin red line down Hawk's left bicep, Billy gasped aloud. She hoped the combatants would not realize they had an audience, for at the moment, she feared Hawk's reaction nearly as much as Maloche's. Her worry was unnecessary.

So intent were the two men on thoroughly destroying each other, bit by bloody bit, that they were oblivious to anything outside that circle. They would not notice, she was sure, if an entire cavalry platoon charged into the fray.

Billy prayed for the battle to end, with Hawk as victor, of course. She simply could not stand to watch much longer. Her stomach hurt, her head ached, and she'd bitten several nails down to the quick. Watching was killing her. She'd have to *do* something. Hawk, armed only with his knife, must have stashed his rifle somewhere. Perhaps she could work her way around the circle and locate it.

There was, no doubt, some primitive rule governing the use of knives only, but enough was enough. Someone had to put an end to this before they whittled each other down to bloody stumps. Having a definite plan of action made Billy feel infinitely more useful as she moved slowly, and she hoped discreetly, toward the pile of rocks where Hawk had unloaded his few possessions before the fight.

Obviously feeling confident of victory, Maloche regaled Hawk at great and vivid length with exactly what he was going to do to him before he died. Billy blanched as she scooted along the ground, ducking low behind rocks and brush. The man was a sanguinary monster, but he definitely had a way with words.

"Then I will track down your woman," Maloche gloated. "You will not die easy knowing what entertainments I have planned for that golden-eyed *puta.*"

Hawk didn't see much point wasting valuable energy and concentration on conversation. Gathering what strength he had left, he plunged his knife in a deadly arc toward Maloche's heart, but missed as the devil floated away.

Either the fight had lasted too long or Hawk was getting too old for such work. His feet were not as sure as they'd been half an hour ago, and his aim was considerably off. Blood and sweat dripped into his eyes, and the combined effect made Maloche appear to swim in front of him in a disoriented pool.

The light was dying, and for the first time, Hawk worried that he just might be too.

The gloom of evening was thick around him when Hawk noted with dismay that the fight was moving progressively closer to the edge of the bluff. Bad news or good? He'd already scouted the area. The sheer rock wall dropped down some forty feet to a rubble-covered ledge that projected over a plunging ravine. It was at least another hundred feet to the rock-strewn bottom.

Seized with a sudden idea, Hawk inched imperceptibly backward, hoping to draw Maloche to the brink. Then an unexpected feint, a well-placed kick, or even a timely shove might finish the job completely, and that would be the end of this crazy, indestructible man called Maloche.

It was time to do some taunting of his own. "So, *cobarde* who attacks helpless women, are you not

strong enough to defeat a man? Can you only boast
of winning?"

As he spoke he caught a slight movement in the
brush, the flicker of light glinting off metal. He
thought for one wild moment that it was Billy sneaking around the circle. It was definitely time to make
his move—he was starting to see things.

Maloche grunted his displeasure at the insult.
"You are a dead man, white-eye. Your life's blood
is draining out of you. But you will linger long
enough to hear your woman's screams when I find
where she has hidden."

Hawk did indeed feel his strength flowing away
and nearly panicked at the thought that he might be
unable to help Billy. Maloche's treachery was legendary. If there was any way to buy her a little extra
time, Hawk would use it.

Dredging up all the bravado he'd lost during the
long fight, he laughed. "I can save you the trouble
of looking, you bastard. I killed her."

Hawk's words had the desired effect on Maloche
because the madman's voice faltered and he snarled.
"I do not believe you. You would not follow all this
way only to kill her."

"She was ruined and of no further use to me."
Hawk was careful to make his tone as contemptuous
as possible. "Now I shall kill you too."

Cheated out of his revenge, Maloche charged at
Hawk out of the darkness with a blood-chilling bel-
low. They grappled on the very edge of the bluff for
a moment that seemed frozen in time. But things
didn't work out as Hawk had planned. His concentration had been broken when he saw the flash in
the brush, and that brief loss of attention had cost
him dearly.

Hawk ran out of ground and felt the bluff crumbling beneath his feet. The world seemed to tilt as
he stumbled in a frantic attempt to regain his footing. But it was too late, and he fell backward. Ma-

loche's leering face loomed before him, and the still
night air was torn by the renegade's yelp of victory.

In a final desperate attempt to correct his downward momentum, Hawk's fingers clawed the air and
stretched toward the Montoya cross that swung
brightly on Maloche's chest. They closed on the cold
metal, and Hawk held on. The thong broke free only
seconds before the dark emptiness swallowed him
up.

In horrified disbelief, Billy watched her beloved
Hawk tumble backward over the cliff. He was gone,
and he'd taken her heart with him. She had come
to these mountains in search of gold and had found
a greater treasure—love. The hours she'd spent in
Hawk's arms were worth more than a lifetime without him, and if it took death's embrace to reunite
them, so be it.

With no thought for her own safety, she screamed
and charged out of her hiding place behind the mesquite.

Maloche whirled. He seemed almost as surprised
to see her as he had been when Hawk fell. "So you
have come back from the dead, eh? I knew the white-
eye lied, and it is thoughtful of you to spare me the
trouble of hunting you down."

He made a move toward her, and Billy looked
around frantically for Hawk's rifle. It was out of
reach, but the pearl-handled knife wasn't. She
shifted it into her other hand and waved it in front
of her.

Maloche leered. "Do you think that puny weapon
can stop me, the great Maloche?"

She glanced nervously from the advancing madman to the slender blade. Probably not. But if she
plunged it into her own heart she could yet cheat
Maloche of his victory and save herself unnecessary
suffering. She sobbed and shuddered as the vision
of Hawk falling played itself back in her mind. Without him she had no desire to live.

"Now that your man is dead, I am free from the medicine man's taboo." Maloche kept one eye on her knife as he slowly stalked her. "You belong to me now, and I shall wait no more."

Billy turned the blade toward her breast, but she could not bring herself to bury it there. Was she such a coward, then? What had Hawk said about using it to protect herself? Hawk! How could he die and leave her? Who would avenge him, if not her? Who would avenge Uncle John?

Suddenly filled with an anguish so powerful that it overcame her sense of reason, Billy screamed Hawk's name and rushed headlong into the startled Maloche. With no other thought than to punish him, she plunged the blade into his chest.

He staggered backward and teetered upon the edge of the cliff exactly as Hawk had staggered and teetered there only minutes before. Shock and disbelief transformed Maloche's grim features and his mouth moved, but no words came out. His fingers searched for the magic amulet, but closed instead around the handle of Billy's knife.

She watched in horror. Was it true, then? When Hawk stole the amulet, had he stolen Maloche's power? It seemed so. The man with nine lives played out his last on a rocky ledge in the Superstition Mountains, and then hurtled into the waiting darkness.

Billy stumbled to the edge of the cliff and looked down into the murky depths of the ravine below. "Hawk," she cried desperately, knowing she would get no answer. She plucked up a pebble and tossed it over the side. It seemed to fall for a very long time. No one could survive such a fall. She had to face reality.

Hawk was dead.

She backed away from the edge in shock. Her legs no longer able to support her, she collapsed to her knees and then crumpled to the ground weeping. She had killed a man, and it hadn't been at all difficult. She hadn't felt barbaric when she took Maloche's life, and she felt no remorse now. She understood that Hawk had been faced with such dilemmas many times before, and it had hardened him. But he'd been hard because it was necessary.

He had also been gentle. His last thoughts had been of her and that is why he had lied to Maloche about killing her. He'd wanted to save her, even when he knew he could not save himself.

Her sobs were the only sound in the early night stillness, and she realized for the first time how truly alone she was. The wildness of the place closed in on her, and she curled onto her side on the sandy ground.

Hawk! Why did you have to die? She missed him so much already that she felt her heart breaking from the pain. She hadn't been allowed to cry for Uncle John so she did that too. She wept from the endless sorrow inside her; for Hawk, for her uncle, for herself.

Grief, exhaustion, and hunger conspired to plunge her into a deep sleep, a sleep haunted by dreams of what might have been.

When she awoke at dawn the next morning, it was with the unshakable feeling that she'd just experienced a terrible nightmare. But when she sat up and rubbed the sleep from her eyes, she knew that what had happened the night before was no dream. It had really happened.

Hawk was dead. Uncle John was dead. She was alone.

She crawled to the edge of the cliff, and what she saw made her head swim and her empty stomach spasm. The rocky cliff face dropped straight down for at least fifteen meters. A jutting ledge, no more that forty inches wide, extended out at that point and was dotted with a few straggly-looking bushes. The bottom of the ravine was another thirty meters below the ledge.

She saw no sign of the bodies and concluded that

they had struck the ledge and rolled off, out of sight in the dense underbrush that choked the ravine.

"Oh, Hawk!" she cried, her voice echoing back to her. "Why did it have to end like this? We were so close, my love, so close."

Hysteria bubbled up inside her like water in an untended kettle. "My biggest regret is that I never had the chance to tell you that I'd rather have you than all the gold in the world. Hawk!"

Wearing Hawk's shirt, she sat cross-legged in the dirt, staring out into the ravine, her tears making twin tracks down her dirty face. With Hawk gone, she had no reason to live. She would sit here until she turned to dust.

The sun climbed steadily higher, and Billy cried until she had no tears left. Her lips were parched, and her body reminded her that it had been too long since her last drink of water. But what was thirst compared to losing Hawk?

She thought about all he had given her. He'd taught her to love, to recognize, and respect her own needs. He'd made her feel the passion she had thought she lacked, and he'd helped her realize her strength.

Where was that strength now? What would Hawk think if he could see her sniveling in the dirt? He wouldn't want her to give up, to let Maloche win. If she did not fight for her own survival, Hawk would have died in vain.

The longer she sat there, the more determined she became. She summoned up her reserves of hauteur and decided that Hawk wouldn't mind if she used him to work up the necessary fervor to get herself going again.

"Bloody hell, Devlin. It wasn't very sporting of you to go and get yourself killed, just when we'd finally decided to admit that we loved each other. Damn you!"

The "Damn you" echoed around her and she wavered. "I don't know how I'll ever make it without you."

Life without Hawk? How could she bear it? "I'll never love anyone else as long as I live," she yelled into the ravine, finally making the commitment she had been unable to make before. "You are the only man for me, you wonderful, lovable rattlesnake-eating brute. You've ruined me for lesser men."

"At least I did something right." The weak reply drifted up from far below.

Billy couldn't believe her ears. That sounded suspiciously like Hawk's voice. She crawled to the edge and peered down. Now she couldn't believe her eyes. It *was* Hawk! He was standing on the ledge. And he was alive!

"Hawk! I thought you were dead." Overcome by emotion, she was laughing and crying at the same time.

"Not only am I not dead," he called up, "I'm rich. And so are you!" He waved triumphantly, and the early morning sunlight glinted off the gold bars in his hands.

Chapter 19

"Where did you get that?" Billy demanded, suddenly and perversely furious.

"There's a cave down here," he called up. "It isn't visible from below, and if I hadn't fallen ass backward off that cliff I never would have found it. Wait until you see what else is in here."

"You jackass!" she screeched. "You inconsiderate, good-for-nothing, worthless jackass."

"Hey! Is that any way to talk to the only man you'll ever love who has miraculously returned from the dead?"

"I thought the fall killed you."

"You sound disappointed that it didn't," he said, wounded by her sudden change of attitude. "There must have been some magic left in that amulet. See that scrubby little tree up there?"

Billy looked down and located the stunted juniper growing horizontally out of the rock face, much like the one that had saved her during the javelina attack.

"I grabbed it going down and it broke my fall."

"Do you mean to tell me you've been alive all this time?" she demanded irrationally.

"Wait a minute. Are you mad because you thought I was dead or because I'm not?"

"Oooh!" Billy stamped her foot. "If I had a gun in my hand, Hawk Devlin, you would be."

"Now, Billy, you don't mean that," he cajoled.

"Why, just a minute ago you were proclaiming your undying love and devotion to me. Forever, as I recall."

"I take it all back. I've changed my mind." Why *was* she angry? Perhaps she'd had one shock too many during the past few hours and had truly lost her mind. As much as she loved him, as glad as she was to see him alive and unharmed, she couldn't regain control of her galloping emotions.

"While you were busy gloating over *my* gold, I could have been lying up here in a pool of blood, for all you knew."

"I wasn't too worried about you," Hawk teased. "Maloche sort of dropped by last night after your little skirmish." Half dazed from the fall, he'd seen Maloche's body tumble over the cliff with his mother's knife protruding from his chest. He'd assumed the rest before passing out completely. "Mortally injured women do not inflict fatal knife wounds."

He smiled. She wasn't really mad at him; she was glad to see him. She just had a funny way of showing it. During the long night, when he was nearly delirious from the concussion he'd received from the fall, all he'd thought of was Billy. Of how he was going to spend the rest of his life making her happy. Of course, the way she was ranting at him now, that might take some doing.

"What were you thinking of, letting me cry my heart out about you all night?"

"Sorry for the inconvenience, Billy, but I was a little unconscious. Hit my head when I fell the rest of the way," he told her.

Still on her hands and knees at the edge of the cliff, she appeared to consider his explanation. "Were you out cold?"

"Pretty damn near. Do you forgive me for not dying?" he teased.

"Yes." She glared down at him. "But if you ever do anything so thoughtless again, I shan't."

"Glad we got that settled. Now we can get to more pressing matters."

"Such as?"

"Such as why you came back. I may have had a bump on the head, but it didn't give me amnesia. I distinctly remember ordering you to leave. But did you obey me? No."

She flashed him a haughty look. "I do not like orders, and I cannot recall taking any vows of obedience." Yet. "You should be glad I had so much initiative. You'd have been in a fine kettle of fish if I hadn't come back and killed Maloche."

"If I hadn't caught sight of you when the firelight glinted on that goddamn knife, I wouldn't have lost my concentration and I could have killed him myself."

"If you hadn't been so stubborn, I never would have had to resort to trickery."

"I give up. There's no arguing with a hardheaded woman like you." Hawk tossed the gold bars aside and held up his arms. "You win, I'm a jackass. Now are you satisfied?"

"With me up here and you down there? Not bloody likely."

Hawk shook his head, no longer trying to suppress his joy that both of them were alive and wealthy. "We'll take care of that satisfaction later."

"Will we now?" she asked sassily.

"Soon," he promised. "Very soon."

"I'm coming down there." She couldn't wait to feel his lips on hers, to press her tired, bruised body into his arms.

"Hey, Billy?"

"Yes?"

"I don't recommend the route I took, so why don't you wait for me to come up? I found some old rope in the cave. I'll secure it here and throw it down. Later, we'll have to climb up from the canyon floor in order to get the gold."

Billy shifted her weight from foot to foot. "I'm

sure I can't wait that long. Is it really the Montoya gold?''

Hawk grinned. "Not anymore. It's the Devlin-Hartford gold now."

She grinned back. The Montoya gold. It had always been a distant dream, just out of reach. Now, suddenly, it was within their grasp. She knew she should be elated. And she was.

Only it wasn't the gold that made her happy. It was Hawk.

She called out reproachfully. "The Hartford-Devlin gold, you mean."

He waved his acquiescence and as she watched, he disappeared into the cave and came out a few minutes later with a length of hemp rope coiled in his hands. He fashioned a loop and wrapped it around a huge boulder, and dropped it over the edge.

Then he started climbing slowly up the cliff. Thousands of years of relentless wind and rain had eroded the face of rock and it provided a number of conveniently spaced hand and toe holds.

He slipped once and Billy gasped. He soon regained his balance, and she watched in fascination as he crawled toward her. Each time he looked up, she saw the happiness in his eyes. It clearly reflected her own. The Superstition Mountains were not such a bad place after all. The guardian spirits had given them another chance. She meant to make the most of it.

When Hawk's head appeared above the edge of the cliff, Billy hurried to help him up and over, onto solid ground. They fell into each other's arms, the struggle to gain their feet hampered by laughter and kisses and tears of joy.

"Are you quite sure you are all right?" she asked him when she saw the dried blood on his head. She touched it tenderly, and he clasped her hand and kissed it. The wounds he had sustained during the

fight had ceased to flow, but he was indeed a gruesome sight.

"I'm fine," he said dismissively. "What about
you?" His features softened as he stroked her sunburned face and smoothed his finger over her
chapped and peeling lips. "Maloche didn't . . ."

"No, Hawk," she assured him. "Maloche didn't
violate me, not the way you mean." She explained
the taboo.

"I'm sorry I had to tell him I'd killed you. I was
only trying to gain the upper hand. You realize that
no matter what happened, I could never harm you,
don't you?"

"Yes, I understand. When Maloche first captured
me, I prayed I would die. Then somewhere along
the way I ceased being a refined lady who could do
nothing but bemoan her fate. I knew I'd do anything
to survive. To avenge Uncle John. To rid the world
of Maloche."

"There are many who will thank you. You'll be a
heroine."

"But even that wasn't why I fought for survival.
I knew I couldn't die because I hadn't yet told you
how much I loved you."

He clutched her in a fierce embrace. The last of
the walls between them crumbled. Hawk, who had
always claimed he needed no one, acknowledged the
precious woman in his arms. "Oh, Billy," he whispered. "Don't ever leave me."

They decided that since the gold had waited for
over two hundred years, it could wait a while longer.
Their first priority was to climb down the Needle
and return to the horses for food and water. After a
quick meal of dried meat and mescal cakes they
found in Maloche's pack, they followed a straggly
line of cottonwoods to a small spring.

It was no more than a hearty trickle, but the tiny
pool it made was sufficient for their purposes. They
cleaned up as best they could. Billy discarded her

filthy undergarments, eager to get rid of everything associated with her captivity. With Maloche dead, the mountains didn't seem so forbidding, and she could relax for the first time in days. She told Hawk all about her ordeal, and his attention allowed her to cleanse her mind as well as her body by sharing the experience with him.

They bathed each other gently, mindful of the cuts and bruises that marred their bodies. They were comfortable with their desire which, for now, could be satisfied with kisses and tender ministrations. The knowledge that they had the rest of their lives to indulge their mutual passion made them patient.

They discussed their plans while they rode the horses around the base of the mountain, looking for the ravine below the cave. Without the camels, they couldn't hope to pack out much of the gold on this trip. They would have to return to the canyon where John was buried, look for the camels, and retrieve their supplies. If they couldn't find the beasts, they'd be forced to ride the Indian ponies back to Tucson to file their claim and return for the rest later.

Hawk found an ancient trail, faint but still visible. They followed it and in the rocky ravine below the cliff where he had fallen, they discovered a primitive mining device. Called an *arrastre* by the Spaniards, the crude machine had barely survived the elements and the centuries. The wooden beam that had pivoted inside the circular rough stone trough was splintered and crumbling.

Hauled around and around, either by man or beast, the beam had dragged boulders through the trough. It was slow and back-breaking work, but the process crushed the ore so that the gold could be extracted.

A short distance away, directly under the cave where Hawk had found the gold, they discovered evidence of the fires used to melt it down. The face of the canyon wall had been carved by time, and it jutted out over a flat shelf of rock. The wall itself was black with ancient soot.

"There's got to be a trail somewhere in all these rocks," Hawk said. "All we have to do is find it."

"What makes you think there is a way up from here?" Billy wanted to know. "Looking down from above, it is a sheer drop."

"Yeah, but the Spaniards dug the ore out of the cave, then carted it down here to be broken up and smelted. Then they lugged it back to the cave. Since they didn't fly up and down, there must be a trail accessible to horses," he theorized.

"Maybe there's another way into the cave," she suggested.

"Maybe. You wait here, and I'll scout around and see what I can find."

As he rode off, Billy wasn't even tempted to follow him. He had said wait. She was dying of curiosity about the gold, but she quelled her excitement by thinking of all the wondrous things she would do with it.

Twenty minutes later she heard Hawk shout her name, and she urged her horse in the direction he had taken. She rounded a wind-twisted spire of rock a few minutes later and saw him grinning triumphantly.

"I found it. The trail. Come on, we can follow this gorge up and around and come out just below the cave."

The trail was rocky and steep, not really fit for horses, but the surefooted Indian ponies didn't seem to mind the climb. Rocks loosened by their hooves clattered down to the canyon floor, and birds that had built nests in the holes eroded in the walls swooped and shrieked at the intruders. The shadows were deep here, deep and inhospitable.

But they couldn't dampen Hawk and Billy's enthusiasm now that they were so close.

When the trail ended, they secured the horses in a hastily constructed corral, not unlike the one they'd built for the camels, and continued on foot. From above, the side of the ravine had looked like a sheer drop, but in truth, the outcrops of rocks made it a relatively accessible climb.

They soon found the spot where Hawk's frayed rope dangled down over the ledge. "We're almost there," he told Billy. "Nothing to it from here on out."

"Spoken like a true intrepid," she commented dryly. She looked doubtfully at the ragged rope that was over two hundred years old. "Are you sure that thing will hold us?"

"We'll soon find out." Hawk snatched the swinging end of the rope and climbed up with practiced ease. He soon gained the ledge. "Just tie it around your waist," he advised her. "I'll pull you up."

Following his directions, she made a sturdy knot and held on so tightly that her knuckles whitened with the effort. She dangled like a spider on a string as Hawk pulled her up and over the ledge.

The mouth of the cave was nothing spectacular, and in fact was almost invisible to eyes scouring the surrounding area. That was why it had remained lost for so long. Billy stared at the black gap in the rocks until Hawk's words interrupted her thoughts.

"What is it, Billy?"

"I was just thinking about destiny again. Do you realize that if Maloche hadn't kidnapped me and brought me to this place, if you had not engaged him in combat, if you had not fallen over that cliff, we might never have found the gold? What do you suppose it all means?"

"It means we're the richest people in the Territory." He grabbed two of the torches he had fashioned and gave one to her. Holding the other aloft, he took her hand and led her inside.

The cave was an eerie place. The smell of decay was heavy in the close air, and Billy held her breath as they moved stealthily past the skeleton sentinels. Apache arrows protruded from the long-dead men, both Pima and Spanish. The helmets and armor were identifiably Spanish and could be dated by experts. In the outer room, they also discovered Spanish coins, rusty muskets, and tarnished swords. It was just as Montoya had described in his journals, and Billy blinked back tears when she realized that this was indeed the fulfillment of a dream.

Hawk led her through the cave to a smaller room. He held his torch high, and the flame glinted off a small mountain of smelted gold. "This is it, Billy."

Carrying her torch, she walked slowly, as if in a trance. She ran her fingers over the glittering bars of gold. The stack was high, almost as tall as she was, and she could not breathe, think, or speak. So much gold in one place was an awe-inspiring sight.

While Hawk marveled over the extent of their riches, Billy couldn't stop thinking about the ancient artifacts that proved once and for all that Ricardo Montoya's tales were true. If only her father and Uncle John could have shared this moment with her. She dashed away her tears, knowing they were smiling down on her from their seats in heaven. She glanced at Hawk, and the look they exchanged communicated their happiness. They would live her father's dream for him. Together.

She walked back to the entrance of the cave, paced sixteen feet to the left, and found a pile of rocks. She removed them one by one and found a dusty sheaf of papers concealed beneath them. The scroll was wrapped in leather and tied with a crumbling cord. She reached for it, but her hand froze in the air and her fingers flexed. If this was what she thought it was, it had lain undisturbed for more than two centuries. Hidden in the secret place, it had waited.

For her.

Overcoming her sense of wonder, she reached for the scroll. Unwrapping it reverently and with the care of a trained scientist, she soon realized its authenticity. "Oh my God," she whispered.

"What is it?" Hawk asked.

"Montoya's log. It was right where his memoirs said it would be." She turned the pages carefully. They contained a complete record of the expedition, up to but not including the final hostile attack. "This is the proof I need for the Bureau of Ethnology. They'll have to take me seriously now."

"Honey, log or no log, they'd have to take a woman this rich seriously. Do you have any idea how much all this is worth?"

She shook her head. "Do you?"

"No, but it's more than we can ever spend."

"I've been thinking. After all we've been through together, I have decided to divide the gold equally. You've earned fifty percent."

Hawk was touched by Billy's generosity. Forfeiting part of her share of the gold proved how much she'd changed. Her offer made them equal partners in every sense of the word. "That's mighty generous of you, Billy," he said with a smile. "I was thinking along those same lines, and you just saved me the trouble of asking."

Billy grinned smugly.

After they finished their explorations, they returned to the horses and retrieved their supplies. Hawk discovered a basin where enough rain water had collected to supply not only their needs but also the horses'. By tying one of the packs to the end of the rope, they rigged up a method for transporting goods and gold up and down.

Late in the day, Billy sat outside the cave. As she pored over Montoya's log, she was caught up in the tragic events that had occurred over two hundred years before. Hawk's hand on her shoulder drew her back to the present.

Looking deep into her eyes, he pulled her to her feet and led her inside. She followed him deep into the cavern where he'd left a torch burning.

"What is this?" she asked.

"A surprise."

The surprise turned out to be a bed of gold. He had arranged hundreds of bars into a platform and padded it with blankets. Hawk dropped her hand and stepped into the middle of it. "Will you make love with me here?"

"I would make love with you anywhere. I was beginning to worry."

"About what?"

"You were so interested in the gold, I was afraid I'd lost my appeal."

Hawk once more offered his hand to her. "The treasure is meaningless without you, but it's only right that we celebrate our love surrounded by the gold of your ancestors and mine."

She smiled and stepped up against him. "I think that is a marvelous idea."

Hawk pulled his shirt over her head and then removed her boots. She stood before him, proud and trembling, wearing nothing but the heavy Montoya cross. The weight of it between her breasts made her feel primitive and uninhibited as she removed his Indian clothing. Here, with Hawk, she was unencumbered by society's restraint, free to do whatever she wanted. They sank onto the bed together, and Hawk's lips slanted over hers with a heat that threatened to melt the gold around them.

Her body quivered with emotion, and she tore her mouth from his to kiss his wounds. He flinched but reveled in the way her lips moved over his body, tasting and exploring. When he could stand it no longer, he thrust his hands into her freshly washed hair and pulled her face up to his.

"Billy, Billy," he chanted against her lips.

His hot hands caressed her breasts with a passionate hunger, and her nerves tingled at his touch. Her head fell back when his lips and teeth nipped her neck.

"Oh, Hawk," she moaned. "All the time I was captured I knew you would find me. I knew we would be together again like this. Those days seemed like years, and I don't want to wait any longer. I cannot," she gasped.

He slipped his hand between her thighs and moved his fingers, lightly, gently. She was wet and warm and ready for him. Hawk lowered his head and covered the peak of her breast with his mouth. With teeth and tongue he teased her nipple while his fingers probed and massaged until she writhed restlessly against him.

Her eyelids drifted shut as Hawk filled her, hard and thick and relentless. The sleek muscles of his buttocks rippled against her palms as his body rhythmically pumped into hers. Finally a dark velvet abyss yawned wider and drew them into a glittering explosion of senses.

They kissed tenderly and curled against each other, replete and content. They were happier than either had ever expected to be.

"Hawk?"

"Yes."

"I feel so glad."

"I know. I feel the same way. We have everything, don't we?" He squeezed her urgently. "We have each other. We have enough gold to last a lifetime; hell, forty lifetimes."

"I wish Uncle John could have lived to see it," she whispered.

"So do I."

After a few quiet minutes passed, she asked, "What will you do with your share of the gold?"

He considered the question. "Well, the first thing I'll do is buy Tucson and give it to the Apaches so they won't have to live on the reservation. What about you?"

"I think I'll make a few endowments in my father's name. The Thomas Hartford Memorial Trust to finance and support the work of promising young ethnologists. Male and female, of course. Then, if we recover Uncle John's plates intact, I'm going to see that his photographs are published."

"It's a little frightening, isn't it?" he murmured. "We can do anything we want. All our dreams can come true."

Billy clung to him. "Can they? Since you've never chosen to reveal much about your past, present, or future dreams, I feel I hardly know you."

"You know more about me than anyone else ever has," he said sincerely.

She kissed the tip of his nose. "But I need to know more. Everything. Can you understand?"

"I understand that you're as greedy as I am, in your way," he teased. Resigning himself to talking now and loving again later, he sighed and pulled her into his arms. They held each other tightly as he spoke.

He told her about his reluctant trip East, about his experiences, first in the preparatory school, then at William and Mary.

"Did you ever make peace with your father's family?" she asked.

"They finally accepted my right to the name, but we never had personal contact. Everything was handled through a lawyer."

"Who was she?" Billy asked unexpectedly.

"What do you mean?"

"Someone hurt you deeply. You turned away from the society where you'd made a place for yourself and returned to Arizona to close yourself off in a tough shell. Only someone you loved could have caused that kind of pain. Who was she?"

Hawk had always known Billy was smart. It appeared she was perceptive too. "Her name was Mariel Davenport. We met during my third year at William and Mary, and I imagined I was in love with her."

"Imagined?"

"Now that I've met and loved you, Billy, I know that what I felt for Mariel was only infatuation. I never presented myself as anything but what I was, and the young lady and her family knew my background. They claimed it made no difference.

"The Davenports were liberals, you see. They'd been against slavery too. The Devlins were a powerful family, and even if Hawk Devlin was a bastard, the name lent credibility. Of course, by this time I had graduated at the top of my class and had a promising future ahead of me."

"What happened?"

"On the eve of our engagement party I was sipping sherry in the Davenport drawing room with Mariel and her parents when the topic of our future plans arose. I mentioned that the first thing I wanted to do, once we got settled in our own home, was send for my mother."

"Of course."

"In my enthusiasm I pulled out a tintype of Mirry that I always carried, and I passed it around, expecting the Davenports to love her as much as I did."

Billy sensed what was coming. She wanted to tell him not to relive the pain, but he seemed determined to do so.

"I thought it was a nice picture of her, but the Davenports were horrified when they saw it. A squaw. That's all Mirry was to them. They couldn't see her beauty, her goodness. They would never know her generous heart because they couldn't get past her dark skin and Indian features."

"Oh, Hawk, I am so sorry."

"Don't be. It was their loss. Although I'd done everything I knew to prove myself, to make myself worthy of their precious daughter, I could see immediately that our marriage would never work. Like others of their class, the Davenports were liberal up to a point. But that point did not include tainting their Mayflower family line with my mongrel blood."

"What of Mariel?"

"Poor little Mariel. She couldn't defy her parents,

and I knew it. I could also see that having an Apache
mother-in-law camped out on her veranda did not
figure in her plans. She was quiet for a long time,
and then she asked if there was any chance our children would look like Mirry. I told her no, they
wouldn't, because there would be no children, no
marriage.

"I left that night. I came back to Arizona and had
a few good years with my mother before she died of
pneumonia."

Billy gathered him into her arms and covered his
face with kisses. "Mariel was a fool to let you go,
but I am glad she did."

Hawk nuzzled her neck and trailed tiny kisses
across her shoulders. "You won't let me get away,
will you?"

"Never!"

He joined himself to her again and their ecstasy,
when it came, was even greater than before. Afterward, she snuggled in his arms. "I don't want to
lose you."

"You won't," he said as his mouth came down
hard on hers. All his love, all his passion spilled
over into the embrace. Hawk buried his hands in her
hair, his fingers tangling in the curly mass. His
tongue delved into the welcoming recesses of her
mouth, urging her sweet response. It was an obsession, he realized, this overwhelming need for Billy.

For all her refined ways, she was nothing like
Mariel. She'd always been strong, but her experiences had forged in her an immutable courage. They
had shown her that civilization was a matter of degree. A few weeks ago, he'd thought her the most
difficult woman he'd ever met. Now he thought her
the most wonderful.

Hawk brushed her bruised face gently. "You're
beautiful."

"So are you," she said shyly.

"You have incredible eyes," he said as he kissed

them. "They're so deep that when I gaze into them I can see all the way to the future."

"Like a hawk." Billy stretched enticingly beneath him, wrapping her arms around his neck. "So tell me, what do you see?"

"I see us together. Forever."

"I've heard that Apaches sometimes take more than one wife. How many will you need?"

"That depends."

"On what?"

Hawk smiled. "How do you feel about children? After all we've been through, do you still think they belong on expeditions?"

"They belong with their parents. And our beautiful, intelligent children will be most happy sharing our exciting lives."

He kissed her again. "That was the right answer. I just need one wife—you. I give my love and my body into your keeping."

"And I give mine to you."

"We are as one in our hearts," he pronounced.

That night they slept on their golden bed, but they rose at dawn and began loading the three horses for their departure. Billy made a bundle out of one of the blankets and wrapped up as many artifacts as it would hold.

Hawk was more worried about the gold and rigged a makeshift framework of tree limbs with which to secure it on the packhorse. The arrangement was a bit shaky, but he was sure it would hold until they could find something better.

After a quick meal, they went back inside the cave for the last time. They stood staring at the stacked gold for several moments.

"I still have trouble believing it's real," Billy said.

"I know how you feel. I have trouble believing it's ours."

"Is it right to take it, do you suppose?"

"Right? Of course, it's right."

"But what about the mountain spirits? What about the Earth Mother?"

"I communed with them this morning. They said they want us to have it. Kind of a wedding gift."

She looked up sharply and caught him grinning. "Why, you . . ." He kissed the words out of her mouth. Slipping his hands down her sides, he pulled up the buckskin shirt and bared her skin to his touch.

Still surprised by her own passion and lack of inhibition, she tugged his breechclout aside and caressed him with her hands.

"Here? Now?" she whispered.

"Standing up," he confirmed.

His lips were soft as they covered hers, then grew more demanding as he rubbed sensuously against her thighs. Billy kissed him back and with his help, wrapped her legs around his waist and wiggled onto him.

Hawk cupped her buttocks in his hands and slipped inside her. She was all heat, all desire, and it was all for him. Spasms of joyous pleasure pulsed through his veins as he filled her body with his own. With more restraint than he thought possible, he used his hands and mouth to tantalize, to build her need to a fever pitch.

"Please, Hawk." The words were little more than a sigh, and her pleasure was an invitation he could no longer resist. He plunged deeper, and Billy clasped him to her with her legs, bringing him even more deeply inside. She churned her hips in wild response to his burning thrusts, until he lost all thought, until the blood pounded in his temples and they were one in body as well as heart.

Weakened by their release, they sank onto the pile of gold, still joined together. Hawk stretched out on his back, and Billy straddled him. The sharp edge of pleasure slowly receded, leaving them spent and happy.

"I've never been so . . ." Billy searched for the right word to describe her feelings. "So moved."

Hawk sighed and spoke without opening his eyes. "Me either."

Billy thought she heard a rumble, like thunder. Maybe if it stormed, they'd have to delay their departure. They might have to spend yet another day, and night, on their golden bed. Just contemplating that made her tingle anew.

She heard another rumble and wriggled out of Hawk's embrace. "The earth trembled."

"Yeah," he agreed with a catbird grin. "Come here and we'll see if we can really make it shake."

"No, listen." Another reverberation, more ominous and louder than the last, penetrated the cave and preceded an earth-rattling tremor. Billy jumped up, her eyes wide. "I hate to disillusion you, Hawk, but that shock we felt had nothing to do with your legendary prowess at lovemaking. I think it's an earthquake."

Chapter 20

The ground shook violently, and a fierce rumbling, like that of an awakening ogre, filled the cave as Hawk and Billy scrambled for the entrance. She grabbed up the bundle of artifacts and looked longingly at the pile of gold bars.

"What about . . . ?"

The thought of abandoning the gold, after all they'd suffered to find it, made Hawk physically ill. But they had no choice. The way the ground was undulating, this was working up to be a first-class earthquake. "Leave it."

"Leave it? Are you insane?"

"You heard me. Maybe we can save what we packed out of here this morning. If we can get to the horses before it's too late, that is."

"Come on, then." She grabbed his hand, and they bolted from the cool dark cave into the scorching cloudless morning, dodging the rocks and debris that tumbled down around them. Billy went down the rope first, sliding so fast she burned her hands. Her feet had scarcely touched the ground before Hawk was beside her.

They fell to the quaking ground several times before they finally reached the makeshift corral. The ponies were still there, but they were half crazy with fear, rearing and screaming and rolling their eyes. Billy tried to calm them while Hawk secured the packs of gold he'd carried out earlier.

After lashing the last strap tight, he looked around and saw her trying to fling one of the heavy Mexican saddles onto her nervous pony's back. "Forget that. There's no time."

Without something to hold on to, Billy wasn't sure she would ever get on the horse, much less stay on it. But this was one time when she followed orders without question. They half led, half dragged the frantic horses toward the head of the trail just moments before a giant fissure split open the earth in the spot where the corral had been.

"That was close," Billy cried over the thunder roaring around them.

Too damn close, Hawk thought as he judged their ever-decreasing chances of making it down the trail in time. Another minute and what little gold they'd managed to salvage would have been lost forever.

The ground quaked and shook as they made for the narrow pass that would take them away from Weaver's Needle. Through some miracle, it was still open. Filled with renewed hope, Hawk began to think they might make it after all.

"Get on your horse, dammit!" he commanded Billy. He'd managed to mount his pony, but in its terror, the pack animal was fighting him, and he had a hard time hanging on to the lead rope.

"I'm trying to!" she yelled back. The horse, whose whole body quivered in fear, was desperate to break free of the rein. "Don't be such a fool," she told the animal. "I'm trying to get you out of here." Try as she would, she simply could not swing her weight onto the constantly moving target.

Hawk finally recognized the problem and raced his horse to her side. Reaching down, he scooped her up and dumped her on her horse's back.

"Thank you very much," she screamed. "For a moment there, I thought you were more worried about the bloody gold than about me!"

"Not a chance!" Hawk wrapped the packhorse's lead rope around his hand and yelled at her to follow. "We have to make it down the trail before the whole damn mountain falls on top of us!"

Their descent was an endless series of close calls; rocks plummeted down, bouncing out over the narrow trail and crashing to the desert floor below. Pinnacles shook and the deep canyons coughed dust as they were filled with tons of rocks. Cracks opened up in the rock walls, and the ground rolled and bucked.

The surefooted Indian ponies finally seemed to understand what was expected of them and charged headlong down the steep path. Billy didn't have time to think about what was going on behind them. She had to focus all her efforts on remaining upright on the pony's back.

Hawk couldn't believe this was happening. An earthquake, of all things! And with a whole big flat damn desert for miles around, they had to pick the highest, rockiest spot the land had to offer. What luck! What timing! He sent Billy down the trail ahead of him so he could keep an eye on her. She was having trouble with her horse, but if she could just hold on for a few more minutes they'd reach the relative safety of the canyon floor.

The pack pony's lead rope was cutting off the circulation to Hawk's hand, but he didn't care. All he could think about was holding on to what little gold they'd managed to save.

Less than half an hour, which seemed more like half a lifetime, passed before they reached the bottom of the mountain trail. The bright day had darkened as the sun was obscured by dust, hanging thick in the air like a storm cloud come to earth. The ground still trembled and roiled beneath them, not unlike the deck of the ship that had brought Billy across the turbulent Atlantic.

With Hawk in the lead, they raced their ponies away from the falling boulders toward a flat stretch of land filled with tumbled saguaros and uprooted agaves.

But even there safety eluded them. A giant crack appeared suddenly in the ground, and Hawk's horse leaped over it. The pack animal, on the other hand, was not so intrepid and balked suddenly, loosening the pack and nearly wrenching Hawk's arm out of the socket at the shoulder when the lead rope drew taut. He grasped the rope and tugged, but the frightened horse refused to jump.

Billy saw what was happening and, clutching her horse's mane in both hands, dug her heels into its sides and urged it over. Sensing the pack animal's distress, her pony also balked and screamed down into the yawning black fissure which had widened to nearly three feet. She jerked on the reins and backed the pony up for another attempt, but again it stopped, almost pitching her over its head.

"Hawk!" she yelled. "Help me!"

Hawk was having his own problems. The pack-horse seemed intent on committing suicide. No matter how hard Hawk yanked and pulled, it would not leap the breach and now seemed determined to shake off the pack, which tilted ominously to the side. He had a disquieting image of the rocky ledge crumbling beneath the frantic hooves and all the gold, including his fifty percent, plunging down into the bowels of the earth.

Not as long as he had a breath left, it wouldn't. "Just a minute!" he yelled back, returning his attention to the stubborn animal.

"Just a minute?" Billy could not believe it. Hawk was so worried about saving the gold that he'd all but forgotten about her. It was nice to know, now that death was so close at hand, exactly where she fit into his list of priorities. If she got out of this alive, she would never speak to him again!

The earth at the edge of the fissure cracked and crumpled, giving her a frightening look down into the abyss. Scared beyond reason, she backed her terrified horse away just before it could fall in. Once on temporarily solid ground, she looked around to see Hawk still trying to pull the packhorse across.

Damn! Hawk hated to do it, but he recognized an impossible situation when he saw it. With a grim sense of resignation, he unwrapped the lead rope from his hand. He tossed it aside with a heartfelt curse and wheeled his horse around, urging it back across the crumbling crack.

An ear-shattering rumble made all three horses rear up in fright, and the packhorse tucked its legs up and leaped across the newly created gorge like Pegasus taking wing.

"Yeah, now you do it, you damn fool," Hawk yelled after the rapidly retreating horse. They'd be lucky if they ever saw it, or the gold, again. He groaned when he thought of the surprise some stranger would have when he found a stray Indian pony laden with gold bars. No doubt that would initiate a whole new round of legends about the Superstition Mountains. Goddammit!

"Hawk!"

Billy's scream reclaimed his attention, and he saw that she had managed to drop her reins in the confusion. Her horse was totally out of control and nearly blind with terror. She had flattened herself on its back and was hanging on to its neck like a monkey in a sideshow. Hawk galloped over and in one smooth motion reached down and scooped up the dangling reins.

Leading Billy's animal, he urged the horses on.

But it was too late. By the time they reached the fissure, it was too wide to leap so he yanked on the reins and sped along its length, trying to find a place still narrow enough to cross.

The earth shook as if a giant were stamping his feet. The horrible cannonade of rocks made the horses even more loco, and they bucked and reared in a frenzy to escape. The bombardment rattled Hawk's and Billy's teeth, and the roar filled their ears. If they were thrown now they would be stomped to death by the flashing hooves, providing they survived the quake.

Another massive rumble rolled down from above, and they looked up at Weaver's Needle just in time to see ten thousand years' worth of accumulated geological debris crash down over the cave entrance. When the thick cloud of dust began to settle, it became clear that the entrance had been obliterated in one of nature's most violent gestures. The Montoya gold and the ghosts of the Indians and Spanish conquistadors were sealed inside forever.

Hawk and Billy coughed and wiped the dust from their eyes. Almost immediately the violent shaking stopped, as suddenly and unexpectedly as it had started. The earth stood still once more. The sudden contrasting silence was oppressive and tomblike, and not even an insect chirped. It was as if all living things were waiting breathlessly to see if it was really over.

It was.

Happy to be alive, Hawk and Billy slid off their horses and fell into each other's arms. He brushed back her tangled hair and searched her face. "Are you all right?"

"Yes," she whispered. "Thanks to you." Then she remembered his reluctant rescue. "I suppose it was a difficult decision to make. The woman you love or the gold?" Her fury and fear made her tremble, and she slapped at his arm in righteous indignation. "What were you waiting for?"

"I was hoping to save you both. You got a problem with that?" He grabbed her hands and pulled her to him in a savage embrace, his lips seeking and finding hers.

His kiss was almost as violent as the earthquake had been, or at least the emotions it created seemed so to Billy. She swayed against him, feeling suddenly weak and light-headed.

"We don't need the gold," she told him, forgetting all about her vow not to speak to him. "We're alive and we have each other."

"Yeah, but the gold would have been nice too. Of all the dirty, rotten, lousy luck. I can't believe the timing."

A feeling of serenity settled over Billy as she stood in the circle of Hawk's strong arms. "Do you think it was really just bad luck and skewed timing that buried the mine?"

"What else?"

"What about fate?"

"Don't start with that again. There's no such thing as fate or destiny."

"How can you say that after all that has happened? Don't you feel the presence of the other world?"

"All I feel is the absence of the gold. Especially my fifty percent."

She looked up at the ravaged mountain through the settling dust. The sun was bright now, and it sent a shower of brilliant light cascading down upon them. "The spirits or the ghosts or whatever forces guard the Earth Mother's gold are no longer restless. They've had their revenge, and they are content in knowing no one will ever uncover it again."

"They should be happy. A ton of dynamite wouldn't move those rocks."

"It's as it should be."

"I don't see how you can accept this so calmly. Haven't you figured out yet that everything you dreamed about is destroyed?"

"Sometimes we must trade in our battered old dreams and dare to hope for unexpectedly wonderful new ones." She planted a kiss on his cheek.

"But what about the artifacts? Don't you still want to tell the Bureau of Ethnology I-told-you-so?"

Smiling slyly, she removed the bundle she'd slung around her shoulder. In it were the map, the logbook, and other relics. "These and the Montoya cross are all I need to prove Ricardo's story was authentic.''

"What about the gold?" He cast a last fond look at the tumbled-down mountain. No existing technology could possibly provide the means to excavate it.

"I don't think the world needs the gold nearly as much as it needs the legend," she told him gently. "Let's give it that much, what do you say?"

He grinned and kissed her again.

"How about you?" she asked.

"What about me?"

"All those dreams of grandeur. Can you be content to be poor again after a brief moment of possessing enough gold to live like a king?"

"Easy come, easy go. Like I always say, *que sera, sera.*"

"We can always look for the packhorse," she suggested.

"We'll definitely do that. On our way back to Tucson. Even that hellhole's going to seem peaceful after this place. And if I never smell a camel again, it'll be too soon."

Sybilla's eyes widened. "The camels! We have to find them."

"To hell with them. If there's any searching to be done, it's going to be for that horse and my gold."

"*Your* gold?" she reproved with a raised brow.

"Did I say *my* gold?" He feigned innocence. "I meant *our* gold.

"How can we face Ahmed and Zora with no gold and no camels?"

"Maybe they can start up a flea circus," he suggested with a cynical laugh. "There's plenty of those in Tucson, and the overhead wouldn't be too high."

"Don't be a tease. I'm deadly serious," she protested. "We have to find those camels. I gave Ahmed my word that I'd take good care of them."

She noticed that he wasn't really listening to her. Nor was he paying attention. He was staring over her shoulder with a look of wonder on his face. She turned to see what was so fascinating.

Her eyes narrowed against the glare, and she stared intently at a tiny moving line on the horizon. Seven indistinct shapes were headed in their direction. Seven humpbacked, long-legged, scrawny-necked shapes.

"The camels!" She jumped up and down in her excitement. "Samson's bringing the girls to us. What impossibly wonderful luck!"

"Yeah, I'm overwhelmed."

Billy turned to Hawk. He still wasn't listening. His eyes were fixed on a point between them and the approaching camels.

"What is it?" she asked curiously.

"Do you see what I see?"

"I see the camels coming."

"Not the damn camels. Over there by that pile of rocks. Tell me I'm not hallucinating. Tell me it's not my imagination and wishful thinking combining to play a trick on me."

She looked to where he pointed and saw the object of his interest. "The packs! Oh, Hawk! The packs must have fallen off the horse."

"Thank you, Lord!" Hawk took off his hat and tossed it into the air. Then he scooped Billy up in his arms and swung her around and around. "You know what this means?"

"It means there are happy endings outside of fairy tales."

"Yeah, that too." He kissed her absently. "We can use the gold to finance another treasure hunt. I heard about this Spanish galleon loaded with silver and gold that sunk off the coast of Florida in 1632. I'm tired of looking at rocks and sand, and the ocean sounds pretty good right now."

"Florida? I should say not. That's your greed talking again. We're going to use the gold to finance an expedition to Crete."

"What's in Crete?"

"Lost civilizations, that's what."

He groaned. "I've seen enough old bones to last a lifetime. And you call me greedy. I think your obsession to uncover what no one else can find is stronger than any case of gold fever I've ever heard about."

They argued about the whys and wherefores and eventual dispersal of *their* gold until they were interrupted by a nasty-sounding *thppt*. They whirled around and found the ugly faces of Samson and his newly acquired harem staring at them.

"They actually look glad to see us," Hawk said.

Billy hugged Delilah's neck. "I know I'm glad to see them. Ahmed and Zora will have their camels plus a nest egg to help them get that circus started."

"And we'll get that trip to Florida."

"Crete."

"Florida."

"You know what Uncle John told me?" she asked him. "He said even if we didn't find the gold, we'd already found a fortune worth far more than all the lost, sunken, or buried treasure in the world."

"Uncle John was pretty smart for an Englishman," Hawk said as he tugged her close.

"Love," she said simply. "Love is the only true fortune known to man. Treasure me, Hawk Devlin, and I will treasure you."

"Forever, Billy," he confirmed with a kiss.

Avon Romances—
the best in exceptional authors and unforgettable novels!